The Second Mrs. Bennet

Pride & Prejudice Chronicles, Volume 1

Gayle Buck

Published by Gayle Buck, 2024.

THE SECOND MRS. BENNET

First edition. October 23, 2024.

ISBN: 978-1952091230

Written by Gayle Buck.

And however uncertain of giving happiness, marriage must be our pleasantest preservative from want. – Jane Austen, Pride & Prejudice

"Oh! We cannot begin too early. You are not aware of the difficulty of procuring exactly the desirable thing." – Jane Austen, Emma

[1]

In Hertfordshire, near the market town of Meryton and outside Longbourn village, stood a stately manor, called simply Longbourn. There resided Mr. Thomas Bennet, a gentleman of intellect and a philosophical nature, who preferred the country to town. He had a comely but foolish wife and too many daughters. Lacking a male heir, the entire property was entailed to a distant relation. The five Bennet girls were therefore the daughters of a gentleman but had no fortunes.

Mr. Bennet's marriage had been imprudent. He had married at a young age, bowled out by a beauty, but his realization of her narrow mind very early in their marriage put an end to all real affection for her. Respect, esteem, and confidence had vanished forever, and all his views of domestic happiness were overthrown.

He was not of a disposition to seek comfort for the disappointment in any of those pleasures which too often console the unfortunate for their folly. He was fond of the country and of books, and from those tastes had arisen his principal enjoyments.

Mr. Bennet was very little otherwise indebted to his wife, except as her ignorance and folly had contributed to his amusement. It was not the sort of happiness which a man would in general wish to owe to his wife; but where other entertainment was wanting, the true philosopher will derive benefit from such as are given.

At Longbourn, Mrs. Bennet ruled the house and all those within its walls. Mrs. Bennet's sole ambition in life was to see all of her daughters wed, and she often complained that the undertaking was a wearisome and thankless task. Mr. Bennet had left the upbringing of his daughters and the settling of their futures to his wife's management.

It was more comfortable for everyone.

Mrs. Bennet suffered great affliction of her nerves at the least hint of opposition.

The summer of 1811 had been an unsettled, cold, and wet one, and it was bidding fare to be another harsh winter. The autumn dawn, heralded by streamers of orange and gold, had barely shown its face when Thomas Bennet arose, dressed, and holding aloft a single flickering candle in a tin holder to illuminate his way, went downstairs to his library, as was his custom, to take advantage of a precious hour or two of quiet before began all the bustle of the new day.

Wearing his drab wool overcoat buttoned up against the cold air, he first lit several tapers in a candelabra before starting a fire in the large fireplace, using the well-stacked wood and kindle that had been put down the night before. His flat-coated spaniel trundled in after him, and in front of the warming hearth, circled twice on a lumpy cushion, before curling tight and tucking its black nose beneath a feathery tail.

Candlelight flickered in the library, shedding a yellow nimbus where Thomas Bennet was seated, occupied at his desk. As he tallied the columns in his expense ledger, he exhaled on a long, wearied sigh. *Bonnets and ribbons – and more ribbons! – and only the good Lord knows what else besides.*

Mrs. Bennet's father had been an attorney in Meryton, and had left her four thousand pounds, giving her two hundred a year from the interest. Her fortune, though ample for her situation in life, could barely supply the deficiency in Mr. Bennet's income. Longbourn produced an income of two thousand a year – a comfortable living for a large household that practiced simple economy.

Mrs. Bennet had never learned economy.

Bennet shook his head. "However many times I tot up the numbers, the sums remain the same."

At hearing the stirring of the household, Bennet set aside his ledgers, extinguished the candles, and went to join his family in the breakfast parlor. The cheerful chattering and loud hubbub of his wife and five daughters greeted him. A fire blazed in the fireplace, warming the room. Shedding his overcoat, he handed it off to the butler before taking his customary place at the head of the table. Mr. Bennet's breakfast preferences were well-known and the footman placed before him a laden plate. Bennet folded back a page of his ironed newspaper, which the butler placed beside his plate. He began to read, while lifting a bite of his morning eggs.

His fork was halfway to his mouth when his wife addressed him.

"My dear Mr. Bennet. Have you heard that Netherfield Park is let at last?"

He sighed. *I am a man of simple wants.* A few minutes of quiet over the breakfast cups was surely not too much to ask; it was a philosophical point he had pondered for all the years of his marriage. "No, my dear, I had not."

"But it is, for Mrs. Long has just been here, and she told me all about it."

Bennet made no answer. His thoughts were acid. It was too early for morning callers. *Mrs. Long must have trotted over in her nightshift!* He carried the fork to his mouth, chewed his eggs, and resolutely returned his attention back to the fine print which presented the news to his inquiring gaze. A gentleman was obligated to keep abreast of serious matters taking place outside his own household.

"Do you not want to know who has taken it?" cried Mrs. Bennet impatiently.

He sighed again. He knew that rising note of irritation. He would have no peace until his wife had emptied her mind of its most recent acquisition. It was a shallow receptacle, indeed, for it seemed she could not hold more than two thoughts in her head at a time. Perhaps he underrated her; she might possess three good thoughts. "You want to tell me, and I have no objection to hearing it."

"Why, my dear, you must know, Mrs. Long says that Netherfield is taken by a young man of large fortune from the north of England, that he came down on Monday in a chaise and four to see the place, and was so much delighted with it that he agreed with Mr. Morris immediately; that he is to take possession before Michaelmas, and some of his servants are to be in the house by the end of next week."

Bennet abandoned his perusal of the newspaper. He looked down the loaded table boards, taking note of his wife's ebullient expression, and that the usual chatter of his daughters had trickled and died away.

This is news, indeed.

A newcomer in the neighborhood meant social obligations. It seemed that he must bestir himself. "What is his name?"

"Bingley."

"Is he married or single?"

"Oh, single, my dear, to be sure!" Mrs. Bennet canted over her plate, her excitement bubbling over. "A single man of large fortune! Four or five thousand a year! What a fine thing for our girls!"

Bennet discerned the trajectory of his wife's convolutions. However, he would give her the illusion he needed to be informed. "How so? How can it affect them?"

"My dear Mr. Bennet, how can you be so tiresome! You must know that I am thinking of his marrying one of them."

He was amused. "Is that his design in settling here?"

"Design! Nonsense, how can you talk so! But it is very likely that he may fall in love with one of them, and therefore you must visit him as soon as he comes."

Bennet shook his head. "I see no occasion for that. You and the girls may go, or you may send them by themselves, which perhaps will be still better, for as you are as handsome as any of them, Mr. Bingley might like you the best of the party."

The mild witticism passed over his wife's head. She preened a little, wagging a forefinger at him. "My dear Mr. Bennet, you flatter me. I certainly have had my share of beauty, but I do not pretend to be anything extraordinary *now*. When a woman has five grown up daughters, she ought to give over thinking of her own beauty."

"In such cases, a woman has not often much beauty to think of, Mrs. Bennet," he responded, somewhat caustically. She *had* once been a great beauty and she had giggled at all of his small jokes. He had been a foolish young man, bookish and reserved, inexperienced with females, and he had equated her agreeable vivacity with intellectual compatibility. After three-and-twenty years, he still felt flattened whenever his wife failed to catch his humorous casts.

Fanny has her own sort of armor.

"But, my dear, you must indeed go and see Mr. Bingley when he comes into the neighborhood."

Thomas Bennet sighed yet again. His wife had taken his teasing not as the absurdity it was meant to be, but as a rebuff. Perversity drove him to provoke her. "It is more than I engage for, I assure you."

"But consider your daughters. Only *think* what an establishment it would be for one of them. Sir William and Lady Lucas are determined to go, merely on that account, for in general, you know they visit no newcomers." The observation seemed to greatly affect Mrs. Bennet and she said urgently, "Indeed you *must* go, for it will be impossible for us to visit him, if you do not."

Bennet set himself to finish his breakfast; there was no reason to let a good plate of eggs and buttered toast grow cold. "You are over-scrupulous, surely. I daresay Mr. Bingley will be very glad to see you, and I will send a few lines by you to assure him of my hearty consent to his marrying whichever he chooses of the girls." He heard a smothered chuckle and knew from whom it originated. "Though, I must throw in a good word for my little Lizzy."

"I desire you will do no such thing," snapped Mrs. Bennet. Spots of color rose in her cheeks. "Lizzy is not a bit better than the others! I am sure she is not half as handsome as Jane, nor half so good-humored as Lydia. But you are always giving her the preference!"

Bennet adroitly muddied the waters. "They have none of them much to recommend them. They are all silly and ignorant like other girls." He allowed himself to smile. "But Lizzy has something more of quickness than her sisters."

Mrs. Bennet threw up her hands. "Mr. Bennet, how can you abuse your own children in such a way? You take delight in vexing me. You have no compassion on my poor nerves."

"You mistake me, my dear," he said dryly. He regarded his wife with some amusement. "I have a high respect for your nerves. They are my old friends. I have heard you mention them with consideration these twenty years at least."

Mrs. Bennet's face darkened with an angry flush. "Ah! You do not know what I suffer."

"But I hope you will get over it, and live to see many young men of four thousand a year come into the neighborhood." Bennet picked up his newspaper, preparing to quit the breakfast parlor.

Mrs. Bennet shook her head, her lips pushed out in a pout. "It will be no use to us, if twenty such should come, since you will not visit them."

"Depend upon it, my dear, that when there are twenty, I will visit them all."

Thomas Bennet was among the earliest of those who waited on Mr. Bingley. He had always intended to visit him, though to the last always assuring his wife that he should not go, and until the evening after the visit was paid, she had no knowledge of it.

He observed his second eldest employed in trimming a hat, and he suddenly addressed her. "I hope Mr. Bingley will like it, Lizzy."

"We are not in a way to know what Mr. Bingley likes," said Mrs. Bennet resentfully. "Since we are not to visit."

"But you forget, Mama," said Elizabeth cheerfully. "We shall meet him at the assemblies, and Mrs. Long has promised to introduce him."

"I do not believe Mrs. Long will do any such thing. She has two nieces of her own. She is a selfish, hypocritical woman, and I have no opinion of her," said Mrs. Bennet with irritation.

"No more have I," said Bennet, entertained by his wife's capacity to speak against her friend when it suited her. "And I am glad to find that you do not depend on her serving you."

Mrs. Bennet screwed up her mouth, but did not deign to reply. However, unable to contain her crossness, she began scolding one of her daughters. "Don't keep coughing so, Kitty, for heaven's sake! Show a little compassion on my nerves. You tear them to pieces!"

"Kitty has no discretion in her coughs," said Bennet lightly. "She times them ill."

"I do not cough for my own amusement," said Catherine fretfully.

Bennet turned back to his second eldest. "When is your next ball to be, Lizzy?"

"Tomorrow fortnight."

"Aye, so it is," cried Mrs. Bennet. "And Mrs. Long does not come back till the day before. So, it will be impossible for her to introduce him, for she will not know him herself."

"Then, my dear, you may have the advantage of your friend, and introduce Mr. Bingley to *her*."

"Impossible, Mr. Bennet, impossible, when I am not acquainted with him myself! How can you be so teasing?"

"I honor your circumspection. A fortnight's acquaintance is certainly very little. One cannot know what a man really is by the end of a fortnight. But if we do not venture, somebody else will. After all, Mrs. Long and her nieces must stand their chance, and there, as she will think it an act of kindness, if you decline the office, I will take it on myself."

The girls stared at him. Mrs. Bennet was much irritated. "Nonsense, nonsense!"

"What can be the meaning of that emphatic exclamation?" Bennet wickedly quizzed her. "Do you consider the forms of introductions, and the stress that is laid on them, as nonsense? I cannot quite agree with you there. What say you, Mary? For you are a young lady of deep reflection, I know, and read great books, and make extracts." Mary looked as though she wished to say something very sensible, but knew not how. He took pity on her and turned back to the others. "While Mary is adjusting her ideas, let us return to Mr. Bingley."

"I am sick of Mr. Bingley," cried Mrs. Bennet.

"I am sorry to hear that, but why did not you tell me so before? If I had known as much this morning, I certainly would not have called on him. It is very unlucky. But as I have actually paid the visit, we cannot escape the acquaintance now."

The astonishment of the ladies was just what he wished, that of Mrs. Bennet surpassing the rest. When her first tumult of joy was over, she began to declare that it was what she had expected all the while.

"How good it was in you, my dear Mr. Bennet! But I knew I should persuade you at last. I was sure you loved your girls too well to neglect such an acquaintance." A delighted smile on her face, she clapped her hands."Well, how pleased I am! And it is such a good joke, too, that you should have gone this morning, and never said a word about it until now!"

"Now, Kitty, you may cough as much as you choose," said Bennet with an ironic smile.

"What an excellent father you have, girls," said Mrs. Bennet, not heeding him. "I don't know how you will ever make him amends for his kindness. Or me either, for that matter! At our time of life, it is not so pleasant, I can tell you, to be making new acquaintances every day, but for your sakes, we would do anything."

"My dear, you speak so eloquently of our decrepitude," murmured Bennet.

As usual, he was ignored by his wife, who had never attempted to puzzle out the meaning of her husband's oblique comments. She had more important things on her mind. "Lydia, my love, though you are the youngest, I daresay Mr. Bingley will dance with you at the next ball."

Lydia tossed her head. "Oh! I am not afraid, for though I am the youngest, I am the tallest."

"I wonder how soon Mr. Bingley will return Mr. Bennet's visit," said Mrs. Bennet, her hands fluttering in the air. "We must ask him to dinner. Oh, I *do* hope he will be available! What an exciting prospect!"

Bennet left the room, fatigued by the raptures of his wife.

Bennet resisted all of Mrs. Bennet's efforts, and those of his five daughters, to draw from him any satisfactory description of Mr. Bingley. They attacked him in various ways, with barefaced questions, ingenious supposition, and distant surmise. But he eluded the skill of them all and they were at last obliged to accept the second-hand intelligence of their neighbor Lady Lucas. Her report was highly favorable. Sir William had been delighted with him. He was quite young, wonderfully handsome, extremely agreeable, and to crown the whole, he meant to be at the next assembly with a large party.

"Nothing could be more delightful!" exclaimed Mrs. Bennet. "A fondness of dancing is a certain step towards falling in love. I entertain very lively hopes of Mr. Bingley's heart."

"Mrs. Bennet, your soaring optimism is an astonishment."

Unheeding of her husband's dry tone, Mrs. Bennet added, "If I can but see one of my daughters happily settled at Netherfield, and all the others equally well-married, I shall have nothing to wish for. Indeed, I shall never wish for anything ever again!"

Bennet poked gentle fun at her exaggeration. "The prospect of a new bonnet or two will soon set you to rights, my dear."

In a few days, Mr. Bingley returned Mr. Bennet's visit. Bennet invited him into his library. Upon this second meeting between them, he was just as impressed as he had been before. Mr. Bingley was modest and gentlemanly. He had a pleasant countenance, and easy, unaffected manners.

After their initial greeting, Mr. Bingley said, "I have heard much of the beauty of your daughters, sir. I was hoping to meet them."

Bennet waved a dismissive hand. "You will be subjected to the whole lot of them soon enough. They are a giggling gaggle of foolish young girls."

"Oh, are they, sir? They are no doubt a merry lot, then."

"Oh, yes, and excitable. They will have already seen you from an upper window, and likely are even now exclaiming about how you wore a blue coat and that you rode a black horse."

Mr. Bingley laughed heartily. "Oh, that is marvelous! I am flattered, sir!"

Altogether, his visit was only a quarter hour, but the two gentlemen were satisfied that their first impressions were correct, and were each gratified by the discovery. Bennet accompanied the gentleman out to the front porch, where his visitor's horse was tethered to the decorative iron post. Mr. Bingley loosened the rein and swung up onto his black gelding.

"It was a pleasure to converse with you, Mr. Bingley."

Mr. Bingley smiled and touched the brim of his hat. "And for me also, sir." He nudged a heel to his mount's side and rode away.

Bennet returned inside the house, to his library. He was well-pleased. *Bingley will make an excellent neighbor.*

When he emerged for the noon meal, he was informed that a dinner invitation had been dispatched to Netherfield Park. "I am pleased to hear it, Mrs. Bennet. Mr. Bingley is just the sort of gentleman I would like to see sit at our table."

Mrs. Bennet had already planned the courses that were to do credit to her housekeeping, when an answer arrived that ruined all of her plans. "Why, Mr. Bennet! Mr. Bingley is obliged to be in town the following day, and consequently will be unable to accept the honor of our invitation!"

"A grave disappointment, to be sure," said Bennet calmly. "But hardly as calamitous as you make it out. There will be other invitations."

Mrs. Bennet paid no heed. "I cannot imagine what business he could have in town so soon after his arrival in Hertfordshire. I fear that he will be always flying about from one place to another, and never settle at Netherfield as he ought."

She kept up a steady stream of complaint and speculation which did not lend itself to good digestion, and Bennet ducked back into his sanctuary as soon as he could get away.

When next Mrs. Bennet saw him, and as soon as she set eyes on him, her lamentations were renewed. "Mr. Bennet, I cannot decide what could have taken Mr. Bingley away. Away on business! What conceivable business can he have, I wonder? It is not at all comfortable, to have all one's plans ruined, I can tell you!"

The shrill spate continues.

Bennet wondered why he had stepped foot outside the quietude of his library. But of course, he did know – from his window he had seen the Lucas carriage arriving and he had wanted to be on hand to greet their visitors. Out of all of his neighbors, he enjoyed a close friendship with Sir William Lucas.

Though Sir William had formerly been in trade in Meryton, where he had made a tolerable fortune, it was not held against him by better-born individuals. He had risen to the honor of knighthood by an address to the king, during his mayoralty, and that was enough to excuse him to the gentry of the county.

The distinction had perhaps been felt too strongly. It had given him a disgust to his business and to his residence in a small market town, and quitting them both, he had removed with his family to a house about a mile from Meryton, denominated from that period Lucas Lodge, where he could think with pleasure of his own importance, and unshackled by business, occupy himself solely in being civil to all the world.

Sir William was by nature inoffensive, friendly, and obliging, and his presentation at St. James's had made him courteous. Though elated by his rank, it did not cause him to be supercilious. It was for these qualities – not the weight of his purse nor his step up in rank – which Bennet valued in their mutual friendship.

Lucas Lodge was within a short walk of Longbourn and there were often visits back and forth between the daughters of both houses, for the families were particularly intimate. Thomas Bennet knew well that Miss Lucas had formed a fast friendship with his eldest daughters, Jane and Elizabeth, while her younger sister Maria seemed fairly close to his daughters Catherine and Lydia. He supposed if there had been another Lucas female of an age with his middle daughter, the girl would have been Mary's bosom-bow. As it was, Mary was an awkward outsider to the other friendships.

"Oh, I am glad you have come!" exclaimed Mrs. Bennet to Lady Lucas as she and her daughter were ushered into the drawing-room by the butler.

Bennet deemed Lady Lucas to be a very good kind of woman, practical but not too clever, which meant she was a valuable neighbor to Mrs. Bennet. Sir William and Lady Lucas had several children but this day she was accompanied only by her eldest daughter, Miss Charlotte Lucas. He experienced disappointment. *A pity Sir William did not come, as well.* He made his bow to the ladies. "I trust you are well, Lady Lucas, Miss Lucas?"

"Very well, sir."

The civilities were dispensed within a few moments, and Mrs. Bennet launched into what so much exercised her mind. Lady Lucas was able to quiet Mrs. Bennet's fears to a degree, earning Bennet's quick gratitude. She said in her comfortable fashion, "I expect Mr. Bingley has gone up to London only to get a large party for the ball."

Mrs. Bennet's exclamations were several and of voluble speculation.

Bennet cast a dispassionate glance at his wife. Not for the first time, he regretted he had not had the good fortune to stumble over a sensible woman when he was looking out for a bride. His wife's excitability was what drove him so often into the solitude of his library. As a consequence, he had, on occasion, an uncomfortable awareness that he knew far less about what went on in his own household than he should. The twinge of conscience was a mild disturbance to his ordered mind, but from long practice, Bennet was able to set it aside. If he acted upon the impression, then it was inevitable he would be led into a confrontation with his wife's nerves, those pains and flutterings and spasms, invariably accompanied by stormy temper – a situation he was determined to avoid.

He asked after Sir William, and it was Miss Lucas who replied. "Papa is set on getting up a hunting party, sir, and asked an invitation be conveyed to you to join him."

"Oh, yes! I was just about to tell you, before I was side-tracked by this talk of Mr. Bingley," said Lady Lucas with a laugh. Her attention was once more demanded by Mrs. Bennet and she turned away again.

Bennet addressed Miss Lucas. "I shall be delighted to participate. Please tell Sir William for me. When is it to be?" He was an avid sportsman and counted himself a fair shot. It was a treat to be included in Sir William's party. He would certainly enjoy the masculine camaraderie, and in addition, he would bag some game for Longbourn's table, which would be a welcome change to their usual fare.

Miss Lucas' pitch of voice was soft and pleasing. "Saturday next."

He smiled at the young woman. He regarded her with an attention he had never accorded her before. She was nothing out of the ordinary. Her features were even, her hair an unremarkable light brown. Her eyes were beautiful, however, being heavily-lashed and a clear gray. She was the particular friend of Elizabeth, but she was older than any of his own daughters, being all of seven-and-twenty years. She was already on the shelf without ever having been off of it.

A pity, of course, but often the natural course of things.

"I look forward to the pleasure." He made an effort to converse with her since Lady Lucas was still commandeered by Mrs. Bennet. Casting another resigned glance in his wife's direction, as her shrill, complaining voice grated on his ears, he said, "Are you as enamored as all the rest of our new neighbor, Mr. Bingley? I hear nothing else but talk of his fortune, and his being situated at Netherfield, and the assembly, at which he must surely make an appearance. It is already quite decided that since he has come into the neighborhood, he must marry one of our young ladies."

Miss Lucas smiled but shook her head. "I am not so fanciful as some of my peers, Mr. Bennet. I am certain Mr. Bingley is everything good that has been said of him. But I beg to differ on his motive for establishing a place at Netherfield Park."

He responded lightly. "Why, how is this? Surely you are as convinced as everyone else that Mr. Bingley has only come among us to find himself a bride!"

She shook her head again, her amusement still evident. "All wishful thinking and speculation, I fear."

He was entertained. "Not a cat set among the pigeons, then."

"No, I believe not."

Miss Lucas' gray eyes held a decided twinkle. Bennet thought she was much improved by her expression of humor. He had not spoken at such length with Miss Lucas before and he was impressed by her. *An altogether delightful young female.* She was an intelligent girl, a fitting companion for his favorite daughter. Elizabeth had inherited some of his own quickness of mind and it was refreshing to discover that she was not the only young woman in the world who could hold a decent conversation.

"Are you not a romantic, Miss Lucas?"

Charlotte let free a small laugh. Interest had lit Mr. Bennet's eyes. It disconcerted her a little. She was not used to having a man's attention focused on her, nor to exchanging banter with him, especially one such as Mr. Bennet. He had always been aloof and reclusive, older than she, the father of her best friend, and altogether beyond a bit of easy conversation. "I am too sensible a creature. No, I have long since given up the notion that a knight on his charger shall appear out of the morning mists. A good marriage to a good man is all I ask. All the rest is the stuff of dreams."

At that moment, Lady Lucas said, "We must be off, Charlotte. I have several things I must do at the Lodge this day."

"If you do not have a need of me, may I stay to visit with Eliza and Jane? I can easily walk back."

"Certainly, my dear girl."

Charlotte took leave of Mr. and Mrs. Bennet and left the drawing-room. She started up the stairs, knowing where to find her friends, in the small upstairs sitting room. Below her, she heard the rustle of skirts and the footsteps of the others moving into the entry hall. Mrs. Bennet's voice was as loud and penetrating as always and traveled up the stairwell. "Your Charlotte is a good girl. It is a pity she is not a beauty, like my Jane."

"Mrs. Bennet!" Mr. Bennet's rebuke held a mix of embarrassment and censure.

Charlotte's cheeks burned. She stopped on the turn in the stairs, closing her eyes as she leaned against the wainscoted wall. She was not spared her mother's regretful rejoinder. "Charlotte would have made some man an excellent wife." She put her hands to her hot cheeks. *Even my own mother rates me low and has regulated me to the dustbin.* It was humiliating that someone like Mr. Bennet was made aware of how little she mattered.

She heard retreating boot steps and the quiet closing of a door. "There goes Mr. Bennet! He positively *lives* in the library." Mrs. Bennet's petulance was easy to discern in her discontented voice.

Charlotte slowly continued up the stairs. She with difficulty mastered her emotions. She had already resigned herself to be a companion to her parents and a support to her brothers and sisters. She would never marry. She was an old maid without fortune or prospects. It was a hard thing to acknowledge that she would always be a burden and financial drain on her family. It was even harder to hear herself spoken of in those same regretful terms.

Then a quick step was coming toward her – a happy exclamation from Elizabeth. "Charlotte! How glad I am to see you!" And she was drawn into the lively company of the elder Bennet sisters.

When Charlotte Lucas left Longbourn and directed her steps homeward, the recollection of her humiliation became fresh. However, an unexpected aside was born out of her reflections and soon consumed her. Though she was unromantic, she did not think she could bear such a marriage as existed at Longbourn. The Bennets were an unequally yoked pair. Mr. Bennet was so odd a mixture of quick parts, sarcastic humor, reserve and caprice. She thought it would take the better part of a lifetime to understand his character. Mrs. Bennet's mind was less difficult to ascertain. She was a woman of mean understanding, little information, and uncertain temper.

Charlotte had been enough around the family to know very well how Mrs. Bennet ruled her household. When Mrs. Bennet was discontented, she fancied herself nervous and she made certain all in her sphere suffered along with her. The business of her life was to get her daughters married, its solace was visiting and gossip. Charlotte was not blind to the impropriety of Mr. Bennet's behavior as a husband. While respecting the gentleman's intellectual abilities, she had often observed how he had made Mrs. Bennet the object of his most satirical witticisms. She could not overlook the continual breach of conjugal obligation and decorum which, in exposing his wife to the contempt of her own children, was so highly reprehensible. She scolded herself for her uncharitable, harsh opinions. After all, she was not privy to everything that had gone into the making of that relationship.

I would know better how to manage a man like Mr. Bennet.

She was shocked by her wayward thought.

But how am I not to think about the man now that he has become a flesh-and-blood individual?

Before, he was simply Mr. Bennet, Elizabeth's father, a rarely glimpsed figure. *Now,* she had spoken with him at length, and he had spoken to *her* as though she was a person worthy of attention. *Now,* she had taken particular notice of his face and his person. He had obviously been a very handsome man in his youth, with a masterful nose and strong chin, and his features had aged well, being still firm with only a few wrinkles around his heavy-lidded keen eyes. His personality had appealed to her. She had liked how he poked gentle fun at the absurd vagaries of his neighbors and even of himself. Mr. Bennet did not physically resemble her father, who was short and portly and jovial; no, his was a long, well-built frame, the shoulders wide under his coat, and his physique showed little of the thickening that came with age. She realized she did not know his exact age. She knew only that her father was several years older than Mr. Bennet, and Sir William was a little over fifty years.

She thoughtfully shook her head. *Mrs. Bennet should count herself lucky to have such a fine figure of a man.*

[2]

A pale orb of sun shone, making a patchy sea of the foggy horizon. Bennet walked the brisk, short mile to Lucas Lodge. His breath streamed in the chill, dampish air. He wore hat and muffler, with a long buff overcoat buttoned close over his frock coat and breeches, the heavy drab wool length brushing the tops of his Hessian boots. His shotgun was broken open and rested over his forearm. His spaniel pranced beside his heel, long low body quivering with excitement. The bitch was a cross between the Sussex and the old-fashioned cocker of Devon; dogs for flushing game needed high energy and an excellent sense of smell, and he knew his well-bred spaniel was one of the best.

At Lucas Lodge, he exchanged cheerful greetings with his host and his fellow hunters, their breaths turned white in the early-morning air. They had congregated in one of the near fields and all carried shotguns and shot bags, while dogs snuffled and whined at their feet.

Bennet cast a measuring glance at the sky. There were heavy, grayish clouds formed overhead but no immediate threat of rain. *If the weather turns nasty, the pheasant will seek refuge in deepest cover.* But he said nothing of that. "It's a fine morning for it."

Mr. Philips, his brother-in-law, married to his wife's sister, aimed an affable grin at him. He was a plump man, a solicitor by trade who seldom left Meryton proper, but nevertheless he could tramp with the best of them. "Aye! Mind you, a bit on the frosty side but we will warm up soon enough, I dare swear."

"Nothing better than pheasant pie," said Mr. Long in anticipation, rubbing his gloved hands together.

Mr. Robinson uttered swift agreement. "I must have at least ten. My cook tells me that she cannot do with less than ten." The gentleman had brought his two liver-spotted pointers, known to be excellent in the field. They would undoubtedly retrieve more than enough pheasant for their master.

"No beaters this morning, gentlemen," said Sir William quietly.

Thomas Bennet was pleased. It was what he had expected, as had the other gentlemen. They had each brought their hunting dogs, all good pointers and flat-coated field spaniels. He preferred rough shooting, where several guns walked through a woodland or a field and shot the birds that their dogs put up. He found it to be more challenging sport than when the game was driven by beaters towards a line of standing guns.

He hoped he would bag a good number of birds. Pheasant for the table would be most welcome. With an experienced eye, he considered the stubbled field, which was bordered by the remains of a cornfield on the far side and hedgerows along the bottom edge. His eyesight was keen; he believed he could see the small movements that meant pheasant were already foraging in the fields and along the edges of the hedgerows.

His own satisfaction was voiced.

"A stand of corn! Oh, excellent, Sir William!"

Bennet knew what Mr. Long meant by his happy exclamation. The pheasants around crop fields tended to be larger in size and were finer eating, after feasting on corn, wheat, hops or other grains, than those around the wilder woodland and wetlands, and which subsisted on a leaner diet.

Sir William drew out his gold pocket watch to consult it, then snapped shut the timepiece and put it away. "It is time, gentlemen. Two hours after sunrise."

Pheasants never varied their habits. Hunters knew when to set out to hunt the birds and where to find them, fall through early spring. The game birds always returned to the thick brush, dense patches of grasses and standing cornfields, wherever there was an abundance of berries, seeds, clover and alfalfa grasses, and grasshoppers, fly larvae and mosquitoes.

Wishing one another good luck, the hunters separated. Bennet walked out into the field, slowly making his way across it through the dense patches of grass towards the cornfield. Near the edges of corn, the dead brush and weeds were about knee high. He heard the first crack of a shot, then another. Then he had his own chance. A bird burst dramatically into startled flight almost at his feet, its wings whirring, alerting its brethren with a *kok-kok-kok* call. He lifted his shotgun, feeling the recoil in his shoulder when he pulled the trigger. His spaniel retrieved the bird from where it fell. "Good girl. A nice hen." The bright-eyed spaniel lolled its pink tongue and wagged its tail vigorously.

Bennet walked slowly on, his narrowed eyes examining every bit of tangled cover. Pheasants hunkered down in the standing corn stalks were hard to hunt because they ran through the brush to avoid their pursuers. Running was the pheasant's preferred mode of escape. However, a wily pheasant would not move, even when a dog's nose was almost upon it. The pheasant's color camouflaged it so well in the shadowed brush that it couldn't be seen. More than once, Bennet almost walked right past one of the birds without ever noticing it until he was alerted by his canine partner. A good hunting dog would point at the pheasant, and in that, his spaniel was invaluable.

By mid-morning, the pheasant had stopped feeding and sought cover in the thickest brush or in trees, where they would remain until late afternoon, when they would return to their foraging. The hunters searched for them resting in their roosting places of grassy stands, along the edges of the fields and ditch banks.

At length, the day's hunting was pronounced to be a success by all of the party "My cook will be pleased, indeed, she will! More than two dozen altogether!" exclaimed Mr. Robinson.

Mr. Long held up one of his best pheasants. "Look at the crop on this one! It is the biggest I have ever beheld! And the breast on it!"

Mr. Philips admired the prized bird. "Corn fed, Long. Corn fed."

Bennet had bagged several birds, both the flamboyantly green-and-gold-and-scarlet cocks and the duller-colored hens. He experimentally weighed the three braces of birds. It would be a hefty burden to carry, but Longbourn was but a short distance away.

Some others were also testing the weight of their birds, with a thoughtful air. Along with guns and shot bags, they would make heavy work of it to get their prizes home. Mr. Robinson had come in his carriage and he said good-naturedly, "Philips! Long! Do you wish a seat back to Meryton?"

The gentlemen took him up on his offer. Mr. Philips in particular was grateful. "Good of you, Robinson."

After the three had expressed their farewells to Sir William and Mr. Bennet, the gentlemen climbed up into the vehicle and left, with their respective dogs loping along behind the rolling carriage.

Thomas Bennet had enjoyed the morning spent with his fellow man, their guns and dogs. *Conversation with sensible men. Manly sport. A rarity, indeed.* It had done him good to be away from the feminine sphere that held sway at Longbourn. Feeling content and pleasantly fatigued, he was moved to quietly quote a favorite poem.

"The whirring Pheasant springs,
And mounts, exulting on triumphant wings:
Ah! What avails his glossy, varying dyes,
His purple crest, and scarlet-circled eyes,

The vivid green his shining plumes unfold,
His painted wings, and breast that flames with gold."

"Pretty, that," remarked Sir William. "What is it?"

"Alexander Pope, 1713."

"You are a marvelously bookish fellow." Sir William's jovial mien faded to a more thoughtful cast. "What think you of all this fuss over Netherfield Park being let? I have heard of little else spoken of whenever Lady Lucas and her friends come together. I am forever being asked what I thought of Mr. Bingley, once I had paid a courtesy call. I liked the man, by the by, he is not at all one of your arrogant gentlemen. And now this upcoming assembly!"

Bennet was willing enough to express his view. "I also took a liking to Mr. Bingley, and my good opinion of him was strengthened upon his returning my own morning call. He seems to be a cheerful, sensible young gentleman. However, that does not change the riptide effect his coming to Netherfield has already had."

"I know well you do not much care for such things, but do you attend the assembly, in light of Mr. Bingley's debut into our local society?"

Bennet shook his head. "No, I think not. I shall stay at home, where I will try to persuade myself all is the same as it ever was."

"I must go, of course, to accompany Lady Lucas and my daughters, Charlotte and Maria. But I don't follow you, Bennet, what do you mean?"

"I fear the neighborhood will never be the same, Sir William," he said ruefully. "This month's assembly, where Mr. Bingley is to put in his first public appearance, is but the beginning. The ladies will be vying to outdo themselves at entertaining. The maidens will preen and put on airs." He lifted his braces of birds to illustrate his point. "All to bag a gentleman of four thousand a year!"

Sir William chuckled at the quip. "I heard it was five thousand!"

"Even worse." Bennet shrugged. "Of course, if Bingley was already married, then no one would care a whit."

"You do have five daughters," said Sir William with a sly grin.

Bennet threw up a gloved hand. "Spare me, I beg you! It is all I hear about until my ears are ringing. Mrs. Bennet insists one of her daughters must wed Mr. Bingley. It is already a settled thing, you know!"

Sir William laughed again.

Bennet thought to turn the tables on his friend. "As I recall, *you* have two daughters of marriageable age. Is not Lady Lucas also plotting?"

Sir William smiled but shrugged. "Oh, well, my poor dear Charlotte is already past the age of expectation for a proposal. As for Maria, she is still young, at sixteen, and not yet fully out. I do not wish her to wed so soon. So, I do in all earnestness yield the field. I shall not compete against you, Thomas."

"Good of you," remarked Bennet dryly.

Sir William grinned. He placed a hand over his heart and made a flourishing bow. "The field of tournament is left wide open for your girls! What knights shall you entertain, oh, king of Longbourn, what favors shall you require for the hands of your beauteous maidens?"

Bennet made a rude remark, punctuated by an even ruder gesture, which greatly amused Sir William.

§

Hunsford, near Westerham, Kent

15th October

Dear Sir,

The disagreement subsisting between yourself and my late honored father, always gave me much uneasiness, and since I have had the misfortune to lose him, I have frequently wished to heal the breach but for some time I was kept back by my own doubts, fearing lest it might seem disrespectful to his memory for me to be on good terms with any one, with whom it had always pleased him to be at variance...

If you should have no objection to receive me into your house, I propose myself the satisfaction of waiting on you and your family, Monday, November 18th, by four o'clock, and shall probably trespass on your hospitality till the Saturday se'night following, which I can do without any inconvenience...

I remain, dear sir, with respectful compliments to your lady and daughters, your well-wisher and friend,

William Collins

[3]

The Meryton assembly ball was anticipated with heady excitement. The evening of it, Thomas Bennet retired early to the library, but even through the closed oaken door, he could hear the sounds that meant the ladies of the household were getting ready. Slamming of doors, cries for Mrs. Hill and Sally the maid, bursts of giggling and excited voices, and above it all, Mrs. Bennet's shrill demanding accents.

Bennet selected one from amongst his many favorite books from his shelves and settled into his comfortable chair beside the warm fireside, crossing his ankles on a well-worn hassock, and began to read. His spaniel bitch had watched these familiar actions, then circled twice on the lumpy pillow, and curled up. Dropping head on paws, the dog shut its eyes, and huffed gently in sleep.

The ormolu mantel clock ticked. A quarter hour passed; then a second quarter. The clock chimed the hour. Shortly thereafter, he heard the pattering of myriad footsteps, bustling and hubbub, and finally, the shutting of the front door. He lifted his head and listened for a few moments. The clattering of the carriage and hoofbeats sounded without, then the rumbling of the carriage wheels faded.

Silence had fallen on the house at last. He heard only the slow *tick-tock* of the clock. Thomas Bennet drew a contented sigh. It would be several hours before the return of his wife and daughters and he looked forward to a peaceful, uninterrupted evening.

Mrs. Bennet, along with her two youngest daughters, often visited her elder sister, Mrs. Philips. The lady resided in Meryton, which was only one mile from Longbourn, and as she was very agreeable to hear whatever gossip was to be had, she was always able to relate the latest. A report had been bandied about that Mr. Bingley was to bring twelve ladies and seven gentlemen with him to the assembly.

Mrs. Bennet had received the news with displeasure. "Oh, sister! I wish Mr. Bingley would leave all the ladies at home!"

However, when the Netherfield party entered the assembly room, it consisted of only five altogether: Mr. Bingley, his two sisters, the husband of the eldest, and another young man. Along with everyone else, Charlotte Lucas surveyed them with a great deal of curiosity.

Mr. Bingley lived up to report; he was good-looking and gentlemanly. He had a pleasant countenance and easy, unaffected manners. His sisters were fine women, with an air of decided fashion. Charlotte could not help envying, just a little, the elegance of their gowns. She formed a lesser opinion of Mr. Bingley's brother-in-law; he ignored all in his path in his beeline for the refreshment table.

Mr. Hurst merely looks the gentleman. Mr. Darcy, however – she heard murmurings around her and she knew it was not only her attention which had been drawn by his fine, tall person, handsome features and noble mien. Within five minutes of his entrance, it was circulating that he had ten thousand a year and a large estate in Derbyshire. Mr. Darcy's popularity was assured. The gentlemen pronounced him to be a fine figure of a man. The ladies declared he was much handsomer than Mr. Bingley. He was looked at with great admiration for about half the evening, until his aloof manners gave a disgust which turned the tide. He was discovered to be proud, to be above his company, and his countenance was described as most forbidding and disagreeable, and he was unworthy of being compared to his friend.

Mr. Bingley soon made himself acquainted with all the principal people in the room, having already met most of the gentlemen through morning calls, and they in turn presented their wives and daughters and nieces. Sir William introduced Lady Lucas and his eldest daughter. Mr. Bingley was so flattering as to lead Charlotte out for the first dance of the evening. It was a triumph, she knew it was, as several disgruntled female gazes proved, following her progress. She was never singled out in such a way by gentlemen and she was grateful to Mr. Bingley for the unique experience. *Indeed, it quite puffs up my own conceit!*

Charlotte found her partner to be lively and unreserved. He gazed about him with unalloyed enjoyment and exclaimed, "What a splendid ball! Everyone has been most congenial! I must give a ball myself at Netherfield!"

"All of your neighbors would delight in such an agreeable entertainment."

"Do you think so? Well, then, I will do it."

After their set finished, Mr. Bingley bowed and flashed a friendly grin. He immediately went across to Mrs. Bennet, where she was standing with her eldest daughter, his obvious object to be introduced, so that he could solicit Miss Bennet's hand for the next set. Charlotte was not surprised. Jane Bennet was quite the loveliest lady in the room. However, she *was* surprised when, through the evening, Mr. Bingley subsequently danced every dance, requesting even the hands of ladies who were not noted for comeliness. There was always a greater number of ladies at these functions and Mr. Bingley's happy progress did not go unnoticed.

His good manners are in direct contrast to his friend.

Mr. Darcy danced only once with Mrs. Hurst and once with Miss Bingley, declined being introduced to any other lady, spok occasionally to one of his party, and spent the rest of the evening in walking about the room.

His character was decided.

"He is the proudest, most disagreeable man in the world," exclaimed Mrs. Bennet to her sister.

Mrs. Philips agreed. "Everybody hopes he will never come again."

Circulating about the room, greeting friends and neighbors, occasionally taking the floor at the behest of a gentleman, Charlotte heard it all. She thought it a pity such a fine-appearing gentleman could so quickly develop such a horrible reputation. However, there was worse to come.

Charlotte and her friend Elizabeth Bennet had sat down for two dances, there being a scarcity of gentlemen, and compared lively observations of the evening. Mr. Darcy had drifted their way and he was standing near enough for them to overhear a conversation between him and Mr. Bingley, which at first was most interesting.

"Come, Darcy, I must have you dance. I hate to see you standing about by yourself in this stupid manner. You had much better dance."

"I certainly shall not. You know how I detest it, unless I am particularly acquainted with my partner. At such an assembly as this, it would be insupportable. Your sisters are engaged, and there is not another woman in the room, whom it would not be a punishment to me to stand up with."

At the gentleman's sweeping denouncement, Charlotte and Elizabeth exchanged significant looks. After Mr. Darcy's appalling lack of civility all evening, they were not surprised that he should express such a harsh opinion.

"I would not be so fastidious as you are for a kingdom! Upon my honor, I never met with so many pleasant girls in my life, as I have this evening, and there are several of them who are uncommonly pretty."

"You are dancing with the only handsome girl in the room, the eldest Miss Bennet."

Charlotte saw that Elizabeth's astonishment equaled her own. Then she looked pleased, that even the proud, disagreeable Mr. Darcy had confessed that Miss Jane Bennet was attractive.

"Oh! She is the most beautiful creature I ever beheld! But there is one of her sisters sitting down just behind you, who is very pretty, and I daresay, very agreeable. Do let me ask my partner to introduce you."

Charlotte and Elizabeth pretended not to have heard a word. Instead, they concentrated on staring at the rows of couples going down the dance on the floor. Out of the corner of her eye, Charlotte saw Mr. Darcy turn and look for a moment at her friend.

"Which do you mean?" Elizabeth apparently couldn't stand the suspense and she slightly turned her head, catching his gaze. Mr. Darcy turned away and coldly said, "She is tolerable, but not handsome enough to tempt me. And I am in no humor at present to give consequence to young ladies who are slighted by other men."

Charlotte saw the sudden flush that rose in Elizabeth's face. Mr. Bingley must have also. "For God's sake, Darcy! She's overheard you. Have a care."

Mr. Darcy appeared self-conscious for an instant, followed swiftly by irritation. "You had better return to your partner and enjoy her smiles, for you are wasting your time with me."

Without uttering a word more, embarrassment in his expression, Mr. Bingley followed his friend's advice.

Mr. Darcy walked swiftly away, his hands clenching and unclenching at his sides.

Elizabeth's head had lowered, her side curls soft against her temples. She was biting her lip. Charlotte reached out and clasped her friend's hand, squeezing it in sympathy. "My dear Eliza! I am so sorry."

Elizabeth shook her head and raised her chin. She slid a laughing glance her way. "Well! I have no vanity left to me. Whatever shall I do since I have not Mr. Darcy's good opinion?"

Charlotte chuckled along with her, but she wondered if the hurtful words had stung more than Elizabeth let on. She feared it, but Elizabeth would never let it show. *Instead, she will make a droll joke of it.* It was precisely what Elizabeth did do, to the entertainment of her friends. Charlotte herself was caught up by laughter at the way Elizabeth held up Mr. Darcy's insult for ridicule.

When Mrs. Bennet heard of it, however, she was not amused. An angry flush mounted in her cheeks. The lady's dislike for Mr. Darcy's general behavior was sharpened into particular resentment by his having slighted one of her daughters. "What a disagreeable man!"

Soon after, the ball ended and the Bennet ladies found their wraps and took cheerful leave of all their departing friends. Many were the promises exchanged to call upon one another on the morrow, to discuss the ball and to compare impressions.

When the wheels of the carriage could be heard, the footman was waiting to open the front door and the butler received Mr. Bennet's family as they re-entered the house on a rush of animated feminine voices and very chilly night air, relieving the ladies of their separate wraps. Thomas Bennet had moved into the large parlor some time before so that he could learn what had taken place at the assembly. With a book he was oblivious of time, but on the present occasion he had a good deal of curiosity as to an evening which had raised such splendid expectations. He had rather hoped that all his wife's views on the new leaser of Netherfield would be disappointed, but he soon found he had a very different story to hear.

"Oh! My dear Mr. Bennet," she said as she entered the room, followed by all of her daughters. "We have had a most delightful evening, a most excellent ball. I wish you had been there. Jane was so admired nothing could be like it. Everybody said how well she looked, and Mr. Bingley thought her *quite* beautiful, and danced with her twice. Only think of that, my dear, he actually danced with her *twice*! And she was the only creature in the room that he asked a second time. First of all, he asked Miss Lucas. I was so vexed to see him stand up with her; but, however, he did not admire her at all. Indeed, *nobody* can, you know; and he seemed quite struck with Jane as she was going down the dance. So, he enquired who she was, and got introduced, and asked her for the two next. Then the two third he danced with Miss King, and the two fourth with Maria Lucas, and the two fifth with Jane again, and the two sixth with Lizzy, and the Boulanger."

"If he had any compassion for me, he would not have danced half so much!" Bennet carefully placed a bookmark of black satin ribbon and snapped shut his book. "For God's sake, say no more of his partners. I wish he had sprained his ankle in the first dance!"

Mrs. Bennet tittered, as though at a particularly good joke. "Oh, my dear, I am quite delighted with him. He is so excessively handsome! And his sisters are charming women. I never in my life saw anything more elegant than their dresses. I daresay the lace upon Mrs. Hurst's gown-"

"I protest against any description of finery," he said firmly. He knew such descriptions of fashion, once embarked upon, would last many, many minutes.

Balked for only a second or two, Mrs. Bennet then related, with much bitterness of spirit and heightened complexion, the shocking rudeness of Mr. Darcy. "*Everyone* was exclaiming over it! But, I can assure you that Lizzy does not lose much by not suiting *his* fancy. He is a most disagreeable, horrid man, not at all worth pleasing. So high and conceited that there was no enduring him!" Mrs. Bennet flung each hand out in a dramatic gesture. "He walked *here*, and he walked *there*, fancying himself so very great! *Not handsome enough to dance with!* I wish you had been there, my dear, to have given him one of your set-downs. I quite detest the man."

Thomas Bennet smiled and took it all in with a grain of salt, knowing well his wife's penchant for exaggeration. However, his curiosity *was* piqued. "Well, Lizzy? What have you to say about this Mr. Darcy?"

"I have no very cordial feelings towards him," said Elizabeth with a shake of her head. She lowered her voice in mimic of a man's tone. "She is tolerable, but not handsome enough to tempt me!" She laughed. "Mama is right, he is not worth pleasing."

"I am glad you can take delight in the ridiculous, Lizzy." Bennet turned to his eldest daughter. "I have heard you were much admired, Jane. So, Mr. Bingley danced with you twice!"

"I was much gratified, and I was distinguished by his sisters," said Jane quietly.

Bennet nodded at her in approval. "You do well in your modesty, Jane."

Elizabeth smiled at her sister. "I was glad of Jane's pleasure.

Mary leaped in, saying, with a touch of pride, "I heard myself mentioned to Miss Bingley as the most accomplished girl in the neighborhood."

"A triumph, indeed," said Bennet gently. This middle daughter of his was the plainest of the five, having inherited his masterful nose and firm jaw; features which had added to his own countenance, but which had detracted from accepted traits of beauty in hers. She had worked to set herself apart from her sisters with accomplishments, unfortunately with little enough to show for her efforts. She had little formal training in voice or on the pianoforte and she had never had anyone to instruct her in intellectual pursuits. *Fordyce's Sermons* was her strong preference and she moralized to all and sundry in such a way that she was ignored or avoided by nearly everyone, and so was explained her obvious, pathetic pleasure in a passing remark uttered to a stranger.

Of a sudden, he felt a twist of unexpected guilt. *I should have at least guided some part of Mary's learning.* But the years had seemed to speed by, swallowed up in his own disappointments and the tempests of his wife. He huffed a low, sardonic laugh for his pitiable excuses. *A sop to your conscience, Bennet!* It was really quite admirable that she had done as well as she had, being mostly self-taught. He supposed it did show some intellect and even more tenacity, which was as much as he could say about her. Nevertheless, he gravely acknowledged what she felt was of such import. "The accolade is one you will treasure for some time, I feel certain."

Mary subsided with a half-smile.

"Well, Kitty and I were never once without partners," said Lydia with a toss of her head.

"And that is all *we* care about at a ball," added Catherine.

§

Maple Grove, near Bristol

17th October

Dear Aunt Lucas,

In answer to all the questions in your letter, I do assure you that you can have no fears in retaining the services of my dear young sister's former governess. You may rely upon my sincere recommendations of Miss Simmons, who is of good character, gentle birth but impoverished means, and possesses exemplary skills of education, and who is, I am certain, fully capable of handling a set of lively boys and able to prepare them for any fine boarding school.

If it were not for Augusta's launch into Bath society, which is much anticipated by her – believe me! – I would certainly have kept Miss Simmons in our household for another year. However, August is adamant that she is matured beyond the services of a governess, which is the reason I first approached you with the notion of hiring Miss Simmons.

I must ask a boon of you, dear aunt Lucas, and that is for August to come stay with you for a fortnight – perhaps two- as I am shortly to enter my first confinement, and I must confess, I am fair exhausted by all of Augusta's exuberance. She will help me, whether I will it or not, you see! I discover I am of a nervous disposition. Her travel arrangements will not be a great inconvenience, for Miss Simmons may accompany her in a hired carriage, with all propriety, and they shall set down at Lucas Lodge on Tuesday, November 18th.

I do know your kind heart, and the kind affability of Sir William Lucas, and I am confident you will welcome my dear sister Augusta with open arms.

I remain your devoted niece,

Mrs. Selina Suckling

When Lady Lucas finished her letter, her forehead was creased. She immediately sought out her husband. "My dear sir, hear is my niece Selena informing me that she is not only sending her former governess, but her sister, too!" She held out the sheet for him to take.

"Miss Hawkins?" Sir William made himself master of the contents of her letter and afterwards handed it back to her. He calmly regarded his wife. "I see nothing in this to disturb you, my dear. Mrs. Suckling explains most adequately her thoughts, and she is quite right, we shall offer Miss Hawkins a most civil hospitality. It is in a good cause, after all. You would not want Mrs. Suckling's mental state during her confinement to be other than composed, rather than to be fretted by her young sister."

"Well, no, of course not! However, I do find it passing strange that Selena never hinted earlier in our correspondence that she wished for such an arrangement."

Sir William shrugged. "What I find strange, as you so eloquently put it, is there is not a word of Mr. Suckling, when she was always before penning a great many things of him."

"Why, whatever do you mean?"

"I am reading between the lines. Depend upon it, my dear, it is not your niece who is fault for this abrupt draw upon our hospitality, but Mr. Suckling! I suspect he is behind it, not wishing for any upset to his wife's equilibrium. So, he has required her to send away Miss Hawkins until after the blessed event."

Lady Lucas was much struck. She glanced back down at her letter. "Augusta's exuberance...her nervous disposition...why, sir, I believe you may very well be right!"

"I have a shrewd business head; I know a thing or two. Mr. Suckling has made his fortune. A few years ago, he purchased a snug property, making of him one of the new gentry class." Sir William smiled at his spouse. "We did the same when we took up Lucas Lodge."

Lady Lucas pursed her lips. "Indeed, that is so."

"Mr. Suckling will not chance his wife's well-being at such a time, for she may birth a fine heir, the first of his family who will be acknowledged as landed gentry."

"I have heard the Bingleys have ties to trade," mused Lady Lucas.

Sir William nodded. "I had the history from Mr. Bingley himself. Mr. Bingley's father sent Bingley and his sisters to be educated with the higher echelons of society. Now, Mr. Bingley is learning to administer an estate, with an eye to buying one, whether it is Netherfield Park or some other. He is friends with Mr. Darcy, who is related to some of the most prestigious families in the kingdom, and his elder sister is married to a fashionable man whose father is a baronet. Miss Bingley is a haughty creature, but she will no doubt make an even more advantageous marriage than her sister."

"And you believe much of this same thinking has passed through Mr. Suckling's mind?"

"Indeed, and I do not fault him for it," said Sir William emphatically. "When I was knighted, my eyes were opened to possible paths for my children that I could never dream of before, which, as you know, is why I removed us out of Meryton and purchased this place. The eldest son, our John, shall have Lucas Lodge, along with the farm, while the rest of our boys shall go away to school, where they will make such connections that must raise them – such a connection as Mr. Bingley has found in Mr. Darcy. So, there you have it! Miss Simmons has her work cut out for her with the youngsters. For the elder boys, we shall continue with the tutor."

"And our dear girls must *share* in the advantages of having a superior governess," admonished Lady Lucas. "I should so like to see Maria and the younger darlings enhance their chances of a good marriage."

"And what have you planned for Charlotte?"

Lady Lucas sighed. "Dearest Charlotte! I fear it all comes too late for her."

[4]

At Lucas Lodge, during a large evening party, Elizabeth confided to Charlotte Lucas her pleased observations. "Whenever Jane and Mr. Bingley meet, it is plain he admires her. It is equally evident that Jane is yielding to the preference which she had begun to entertain for him from the first. She is in a way to be very much in love."

Charlotte gently plied her open fan. "Jane appears very cheerful."

Elizabeth was watching as Mr. Bingley and her sister went down the dance. In all earnestness, she said, "It is not likely to be discovered by the world in general, of course, since Jane unites with great strength of feeling a composure of temper and a uniform cheerfulness of manner, which will guard her from the suspicion of the impertinent."

Charlotte had already noted Mr. Bingley's assiduous attentions, and agreed that he admired her. "But I do not see Jane's happy demureness in the same way. It may perhaps be pleasant to be able to deceive the public in such a case, but it is sometimes a disadvantage to be so very guarded."

Elizabeth looked at her, surprised. "Why, whatever do you mean?"

Charlotte discreetly gestured with her fan at the couple. "If a woman conceals her affections with the same skill from the *object* of it, she may lose the opportunity of fixing him. And it will then be but poor consolation to believe the world equally in the dark. There is so much gratitude or vanity in almost every attachment, that it is not safe to leave any to itself."

"What are these sentiments? I do not recognize them." Elizabeth said lightly, "Surely, your opinion takes too dim a view of the chance for love."

Charlotte shook her head. "I do not believe so. We can all begin freely – a slight preference is natural enough. But there are very few of us who have heart enough to be really in love without encouragement. In nine cases out of ten, a woman had better show more affection than she feels. Mr. Bingley likes your sister, undoubtedly, but he may never do more than like her, if she does not help him on."

Elizabeth's smile slipped. "But she *does* help him on, as much as her nature will allow. If I can perceive Jane's regard for him, he must be a simpleton indeed not to discover it, too."

"Remember, Eliza, he does not know Jane's disposition as you do."

"But if a woman is partial to a man, and does not endeavor to conceal it, he must find it out."

Charlotte lifted her shoulders in a slight shrug. "Perhaps he must, if he sees enough of her. But though Mr. Bingley and Jane meet tolerably often, it is never for many hours together, and as they always see each other in large mixed parties, it is impossible that every moment should be employed in conversing together. And that is what is needed."

At her friend's open doubt, Charlotte smiled a little. She thought Elizabeth's naivety was understandable but mistaken. It was so obvious to her that Elizabeth had not yet given much reflection to what their situation as impoverished gentlewomen actually meant. *We are very unlike Miss Bingley. Our birth is better but we have not got thirty thousand pounds.*

Though Mrs. Bennet was beyond foolish, and her methods were vulgar, the lady *was* in the right of it that a push must be made if her daughters were to enter into respectable marriages. "Jane should make the most of every half hour in which she can command Mr. Bingley's attention. When she is secure of him, there will be leisure for falling in love as much as she chooses."

Elizabeth said playfully, "Your plan is a good one, Charlotte, where nothing is in question but the desire of being well married; and if I were determined to get a rich husband, or any husband, I daresay I should adopt it."

Charlotte laughed softly. "Nothing in question, indeed! I believe you would question your heart most earnestly!"

Elizabeth's amusement had swiftly faded. She furrowed her brows. "But these are not *Jane's* feelings. She is not acting by design. As yet, she cannot even be certain of the degree of her own regard, nor of its reasonableness. She has known him only a fortnight. She danced four dances with him at Meryton. She saw him one morning at his own house, during a courtesy call after the assembly, and has since dined in company with him four times. This is not quite enough to make her understand his character."

Charlotte gave a nod of agreement. "Not as you represent it. Had she merely dined with him, then she might only have discovered whether he had a good appetite. But you must remember that four evenings have also been spent together – and four evenings may do a great deal."

"Yes, these four evenings have enabled them to ascertain that they both like Commerce better than any other parlor game," retorted Elizabeth. "But with respect to any other leading characteristics, I do not imagine that much has been unfolded."

Realizing Elizabeth was becoming ruffled, Charlotte said pacifically, "Well, I wish Jane success with all my heart. If she was married to him tomorrow, I should think she had as good a chance of happiness, as if she was to be studying his character for a twelvemonth."

Charlotte had given over much time to consider her own unwedded state and had long since, with wistful resignation, put aside romanticism as a girl's fantasy. She expressed the result of her introspection. "Happiness in marriage is entirely a matter of chance. If the disposition of the parties are ever so well-known to each other, or ever so similar beforehand, it does not advance their felicity in the least. They always continue to grow sufficiently unalike, afterwards to have their share of vexations. It is better to know as little as possible of the defects of the person with whom you are to pass your life."

At the end of her little speech, Elizabeth shook her head, smiling fondly at her. "You make me laugh, Charlotte, but it is not sound. You know it is not sound, and that you would never act in this way yourself."

Charlotte said no more. It was obvious to her that Elizabeth could not enter into her feelings. She was seven years older than her friend. *Eliza is still of a romantic turn of mind.* She was not yet officially on the shelf, unlike Charlotte herself. Elizabeth had yet to accept the harsh realities of being a woman of no fortune or prospect.

A comfortable silence fell, occasionally broken by whatever desultory remarks that occurred to either of them or about their conversations with others.

"Your cousin, Miss Hawkins, who comes on 19th November, do you know her well?"

"I have never met her." Charlotte related what she had been told. "Mama knew the family when the parents still lived. The eldest daughter is wed to a Mr. Suckling. I have a curiosity to make Augusta's acquaintance."

Elizabeth murmured a response, but her thoughts were obviously elsewhere, for she said suddenly, "What does Mr. Darcy mean by listening to my conversation with Colonel. Forster? Indeed, he has attended to my conversations with others, as well."

"That is a question which only Mr. Darcy can answer." Charlotte was surprised by her friend's comment. She had not herself observed such odd behavior but she accepted Elizabeth's perception. Elizabeth was always watching everyone around her, her lively humor finding much to amuse her in her fellow creatures. If Mr. Darcy was indeed paying such close attention to her, Elizabeth would certainly be aware of it, and it set Charlotte to wonder. She slid a speculative glance at her friend.

Such decided attention sets up a very interesting possibility.

She expressed her audacious supposition "Perhaps you are becoming an object of some interest in his eyes. He begins to wish to know more of you, and it is a step towards conversing with you himself."

"Oh, Charlotte, what fancy is this? I cannot agree with you! Recall his opinion of me," said Elizabeth, shaking her head and smiling. "But if he does it any more, I shall certainly let him know that I see what he is about. He has a very *satirical* eye, and if I do not begin by being impertinent myself, I shall soon grow afraid of him."

Charlotte laughed. "Oh, come! Surely, it is quite the opposite. No sooner had Mr. Darcy made it clear to himself and his friends that you have hardly a good feature in your face than he began to find it was rendered uncommonly intelligent by the beautiful expression of your dark eyes. To this discovery succeeded some others equally mortifying."

Elizabeth looked arch. "He has been forced to acknowledge my figure to be light and pleasing, I suppose!"

"Precisely! In addition, though your manners are not those of the fashionable world, he is caught by their easy playfulness."

"You are in a strange, teasing mood this evening, Charlotte."

"Am I, indeed? But you are of a romantic nature, Eliza! Surely you must admit my nonsense to be most agreeable to your imagination."

"Oh, it is! But you have chosen the wrong gentleman for the hero of your silly piece. Mr. Darcy is the man who has made himself agreeable nowhere, and who did not think me handsome enough to dance with, so to me, he is only that and can never be anything more, even in imagination."

Mr. Darcy approached them soon afterwards, though without seeming to have any intention of speaking. Behind her gloved hand, Charlotte defied her friend to mention her previous observation to him, which immediately provoked Elizabeth's high spirit. She turned and said, "Did not you think, Mr. Darcy, that I expressed myself uncommonly well just now, when I was teasing Colonel Forster to give us a ball at Meryton?"

Mr. Darcy appeared astonished to be addressed. Charlotte awaited with suspended alarm the outcome of her friend's bravado. She expected a strong set-down from such a proud man. Mr. Darcy's measured reply came as a surprise. "With great energy. But it is a subject which always makes a lady energetic."

"You are severe on us," said Elizabeth, looking a little taken aback. A lurking smile then touched her countenance. "But I have a suspicion you are twitting me, Mr. Darcy."

"Not at all, Miss Elizabeth. Your lively manner is enjoyable."

At having won such a compliment – from Mr. Darcy! – Elizabeth's lips parted. Speech appeared beyond her; she could only stare up at the gentleman. She glanced rather helplessly at Charlotte. Though astonished herself by Mr. Darcy's unexpected and unprecedented civility, Charlotte rose to the occasion. "It will be her turn soon to be teased, Mr. Darcy. I am going to open the instrument, Eliza, and you know what follows."

"You are a very strange creature by way of a friend! Always wanting me to play and sing before anybody and everybody!" exclaimed Elizabeth, in command of herself again. "If my vanity had taken a musical turn, you would have been invaluable, but as it is, I would really rather not sit down before those who must be in the habit of hearing the very best performers."

"Oh, but I insist."

"Very well. If it must be so, it must." Glancing gravely at Mr. Darcy, Elizabeth added, "There is a fine old saying, which everybody here is of course familiar with – keep your breath to cool your porridge – and I shall keep mine to swell my song."

Along with everyone else, Charlotte listened to her friend's lively, pleasing performance. After a song or two, and before Elizabeth could reply to several entreaties that she would sing again, she was usurped at the instrument by Mary Bennet.

Charlotte sighed, thinking it was regrettable. She thought she understood, however. In consequence of being the plainer one in the family, Mary was always impatient for display. The young woman worked hard for knowledge and accomplishment, but she had neither genius nor taste. Vanity had given her application, but it had also given her a pedantic air and conceited manner, which would have injured a higher degree of excellence than she had reached. Elizabeth, easy and unaffected, had been listened to with much more pleasure, though not playing half so well. Mary, at the end of a long concerto, was glad to purchase praise and gratitude by playing Scotch and Irish airs, at the request of her younger sisters, who with some of the Lucases and two or three officers joined eagerly in dancing at one end of the room.

Charlotte was still standing beside Mr. Darcy when her father came up and addressed the gentleman. "What a charming amusement for young people this is, Mr. Darcy! There is nothing like dancing, after all. I consider it as one of the first refinements of polished societies."

"Certainly, sir, and it has the advantage also of being in vogue amongst the less polished societies of the world. Every savage can dance."

Charlotte winced at Mr. Darcy's acidic reply. It was meant as a sharp set-down for her father.

However, Sir William only smiled. His congeniality was unimpaired by Mr. Darcy's cold reply. "Your friend Bingley performs delightfully and I doubt not that you are an adept in the science yourself, Mr. Darcy."

"You saw me dance at Meryton, I believe, sir."

"Yes, indeed, and received no inconsiderable pleasure from the sight. Do you often dance at St. James's?"

"Never, sir."

"Do you not think it would be a proper compliment to the place?"

"It is a compliment which I never pay to any place if I can avoid it."

"You have a house in town, I conclude."

Mr. Darcy bowed.

"I had some thoughts of fixing in town myself, for I am fond of superior society. But I did not feel quite certain the air of London would agree with Lady Lucas." Sir William paused, obviously in hopes of an answer, but this time Mr. Darcy did not respond.

Charlotte saw that Elizabeth was threading her way towards them through the company. Sir William called out to her. "My dear Miss Eliza, why are you not dancing? Mr. Darcy, you must allow me to present this young lady to you as a very desirable partner. You cannot refuse to dance, I am sure, when so much beauty is before you."

Charlotte nearly dropped her fan. She stood stock-still, unable to do anything to avert what was surely a disaster to unfold before her very eyes. It did not matter that several minutes before, Mr. Darcy had unbent enough to pay her friend a compliment. This was something altogether different. *Oh, Papa, your good intent presses too much!* Mr. Darcy's disagreeableness was well-known and he would certainly squelch such presumption.

Sir William took Elizabeth's hand and he would have given it to Mr. Darcy, when she instantly drew back and said with some discomposure to Sir William, "Indeed, sir, I have not the least intention of dancing. I entreat you not to suppose that I moved this way in order to beg for a partner."

Mr. Darcy had appeared surprised, then amenable to Sir William's gallant suggestion. With grave propriety he requested to be allowed the honor of her hand, but in vain. Elizabeth was determined in her refusal and Charlotte had a very fair notion of why. *Eliza's pride was wounded by Mr. Darcy's comments at Meryton.* She had not forgotten what he had said about her being only tolerable, and so could not tempt her to dance with him.

Sir William tried to persuade her. "You excel so much in the dance, Miss Eliza, that it is cruel to deny me the happiness of seeing you. And though this gentleman dislikes the amusement in general, he can have no objection, I am sure, to oblige us for one half hour."

"Mr. Darcy is all politeness," said Elizabeth with a small smile.

"He is indeed. But considering the inducement, my dear Miss Eliza, we cannot wonder at his complaisance, for who would object to such a partner?"

Elizabeth looked archly and turned away, catching Charlotte's gaze. "Come, Charlotte. I have something I wish to say to you." She firmly linked her arm in Charlotte's and the two walked away.

"That was very brave and very rude of you, my dear Eliza," said Charlotte in a low voice. She was much relieved by Mr. Darcy's unexpected forbearance. *That is twice in one evening. Eliza must surely be cognizant of it.* "Mr. Darcy must have gathered a strange opinion of you just now."

"What have I to do with Mr. Darcy? I care not for that gentleman's good opinion!"

[5]

Breakfast was interrupted by the entrance of the footman with a note for the eldest Miss Bennet. It came from Netherfield Park and the servant who had carried it waited for an answer.

Thomas Bennet quirked a brow. *A note. For Jane.* Mr. Bingley would not have written directly to his daughter. Such a thing was not done between a lady and an unrelated gentleman. The note could only have come from one of the Netherfield ladies, proffering a social invitation. His interest was lukewarm at best; it was otherwise with his wife.

Mrs. Bennet's eyes sparkled with pleasure. "Well, Jane, who is it from? What is it about? What does he say? Well, Jane, make haste and tell us. Make haste, my love."

Ah, she leaps to fanciful conjecture. What does he say, indeed!

"It is from Miss Bingley. She asks me to dine today with herself and Mrs. Hurst."

Mrs. Bennet threw up her hands. "Really, Jane! It is alike to pulling teeth! What of Mr. Bingley? Does she say anything of him?"

"Her brother and the gentlemen are to dine with the officers."

"With the officers!" cried Lydia. "I wonder my aunt did not tell us of *that!*"

Mrs. Bennet pursed her lips. "Dining out. That is very unlucky."

"May I have the carriage?"

Mrs. Bennet shook her head. "No, my dear, you had better go on horseback, because it seems likely to rain. And then you must stay all night."

Jane's eyes widened. "Likely to rain? Stay the night? Mama, you cannot mean it!"

Bennet's spurious attention sharpened. He leaned back in his chair to observe the overall reaction to Mrs. Bennet's absurd stratagem. He heard a soft snort from Mary. *She may have gathered the import, but she will say nothing.* The two younger sisters responded just as he would have expected. Catherine's brow wrinkled, as though she was puzzled, and she exchanged a look with Lydia, who shrugged her shoulders.

It was left to Elizabeth to dare a mild observation. "That would be a good scheme, Mama, if you were sure that they would not offer to send her home."

Mrs. Bennet's eyes flashed. She never liked to be questioned. "The gentlemen will have Mr. Bingley's chaise to go to Meryton, and the Hursts have no horses to theirs."

Jane's discomposure was visible, unusual for one with such a placid nature. "I had much rather go in the coach."

"But, my dear, your father cannot spare the horses, I am sure. They are wanted in the farm, Mr. Bennet, are they not?"

Bennet frowned as he regarded his wife. The sturdy carriage horses were useful as extra animals to pull wagons to and from the fields. The chill, wet summer had played havoc with the growing season. It had made for a delay in some of the harvest, and he had indeed been using the team. For several days, worry had begun to ride him that all the crops would not be got in before the first freezes. The signs all harbingered another harsh winter. But it was not in him to express such concerns.

"They are wanted in the farm much oftener than I can get them."

His response was acerbic. Mrs. Bennet often commandeered the team for carriage-use to make visits to her sister Philips and to the shops in Meryton. There was never a set time or day for these weekly excursions and the farm work was hindered and held hostage by her caprice. He had long since given up objection, however, for it always ended in a shattering tantrum by his dear helpmate.

Elizabeth's shrewd gaze met his narrowed eyes. Her observation was exceedingly dry. "But if you have got them today, then my mother's purpose will be answered."

Bennet covered his appreciative grin with his hand. Elizabeth's wit was one of his chief pleasures in what was a rather barren intellectual life. Mary huffed a laugh and he glanced at her, surprised. His middle daughter seemed to have unexpected depths today. "Exactly so, Lizzy."

Mrs. Bennet glared at Mary, but she reserved the daggers of her displeasure for Elizabeth. "Lizzy, you are grown altogether too pert these days, and it is most trying of you! My nerves, my poor nerves! Was there ever a mother more beset! You are enough to try a saint! But there, I shall not allow you to put me out of temper. Jane, you will go by horseback."

At the appointed time, Jane was therefore obliged to go on horseback, and her mother attended her to the door with many cheerful prognostics of a bad day. Her hopes were answered. Jane had not been gone long before it rained hard, a cold driving rain that sucked the light out of the day. As the servants lit all of the candelabras and fed the hearth fires, Bennet gathered the general consensus. Jane's sisters were uneasy for her, but her mother was delighted. The rain continued the whole evening without intermission. Jane certainly could not come back.

"This was a lucky idea of mine, indeed!" said Mrs. Bennet, more than once, as if taking credit for making it rain. Until the next morning, however, she was not aware of all the felicity of her contrivance. The family had not yet risen from the breakfast table when a servant from Netherfield brought a note for Elizabeth from Jane.

Mrs. Bennet was impatient. "Well, well, what does it say?"

Elizabeth looked up, her brow furrowed. "Jane says she is unwell from getting wet through yesterday. She has a sore throat and headache. She is laid down in bed and the Bingleys have had the apothecary in to see her."

Bennet, not at all pleased by the intelligence, addressed his wife. "Well, my dear, if your daughter should have a dangerous fit of illness, if she should die, it would be a comfort to know it was all in pursuit of Mr. Bingley, and under your orders."

The sharp edge of his observation caused gasps from all of his daughters. Even Mrs. Bennet was not incognizant, but she shrugged. "Oh! I am not at all afraid of her dying. People do not die of little trifling colds. She will be taken good care of. As long as she stays there, it is all very well. I would go and see her, if I could have the carriage."

Thomas Bennet looked long at his wife. Her mendacity did not surprise him, but it disgusted him that she would make the *carriage* her excuse for not going to Netherfield. Mrs. Bennet had no compunction at ordering out the carriage when it came to her pleasures. It simply did not suit her to go to her daughter.

Elizabeth was still frowning. "I am determined to go to Jane, though the carriage is not to be had."

"How can you be so silly as to think of such a thing, in all this dirt!" cried her mother. "You will not be fit to be seen when you get there."

"I shall be very fit to see Jane, which is all I want."

Elizabeth was no horsewoman, so walking was her only alternative if she did not have the carriage. Bennet regarded her with a faint smile. "Is this a hint to me, Lizzy, to send for the horses?"

She shook her head. "No, indeed, I do not wish to avoid the walk. The distance is nothing, when one has a motive, only three miles. I shall be back by dinner."

However, Elizabeth was not back by dinner. Instead, a note was delivered to Longbourn to acquaint the family with what was going forward at Netherfield Park. Mrs. Bennet perused the note with delighted complaisance. "Lizzy says Jane could not bear to part from her, and so Miss Bingley, who would have ordered the chaise for her, instead invited her to prolong her stay. Oh, how fortunate that Jane is an affectionate sister! Otherwise, Lizzy would have been obliged to leave. Now I have two daughters at Netherfield! It could not have turned out better! How glad I am that Lizzy went to see dear Jane!"

With a satisfied smile, she turned to her husband. "My mind is quite set at ease. Lizzy may engage Miss Bingley's and Mrs. Hurst's interest, which will leave Jane free to enjoy Mr. Bingley's conversation."

"A wonderful thing, indeed," he agreed sardonically. "Does she say anything else?"

Mrs. Bennet dropped the note on the occasional table beside her chair and bustled to her feet. "Lizzy asks we send back a supply of clothes. I am sure there is nothing to wonder at in that! She must have been covered in mud when she arrived at Netherfield. Mrs. Hill must see to the packing of a valise."

"I was hoping to hear when she and Jane mean to return to us."

"Oh, my dear Mr. Bennet! I hope not to see them for a week, at least." Mrs. Bennet rushed away, calling for the housekeeper. "Mrs. Hill! Mrs. Hill! Come at once! I have need of you!"

Bennet was displeased but resigned himself. It was not worth the confrontation that would ensue if he were to insist on sending for a more definitive answer. *She has the management of her daughters.* The time would pass soon enough, and much more pleasantly, if he did not agitate his wife's 'nerves'. There would be no harm in letting Mrs. Bennet have her way in this; it was a small matter, after all.

He turned his attention to his estate business with a good conscience. It was with sound satisfaction that he oversaw the repair of a tenant cottage, chinking it against the coming winter, and made full use of the carriage horses at the farm. Barns began to fill; stacks of cut cordwood grew. He also took out his shotgun and, with his spaniel, succeeded in bagging some partridges and a couple of red grouse. Braised partridge, simmering in a savory broth, and the rich, gamey flavor of roasted grouse breast were quite the treat. He was able to forget about the absence of his eldest daughters until it was brought back to his attention, a few days later.

"I have had a very proper note from Lizzy. She wishes me to come to Netherfield to judge Jane's condition for myself." Mrs. Bennet gave a nod, and smiled with satisfaction. "Yes, very proper, indeed! I shall go at once."

"Mama, may I come? I should *so* like to see Netherfield!"

"Of course, Lydia. Yes, yes, Kitty, you may come, too. And Mary, well, I suppose you might as well accompany me as not."

At the shrill outbursts of glee from his two youngest daughters, Thomas Bennet winced. Lydia and Catherine ran from the room, in a hurry to put on their bonnets and cloaks, and were followed at a decorous pace by their sister Mary. He turned to his wife. "Mrs. Bennet, what does Lizzy say of Jane?"

Mrs. Bennet shrugged. "Nothing very much, Mr. Bennet. The Bingleys have sent for the apothecary. Lizzy writes that Jane is easier since his first visit, but she wishes my opinion on whether Jane is well enough to be removed from Netherfield. Well! I am very sure already that Jane should stay just where she is for now."

Bennet gently mocked. "What! Are you already so certain? Why, it is marvelous, indeed, that you can discern it from such a distance." He knew very well why his wife wanted Jane to stay at Netherfield, and it had little to do with her health and everything to do with Mrs. Bennet's ambition to see Jane established as the future mistress of Netherfield Park. He offered a mild suggestion. "Perhaps Jane will be more comfortable in her own bed."

Mrs. Bennet sniffed and tossed her head. "Nonsense, nonsense! I know you are teasing me, Mr. Bennet. But I shall not let you provoke me today, for I must be making ready to go to Netherfield."

"Mrs. Bennet, I doubt I could provoke anyone as much as you."

Mrs. Bennet eyed him with suspicion.

He blandly returned her gaze. "Will you walk as Lizzy did?"

Mrs. Bennet reddened with temper. "Of course not! Three miles! Whatever are you thinking, Mr. Bennet? I shall order out the carriage."

"But you told Jane that I have use of the horses on the farm," he murmured with a twist of his lips.

Mrs. Bennet turned sharply about and stalked from the drawing-room.

With a sigh, Bennet also left the drawing-room. *Sometimes it wearies me to the soul to deal with Fanny.* He walked slowly into his sanctuary, shadowed at his heels by his faithful spaniel, and with a firm backward thrust of his hand shut the door. He sat down behind his desk and began to go through his neglected correspondence. On most common occasions, he was a negligent and dilatory correspondent; but once begun, he would work through the whole, and pen those letters he deemed worthy of reply. He ignored the loud, excitable exclamations and bustling of leave-taking.

His wife and daughters were not gone long when there was a respectful knock on the library door and it opened under the butler's hand. "Mr. Bennet, Miss Lucas has come to call."

"Thank you, Hill. I will come." Thomas Bennet exited the library and crossed through the entry hall to turn into the small front parlor, where he found Miss Lucas sitting on the settee. She rose to her feet when he entered the room and made a graceful curtsy. He bowed and gestured in invitation for her to resume her seat. She sank down again as he took a chair opposite. "Good day, Miss Lucas. I hope you are well."

"Very well, Mr. Bennet. I had hoped to hear that Jane was better."

"Mrs. Bennet and her daughters have gone to Netherfield to ascertain for themselves the state of Jane's health. Lizzy wrote this morning to say that Jane *is* better, but Mr. Bingley had sent for the apothecary again to see her.

"Oh, I am glad that Jane is improved!" exclaimed Miss Lucas with a sincere expression. "When does she return home?"

"Lizzy requested that Mrs. Bennet come to Jane and determine whether she should come home." He did not add Mrs. Bennet's conviction that Jane should remain where she was and why. *It is not a thing to be aired.*

"I see." Miss Lucas' tone was thoughtful. "I expect Eliza is very ready to return home, but she will not come without bringing Jane with her."

"You know her well, Miss Lucas. Lizzy will not abandon her sister. All she lacks is her mother's authority to remove Jane from the benevolent hospitality of Mr. Bingley's household."

"She *hopes* to persuade Mrs. Bennet." A blush rose in her cheeks as she realized her *faux pas*. She smiled suddenly. "Forgive me, Mr. Bennet, but it could prove to be a formidable task."

Miss Lucas had a twinkle in her gray eyes, which he found himself responding to with a smile. Warmth suffused his chest. He was not used to such percipience. It was pleasant to share a mutual amusement, knowing the other person had discerned exactly what was so diverting. "That is it precisely, Miss Lucas. And if Mrs. Bennet has her way, Jane will be a guest at Netherfield for an indefinite period. I daresay a year at least."

Miss Lucas laughed, a low musical sound that was pleasant on his ear. "Yes, I would not be surprised." She gathered the strings of her reticule and rose to her feet.

He was sorry to see that she meant to take her leave. He reluctantly stood.

"I shall not trespass any longer, Mr. Bennet. Pray tell Jane, when she comes home, that I am glad she is recovering. I shall expect a visit from Eliza. I bid you good day."

She held out a slender gloved hand and he gently took it. He smiled down at her, retaining her fingers for just a moment. "Thank you, Miss Lucas. I will relay your kind messages." He accompanied her to the front door. He waved aside Hill and opened the door in the butler's stead. "Did you come in your father's carriage?"

She shook her head. "No, I walked here."

"There is a blustery wind."

"I am used to it, sir."

"Relate my compliments to Sir William and Lady Lucas."

"I will do so, Mr. Bennet."

Then she was gone, her skirts catching and billowing in a whirl of wind.

[6]

Elizabeth's short note to Longbourn, desiring her mother to visit Jane, and form her own judgment of her sister's situation, was quickly complied with; Mrs. Bennet, accompanied by her girls, reached Netherfield Park soon after the family breakfast. The Bennet ladies were escorted up to Jane's bedchamber, and there left, to enjoy a reunion amongst themselves.

"My dear Jane! You are looking pale but lovely still. I am glad of it, for Mr. Bingley's sake!" exclaimed Mrs. Bennet. "I can see your illness is not alarming. I would have been very miserable if it had been otherwise!"

"Then should not Jane be carried home, Mama?"

"Lizzy, how you do take one up! Jane is not restored, not one whit! She cannot be moved," exclaimed Mrs. Bennet. Meeting the look in her second daughter's eyes, she shook her head. "No, Lizzy, not another word! I will not listen to you!

The apothecary, who had arrived at about the same time, concurred in Mrs. Bennet's opinion. "I do not think it at all advisable, madam."

"There! We must listen to Mr. Jones," said Mrs. Bennet in triumph. "Jane, you must abide here at Netherfield yet awhile, until you are fully restored in health."

Elizabeth sighed and bowed to the inevitable.

A couple of days later Mrs. Bennet made much of another note she received from Elizabeth, and she was not as pleased with it as the last one. "What is Lizzy thinking! My patience with her is quite at an end! She begs that the carriage might be sent for them sometime in the course of today. But I had calculated on my daughters remaining at Netherfield until Tuesday, which will exactly finish Jane's week there. I could not bring myself to receive them with pleasure before."

"I am very willing to send the carriage." Bennet would be glad to see his eldest daughters. He had felt their importance in the family circle. The evening conversation when they were all assembled in the drawing-room had lost much of its animation, and almost all its sense, by the absence of Jane and Elizabeth.

"Nonsense, nonsense! I have already sent them word they could not possibly have the carriage before Tuesday. Indeed, I wrote that if Mr. Bingley and his sister pressed them to stay longer, I can very well spare them."

Bennet tightened his lips, controlling his irritation. "But I cannot, my dear. I have felt their absence. However, even if they are asked to remain, I believe Lizzy and Jane have more sense than to overstay themselves. I shall hope to see them before ere long."

Mrs. Bennet huffed and turned her shoulder. "I am off to visit my sister Philips. I have not called on her all of the week and no doubt she will have news to relate."

Bennet was not sorry at his wife's exit, and when it became obvious, from various overheard excited statements and giggles, that Lydia and Catherine had decided to accompany their mother to Meryton to pay a call on Mrs. Philips, he was moved to release a long sigh. The only discordance to be heard was Mary's pianoforte practice from the upstairs sitting-room, the complicated notes penetrating the far reaches of the house, and it was no great thing to ignore it, as he had become quite accustomed to doing over the years.

The next day, Bingley's carriage was driven up to the house and rolled to a stop in front of the porch. It had come on to drizzle, but nevertheless, Bennet stepped out and himself met his daughters as they alighted from the vehicle. He was laconic in his expression of pleasure at their return, but he was sincerely glad of it and he showed it by the warmth of his welcome. He kissed his favorite daughter's cheek. "Well, Lizzy? How did you like Netherfield?"

Elizabeth's eyes sparkled. "Oh, I found much to amuse myself. I shall tell you all about it later, Papa. Here is Jane! She is well again at last."

He kissed his eldest daughter's cheek, and smiled at her. "I am happy you are recovered, Jane. Welcome home, my dear."

"Thank you, Papa. I am very well again."

"Mrs. Bennet had formed the intention that you would not be seen again by us until Tuesday. You have cut up all her hopes," said Bennet lightly as he ushered them out of the wet and into the house.

Elizabeth and Jane exchanged a look; Jane murmured, "Oh, dear!"

The footman followed them, carrying a medium-sized valise that he had taken from the carriage, and which he proceeded to carry through the entry hall and up the stairs. Hill shut the front door and sent another servant off to inform the maid of the Miss Bennets' arrival.

"I was impatient to get home. I was positively resolved, and my mother's note was not propitious, at least not to my wishes! I urged Jane to borrow Mr. Bingley's carriage and so here we are!" said Elizabeth cheerfully, divesting herself of spencer and bonnet and handing them to the waiting butler. She began to pull off her gloves.

"And what of you, Jane? Were you as eager as Lizzy to leave Netherfield?" Thomas Bennet wondered a little. He thought he had seen what he took to be regret flicker across his eldest daughter's face as she watched the Bingley carriage depart. Then he thought he must have been mistaken. Jane had turned her clear gaze back to him and smiled with her usual serenity.

"It is nice to be back at home, Papa." Jane had also removed her bonnet and began with the ties of her cloak.

Mrs. Bennet emerged from the drawing-room before her daughters had finished putting off their outer garments. She did not extend a cordial welcome; her eyes were narrowed and her lips pouted. Mrs. Bennet unerringly placed the blame where it belonged, and said pettishly, "I wonder at your coming, Lizzy, and think you very wrong to give so much trouble. I am sure Jane will have caught cold again."

Jane said at once, "Oh, I am very well, Mama." She gave her outwear into the returned footman's care, along with a quiet word of thanks.

"Did Charlotte call here?" asked Elizabeth, fluffing her dark curls as she made for the warmth of the large drawing-room. "Oh, I am glad we had a brick to our feet! The heavy cold seeped through every seam in the carriage."

Mrs. Bennet followed her second daughter, her voice sharp. "Why, I told you so at Netherfield, but you never listen, Lizzy."

Bennet offered his arm to his eldest daughter and together they walked into the drawing-room, remaining silent under Mrs. Bennet's continuing scold.

"Sir William and Charlotte Lucas called the day after you went to Netherfield. She was most astonished! I am sure it was at your walking all that way, just because Jane had taken a trifling cold. It is not to be wondered at, when you go careering all over the countryside as you do! It is *most* unbecoming. I fear my nerves are quite overset at what Lady Lucas must have thought when she heard of it! Such palpitations, and flutterings, and pains that I am made to suffer! You will be the death of me, Lizzy!"

Elizabeth ignored her mother's plaintive complaints. "Yes, Mama, I recall what you said very well. I was asking if she has been here again."

"Miss Lucas has paid another visit." Bennet replied in a studied, casual manner, for it would not do to reveal he had taken pleasure in meeting with Miss Lucas again and exchanging conversation with her. He privately conceded he had indeed missed the rational conversation of his two eldest daughters, and in an otherwise stale environment, Miss Lucas had seemed like a small breath of fresh air. *I would have liked to talk longer with her. She has a gentle, piquant humor which is endearing.* Bennet did not reveal anything of his thoughts. "She came to inquire if we had any further word of *you*, Jane, and expressed her concern. She also said she expects a visit from you, Lizzy."

"Then I must go see Charlotte! Come, Jane! I will accompany you upstairs before I set off. Sally will have unpacked the valise and I want to get my other shawl."

Thomas Bennet stayed her for a moment. "This mizzle might well turn to rain. I shall order out the carriage for you, Lizzy."

Elizabeth's dark eyes sparkled. She smiled her pleasure. "Thank you, Papa."

Mrs. Bennet ignored the exit of her daughters, who were softly speaking to one another in an undertone. She stared at her husband, and exclaimed accusingly, "Mr. Bennet, you never told me that Charlotte Lucas was here again!"

He was imperturbable. "I just did so, my dear."

"While I was gone! I am quite put-about that I missed her! I could have told her all about Netherfield and the elegant curtains and number of furniture and how many servants there were. The affability of Mr. Bingley and his sisters! As for Mr. Darcy, he is the most disagreeable man! So proud and holding his nose up at our country society! Of course, Lizzy *would* put her oar in! She is grown so pert, there is no bearing it."

"What is this? About Lizzy and Mr. Darcy, was it?"

"Nothing, nothing! How you do catch one up, Mr. Bennet." Mrs. Bennet shook her head. "I would have told it all to Charlotte Lucas and she could have told it to dear Lady Lucas." Mrs. Bennet's clouded features lightened. "Oh, I am *glad* that I missed Charlotte, for now I may tell everything to Lady Lucas myself!"

"I have promised the carriage to Lizzy. She will not be overlong. And I expect you will not wish to hurry your own visits."

Mrs. Bennet pouted but she dipped a begrudging nod. "It is true, I should not like to go with Lizzy. She *will* express her opinions! Well! I shall have to visit Lady Lucas as soon as may be. And my sister Philips, for she will be very glad to hear all about my visit to Netherfield. Perhaps I shall stop in on Mrs. Long and Mrs. Robinson."

Bennet could not resist a barb of sarcasm. "I suppose that must mean I have no further need for the horses on the farm this week."

§

The small sitting room was made cozy by candles and a fire, by which extra light, Charlotte was embroidering a handkerchief. When Elizabeth was ushered in by a servant, Charlotte was delighted to see her. She set aside her needlework and stepped forward, holding out her hands. "Eliza! But how glad I am to see you! So, you have returned from Netherfield Park at last. How is Jane?"

Elizabeth rushed over, ignoring her outstretched hands, and instead hugged her. "My dearest friend! How I have missed you!" She drew back and beamed at her. "Jane is fine. It was a bad feverish cold, but she is well again. Oh, Charlotte! I have so much to tell you!"

Charlotte drew her down to the settee. "I am happy to hear Jane is recovered. I was most astonished to learn of her illness and that she was at Netherfield. How did this come about?"

"It was all my mother's doing. You know how she is, Charlotte, when she is determined to have her way." Elizabeth swiftly removed her gloves and smoothed them together on her lap. "Jane received an invitation from Miss Bingley and Mama would have it that she must go by horseback, even though it was coming on to rain. She *hoped* Jane would have to remain the night!"

Charlotte shook her head. "I may guess at the rest. Jane took ill and so you also went to Netherfield."

"Yes, and it was most amusing, except that Jane was sick. She was tied to her bed, so I was obliged to go downstairs alone in the evenings."

"I know you do not much like Mr. Bingley's sisters." Charlotte raised her brows in question."I hope they were civil to you."

"Jane has always liked them, but I thought their manners too high for their company," said Elizabeth, with a small shrug. "But I must credit them just a little. They joined Jane and me in her room at times, and when I saw how much affection and solicitude they showed for Jane, I began to like them myself. The evening Jane was finally able to go downstairs to the drawing-room, I had never seen them so agreeable as they were during the hour which passed before the gentlemen appeared. Their powers of conversation were considerable. They could describe an entertainment with accuracy, relate an anecdote with humor, and laugh at their acquaintance with spirit."

Charlotte was amused. "Why, Eliza, this is *lofty* praise!"

"Oh, but when the gentlemen entered, Jane was no longer the first object," said Elizabeth with the flash of a smile. "Miss Bingley's eyes were instantly turned to Mr. Darcy. She had no more time for Jane! Mrs. Hurst's manners were a trifle better. She was principally occupied with playing with her rings and bracelets, but she joined now and then in her brother's conversation with Jane."

Charlotte gave a ripple of laughter. "What disgust you convey! But I notice you do not criticize Mr. Bingley's manners, nor those of the other gentlemen."

"Mr. Darcy was all politeness. Mr. Hurst was indifferent," said Elizabeth, disposing handily of those two gentlemen. Her face lit up with enthusiasm. "But I can say nothing but good of Mr. Bingley! He was all attention toward Jane. The first half hour was spent in piling up the fire, lest she should suffer from the change of room; and she removed at his desire to the other side of the fireplace, that she might be farther from the door, away from any draft. Then he sat down by her, and talked scarcely to anyone else. I was at work with my embroidery in the opposite corner and I saw it all with great delight, as you may imagine!"

Charlotte smiled at Elizabeth's pleased expression. "Mr. Bingley's kindness speaks well for him. I am sure Jane was conscious of it. She must have regretted leaving Netherfield."

Elizabeth's dark brows creased, her face showing mild surprise. "Jane was recovered. Though Mr. Bingley and his sister urged us to stay a few days more, I felt we could not trespass longer on Mr. Bingley's hospitality."

"No, of course not." Charlotte said no more. Her observation had a little deflated Elizabeth's pleasure. To her mind, the opportunity to engage Mr. Bingley's interest had been an invaluable one for Jane. It was regrettable the visit had not been extended a little longer. In her opinion, Elizabeth had not helped her sister's cause. *Surely she is aware of it. If not then, she is now!* Instead, she turned to another point of curiosity. "What of Mr. Darcy? Did he make a practice of listening to your conversations as he did at our last party?"

Elizabeth shook her head. A mischievous smile peeped out. "Oh, no! Mr. Darcy was not granted the opportunity. He and I engaged in several bantering exchanges. This did not suit Miss Bingley! She reveals jealousy of anyone able to hold, even for a few moments, that fine gentleman's attention!"

Charlotte wondered what her friend and 'the most disagreeable gentleman that Hertfordshire had ever seen' had found to converse about – no, *banter* about! She looked speculatively at her dear companion. Perhaps there was more here than she had ever suspected. "Were you flattered by Mr. Darcy's attention?"

"I was not *flattered*, for I have not changed my opinion of him," said Elizabeth quickly. "I was surprised by Mr. Darcy's willingness to engage in conversation, though, and amused by his swift wit."

"I am glad. At least you were not bored in Mr. Darcy's company."

Elizabeth paused, a look of mild astonishment crossing her face. As though it had not occurred to her before, she said slowly, "No, it is true, I was not bored."

[7]

At breakfast the next morning, Bennet addressed his wife. "I hope, my dear, that you have ordered a good dinner today, because I have reason to expect an addition to our family party."

"Who do you mean, Mr. Bennet? I know of nobody that is coming, I am sure, unless Charlotte Lucas should happen to call in, and I hope my dinners are good enough for her. I do not believe she often sees such at home."

"The person of whom I speak is a gentleman and a stranger."

Mrs. Bennet's eyes sparkled. "A gentleman and a stranger! It is Mr. Bingley, I am sure. Why, Jane, you never dropped a word of this, you sly thing! Well, I am sure I shall be extremely glad to see Mr. Bingley. But how unlucky! There is not a bit of fish to be got today. Lydia, my love, ring the bell. I must speak to Mrs. Hill this moment!"

"It is not Mr. Bingley. It is a person whom I have never seen in the whole course of my life." Bennet's declaration roused general astonishment, which pleased him, and he derived even greater pleasure from the eager questions that were flung at him. He drew a folded sheet from out of his coat pocket and unfolded it. "About a month ago, I received this letter, and about a fortnight ago I answered it, for I thought it a case of some delicacy, and required my attention. It is from my cousin, Mr. Collins, who – when I am dead – may turn you all out of this house as soon as he pleases."

Mrs. Bennet at once exclaimed in distress. "Oh! I cannot bear to hear him mentioned. Pray do not talk of that odious man. I *do* think it is the hardest thing in the world, that your estate should be entailed away from your own children. I am sure if I had been you, I should have tried long ago to do something or other about it."

Bennet treated his wife's unhappy declaration as he had always done. He said, with a faint smile, "I entertain not a doubt of it."

Mrs. Bennet seemed incapable, or perhaps unwilling, to comprehend the entail; but Jane and Elizabeth tried to explain it to their mother yet again. However, Mrs. Bennet did not cease in her bitter railing. "It is cruel to settle an estate away from a family of five daughters, in favor of a man whom nobody cares about!"

"It is certainly a most iniquitous affair." He thought the amusing little sideshow had gone on long enough. "Nothing can clear Mr. Collins from the guilt of inheriting Longbourn. But if you will listen to his letter, you may perhaps be a little softened by his manner of expressing himself."

"No, that I am sure I shall not, and I think it was very impertinent of him to write to you at all, and very hypocritical," exclaimed Mrs. Bennet petulantly. "I hate such false friends. Why could not he keep on quarrelling with you, as his father did before him?"

"Indeed, he does seem to have had some filial scruples on that head. I shall not read it all, for the gentleman is fond of long periods." Bennet swiftly scanned the letter. "Ah! Here it is! '*As a clergyman I feel it my duty to promote and establish a blessing of peace in all families within the reach of my influence; and on these grounds I flatter myself that my present overtures of good-will are highly commendable, and the circumstance of my being next in the entail of Longbourn estate, will be kindly overlooked on your side, and not lead you to reject the offered olive branch. I cannot be otherwise than be concerned at being the means of injuring your amiable daughters, and beg leave to apologize for it, as well as to assure you of my readiness to make them every possible amends.*'"

He looked up and regarded his wife's expression, taking note that she was looking far less irritable. "There, Mrs. Bennet, does not my cousin express himself well?"

"There is some sense in what he says about the girls, and if he is disposed to make them any amends, I shall not be the person to discourage him," said Mrs. Bennet slowly.

Jane furrowed her brow. "Even though it is difficult to guess in what way he can mean to make us the atonement he thinks our due, the wish is certainly to his credit."

Elizabeth frowned thoughtfully. "He must be an oddity, I think. I cannot make him out. There is something very pompous in his style. And what can he mean by apologizing for being next in the entail? We cannot suppose he would help it, if he could. Can he be a sensible man, sir?"

Thomas Bennet smiled. His cleverest daughter had put her finger on the crux of it. "No, my dear, I think not. I have great hopes of finding him quite the reverse. There is a mixture of servility and self-importance in his letter, which promises well. I am impatient to see him."

Mary was quick to offer up her opinion. "But Papa, in point of composition, his letter does not seem defective. The idea of the olive branch perhaps is not wholly new, yet I think it is well expressed."

Mrs. Bennet re-entered the conversation, in a way that astonished them all. "For once, Mary, you speak truly. I have been thinking, and I shall be glad to meet the man."

Bennet raised his brows, examining his wife in some surprise. Several other pairs of eyes turned to Mrs. Bennet. Even Catherine and Lydia, who did not hide that they were not very interested in the letter or its writer, looked fixedly at their mother.

Mrs. Bennet looked around the table at her family. "Why, what are you all staring at me for? I think it a very good thing that Mr. Collins is so conciliatory. When is he to come, Mr. Bennet?"

"At four o'clock, we may expect this peace-making gentleman." Bennet folded up the letter, to replace it inside his coat pocket. "He seems to be a most conscientious and polite young man, upon my word. I doubt not he will prove a valuable acquaintance, especially if Lady Catherine de Bourgh, his patroness, whom he refers to with the most extraordinary deference, should be so indulgent as to let him come to us again."

Mr. Collins was punctual to his time and was received with great politeness by the whole family. Once they were all seated in the drawing-room, Thomas Bennet said little, content to sit back and listen. However, there was no lag in conversation. The ladies were ready enough to talk, and Mr. Collins seemed neither in need of encouragement, nor inclined to be silent himself. Bennet judged him to be about five-and-twenty years. He was a tall, heavy-looking young man, possessing a grave and stately air, and his manners were very formal.

Mr. Collins had not been long seated before he complimented Mrs. Bennet on having so fine a family of daughters. "I have heard much of their beauty, but in this instance, fame has fallen short of the truth, madam. I do not doubt you shall see all of them well-disposed of in marriage in due time."

Bennet regarded his cousin with derision. *Famed for their beauty, indeed! What flummery!* It was apparent Mr. Collins' fulsome praise struck a discordant note with some of his daughters, as well. Neither Jane nor Elizabeth appeared to be complimented. As for Mary, she was regarding Mr. Collins with a most scornful expression.

However, Mrs. Bennet never questioned compliments. "You are very kind, sir, I am sure. And I wish with all my heart it may prove so, for else they will be destitute enough. Things are settled so oddly."

Bennet sighed. The subject of the entail was worn to threads – over the whole time of their marriage, his wife had never let it go. He had long ago formed the opinion that she enjoyed complaining about a matter that could not be altered, and which always set him at fault.

"You allude perhaps to the entail of the estate."

"Sir, I do indeed. It is a grievous affair to my poor girls, you must confess. Not that I mean to find fault with you, for such things I know are all chance in this world." Mrs. Bennet brought up her lace handkerchief and dabbed at the corner of one eye. "There is no knowing how estates will go when once they come to be entailed."

Mr. Collins gave a solemn nod. "I am very sensible, madam, of the hardship to my fair cousins, and could say much on the subject, but that I am cautious of appearing forward and precipitate. But I can assure the young ladies that I come prepared to admire them. At present I will not say more, but perhaps when we are better acquainted –"

He was interrupted by a summons to dinner by Hill.

Mr. Collins appeared amazed. "Your household extends to a butler! Why, it is most gratifying, most gratifying, indeed!"

Bennet, greatly entertained by the man's deficiency in sensibility, noted that the girls, and household staff, were not the only objects of Mr. Collins' admiration. Their progress to the dining-room was dawdling. His heir's lack of proper feeling was amply displayed. The artwork hanging in the hall, the dining-room and all its furniture, the table settings and cutlery, all were examined and praised. His commendation of everything must have touched the hearts of all who heard him, he thought cynically, except for the mortifying supposition of his viewing it all as his own future property.

In that light, it only offends.

The three-course dinner in its turn was highly admired, an especial attention given to the two soups, the leg of lamb with boiled cauliflower, and a remove of almond cheesecakes and custards. Mr. Collins turned to Mrs. Bennet. "I beg to know which of my fair cousins is owed for the excellence of the cooking."

Bennet was not surprised when Mrs. Bennet took exception to his cousin's assumption. Mrs. Bennet took pride in the amenities of their household, and she said sharply, "We are very well able to keep a good cook, and my daughters had nothing to do in the kitchen."

"I beg pardon for having displeased you, Mrs. Bennet."

Mrs. Bennet declared herself, in a softened tone, not at all offended; but Mr. Collins continued to apologize for about a quarter of an hour.

Thomas Bennet scarcely spoke at all; but when the servants had withdrawn, he thought it time to have some conversation with his guest, and introduced a subject in which he expected him to shine, by observing he seemed very fortunate in his patroness. "Lady Catherine de Bourgh's attention to your wishes and consideration of your comfort appear very notable."

Bennet could not have chosen better. Mr. Collins was eloquent in her ladyship's praise. The subject elevated him to more than usual solemnity of manner, and a self-important expression. "I protest that I have never in my life witnessed such behavior in a person of rank – such affability and condescension, as I have myself experienced from Lady Catherine. She was graciously pleased to approve of the discourses which I have already had the honor of preaching before her. She has asked me twice to dine at Rosings, and sent for me only the Saturday before, to make up her pool of quadrille in the evening."

"Remarkable," Bennet murmured, not referring so much to what he was being told as by the man's ability to speak at such length with scarcely a pause to catch a breath. He suspected a Sunday sermon by Mr. Collins would be extremely lengthy and rather tedious, and was glad his own rector was of a different cut.

Mistaking Mr. Bennet's interjection for interest, Mr. Collins earnestly continued. "Lady Catherine is reckoned proud by many people, I know, but I have never seen anything but affability in her. She has always spoken to me as she would to any other gentleman.

She makes not the smallest objection to my joining in the society of the neighborhood, nor to my leaving my parish occasionally for a week or two to visit relations. She has even condescended to advise me to marry as soon as I could, provided I choose with discretion, and has once paid me a visit in my humble parsonage, where she perfectly approved all the alterations I had been making, and even vouchsafed to suggest some herself – some shelves in the closets upstairs."

"All very proper and civil, I am sure," said Mrs. Bennet. "And I daresay she is a very agreeable woman. It is a pity that great ladies in general are not more like her. Does she live near you, sir?"

Mr. Collins inclined his head to her. "The garden in which stands my humble abode is separated only by a lane from the grounds of Rosings Park, her ladyship's residence."

Mrs. Bennet's curiosity was open. "I think you said she was a widow, sir? Has she any family?"

Mr. Collins' face lengthened into solemn lines. "Her ladyship had one daughter, the heiress of Rosings, and of very extensive property, who passed away not very many months past. Alas, such a tragedy! My great patroness, Lady Catherine de Bourgh, is naturally quite stricken with grief."

Bennet addressed his visitor with grave courtesy. "I am sorry to hear of Lady Catherine's loss."

"Indeed, sir, it was a most terrible blow."

"What sort of young lady was she? Was she handsome? Was she ever presented? I do not remember her name among the ladies at court."

Mr. Collins turned back to Mrs. Bennet to reply to her spate of questions. "Miss de Bourgh was a most charming young lady. She was unfortunately of a sickly constitution, which prevented her making that progress in many accomplishments, which she could not otherwise have failed of, as I was informed by the lady who superintended her education, and who still resides at Rosings. But she was perfectly amiable. She often condescended to drive by my humble abode in her little phaeton and ponies."

"So she was not presented at court?"

Mr. Collins shook his head in sorrow. "Her indifferent state of health unhappily prevented her being in town, and by that means, as I told Lady Catherine myself one day, deprived the British court of its brightest ornament. Her ladyship seemed pleased with the idea."

Mrs. Bennet, obsessed with her own daughters, fastened onto what seemed to her a very important point "Never out in society, never presented! An heiress, if she be ever so sickly, should at least be known to the company of her peers. Indeed, it seems very odd."

Bennet intervened. Mr. Collins was not the only one insensible to the inappropriate. *Let be, Fanny! Lady Catherine's daughter is dead.* "My dear, I think you have inquired enough into the affairs of the de Bourghs."

"Nonsense, Mr. Bennet, nonsense! I am certain Mr. Collins is glad to relate all he knows of such great people."

Mr. Collins frowned a little, before he offered, "I more than once observed to Lady Catherine that her charming daughter seemed born to be a duchess, and that the most elevated rank, instead of giving her consequence, would be adorned by her."

Mrs. Bennet appeared struck to silence at last.

Mr. Collins looked complacently around him but addressed himself to his host. "These are the kind of little things which please her ladyship, and it is a sort of attention which I conceive myself peculiarly bound to pay. You may imagine that I am happy on every occasion to offer those little delicate compliments which are always acceptable to ladies."

Bennet was amused by the man's pomposity. "You judge very properly and it is happy for you that you possess the talent of flattering with delicacy. May I ask whether these pleasing attentions proceed from the impulse of the moment, or are the result of previous study?"

"They arise chiefly from what is passing at the time, and though I sometimes amuse myself with suggesting and arranging such little elegant compliments as may be adapted to ordinary occasions, I always wish to give them as unstudied an air as possible."

Bennet's expectations were fully met. His cousin was as absurd as he had hoped, and he listened to him with the keenest enjoyment, maintaining at the same time the most resolute composure of countenance, and except in an occasional glance at Elizabeth, who was as ready as he to derive amusement from the ridiculous, required no partner in his pleasure.

Mr. Bennet's usual routine was to retreat to his library, where he generally spent much of the day with his books and his studies. However, this day he invited his visitor to join him in a walk about the near property before they repaired back to the manor house, when he would offer a measure of liquid refreshment. "As my heir, you will naturally have an interest in the estate and the workings of it. I trust it is not too cold a day for you?"

Mr. Collins bowed. "Your care to my health is noted and most appreciated, Mr. Bennet. I assure you, I shall bundle up to protect myself from the cold, for I should not wish to inconvenience anyone by becoming ill. You are most gracious in this invitation, sir, and indeed, you have pinpointed my desires precisely. I shall be most happy to accompany you, and I do promise to veritably hang upon your every utterance, for I feel certain many pearls of wisdom must drop from your lips."

"Since I *am* such a wise graybeard," said Bennet dryly. His quip earned him another solemn assurance from Mr. Collins of his being most attentive to all Mr. Bennet had to show to him. Bennet had difficulty in scaling back a grin. He expected to derive more amusement from his interactions with his heir. "Then let us be off,

Mr. Collins. I hope you are a good walker, for I mean to tour the gardens and the orchards, perhaps even the farm, before our return."

By tea-time, however, the dose had been enough, and he was glad to take his guest into the drawing-room again, and when tea was over, glad to invite him to read aloud to the ladies. Mr. Collins readily assented, but he would not read from a novel but chose a sober text instead. This did not suit Lydia, who interrupted after barely three pages.

"Do you know, Mama, that my uncle Philips talks of turning away Richard, and if he does, Colonel Forster will hire him. My aunt told me so herself on Saturday. I shall walk to Meryton tomorrow to hear more about it, and to ask when Mr. Denny comes back from town."

Mr. Collins was greatly offended. "I have often observed how little young ladies are interested by books of a serious stamp, though written solely for their benefit." He then turned and offered to play backgammon with his host.

Bennet accepted the challenge, remarking, "You have acted very wisely in leaving the girls to their own trifling amusements."

"I do apologize for Lydia's interruption, Mr. Collins. I promise that it shall not occur again, if you would but resume your book," said Mrs. Bennet, casting a minatory frown at her youngest daughter.

But Mr. Collins declined and seated himself at another table with Mr. Bennet, and prepared for backgammon. Bennet did not expect much, so he was pleasantly surprised when Mr. Collins proved to be a very good player. He was able to derive true enjoyment from their several matches.

The evening passed in inconsequential conversation between the ladies.

[8]

At Lucas Lodge, there arrived a hired chaise, well-covered with dirt, from which descended two ladies, one dressed very fine in a feathered blue velvet hat, perfectly matching her velvet spencer, and carrying a large fur muff into which she had thrust her hands. The other lady was outfitted in a sensible beribboned velvet bonnet and serviceable spencer of a subdued brown, wearing gloves and carrying a small reticule. They were admitted and their baggage was carried in, with a disparity in quality and number of pieces between them.

In the vestibule, Miss Augusta Hawkins and Miss Simmons were graciously received and invited to refresh themselves in their rooms before rejoining their hosts. Lady Lucas assured them that maids were waiting to serve them and a footman showed the way upstairs. After the first greetings and introductions, Sir William excused himself, saying that he had some business to attend to, but he was certain the ladies would do very well without him.

Charlotte was also on hand to welcome and meet her cousin and the new governess, and afterwards followed her mother into the drawing-room, where the two women were to join them. She was curious about both, her initial impressions having been so fleeting. She had been dazzled by the fashionable ensemble worn by her cousin, and could recall nothing else, either her features or the tone of her voice. However, she had liked the quiet character in Miss Simmons' face.

Charlotte's sister Maria, the one closest in age to her, came into the drawing-room, with equal parts apologies and an expressed curiosity to meet the newest members of the household. "Besides, the schoolchildren will be glad to hear all about them before dinner!"

A half hour later, the butler showed in the two arrivals, each of whom had changed their dresses and tidied their hair. With a smile and a gesture, Lady Lucas invited them to sit down and partake of fresh tea and cakes. "Such a long journey, you must be famished. You must tell us all about yourselves."

Miss Hawkins was nothing loathe. The very first subject after being seated was Maple Grove. "My brother Mr. Suckling's seat, you know. I could see from my bedchamber window, the grounds of Lucas Lodge are very like, neat and pretty, and though not so modern, the house is well-built. I am most favorably impressed by the size of the room, the entrance, and all that I have seen or imagine. Very like Maple Grove, indeed!"

Miss Hawkins appealed to Miss Simmons. "Was not it astonishingly like? I could really almost fancy myself at Maple Grove!" She did not wait for a reply but swept on. "And the staircase! You know, as I came in, I observed how very like the staircase was, placed exactly in the same part of the house. I really could not help exclaiming! I assure you, Lady Lucas, it is very delightful to me, to be reminded of a place I am so extremely partial to as Maple Grove. I have spent so many happy months there!"

Lady Lucas appeared somewhat shell-shocked. "To be sure, my dear."

Maria sat open-mouthed. She was generally considered a lively girl but she had been struck mute since her introduction to her erstwhile-unknown cousin and the governess. Her wide eyed attention was riveted upon Miss Hawkins.

Miss Hawkins sighed, a little wistful smile on her lips. Her gaze swept to Charlotte, including her in the net of her voluble conversation. "A charming place, undoubtedly. Everybody who sees it is struck by its beauty; but to me, it has been quite a home. Whenever you are transplanted, like me, Miss Lucas, you will understand how very delightful it is to meet with anything at all like what one has left behind. I always say this will be quite one of the evils of matrimony, leaving a beloved home for the sake of a *caro esposo*."

Charlotte was astonished and turned her gaze to the woman seated beside her, who had been charged with the responsibility of turning her cousin out as a refined young lady, and in Charlotte's private opinion, it was a responsibility she had singularly failed. It seemed the governess easily discerned the trajectory of her thoughts.

"Mr. Suckling engaged me but two years ago," murmured Miss Simmons.

Charlotte understood the underlying message. *My cousin's character was already set.* And Augusta was a natural force of nature, a hurricane which took no notice of sensibilities or proper boundaries.

"Oh, yes, that is so! Dear Miss Simmons! When we removed to Maple Grove, my brother Mr. Suckling had the very odd notion that I should have a governess." Miss Hawkins gave a trill of laughter. "I told him it was not so, yet he insisted, and now, at last, I have carried my point. But I said to my sister Selena something must be done, we simply had to do something for Miss Simmons. A situation such as you deserve, Miss Simmons, and your friends require for you, was no everyday occurrence, and was not to be obtained at a moment's notice. Indeed, indeed, we had to begin inquiring directly."

"There are advertising agencies, and by applying to them I should have had no doubt of very soon meeting with something that would do," said Miss Simmons, with something of a heightened color.

Charlotte was cognizant that the governess had been embarrassed, and she sympathized. Her cousin had revealed an unfortunate tendency to excessive patronization.

"Something that would do!" repeated Miss Hawkins. "*That* may have suited your humble ideas of yourself. I know what a modest creature you are, but it would not satisfy your friends to have you taking up with *anything* that may offer, any inferior, commonplace situation, in a family not moving in a certain circle, or able to command the elegancies of life."

"Then it was a happy thought of Selena's to inquire of *me*," said Lady Lucas with such emphasis that Miss Hawkins decried having ever a doubt of it, or indeed, would challenge anyone else to doubt it.

"No, indeed! I give you notice. You will find me a formidable opponent on that point. And I assure you, if you knew how Selena feels with respect to dear Miss Simmons, you would be flattered that her choice fell on *you*, dear Aunt Lucas. You do not know how many candidates there always are for the *first* situations. I saw a vast deal of that in the neighborhood round Maple Grove. A cousin of Mr. Suckling, Mrs. Braggs, had an infinity of applications; everybody was anxious to be in her family, for she moves in the *first* circle. Wax-candles in the schoolroom! You may imagine how desirable!"

Charlotte could only sit and wonder at the young woman's obliviousness. *How she runs on like a fiddlestick! How she offends so indiscriminately!*

Upwards of an hour later, during which time Miss Hawkins had done her best to dominate the conversation, she and Miss Simmons had exited the drawing-room, to go back upstairs to rest after their journey, with the understanding of all coming together again over dinner.

Maria scarcely waited for the door to shut behind the two ladies, before she exclaimed, "Our cousin! Is she not very charming?"

There was a little hesitation in Lady Lucas' answer. "Oh! Yes, very...a very pleasing young woman."

"I think her beautiful, quite beautiful."

"My dear Maria, why do you not go up to inform your brothers and sisters of your impressions?"

Maria agreed to go at once.

Left alone with her eldest daughter, Lady Lucas looked at her and raised her brows. "Well, Charlotte, what do you think of her?"

Charlotte had no doubts of whom her mother was speaking, and it was not of the governess. She *had* formed a very good impression of that ladylike young woman. Charlotte hesitated. She did not really like her cousin. However, it would not do to be quite so forthright as that. "Oh! I have but just met her. I think her very nicely dressed; indeed, a remarkably elegant gown."

"*There* is nothing to surprise one at all. A pretty fortune, all of ten thousand pounds."

"Ten thousand!" Charlotte shook her head, a smile hovering over her lips. The world could be cruel, indeed. *Superior females, such as Miss Simmons, are often snubbed by the whims of fate. A thousand pities.* "Well! My cousin will not be shunned, despite her volubility, at any event we choose to host or attend." As she spoke, she realized how much her inflection reflected her disapprobation.

"Old cattish of you, Charlotte, and quite beneath you."

Charlotte inclined her head in acknowledgement of the mild rebuke. "I do apologize, Mama." *My swift dislike is not so hidden as I supposed.*

Lady Lucas said loftily, "I will not be in a hurry to find fault."

"No, indeed, Mama," murmured Charlotte.

Lady Lucas drew in a deep breath. "*But* there is no elegance – ease, but not elegance. For a young woman, a stranger, there is too much ease. Her person is rather good; her face not unpretty; but neither feature, nor air, nor voice, nor manner, are elegant. *Nothing* like yourself, or Jane and Eliza Bennet."

Charlotte blushed fierily. "Mama! You flatter me beyond measure." Indeed, she was amazed by the unexpected compliment, especially coming so swift on the heels of a rebuke. *Me! Elegant! Mama would never say so if she did not believe it.* Warmth filled her whole being, along with a wash of gratitude. The words did much to counter the hurt of those others she had overheard at Longborn. *Mama may think me beyond praying for, but at least I shall be an elegant spinster!*

"You are a good, sensible young woman, Charlotte. Maria seems to have formed an unfortunate girlish crush upon her – I trust it does not long last!" Lady Lucas shook her head and snorted. "This maternal niece of mine – new money and not the sense to recognize her betters! She shall mortify us with our more genteel neighbors, make no mistake!"

Charlotte feared it would be so, indeed. "She is scarcely a *restful* person, is she, Mama? I am only thankful that I do not have to share a bedchamber with her."

Lady Lucas stared at her, before she chortled. "Just so, my dear! Quite the joke you have made!"

§

Tossing aside the novel she had been reading, Lydia exclaimed, "I do so long to visit my aunt Philips! She must have *some* news to give us. I am determined to walk there today. *Do* let us go!"

Lydia's intention of walking to Meryton to visit her aunt Philips was not forgotten, nor was it despised as a way to while away a few hours, and every sister agreed to go with her. Bennet's civility was most prompt in inviting Mr. Collins to attend his daughters in their walk.

Bennet was most anxious to get rid of him, and have his library to himself. Mr. Collins had followed him there after breakfast, and there he would continue, nominally engaged with one of the large folios in the collection, but really talking with little cessation of his house and garden at Hunsford. Mr. Collins, being in fact much better fitted for a walker than a reader, was well-pleased to close his large book and go.

Such doings discomposed Thomas Bennet exceedingly. In his library, he had been always sure of leisure and tranquility. "Though I am prepared," he said in an acid aside to his daughter Elizabeth, as the walking party was setting out, "to meet with folly and conceit in every other room in the house, I am used to be free from them there."

Elizabeth laughed gaily and hurried to catch up with her sisters.

Mr. Collins, on his return to Longbourn, expressed gratitude for his cousins' generous introduction to their aunt, and he spoke admiringly of Mrs. Philips' manners and politeness. "Except for Lady Catherine and her daughter, I have never seen a more elegant woman, for she did not only receive me with the utmost civility, but even pointedly included me in her invitation for tomorrow evening, although utterly unknown to her before. I suppose it might be attributed to my connection with my cousins, but yet I have never met with so much attention in the whole course of my life."

Mrs. Bennet bestowed a pleased smile on him. "I am highly gratified, Mr. Collins, by your opinion of my sister Philips."

Thomas Bennet was astonished. Mrs. Bennet was *pleased* by his cousin's obsequious speech. Perhaps that in itself was not marvelous, but what it betokened certainly did. The man whom she could not bear to speak of the day before was now in her good graces. His wife's turnabout was inexplicable until he recalled that Mr. Collins was not married and was well-situated in his profession with a very tolerable income. He grimaced. *That is explanation enough.* He was fully aware of the inexorable trend of his wife's mind.

Mrs. Bennet was naturally scheming to get one of her daughters off her hands. The thought of having Mr. Collins for a son-in-law was by no means agreeable, and he hoped none of his daughters had been impressed by Mr. Collins' incessant talk of his snug abode and his garden at Hunsford.

Perhaps his mild disquiet was needless. Upon returning from their walk, his two youngest daughters could speak of nothing but the new young officer they had met in Meryton, walking along the street with Mr. Denny. It seemed there had never been such a fellow. His appearance was greatly in his favor; he had all the best parts of beauty, a fine countenance, a good figure, and very pleasing address. In comparison to this paragon, according to Lydia, "All the other officers have become disagreeable, stupid fellows."

Bennet asked with acerbity, "Did you not see anyone of note? Surely, the whole town of Meryton was not littered solely with red coats!"

Not at all affected by his sarcasm, Lydia and Catherine giggled together, protesting that was indeed the case. "Really, there was no one else that *we* saw!" But Jane spoke up, saying, with a blush, "Mr. Bingley and Mr. Darcy rode into town and stopped to speak. Mr. Bingley kindly asked after my health."

"Well! *That* is something!" exclaimed Mrs. Bennet, most pleased. "Mr. Bingley's attentions are just what they ought to be, Jane. Oh, my dearest girl, I shall soon see you established at Netherfield Hall!""

Mr. Collins frowned.

"Yes, and I believe he would have stayed to talk longer, except Mr. Darcy rode away, as soon as he beheld the officers," said Elizabeth, furrowing her brows. "Indeed, it was rather strange. Mr. Darcy appeared to be affected by the sight of one man in particular. They each changed color, one going pale and the other turning red."

Bennet gave her remarks light dismissal. "I cannot say that I blame him, with such silly girls all talking at once to the officers!"

"*I* did not make such a spectacle of myself, Papa."

"Then you did well, Mary."

With a bow, Mr. Collins addressed his hostess. "Mrs. Bennet, if you will be so kind, I should like to have a word – a *private* word."

Mrs. Bennet was all acquiescence. "Certainly, Mr. Collins. Let us go into the front parlor. There is a fire there as well and we will be quite comfortable, I am sure!"

Thomas Bennet's eyes narrowed as he watched his wife and Mr. Collins retreat from the drawing-room into the hallway. Already their heads were close together, and he could discern low, indistinguishable conversation. He was amused by their stratagem, being quite certain that there was a plot afoot. He suspected he knew of what the general outlines consisted. However, it was of small concern. Mrs. Bennet was incapable of keeping a secret. He was confident before very little time had elapsed that his wife would let fall whatever occupied her shallow mind.

It was but a few minutes later, when Bennet left the drawing-room and hid himself away in the library. He could no longer abide all the sprightly talk of the newest officer of the corps – this Mr. Wickham – whom Catherine and Lydia were in alt over. Elizabeth had few remarks to make. However, unless he much mistook the matter, he believed even she was infected with the same admiration, though her enthusiasm was expressed with more restraint than her younger and sillier sisters.

[9]

Lady Lucas had thought it necessary to begin introducing Miss Hawkins into the neighborhood and though as a general rule, she would not consider a governess on a social par, it had not taken her long to take her niece's measure. In the privacy of their sitting room, she spoke her mind to Sir William. "She means to rule the roost, and I cannot very well regulate her to the schoolroom. Well! If she thinks she will be allowed to queen over our society, she will swiftly discover that I disapprove of strong-willed girls who believe they can go about without a proper chaperone! I have already informed Miss Simmons that her chief duty, as long as my niece is with us, will be to act as her chaperone. And that means to go about into society, as well."

"You must arrange all as it seems best to you, my dear. She is your niece, after all," said Sir William mildly. "Miss Simmons is an exceptionally well-bred young woman. She will not disgrace us with our neighbors, I am sure."

Lady Lucas' particular friends, Mrs. Long and Mrs. Robinson, upon making a morning call, were the first to meet Miss Augusta Hawkins. It was not known what the ladies thought of her – their well-bred civility was all it should have been – but at being introduced to Miss Simmons, and learning her role, their nods and smiles held perfect understanding.

Charlotte paid an overdue visit to the Bennets. She would have wished to go alone because she had so much to relate to Elizabeth and Jane, but it was not to be. She was accompanied by her younger sister Maria, her cousin Miss Hawkins, and Miss Simmons. They did not walk the short distance, Miss Hawkins protesting in horror at the proposed exercise. "Such a barbarity in the cold!" So, the Lucas carriage was put to use for the short distance and the ladies scarcely had time to feel the November chill before their arrival at Longbourn. There was already a carriage before the door, which proved to be that of the Bingleys, as was discovered when the Lucas party entered the warmth of the manor house.

In the drawing-room, there were exclamations of welcome, greetings, and introductions. Mr. Bennet was amongst those who greeted the Lucases and their companions. In a fleeting upward glance, Charlotte saw that the gentleman was wearing what she interpreted as a rather sardonic amusement. She wondered what was the cause of it.

Mr. Bennet smiled down at her, his eyes glinting, as though he was asking her to share in a joke. "Miss Lucas, a pleasure to welcome you and your party. Allow me to show you to the settee, here beside Lizzy. Miss Maria, Miss Hawkins, Miss Simmons, pray do sit down. We are quite informal, as you see."

"I am very happy to meet you," said Mr. Bingley, addressing Miss Hawkins and Miss Simmons. His affable manners towards the two ladies were much better than those of his sisters. Miss Bingley could not be bothered with anyone so provincial as the Miss Lucases, and by extension, the rest of her party. Mrs. Hurst at least unbent enough to compliment Miss Hawkins' bonnet, which sported a trio of white osprey feathers.

"Mr. Bingley and his sisters have come to give their personal invitation for the long expected ball at Netherfield," said Bennet. The prospect of the ball was extremely agreeable to every female of his family, and the subject had already been well canvassed. *It has quite buried all the talk of Mrs. Philips' card party on yester evening.* "Mrs.

Bennet has chosen to consider it as given in compliment to her eldest daughter, "

Mrs. Bennet's self-complacence was evident. "I was particularly flattered by receiving the invitation from Mr. Bingley himself, instead of a ceremonious card."

Miss Bingley and Mrs. Hurst exchanged telling looks.

Charlotte at once grasped the source of Mr. Bennet's amusement. She could not quite suppress a smile. "A compliment, indeed, Mrs. Bennet."

Mr. Bingley turned his agreeableness to Miss Hawkins and Miss Simmons. "You must certainly come; it is fixed for Tuesday next. I would certainly have added your names to the invitation card, had I known you were at Lucas Lodge.".

Miss Simmons demurred but her genteel voice was lost beneath Miss Hawkins' overriding assurance. "Indeed, I shall attend, for I am always for a ball! We held such delightful ones at Maple Grove! Have you heard of Maple Grove, sir? My brother Mr. Suckling has been eleven years a resident at Maple Grove, and his father had it before him – I believe, at least – I am almost sure that old Mr. Suckling had completed the purchase before his death."

At the turn in her conversation, Miss Bingley and Mrs. Hurst stiffened. It was always a sore point with them that the Bingleys had not elevated themselves by taking up an estate. However, Mr. Bingley did not take the same affront. "I am leasing Netherfield presently, but I am myself looking to purchase an estate."

"An excellent endeavor, Mr. Bingley!" cried Miss Hawkins. "I hope you may find a seat as fine as Maple Grove. Such an immense plantation all around it! Oh! Do not mistake me, Mr. Bingley! I suppose Netherfield must have an excellent prospect."

Miss Bingley pointedly turned away from Miss Hawkins. "We are delighted to see you again, dear Jane."

"Indeed, it has been an age since we met," agreed Mrs. Hurst. "What have you been doing with yourself, dear Jane?"

"Yes, what *have* you been doing?" echoed Miss Bingley.

The two ladies paid little attention to the rest of the family; avoiding Mrs. Bennet as much as possible, saying not much to Elizabeth, and nothing at all to the others. They were soon gone again, rising from their seats with an activity which took their brother by surprise, and hurrying off as if eager to escape from Mrs. Bennet's civilities. Mr. Bingley bowed, made his goodbyes, and exited in the wake of his sisters.

Miss Hawkins observed the hasty departure of the Bingleys, and delivered her opinion to no one in particular. "I have quite a horror of upstarts. Maple Grove has given me a thorough disgust of people of that sort; for there is a family in that neighborhood who are such an annoyance to my brother and sister from the airs they give themselves! People of the name of Tupman, very lately settled there, and encumbered with many low connections, but giving themselves immense airs, and expecting to be on a footing with the old established families."

"Augusta! Pray recall where you are – your company!" exclaimed Miss Simmons in an urgent undertone.

Miss Hawkins did not seem to hear her former governess. She shook her head. "A year and a half is the very utmost that they can have lived at West Hall, and how they got their fortune nobody knows. They came from Birmingham, which is not a place to promise much. Are the Bingleys from there? One has not great hopes from Birmingham. I always say there is something direful in the sound, but nothing more is positively known of the Tupmans, though a good many things I assure you are suspected; and yet by their manners they evidently think themselves equal even to my brother, Mr. Suckling, who happens to be one of their nearest neighbors. It is infinitely too bad."

An appalled silence was fallen, except for the giggles escaping Catherine and Lydia. Charlotte looked down at her hands, which she clasped together in her lap. Mortification scorched her cheeks. *Mama was right! She is not fit to be let off a leash!*

"I believe the Bingleys are from the north," said Elizabeth in a rather smothered-sounding voice. She resolutely did not meet her father's eyes, or otherwise she thought she might laugh.

"They have relations in Scarborough," offered Mary.

Miss Hawkins considered it. "I know nothing of Scarborough."

Mrs. Bennet huffed. "The Bingleys are perfectly respectable, I shall have you know! Why, Mr. Bingley is as fine and amiable a gentleman as anyone could wish! We are happy to have him, and his sisters, as our neighbors, Miss Hawkins."

"Oh, I do agree, Mrs. Bennet. All of his friends must agree! Mr. Bingley is an amiable gentleman. I found *his* manners to be all that they should be." Her omission of Mr. Bingley's sisters was glaring.

Charlotte released a sigh over her cousin's underbred behavior.

Thomas Bennet cleared his throat and said lightly, "Well, Jane, you must picture to yourself a happy evening in the society of your two friends, and the attentions of their brother." His eldest daughter only blushed, so he turned to his second. "Lizzy, you must be thinking with pleasure of dancing with Mr. Wickham."

Charlotte cast a look toward her. *Wickham? Who is Wickham?*

Elizabeth lowered her eyes but a smile curved her lips. "Oh, I dare say you are right, Papa! Though I also intend to observe Mr. Darcy's looks and behavior, all to see whether he has improved any in them since the Meryton assembly."

"A worthy goal, my dear Lizzy."

. Charlotte chuckled low in her throat. There was enough here to entertain. And she was grateful to the gentleman. Mr. Bennet had skated over the uncomfortable interlude with consummate skill, and changed the tone of the atmosphere.

The happiness anticipated by Catherine and Lydia depended less on any single event, or any particular person, for though they each declared they meant to dance half the evening with Mr. Wickham, he was by no means the only partner who could satisfy them, and a ball was at any rate, a ball. And even Mary could assure her family that she had not disinclination for it.

"While I can have my mornings to myself, it is enough," said Mary. "I think it no sacrifice to join occasionally in evening engagements. Society has claims on us all, and I profess myself one of those who consider intervals of recreation and amusement as desirable for everybody."

As Charlotte already knew, Elizabeth did not often volunteer speech to Mr. Collins, so she was a little surprised when Elizabeth gaily addressed her clerical cousin.

"I cannot help asking, Mr. Collins, whether you intend to accept Mr. Bingley's invitation, and if you do, whether you think it proper to participate in the evening's entertainment."

"I entertain no scruple whatever on that head, Miss Elizabeth."

Elizabeth looked rather surprised. "But do you not dread a rebuke, either from the Archbishop, or Lady Catherine de Bourgh, by venturing to dance?"

"I am by no means of opinion, I assure you, that a ball of this kind, given by a young man of character, to respectable people, can have any evil tendency; and I am so far from objecting to dancing myself that I shall hope to be honored with the hands of all my fair cousins in the course of the evening," said Mr. Collins, with a glance and smile bestowed on the company at large.

Catherine and Lydia looked horrified by the prospect.

He performed a bow. "And I take this opportunity of soliciting yours, Miss Elizabeth, for the two first dances especially, a preference I trust my cousin Jane will attribute to the right cause, and not to any disrespect of her."

Mrs. Bennet cried out, "Why, no apologies are necessary, Mr. Collins! No, indeed! Dear Jane will not mind in the least giving way for Lizzy, I assure you. They are such dear sisters! And Lizzy will be most pleased to accept the honor that you do her!"

Under cover of her mother's loud assurances on her behalf, and Mr. Collins' subsequent protestations of happiness upon earning Mrs. Bennet's approval, Elizabeth muttered in Charlotte's ear. "I feel completely taken in. I had fully proposed being engaged by Wickham for those very dances, and to have Mr. Collins instead – !"

"Your liveliness has never been worse timed," returned Charlotte softly.

Elizabeth cast a sideways glance at her and sighed. "There is no help for it. Mr. Wickham's happiness and my own must be delayed a little longer, and Mr. Collin's proposal accepted with as good a grace as I can."

Charlotte laughed but not without sympathy. *Eliza's preference is clear.* She had not yet met Mr. Wickham, but she had little doubt that he was a finer specimen of manhood than Mr. Collins, who had already demonstrated that his intellectual faculties were not such as to match Elizabeth's lively wit. Charlotte believed Elizabeth was not pleased with his gallantry, especially in light of Mrs. Bennet's encouragement of him, and the idea that it suggested of something more.

Soon thereafter, she and her sister, along with Miss Hawkins and Miss Simmons, bid the Bennets good day and went out of the drawing-room, and made their way to the entry hall, where they would collect their outer garments. Mrs. Bennet accompanied the departing visitors, talking incessantly, while Mr. Bennet went along to direct a footman to run to the stables with an order to bring the Lucas carriage to the front door. Jane and Elizabeth stood in the hall to bid Charlotte a fond farewell, while Mary extended a polite one to Miss Hawkins and Miss Simmons. Catherine and Lydia hugged Maria Lucas, promising her that they would all go together to Meryton to buy new shoe roses. Mr. Collins trailed behind, making several bows and professing himself very well-satisfied with the delightful company.

In the carriage, Miss Hawkins turned her head and smiled at Charlotte. "Dear cousin, I am so glad to have met your friends, such dear friends, indeed, who bear such affection for you! And also Mr. Collins, who is as I understand it, Longborn's heir, with already a good living. He was telling me in *such* wonderful detail of his esteemed patroness, Lady Catherine de Bourgh, and his quaint parsonage and garden, surely just such an establishment to be coveted by any female of humble circumstance. Not by me, of course – I am not yet out and I have ten thousand pounds – yet how perfect, for *you*, Charlotte! Oh, we must promote this match, Cousin Maria, Miss Simmons, we really must promote this match of our dearest Charlotte to Mr. Collins! Such felicity it must bring to her! All her family and friends must wish for it!"

Charlotte's face burned. She was astonished, embarrassed, and humiliated to be addressed in such a way. *Such an insidious attack!* She responded with restraint. "I thank you for your thoughts, Augusta. I do not, however, look for such fortune as you describe."

Miss Hawkins trilled laughter. "You are too modest, dear Charlotte, is she not, Miss Simmons? I am certain Maria must agree with me, we must encourage Charlotte to recommend herself to Mr. Collins in every possible way! Maria, what say you? Have I not devised a perfect remedy to your dear sister's unwed state? She must have the security of a good marriage! Or otherwise hang upon the coat sleeves of her brothers for the entirety of her life! Oh, we must prevent it, Maria, Miss Simmons, we must all agree!"

Round-eyed, Maria suddenly turned red. She stuttered embarrassed protest on her sister's behalf. Miss Simmons laid a hand on her arm, and she turned to that lady with abject relief, subsiding into fuming silence.

"Security is something for which every woman hopes, certainly," said Miss Simmons quietly. "However, I believe each of us has a different idea of what that blessed state consists of and in what form it takes."

"I could not have said it better, Miss Simmons," said Charlotte in a chilly, firm voice. *The insolence!* She had been caught by the throat with such an anger she had never felt before. *And not all for my own dignity, but for the terrible place she has put my poor Maria!*

"Miss Simmons neglects the obvious, does she not? Marriage is our surest preservation, dear cousin, you must agree! And here is your best opportunity, in the person of Mr. Collins!"

The carriage gave a lurch as it was drawn to a standstill. *Thank God! We are home!* A footman opened the door and put down the step, then was ready to give a steadying hand to each of the ladies in descending from the carriage. Charlotte was never gladder of anything than to get out of the close confines of the vehicle, away from her obnoxious cousin. She linked arms with her sister and marched up the front steps of Lucas Lodge.

Maria gave an angry half-sob. "Oh, Charlotte! To say such a thing about you!"

"Hush, dearest. We shall speak presently, in the privacy of my room."

Behind her stiffened back, Charlotte heard the clear, carrying accents of her cousin's voice. "Oh! It so very like Maple Grove, the front entrance, very like it, indeed! Is it not, Miss Simons?"

§

Before the front door had fully closed, Catherine and Lydia squealed and rushed for the stairs, declaring that they must look at their wardrobes to decide what could be worn to the Netherfield ball. Jane and Elizabeth followed them upstairs more sedately, probably with much the same intention, though they did not say so. Mary went off to practice her pianoforte.

Mr. Collins offered a solemn smile to his hosts. "You will excuse me, Mr. Bennet, Mrs. Bennet. I trust it will not offend that I leave your benevolent company. I must go up to my room to write to Lady Catherine de Bourgh, as is my solemn duty, which I do every morning without fail."

Bennet was quick to reassure his guest. "Not at all, sir! Pray do not let us keep you, Mr. Collins." The younger gentleman bowed and hurried away, leaving him with a feeling of relief that his heir had not proposed joining him in the library.

Before he had quit the entry hall, Mrs. Bennet detained him by the simple expedient of plucking at his coat sleeve. She exclaimed in her usual carrying tones. "Well! Mr. Bennet, what have you to say about Mr. Collins? My opinion is well-formed, I can tell you, and I shall voice it so there is no mistaking my intentions!""

"Yes, my dear, I am certain you *do* have an opinion! Let us go in by the fire and you can tell me what is in your mind." Bennet guided her across into the small parlor, away from the ears of the servants in the entry hall. As he shut the door, his reflection was cynical. *Not that there is anything ever kept private in this house.*

Mrs. Bennet settled on the settee, arranging her skirts to her satisfaction. "I am very glad of your civility, Mr. Bennet. It is not often you accord it to me, for I am sure I may count on my hand any number of times that you have not!"

Bennet sat down in the armchair opposite his wife. "Forgive me, Fanny, but did you not allude to your opinion of Mr. Collins?"

"Indeed, sir! I am most pleasantly surprised by him. He is in a very good living and unmarried and will one day inherit Longborn. What could be better for one of our girls? Marrying the heir of Longborn! Why, we would all be saved! He would never throw his near relations out into the hedgerows, once you are dead, for that would bring down the scorn of our society upon his head. No, no, I have thought it all out and we must make him marry one of his cousins!"

"I can scarcely force him to do so." Bennet's reply was at his driest. "And I am not at all certain that any of your daughters would be so foolish to accept his proposals, if they were made."

With her lace handkerchief, Mrs. Bennet waved off such minor obstacles. "I do not regard it in the least, Mr. Bennet! Mr. Collins has confided in me that he is looking for a wife. We shall come to a happy conclusion, I do assure you!"

"I suppose it will not adjust your thinking if I was to express my reluctance to accept such a son-in-law?"

At his mildly-put question, Mrs. Bennet's eyes widened, then narrowed. She tightened her lips. "Now you are teasing me, Mr. Bennet. Oh, my poor nerves! It is not at all kind and so I shall tell you!"

Bennet saw his wife's indignant, reddening face, the swell of her bosom, and he hastened to escape the impending storm by removing himself. He arose from his chair. "Yes, yes, you have told me enough. I shall be in the library until tea-time."

Elizabeth had not been long in ignorance of her mother's plan to wed one of them to Mr. Collins. Certain remarks made by Mrs. Bennet over the passing days, ever since the man's arrival, had made of her surmise more than conjecture. She had discussed the notion with Jane. Her brows creased as she recalled how effusive her mother had been at Mr. Collins' solicitation of her hand for the dance. It now struck her, as almost a thunderbolt. "*I* am selected from among my sisters as worthy of being the mistress of Hunsford Parsonage, and of assisting to form a quadrille table at Rosings, in the absence of more eligible visitors."

The unpalatable idea soon reached to conviction, as she observed his increasing civilities towards herself, and heard his frequent attempt at a compliment on her wit and vivacity; and though more astonished than gratified herself, by this effect of her charms, it was not long before her mother gave her to understand that the probability of their marriage was exceedingly agreeable to *her*.

Elizabeth however did not choose to take the hint, being well aware that a serious dispute must be the consequence of any reply. Mr. Collins might never make the offer, and till he did, it was useless to quarrel about him.

If there had not been a Netherfield ball to prepare for and talk of, the Miss Bennets would have been in a pitiable state at this time, for from the day of the invitation, to the day of the ball, there was such a succession of rain as prevented their walking to Meryton once.

The incessant complaints from the youngest sisters earned the mild mockery of their father. "No aunt, no officers, no news can be sought after – the very shoe roses for Netherfield must be got by proxy. The sufferings you endure, my silly girls!"

Even Elizabeth might have found some trial of her patience in weather, which totally suspended the improvement of her acquaintance with Mr. Wickham; and nothing less than a dance on Tuesday, could have made such a Friday, Saturday, Sunday, and Monday, endurable to Catherine and Lydia.

[10]

Mr. Bennet accompanied his wife, his daughters, and Mr. Collins to the Netherfield ball. He looked forward to the evening. He was not against socializing with his fellow man, merely against spending too much time in the company of the boring and foolish. *I was once very young and very foolish, to my infinite regret.* However, Mrs. Bennet would not remain long at his side. She would flit away and enjoy the exchange of gossip with her friends and neighbors and acquaintances, leaving him to seek out those individuals for whom he had some particle of respect. Otherwise, failing intelligent conversation, he would be kept tolerably amused by the foibles and antics around him.

Thomas Bennet was in a mood to please and to be pleased.

He liked Mr. Bingley. He even liked Mr. Darcy, to a degree, despite the gentleman's disparagement of his daughter Elizabeth at the Meryton assembly. *Lizzy made a joke of it, just as she should.* Mr. Darcy, when he descended from Olympian heights, was an intelligent conversationalist. Bennet's opinion of Mr. Darcy differed from that of the majority of his neighbors. He did not see a disagreeable, overly-proud man but one who simply preferred to hold himself at a distance from his fellows. He saw nothing to cavil in that, for he was himself not overly fond of the half-witted or conceited. However, he did derive some amusement from their company, which Mr. Darcy seemed incapable of doing.

Bennet greeted his host with genuine warmth. "Ah, Bingley! A fine night for a ball, sir! I hear the string quartet already playing. An agreeable harmony, indeed."

"Mr. Bennet, I am glad you have come. And all of your family with you! Welcome!" Though Mr. Bingley's good manners led him to greet all of the Bennet ladies with equal civility, his blue eyes strayed often to Miss Jane Bennet's lovely, gentle smile.

Bennet observed it, and for once, he could give some credence to his wife's understanding. Mrs. Bennet had not been speaking entirely from whole cloth, for there was indeed a spark between his eldest daughter and Mr. Charles Bingley. *If the gentleman has struck dear Jane's fancy, I do not mind it.* Mr. Bingley was amiable, fairly intelligent, and a kind man.

Bennet moved down the receiving line to greet Mr. Bingley's sisters. Miss Bingley and Mrs. Hurst would have been astonished and indignant that Mr. Bennet catalogued them very much as he did his own wife, as empty-headed females of no particular consequence. *Insufferable, proud, dressed as fine as peacocks, and gently waving their fans beneath their superior smiles.* As he made his bows to Miss Bingley and Mrs. Hurst, he corrected himself. These tonnish ladies would no doubt laugh themselves into stitches at his opinion, if it was known to them, and wonder that he dared to have an opinion about them at all. Mr. Hurst stood at his wife's shoulder, an expression of boredom on his face, and he exchanged a nod with the fashionably-dressed gentleman.

Bennet passed on into the bright, candlelit ballroom, where he soon crossed paths with his nearest neighbors, Sir William and Lady Lucas. After they had exchanged civilities, Lady Lucas said, "It will be a sad crush before the end."

Bennet agreed cheerfully. "Yes, indeed! The whole county is here. I hope to indulge my sense of the ridiculous very much this evening."

Lady Lucas smiled at him and shook her head, before moving away to greet another friend.

Sir William chuckled. "You have the right of it, Bennet. We'll see some pretty doings, I make no doubt. The anticipation for the evening is running high."

"My girls will be in the thick of it, and Mrs. Bennet, who is in fine fettle, will have a great deal to say for years to come." Bennet flashed a grin at his portly companion. "All about yards of lace, and whom danced with whom, and how agreeable were the *rich single men*. All except for Mr. Darcy, of course, whom she holds in aversion for insulting one of *her* daughters. But she would come about if the despised Mr. Darcy would bestow the handkerchief on any one of them, for he has ten thousand pounds a year."

Sir William laughed heartily. "You've a wicked tongue, Thomas!"

"Do I?" he murmured, and shook his head. "And here I flattered myself that I was only being remarkably clear-eyed."

Sir William looked at him with a tolerant, bemused smile. "Sometimes I do not know just how to take you."

Bennet clapped him on the shoulder. "Why, with a grain of salt, my friend."

Sir William laughed again.

Before the Netherfield ball, Charlotte Lucas had not seen Elizabeth Bennet for a week; from the day of the invitation, to the day of the ball, there was such a succession of rain as prevented walking anywhere. Through the noisy throng, she glimpsed Elizabeth enter the ballroom and pause on the threshold, looking around, as though in happy search for someone. Charlotte waved to her and Elizabeth at once came to join her. She saw that Elizabeth had dressed with more than usual care for the ball. Her dark hair was twisted up behind her head, full curls in front, with a bandeau. "Why, Eliza, how well you look! Is it for that cluster of red coats assembled over there?"

"Not for all, just one. Indeed, I prepared in the highest spirits for the conquest that remained unsubdued of his heart, trusting that it was not more than might be won in the course of the evening," said Elizabeth lightly, yet a tiny frown was formed between her brows. "Until I entered the ballroom and looked in vain for Mr. Wickham, a doubt of his being present had never occurred to me."

"Well, it is unfortunate, but certainly not grievous." Charlotte gestured with her folded fan. "There are other officers and several respectable gentlemen, besides. I daresay we shall be dancing all the evening. How delightful!"

"I have the dreadful suspicion of his being purposely omitted in the Bingleys' invitation to the officers," said Elizabeth with a flash in her dark eyes. "All for Mr. Darcy's pleasure!"

Charlotte was astonished. *Eliza is in a fine taking. This is serious, indeed.* She turned full-face to her friend. "Why, what do you mean? Why should Mr. Wickham be so slighted by Mr. Bingley or Mr. Darcy?"

Elizabeth looked vexed with herself. "I should not have said so much."

"There is Mr. Darcy." Charlotte watched the gentleman's progress. He did not turn aside to speak to anyone but made his way through the crowded room as though toward a set goal."He is directly approaching. I believe it is a compliment to yourself, Eliza."

"Attention, forbearance, patience – with Darcy! It is injury to Wickham."

"Pray do not be such a zany!" begged Charlotte.

"I am resolved against any sort of conversation with him."

Mr. Darcy reached them then and made polite inquiries, to which Charlotte graciously responded, but Elizabeth seemed hardly able to reply to him with tolerable civility. When Mr. Darcy bowed and left them, Charlotte took her to task. "I do not know what strange notion you have taken into your head! You have turned Mr. Darcy away with such coldness! This ill-humor is unlike you, Eliza."

"I could not wholly surmount it even in speaking to Mr. Bingley, whose blind partiality provokes me," said Elizabeth, shutting and opening her ivory fan. "He is too amiable in his friendship with Mr. Darcy."

Charlotte was concerned by her friend's irritated state of mind. "Eliza, I shall tell you plain. If you have taken a pet because you favor Mr. Wickham, and there is some dispute between him and Mr. Darcy, you are behaving very stupidly."

Elizabeth looked at her, somewhat taken aback. She suddenly smiled. "I apologize, Charlotte. I am treating you to a Cheltenham tragedy, am I not? Though every prospect of my own is destroyed for the evening, I should not let it dwell heavy on my spirits." She pointed with her closed fan. "There is my cousin, Mr. Collins. You have not yet met him in a social setting, outside your brief visit."

Charlotte was vexed to find, flashing to the forefront of her mind, her cousin Augusta's declaration that she must somehow secure Mr. Collins' suit. The remembrance still stung her sensibilities and her pride. She said firmly, "There is no need to call me to his attention."

Elizabeth sighed. "I would infinitely prefer to spare you the acquaintance. He is an oddity, I assure you. He is awkward and solemn, and most unfortunately, I am engaged to him for the first two dances. I do not expect any great pleasure in my partner."

"Have you seen my cousin, Augusta Hawkins, this evening? I suppose she is already circulating amongst the company. Mama permitted her to come, with Miss Simmons as her chaperone. I have never seen such...such ease before, especially in one not yet out." Charlotte thought she had better give voice to a compliment, or otherwise she was in danger of saying more than she should. *Old cattish, Mama would say!* "She is a well-looking girl and will not go without a partner."

Elizabeth gave her a droll look. "I *have* seen her and I am quite envious of her gown, which I am persuaded is in the high kick of fashion!"

"If by that, you mean the quantity of lace on her gown would be enough to trim a half dozen dresses, you are in the right of it!"

Elizabeth laughed and shook her head. "You must not attribute your own opinions to me!"

Charlotte lightly tapped her friend's arm with her closed fan. "What I had meant to tell you, dear Eliza, is this – my cousin Augusta Hawkins was quite taken by Mr. Collins and all he had to say. She had occasion to expound upon the benefits of his situation and-and gave it as her opinion that he would be a most suitable matrimonial partner."

"His parsonage and his garden, separated by only a lane from Rosings Park, the great estate owned by his noble patroness, Lady Catherine de Bourgh!"

Charlotte loosed a soft ripple of laughter. "The very same."

"Miss Hawkins is very welcome to it and Mr. Collins!"

"Oh, she does not want him for herself. She wants him for me!"

"For you!" Elizabeth stared.

Charlotte unfurled her ivory fan and cooled her face. "Augusta was insufferable."

The music started up for the first set, and Mr. Collins was seen approaching. Elizabeth squeezed her friend's arm. "You interest me exceedingly, Charlotte. We must visit on the morrow!" There was no time to say more.

Mr. Collins performed a solemn bow. "Miss Elizabeth, it is my very great pleasure to lead out the fairest lady in the room."

"Mr. Collins, allow me to recall to your memory Miss Charlotte Lucas, who is my dearest friend. Charlotte, my cousin Mr. William Collins is staying with us for a se'enight."

Polite civilities were exchanged, Mr. Collins' being expressed at elaborate length. Finally, the formalities were done with and Mr. Collins led off the lady of his choice. Elizabeth's face reflected polite resignation. Charlotte was herself solicited for the set and she accepted graciously, taking her place in the line with her partner. She watched with interest her friend's standing up with Mr. Collins. He often moved wrong without being aware of it, and Elizabeth's expression was one of distress and mortification. The second set was performed no better. Afterwards, Elizabeth was solicited by an officer and she appeared to be in far more agreeable company.

When the three sets were over, she returned to Charlotte, who addressed her with some amusement. "Mr. Collins did not acquit himself very well. What persuaded the man to get onto the dance floor at all, if he did not know the steps?"

"It gave me all the shame and misery which a disagreeable partner can give. The moment of my release from him was *ecstasy*," said Elizabeth. "My dance with Mr. Pratt had the refreshment of talking of Mr. Wickham, and of hearing that he is universally liked. I discovered that Mr. Wickham had been obliged to go to town yesterday on business."

"Then your surmise was not just."

Elizabeth had the grace to concede. "Mr. Darcy was less answerable for Mr. Wickham's absence than I believed."

Suddenly, Mr. Darcy was standing before them. "Miss Elizabeth, I request the favor of the next set."

Elizabeth looked startled. *As well she might!* Charlotte was horrified that Mr. Darcy might have overheard his name on their lips. Elizabeth must have been as completely taken aback by Mr. Darcy's appearance as she was. She did not reject him, but answered in the affirmative. He walked away again immediately, and Elizabeth was left to fret over her own want of presence of mind. "I was taken so much by surprise in his application for my hand, that, without knowing what I did, I accepted him!"

Charlotte tried to console her, even as she laughed. "I daresay you will find him very agreeable."

"Heaven forbid! *That* would be the greatest misfortune of all!" exclaimed Elizabeth. "To find a man agreeable whom one is determined to hate! Do not wish me such an evil!"

When the dancing recommenced, however, and Darcy could be seen approaching to claim her hand, Charlotte cautioned her, in a whisper behind her fully-spread fan. "Do not be a simpleton and allow your fancy for Mr. Wickham to make you appear unpleasant in the eyes of a man of ten times his consequence."

Elizabeth made no answer, except by a speaking look, but went to take her place in the set. Charlotte was left to circulate amongst her neighbors and acquaintances. She made her bows and spoke her civilities until she came to Mr. Bennet. "I trust you are enjoying the evening, sir."

"I am, indeed. The foibles of my neighbors have afforded me amusement, and I am taking unaccustomed pleasure in the excellent music and the exercise this evening. This set is ended and the next is commencing. Miss Lucas, will you do me the honor?"

Mr. Bennet held out his hand.

Charlotte felt warmth rise in her face. He was being very civil to her. It was not unusual for married gentlemen to dance with others once they had performed their duty to their spouses and those of social prominence. She was often asked by respectable gentlemen to partner them, much more often than by the younger men. However, this was the first time Mr. Bennet had requested her hand. He was not often at the lesser assemblies, and when he was, he did not often join in the dancing. The Netherfield ball appeared to have worked upon his usual avoidance of the dance.

She inclined her head. "I will be delighted, Mr. Bennet."

[11]

Charlotte did not see Elizabeth again for more than half an hour, which she spent very agreeably with Mr. Bennet on the dance floor. He was a competent partner and their shared conversation was interesting to her. She had a fleeting glimpse of Elizabeth talking animatedly with Jane. At the end of the set, Mr. Bennet bowed and said a civil word to her and strolled away. Elizabeth returned and Charlotte said at once, "I saw you earlier with Jane. What has Jane to say? She is in very good looks this evening."

Elizabeth's eyes glowed and she was smiling. "Oh, Charlotte! I listened with delight to the happy, though modest hopes that Jane entertains of Bingley's regard. I said all in my power to heighten her confidence in it."

"It is gratifying to each of us that Jane seems to be securing Mr. Bingley's affections. We can have no difference in sentiment there," said Charlotte with a smile. "But tell me, what of your dances with Mr. Darcy? Was he an agreeable partner?"

Elizabeth chuckled and rolled her eyes. "I took my place in the set, amazed at the dignity to which I was arrived at in being allowed to stand opposite to Mr. Darcy! *And* reading in my neighbors' looks their equal amazement in beholding it."

"Well, that is scarcely surprising. It was much talked of when he insulted you at the Meryton assembly," said Charlotte with a nod. "But go on!"

"We stood for some time without speaking a word. I began to imagine our silence was to last through the two dances and at first resolved not to break it, until suddenly fancying that it would be the greater punishment to my partner to *oblige* him to talk."

Charlotte laughed. "Poor Mr. Darcy! I am able to guess the rest, I believe."

"Yes; it took some resolution and effort, but the gentleman was persuaded to indulge me," said Elizabeth with a droll look. "One must speak a little, you know. It would look odd to be entirely silent for half an hour together, and yet for the advantage of *some*, conversation ought to be so arranged so that they may have the trouble of saying as little as possible."

"Wicked, Eliza!" Charlotte shook her head, smiling. "But whatever did you speak of?"

"Oh, I cannot tell it all to you," said Elizabeth lightly. "I teased Mr. Darcy a little to provoke him into response, and it was enjoyable. Then, he asked if I and my sisters did not often walk to Meryton. I agreed that we did, and I was unable to resist – I told him that we had just formed a new acquaintance." Elizabeth hesitated fractionally. "He knew of whom I spoke, for he and Mr. Bingley chanced by when we met Mr. Wickham."

Charlotte was swift to comprehend. *Mr. Darcy took it in bad part. And she knew he would. Such temerity!* She exclaimed, "All of your good sense must have fled!"She could not stem her morbid curiosity. "What was Mr. Darcy's response?"

"The effect was immediate, Charlotte. A deeper shade of hauteur overspread his features, but he said not a word. Though blaming myself for my own weakness, I could not go on. Then Mr. Darcy made a cutting remark about Mr. Wickham's happy manners ensuring his *making* friends but whether he was equally capable of *retaining* them was less certain. I could not let it pass, not when Mr. Wickham has told me of all he has suffered at Mr. Darcy's hands."

"Eliza." Charlotte was truly in horror at such reckless behavior. "Your partiality for Mr. Wickham carried you too far. Was this wise?"

Elizabeth shook her head, a small, wry smile flickering. "You need not say it, Charlotte, for indeed, I know it was foolish. I have made myself repulsive to Mr. Darcy. But I do not repine! I subjected him to a catechism on forgiveness and resentment and prejudice."

Charlotte eyed her, in some fascination. "And to what did these questions tend?"

"Merely to the illustration of his character. I was trying to make it out."

"And what is your success?"

Elizabeth shook her head. "I did not get on at all. I hear such different accounts of him as puzzle me exceedingly! I may never have another opportunity to take his likeness, so I came away dissatisfied."

She had scarcely finished speaking when Mr. Collins came up to them and told her with great exultation that he had just been so fortunate as to make a most important discovery. He had overheard a gentleman mentioning his aunt, Lady Catherine de Bourgh, to the young lady of the house. "You may imagine my feelings, dear cousin! I am most thankful that the discovery is made in time for me to pay my respects to him, which I am now going to do, and trust he will excuse my not having done it before. My total ignorance of the connection must plead my apology."

Charlotte recognized Miss Bingley in his brief description, but she failed to identify the gentleman. However, her friend had no such difficulty and Elizabeth's face paled.

"You are not going to introduce yourself to Mr. Darcy?"

"Indeed, I am. I shall entreat his pardon for not having done it earlier. I believe him to be Lady Catherine's *nephew*. It will be in my power to assure him that her ladyship was quite well yesterday se'enight."

Charlotte was as astonished as Elizabeth by Mr. Collins' intention. It would be a breach in protocol. She wasn't surprised when Elizabeth tried hard to dissuade him from such a scheme, assuring him that Mr. Darcy would consider his addressing him without introduction as an impertinent freedom, rather than a compliment to his aunt; that it was not in the least necessary there should be any notice on either side, and that if it was, it must belong to Mr. Darcy, the superior in consequence, to begin the acquaintance.

Mr. Collins listened with the determined air of following his own inclination. At the end of her urgent reasoning, he made a pompous speech. "Pardon me for neglecting to profit by your advice, which on every other subject shall be my constant guide, though in the case before us, I consider myself more fitted by education and habitual study to decide on what is right than a young lady such as yourself." With a low bow to Elizabeth, he left them and walked toward the unwitting gentleman.

"He goes to attack Mr. Darcy!" cried Elizabeth despairingly.

"He is certain to meet with rebuff." Charlotte watched as Mr. Collins prefaced his speech with a solemn bow. Mr. Darcy's reception of Mr. Collins' advances was obvious. "Mr. Darcy's astonishment at being so addressed is very evident. It is a pity we cannot hear a word of it."

Elizabeth clutched her arm. "There! I see in the motion of my cousin's lips the words 'apology', 'Hunsford', and 'Lady Catherine de Bourgh'. I feel as if I was hearing it all. It vexes me to see him expose himself to such a man!"

"Mr. Darcy is eyeing him with unrestrained wonder," said Charlotte, intently studying the gentleman's expression. When at last Mr. Collins allowed him time to speak, Mr. Darcy seemed to reply with an air of distant civility. Charlotte was relieved to see it and acknowledged to herself that she was surprised. Mr. Darcy's reputation for insufferable, disagreeable pride had not led her to believe he would deal so well with Mr. Collins.

"Can it be *any wonder*, when Mr. Collins is so insensible of his insult? See Mr. Darcy's contempt of him!"

Charlotte turned her head and looked at her friend. Elizabeth's eyes held an indignant gleam and her cheeks had colored. She entirely sympathized with Elizabeth's feelings and she offered what comfort she could. "One can only respect Mr. Darcy's forbearance, Eliza. He has not given the cut direct to Mr. Collins, but has made him a slight bow and moved away. He may be known as a disagreeable man, but his manners are very good."

Elizabeth was still flushed. "I am mortified! Mr. Collins is a near relation – my father's heir! – and his ill-considered behavior must reflect on my family."

"I think you make too much of it, Eliza. No, I know what you would say, but only consider! Mr. Collins is not long in the neighborhood; therefore, he cannot do much more harm, and I doubt Mr. Darcy will hold the encounter of such importance that he will even recall it."

"I hope you are right, Charlotte."

"Whatever does it matter, Eliza? After all, you said it yourself. What is Mr. Darcy to you?"

Elizabeth did not answer her, only glancing away and biting her lip. Charlotte did not pursue it, preferring to let the matter drop, but she did wonder at Elizabeth's reaction. It seemed strangely intense. Perhaps it was as she had suspected and Elizabeth had been much more hurt by Mr. Darcy's insult than she had let on, and as a consequence, she was made more sensitive to the gentleman's opinion.

When the dancing was done and they sat down to dinner, Charlotte swiftly realized that further humiliation was to lacerate her friend's sensibility. Mrs. Bennet was talking freely, openly, and of nothing else but of her expectation that Jane would be soon married to Mr. Bingley. It was an animating subject, and Mrs. Bennet seemed incapable of fatigue while enumerating the advantages of the match.

Poor Eliza! To have such a mother!

Mrs. Bennet was addressing Charlotte's own mother, and since she was seated nearby, Charlotte herself was privy to every word. Actually, there was no difficulty at all. Mrs. Bennet's conversation was audible to everyone around, including Mr. Darcy who was seated opposite, and whose expression changed gradually from indignant contempt to a composed and steady regard.

The stupid woman can speak of nothing else but her expectation that Jane will soon be married to Mr. Bingley.

The claim was a spurious, high flight of fancy, since nothing had been said or even hinted at by the parties involved, but Mrs. Bennet spoke as though it was already a settled thing. It was an embarrassing want of discretion and showed the vulgarity of Mrs. Bennet's mind and character.

"Mr. Bingley is such a charming young man, and so rich, and living but three miles from us. It is such a comfort to think how fond the two sisters are of Jane, and I am certain they must desire the connection as much as I do." Mrs. Bennet's air of self-congratulation was flagrant. Her shrill declarations swept on like an incoming tide. "It is, moreover, such a promising thing for my younger daughters, as Jane's marrying so greatly must throw them in the way of *other* rich men, and it is so pleasant at my time of life to be able to consign my single daughters to the care of their sister, that I might not be obliged to go into company more than I like."

Charlotte allowed herself a small, disbelieving smile. It was necessary to make *this* circumstance a matter of pleasure, because on such occasions it was the etiquette, but no one was less likely than Mrs. Bennet to find comfort in staying at home at *any* period of her life.

"For heaven's sake, madam, speak lower. What advantage can it be to you to offend Mr. Darcy?" Elizabeth, her cheeks flaming, was doing her utmost to hush her mother. "You will never recommend yourself to his friend by so doing."

However, her efforts went awry. Her mother only scolded her for being nonsensical and her next words were devastatingly clear. "What is Mr. Darcy to me, pray, that I should be afraid of him? I am sure we owe him no such particular civility as to be obliged to say nothing *he* may not like to hear." She continued to enumerate the many advantages of the marriage between her daughter and Mr. Bingley, repeating them over and over to Lady Lucas, who showed by her lack of response that she was far better bred.

Elizabeth blushed and blushed again. She frequently glanced at Mr. Darcy, which was of course no surprise. Charlotte believed her to be in an agony of shame and vexation. At length, however, Mrs. Bennet had no more to say and concluded with a malicious dig at her near neighbor. With a patently false smile, Mrs. Bennet said, "Many good wishes to you, dear Lady Lucas, that you might soon be equally fortunate." She evidently and triumphantly believed there was no chance of it.

Lady Lucas, who had long been yawning at the repetition of delights that Mrs. Bennet saw coming out of the supposed marriage, now shot a swift, regretful glance at her eldest daughter.

Charlotte felt heat bloom on her own cheeks, as Mrs. Bennet's broad injurious brush swept heedlessly across her own sensibilities, leaving the raw acknowledgement that she was destined for lonely spinsterhood.

She was left to the comforts of cold ham and chicken.

When dinner was over, singing was talked of, and Mary, after very little entreaty, prepared to oblige the company. Elizabeth quietly attempted to dissuade her sister but failed, and came to stand beside Charlotte. "Oh, I did hope to prevent Mary's complaisance," she said in a lowered voice. "Mary's powers are by no means fitted for such a display."

"Such an opportunity of exhibiting is delightful to her."

"Her voice is weak and her manner affected," stated Elizabeth flatly. "I am in agonies of embarrassment for her! I hope Jane can bear it. Oh, what must Mr. Bingley think! But only look at his sisters – they are making signs of derision at each other! And Mr. Darcy bears the same grave expression that he wore while listening to my mother's foolish speaking."

"Jane is very composedly talking to Mr. Bingley. You worry overmuch, Eliza." Again, Charlotte wondered at her friend's being so mindful of the reactions of Mr. Darcy and the others residing at Netherfield. *How strange it is that she cares so for their opinions.* It was certainly out of character for such an independent, assured creature as Elizabeth Bennet, and she gave voice to her observation. "This fretfulness is unlike you, Eliza; it is more habitual of you to derive amusement at the foibles of your fellow beings."

"Is it any wonder, if I fret this evening, an evening sponsored by such personages and at which all the county is in attendance, at the consequential follies of my family? My younger sisters, my mother – and now my father! – stopping Mary in such a disconcerting way! He should have gone up to her to whisper in her ear, after her second song, rather than called out from a distance for her to give others an opportunity to exhibit!"

"Mr. Bennet could have handled it better, it is true. But still, you have known for years how some members of your family behave in company and you have regarded it all with tolerance."

"Perhaps I begin to see with different eyes," said Elizabeth in a low, vibrant voice.

In the middle of the floor, Mr. Collins drew himself up and looked about him. "If I were so fortunate as to be able to sing, I should have great pleasure, I am sure, in obliging the company with an air; for I consider music as a very innocent diversion, and perfectly compatible with the profession of a clergyman. I do not mean however to assert that we can be justified in devoting too much of our time to music, for there are certainly other things to be attended to." He went on to describe in much detail the duties of a rector." Then with a bow to Mr. Darcy, he concluded his speech, which had been spoken so loud as to be heard by half the room.

Elizabeth shook her head. "My cup runneth over."

Charlotte reached out to squeeze her hand. "Never mind, Eliza! The music will resume at any minute and you will feel the better for dancing again."

"Oh, I wish it so! However, I suspect I shall derive little amusement the rest of the evening. Here comes Mr. Collins! I am persecuted, Charlotte! *Nothing* shall prevail upon me to stand up with him again!"

"If you deny him the set, it will be put out of your power to dance with others. You shall have to refuse every other offer."

Elizabeth bestowed a droll, yet frustrated, look upon her. "Your logic is irrefutable, Charlotte! I *do* like to dance. Very well! I shall allow him to trod on my toes once again, only to please you!"

Charlotte chuckled and waved her off, when Mr. Collins claimed her hand. Having no partner of her own, she slowly promenaded, eventually coming across her cousin with her chaperone. Charlotte nodded in a friendly way to Miss Simmons before addressing her cousin. "Do you enjoy the ball, Augusta?"

"Indeed! Such a pleasant evening, do you not agree! I would not for worlds trade a ball for anything else, though Maple Grove is closest to my heart. Oh, dear cousin, you have not *lived* until you have the sublime experience of an entertainment at Maple Grove. I know you agree, Miss Simmons, you must. There is nothing like Maple Grove dressed up of an evening! How do you like my gown – Selena's choice – handsome, I think, but I do not know whether it is not over-trimmed. I have the greatest dislike to the idea of being over-trimmed – quite a horror of finery. I have some notion of putting such a trimming as this to my white and silver poplin. Do you think it will look well?"

"Miss Lucas has never seen your white and silver poplin," remarked Miss Simmons quietly.

Charlotte replied with the aplomb of a diplomat. "Though I have not seen it, I am certain you must be pleased with the effect."

Miss Hawkins trilled laughter. "Oh, charmingly said! You must agree, Miss Simmons, my dear cousin is most charming! But what is this – Miss Elizabeth dancing with Mr. Collins! We agreed between us– did we not? – we agreed that you must make an effort for Mr. Collins. I get anxious for you. Oh! My dear cousin, we cannot begin too early. You are not aware of the difficulty of procuring exactly the desirable thing."

Charlotte felt the blush coming into her face. She glanced about, hoping that no one of her acquaintance was near enough to overhear such a conversation. *The absurdity!* "I never fixed on Mr. Collins. Indeed, I wish you will not give it another thought, Augusta. I would not wish you to take the trouble to yourself."

"Trouble! I know your scruples. You are afraid of giving me trouble; but I assure you, my dear cousin, your own family can hardly be more interested about you than I am."

Astonished indignation flashed through her. Her fingers tightened around the sticks of her folded fan. *Such a set-down I should like to give her!* She was quivering and knew herself to be on the cusp of doing something outrageous. Charlotte wished to turn sharp about and leave her cousin, but she *could not* give the cut direct – such would create a scandal.

Miss Simmons stepped forward, and her quiet voice cut through the tumult that had torched Charlotte's rational mind. "Miss Lucas,

I believe you have a torn flounce. Do you accompany me to the repairing room and I shall pin it up for you."

"Yes, yes, of course." Charlotte allowed the lady to take her arm and moved away with her. She drew in a deep breath. "Thank you, Miss Simmons!" After a moment, she said, "I have not torn a flounce."

Miss Simmons laughed a little. "Yes, I know but it was all I could think of as an excuse to bring you safe away. There is the repairing room; we shall duck in for a few minutes until you have regained your composure."

Charlotte agreed to this and when they had entered, she sat down on a padded stool. She meticulously smoothed a wrinkle out of her skirt. She repressed her emotion, with the control of long practice, and smoothed out her expression. "I have always believed myself to be of an even temper. However, there is something about my cousin which sends me straight into the boughs. I am heartily ashamed of myself."

Miss Simmons had also sat down. "Oh, do not be ashamed of your feelings, Miss Lucas. Otherwise, I shall have to take up that cross of shame for myself."

Charlotte glanced at her in some surprise. "Why, whatever can you mean?"

Miss Simmons smiled faintly. "Maple Grove is indeed a pleasant abode, but I was never more glad in my life than to leave my situation there. It will please me greatly when my duties as companion can be put off for those of a mere governess."

"Oh, I see!" Charlotte slid another glance at the lady, and when their glances met, they both burst into chuckles. Charlotte felt the release of her former tension. "I believe I am to count you as a friend, Miss Simmons."

"I should like that."

Another lady entered in impetuous haste. "Here you are, Charlotte! A very good idea – I wish I had thought of it before Mr. Collins asked me for that last set!" Elizabeth plopped down on another bench, and with a groan, she took off one of her dancing sandals to massage her stockinged toes.

"Why, Eliza, has Mr. Collins indeed been so maladroit?"

"Bruised and crushed, I assure you! Miss Simmons, how do you do? I have not spoken to you before this moment, you must forgive me."

"I apprehend I am doing better than you, Miss Elizabeth. *My* toes are intact." Miss Simmons rose to her feet. "I shall leave you now, for I have the task of tracking down my charge and attempt to lead her into comely behavior. Not that I can do much in that respect."

Charlotte and Elizabeth laughed at the lady's wry sally, and when she had exited, they enjoyed a comfortable coze, during which Charlotte repeated the conversation she'd had with her cousin. Elizabeth was indignant on her behalf and entered into all of her feelings. "Such effrontery! I am not at all surprised it put you out. Well! Between my family and your cousin, I must say we have each had a memorable ball! We must return, unfortunately, for we shall be missed."

Charlotte agreed and once Elizabeth had replaced her sandal, they sallied forth. The ballroom seemed rather sparser of company than before, though the string quartet still played. "I gather we stayed rather longer in the repairing room than we knew," she observed.

Elizabeth nodded. With a wry look, she said, "I was quite ready to sit out any further sets. My poor toes!"

Almost immediately, they were approached.

Miss Hawkins spoke out merrily. "Here is the hour come!" She was trailed by Miss Simmons. Charlotte looked a question at the other lady, who did not disappoint. With a smile, Miss Simmons said, "Lady Lucas bids us to say she is ready to depart."

"Then I shall come to say my goodbyes to our hosts." Charlotte turned to Elizabeth and held out her hands. "We shall visit. Perhaps on the morrow."

"Yes," agreed Elizabeth, catching hold of her gloved fingers and giving them an affectionate squeeze before letting go. "I must find my mother. It grows late, does it not? I am certain we shall also be saying our goodbyes."

The Longbourn party were the last of all the company to depart Netherfield; and by a maneuver of Mrs. Bennet had to wait for their carriages a quarter of an hour after everybody else was gone, which gave them time to see how heartily they were wished away by some of the family. Mrs. Hurst and her sister scarcely opened their mouths except to complain of fatigue, and were evidently impatient to have the house to themselves. They repulsed every attempt of Mrs. Bennet at conversation, and by so doing, threw a languor over the whole party, which was very little relieved by the long speeches of Mr. Collins, who was complimenting Mr. Bingley and his sisters on the elegance of their entertainment, and the hospitality and politeness which had marked their behavior to their guests.

Darcy said nothing at all. Bennet, in equal silence, was enjoying the scene.

Mr. Bingley and Jane were standing together, a little apart from the rest, and talked only to each other. Elizabeth preserved as steady a silence as Mrs. Hurst and Miss Bingley, and even Lydia was too much fatigued to utter more than the occasional exclamation, accompanied by a violent yawn. "Lord, how tired I am!"

When at length they rose to take their leave, Mrs. Bennet was most pressingly civil in her hopes of seeing the whole family soon at Longbourn, and addressed herself particularly to Mr. Bingley. "I assure you, sir, how happy you will make us, by eating a family dinner with us at any time, without the ceremony of a formal invitation."

Bingley was all grateful pleasure. "I readily engage for taking the earliest opportunity of waiting on you, Mrs. Bennet, after my return from London, where I am obliged to go tomorrow for a short time."

At last able to quit the house, Bennet handed his wife into their carriage. The hired one containing his daughters and Mr. Collins was already bowling away with clopping hooves and creaking wheels.

Mrs. Bennet was perfectly satisfied, under the delightful persuasion that, allowing for the necessary preparations of settlements, new carriages and wedding clothes, she should undoubtedly see her daughter settled at Netherfield, in the course of three or four months. "It is all but settled, Mr. Bennet. And I shall have another daughter married to Mr. Collins; yes, indeed, he will do very well for Lizzy!" Mrs. Bennet spoke of the imagined second marriage with considerable, though not equal pleasure, for Mr. Collins' prospects, his situation at Hunsford, and his gardens, were all eclipsed by Mr. Bingley and Netherfield Park.

The outside lamps had been lit and with every sway of the carriage, the dim beams flickered in the windows. *What flights of fancy! I am glad to have the carriage to ourselves* Thomas Bennet turned his head, to regard, with mild irritation, his wife's shadowed face. *But I suppose she will repeat it to all and sundry on the morrow!*

"My heir is a foolish man."

Mrs. Bennet sharply inhaled, bridling. "I know what you would say, Mr. Bennet! *Clever* Lizzy! *So* quick of wit! Mr. Collins is not *worthy* of her! Well, Jane is beautiful, Lydia is lively, and Lizzy is impertinent! I shall count myself fortunate to *ever* have her off my hands, let me tell you! No, no, she must hear Mr. Collins on the morrow. I shall see to it. The man and the match are quite good enough for *her*."

As Thomas Bennet knew, Elizabeth was the least dear of all her children, so it did not surprise him that Mrs. Bennet would have a total disregard for, nor give any thought to, Elizabeth's sensibilities or preferences. He knew any attempt on his part to reason with her would only elicit shrill repudiations. He was silent. He had no wish to travel home, locked in a carriage, enduring as his dear wife suffered from flutterings and spasms all up and down her sides!

[12]

Though the Bennets returned very late to Longbourn from Netherfield Park, it was but shortly after dawn when Thomas Bennet rose and set out for a tramp with his faithful spaniel. Not surprisingly, he was joined in his exercise by his second daughter, for she had always loved walking the countryside. Elizabeth was bundled against the cold in a warm woolen cloak, with the hood pulled well over her velvet bonnet.

"For the most part, I enjoyed the Netherfield ball," he remarked.

Elizabeth's reply was short and remarkably unencouraging. "Did you, Papa?"

He slanted a sardonic glance at her. "Why, Lizzy, I am surprised. Surely you took as much amusement in the ridiculous as I did. Your younger sisters' antics, your cousin Collins – why, even myself! – in responding to your silent entreaties to rescue us all from Mary's inadequate performance. As for high farce, your dear mother surely brought down the curtain! I do not think anyone was spared her proclamations that Bingley and Jane were to wed!"

"It appeared to me, sir, that had my family made an agreement to expose themselves as much as they could during the evening," said Elizabeth with some bitterness, "it would have been impossible for them to play their parts with more spirit or finer success."

He barked a laugh. "Come, Lizzy! You have long known of your family's penchant for embarrassing themselves. Why should it matter so much? Unless it was the exalted company which has caused this excess of emotion?"

Two spots of bright color bloomed in his daughter's cheeks, which owed nothing to the cold or the exercise. Elizabeth was an honest creature and she did not pretend a misunderstanding of his questions. Dropping her gaze, speaking in a low tone, Elizabeth said, "That Mr. Bingley's sisters and Mr. Darcy should have such an opportunity of ridiculing my relations was bad enough, but I could not determine whether the silent contempt of the gentleman, or the insolent smiles of the ladies, were more intolerable."

Bennet took pity on her. "Then take consolation for Bingley and your sister. Some of the exhibition escaped his notice, and it seemed his feelings are not of a sort to be much distressed by the folly which he must have witnessed."

"Oh, I am happy to think it!"

Elizabeth's stormy expression vanished, and her lips curled with delight at the reminder that a beloved sister had engendered such distinguished admiration. Bennet was glad to see it; it was a particular boon to his sensibility that his dearest daughter was of a cheerful disposition and could not long sustain melancholia.

After a companionable moment, Thomas Bennet spoke again. "I fear you are in for it this morning, Lizzy. In the carriage last night, Mrs. Bennet assured me that she has granted permission for Mr. Collins to address you."

Elizabeth checked in midstride. Bennet stopped, half-turning to wait for his daughter. She was staring at him with a shocked expression. He smiled at her and beckoned her forward. As she slowly resumed their walk, he said gently, "Come, come, it can be of little surprise to you. Mr. Collins is a single gentleman, well-placed in his profession, and has told us all, in exhaustive detail, of Hunsford and his garden. Moreover, almost from the first moment of entering the house, he has made you the object of his admiration. How can you doubt there is not a proposal in the offing?"

"I observed his increasing civilities towards myself, and heard his frequent attempt at compliment on my wit and vivacity, but I was more astonished than gratified," she said unhappily.

"Mrs. Bennet will arrange a private audience after breakfast."

Elizabeth's eyes widened. She stammered, "Oh, no, no! Mr. Collins must excuse me! He can have nothing to say to me that anybody need not hear."

Bennet smiled at her, sympathetic to her feelings. *Indeed, who can blame her in wishing to avoid such a declaration? Collins is a foolish man, unequal to her in every way.* "Pray do not look so appalled, my dear girl. You will survive, I assure you."

"I shall not stay for breakfast. I am going away." She waved her arms wildly at the hedgerows and the glimpses of winter-browned fields.

"I am sorry for it, Lizzy, but I insist upon you staying and hearing Mr. Collins. Otherwise, you will cause a virulent attack of Mrs. Bennet's nerves. There will be nothing like it. Such flutterings and pains and shrill complaints! No, no, you must lend a patient ear to Mr. Collins. It will be wisest to get it over with as soon and as quietly as possible."

Papa – I beg of you!" She appeared vexed and embarrassed and bit her bottom lip. When she had better command of herself, she said with an attempt at lightness, "My feelings are divided between distress and diversion."

"I understand," said Bennet dryly. He reached out for his daughter's gloved hand and squeezed it. "My dear Lizzy, though Mrs. Bennet will insist you marry Mr. Collins, I *do not* wish for it. You will be subjected, yes, to Mrs. Bennet's nerves, but content yourself that I shall share in those same sufferings, for I shall withhold my consent.

Perhaps by that dilution, we might see a swifter exhaustion of the inevitable tantrum."

He could see she was taken aback by his frank discourse; he was not in the habit of explanation or, indeed, indulging in any serious conversation with the females of his family. It was a rarity and he was half-embarrassed that he had entered into it at all. However, she was his favorite daughter and he had felt a singular impetus to lend her what support he could offer without greater inconvenience to himself.

Elizabeth sighed. "I shall do as you bid me, sir. But I do not feel a happiness for the interview."

"Thank you, my dear. All will be well, you will see." Bennet was sanguine. *She will refuse Collins, Mrs. Bennet will spout and sputter for a bit, and then we may be comfortable again.*

Turning their steps, and with the spaniel frisking at their heels, they returned to Longbourn.

Bennet breakfasted with his family and his heir, listening and watching. When he saw the significant looks which passed between Mrs. Bennet and Mr. Collins, he excused himself from the breakfast parlor. He caught Elizabeth's quick glance, pained and resigned, and he smiled slightly to himself. This daughter of his was strong enough to withstand the importunities of Mr. Collins, and when Mrs. Bennet came to him, as certainly she would, to complain, he would have an answer for her.

§

Charlotte took advantage of the chilly, bright day and walked to Longbourn, eager to exchange impressions of the Netherfield ball with her two closest friends, Jane and Elizabeth Bennet. In addition, she would most willingly unburden herself over her cousin August Hawkins, and her awful pretensions and pronouncements, from the time of her arrival to the previous evening. *Since her coming, Augusta has abraded my feelings, as well as Maria's, and been insulting of our home and our neighborhood society.* Jane would be shocked but she would not pass judgment, being such an amiable person herself that she looked for good in everyone else. However, Elizabeth would surely enter into all of her exacerbated feelings and have something pithy to say.

Strangely, Longbourn's front door stood open. Charlotte climbed the shallow steps but hesitated before she stepped across the threshold, as her ears were at once assaulted by shrieks and wails and lamentations. Her heart bumped, before it speeded up. *That is not Mrs. Bennet! Oh, something terrible has happened.*

Two officers in red regimentals, standing just inside, their heads lifted high, blocked her way...they, too, were listening. Past them, Charlotte saw Elizabeth and Catherine, their faces whitened, come running up the hall, their skirts flying, before they veered sharply into the front parlor. The housekeeper ran in the opposite direction, screaming for the master.

"Mr. Bennet! Mr. Bennet!"

He had been expecting his wife's shrill accents; it disconcerted him to identify instead his housekeeper's raised tones. The urgent summons was accompanied by an agitated knocking on the sturdy library door. He slammed shut his book. Behind the housekeeper's pounding fist, he became aware of other noises, and an awful, high-pitched screeching.

"Cannot a man have a bit of peace?" His spaniel stood up and whined. He sighed, and getting up from his chair, he went to open the door. "What is it, Mrs. Hill?"

The housekeeper's eyes were rounded and glary; her voice was shaking. She wrung her hands. "It is awful, sir! Mrs. Bennet is all over blood and Miss Jane has fainted dead away!"

"What!" He strode out of the library, the heels of his boots striking hard on the floor. Distress having rendered her incoherent, Mrs. Hill trotted behind him. In the entrance hall, cold air rolled over him, making him involuntarily shiver – oddly, the broad front door was standing open. He brushed by two young officers who were simply standing there, alongside the butler and footman. Appearing shaken, Hill flicked his hand in their direction.

Bennet gave a sharp acknowledgement of the officers. "Mr. Wickham. Mr. Denny." *They must have come to call.* He paid them no more heed but was drawn on by the terrible keening noise – yet, was aware that they hesitantly followed him, as though pulled forward by his clipped acknowledgement.

Going along with the officers, went Charlotte, dreading and hesitant. A horrific scene burst upon their combined sight. One of the officers uttered a shocked, incoherent exclamation. Charlotte turned away, hands pressed to her mouth, sickened.

On the threshold of the front parlor, Thomas Bennet had abruptly checked. His shocked gaze fell on Mrs. Bennet sprawled on the carpet, her limbs resting at awkward angles. Her head and face were covered with dark blood. *As though she was wearing a bright red bag over all,* was his horrified impression. Nearby, Jane lay in a deathly-pale swoon. Elizabeth crouched beside her, chafing her sister's limp hand. She was urgently calling her sister's name, but it was not that which he had heard.

It was Lydia, wailing in an awful animalistic way. *"Mama! Mama!"*

Catherine hovered near Jane and the inert body of their mother. Her face was stark-white, her glistening gaze swiveling from one to the other, while all of her fingers pressed hard against her lips.

Transfixed by horror, Bennet stood rooted to the spot. His faculties were suspended by the ghastly scene. He heard the laments and Lydia's hysterics, but he could not act.

A light touch on his sleeve – he started violently.

Miss Lucas stood beside him, attired in bonnet and outer-garments. Her low voice was urgent. "Mr. Bennet, you must send for a physician."

"Yes, yes, of course." He passed a shaking hand over his face and gathered himself. He did not know where Miss Lucas had popped up from, he had not seen her before, but he felt a lightning bolt of relief at her appearance. He peeled away to order the footman to run and send a stable hand to ride immediately to Meryton for the physician. Once more ignoring the presence of the two red-coated militiamen, he snapped at the butler. "And for God's sake, Mr. Hill, close the door! You are letting in the cold!"

When he returned, he could again only stand by, helpless, just inside the doorway of the parlor. He did not know what to do next. Catherine, white-faced, tearful, and fragile-looking; Miss Lucas was speaking to her, holding her hand between both of her own. Jane was being lifted onto a settee – he registered that it was Denny and Wickham who were carefully moving her limp, unconscious form. Elizabeth rose, following close beside them, all of her attention focused on her elder sister's ashen countenance. Mary was prosaically picking up an empty water pitcher and turning away from a drenched, sobbing Lydia, who was huddled in a heap on the floor. He shuddered, so very thankful that his youngest daughter's wild keening had been aborted.

He uttered a stunned query, scarcely aware he did so. "What happened?" There came a flurry of disjointed explanations, from Catherine, from Elizabeth and Mary. The rational part of his brain pieced it all together. Mr. Collins had been left to make his proposals to Elizabeth in the breakfast room. In the parlor, caught up in a welter of excitement, Mrs. Bennet had been swiftly pacing. Round and round she had gone, until she had caught her shoe heel in a worn turn of the rug, just by the fireplace. Mrs. Bennet had taken a hard tumble, striking her head on the hearthstone. Bennet's starting gaze was irresistibly drawn. With rising horror and gorge, he realized that even from where he stood, he could see on the corner stone the trailing, slimy smear of gore.

Mr. Collins was suddenly come up close beside him, speaking in an urgent tone at his right ear. His voice was pitched rather higher than normal, bleating in an aggrieved fashion. "Cousin Bennet, this is most irregular. My leave only extends to Saturday. I set about it in a very orderly manner, with all the observances which I supposed to be a regular part of the business. I was making my declarations in form, addressing to Miss Elizabeth my reasons for marrying."

Bennet was benumbed; the buzz of complaints irritated. He barely glanced at his heir presumptive, just gently set him aside. "Not now, there's a good fellow. It is not a good time."

The household was still in an uproar but things were getting sorted. Miss Lucas was everywhere with a word or an instruction. Catherine and Mary supported a staggering, weeping, Lydia upstairs. All of the girl's exuberance seemed to have shattered to pieces. *Her mother's favorite daughter...the accident has hit her hard.* The military fellows said their adieus – he heard them through the daze of his shocked brain – and left. Elizabeth remained crouched at her station beside her sister, who was beginning to come round and was being persuaded to take a few sips of wine.

I cannot bear it any more. He rushed forward, tugging his handkerchief from his coat pocket. He bent and laid the large square gingerly over his wife's bloodied, still face. The simple, respectful act served to pull him out of his paralysis.

Bennet overheard Miss Lucas offer the hospitality of Lucas Lodge to Mr. Collins and to his infinite relief, the man accepted. The discomposed clergyman went upstairs to pack his portmanteau and trunk. The stable hand returned from his errand, stuttering that the physician was following as soon as he might in his gig. Bennet acknowledged he had heard and ordered out his own gig for transport, directing the stable hand to have a groom convey Mr. Collins to Lucas Lodge. He dispatched the hovering footman to see to bringing down the clergyman's baggage. Then he turned to the ashen-faced butler. "Hill, refreshments shall be wanted for the physician when he is...is finished. See to it. A cold collation, some brandy."

Elizabeth and Jane, with arms wrapped in support about one another's waists, tottered upstairs at last. Miss Lucas followed close behind them, her soft encouragements trailing her. Passing the three ladies in the turn of the stair, Mr. Collins descended, accompanied by the burdened manservant. The footman strapped the baggage onto the gig waiting at the door. Bennet ushered out his heir presumptive, scarcely lending ear to the man's voluble regrets, condolences, assurances of support, and multiple goodbyes.

The physician arrived, giving hat, gloves and drab wool overcoat into the butler's care. Bennet exchanged abbreviated greetings with him, and then the medical man with his black bag was escorted by Mrs. Hill upstairs to his patient's bedchamber. Bennet puzzled over that – *Mrs. Bennet had been in the front parlor, had she not?* – but then, he recalled holding one end of a board, upon which lay his unconscious wife, supported by someone else on the other end. He could not recall who it had been. They had carried Mrs. Bennet up to her chamber to her own bed.

He had come back down to his library again and entered the familiar room – he just stood there, looking around, feeling strangely untethered. All strength suddenly gone, he dropped into a near armchair. His spaniel crossed to him and laid her muzzle on his knee, looking up at him with soft, anxious eyes. He placed a quivering hand on the dog's head and gently stroked the long silky ears between his fingers. The soft fur seemed to him to be the only thing that anchored his turbulence of mind and spirit.

Miss Lucas appeared at the open doorway and said something about seeing that tea was made for him and went away. He did not see her again.

The house at last fell more or less quiet. The inexorable ticking of a clock seemed too loud. His spaniel, which shivered continually, was his sole company. The dog pressed close against his leg. Mrs. Hill brought a tea tray and set it down on the side table, but he ignored it. Apprehension clouded his mind, spread inside him with every heartbeat, to become sludge in his veins.

"I cannot bear it." He *could not* bear to remain, seated in his sanctuary, listening to the damnable tick of the clock. He surged up out of his chair and left the room, to pace the entrance hall, where his boot heels marked a slow, hollow-sounding beat. More than once, he consulted his fobbed gold watch, digging it out from his waistcoat pocket and flicking it open.

A half hour and more passed before the physician reappeared on the staircase. Bennet watched the man's descent, discerning at once from his gloomy expression there was no good news. The weight of dread in his chest oppressed him. He would not allow it to abridge his good manners, however. He urged the man of medicine into his library. "Sit, sir, sit! A cold collation, as you see. The tea is cooled but can be refreshed. Perhaps a brandy, instead?"

The physician declined the offer of all refreshment and came directly to the point. He spoke heavily. "Mrs. Bennet has sustained a terrible blow, Mr. Bennet. Her skull was broken. A piece of the bone was driven inside. There is nothing to be done for her."

Thomas Bennet held his shoulders rigid. He spoke through suddenly stiff lips. "What are you saying, sir?"

"I am saying you must prepare yourself and your daughters, Mr. Bennet."

He bore up well, outwardly. He was a gentleman with a gentleman's well-bred control, after all. He went through the motions of thanking the physician, paying his fee, and seeing the medical man out to the gig. A fugue swamped him, held him motionless. The creaking wheels, the clopping of hooves startled him. He walked jerkily like an automation back into the house.

The butler closed the door behind Longbourn's master. "Mr. Bennet, sir? Is there anything I can do, sir?"

Standing in the front vestibule, Thomas Bennet gazed helplessly about him. It felt as though there had been a seismic shift. A jumble of thoughts and emotions were tearing through him. *Wretched am I!* He had not loved her for many years. He had come to barely tolerate her. He had been unbearably chafed by her voluble stupidity and temper.

"No. No, Mr. Hill. There is nothing."

Bennet grimaced at a sudden spearing of grief and shame. *No, I did not love her anymore.* But he still owed her the respect of a husband for a wife. He could at least sit at her bedside. *It will be my penance.* It was little enough. He could do no more for her. Mrs. Bennet was dying.

Poor, poor Fanny.

He straightened his shoulders and slowly climbed the stairs.

[13]

Charlotte awakened and rolled over on her pillows She blinked up into the shadowy pleats of the canopy overhead. Memories rushed back; she shuddered. *Such a terrible, horrible nightmare. Eliza and Jane...Longbourn!* She threw back the coverlets and pushed aside the heavy bed curtains. As she emerged from the four-poster bed, she saw that the draperies on the windows had been drawn back and tied in place, allowing daylight to stream into the chamber. A new fire burned behind the grate. *The maids have been in.* Charlotte cast a look at the mantel clock, and she was horrified to discover the advanced hour. Some time past, the family had been seated at table in the breakfast parlor! "Near eleven! Why was I not wakened?"

She attended to her ablations, shivering at the chilly water in the bowl. She dressed quickly, pinned up her hair, and left her bedchamber, to tread swiftly downstairs. Her mind was taken up by all that had happened. *Poor Mrs. Bennet! Such chaos, so much to do at Longbourn!*

When she had returned home, the sun had dipped low on the gray winter horizon. She barely had time to change into a fresh gown before sitting down to dinner with her family, along with Miss Hawkins and her companion, and their unexpected guest, Mr. Collins.

It did not require many minutes before Charlotte discovered that the happenings at Longbourn were already much discussed.

In her absence, Lucas Lodge had become a hotbed of speculation. Without any prompting whatever, Mr. Collins had given his own lurid version of the unhappy situation, which naturally threw his horrified audience into a tumult of agitated curiosity, and it was not much satisfied by what he related. Mr. Collins had much to say but he actually knew very little.

In a grim aside to his wife, Sir William had said, "In short, we must wait upon Charlotte's report."

Sir William and Lady Lucas had received Mr. Collins with perfect civility, being agreeable, kind and hospitable, and were much too polite to inquire into the peculiarity of the clergyman's removal from Longbourn to Lucas Lodge. Not so her cousin, whose *sotto voce* questioning whispers had greatly vexed her. Charlotte had put off Augusta with such grace as she could muster. It was impossible to divulge everything in all the company; the gentleman was sitting at table with them!

Charlotte knew more would be required of her than the brief, hurried aside she had given her mother as the ladies removed afterwards to the drawing-room – Mr. Collins was at Lucas Lodge at her suggestion. Lady Lucas gave a nod. "We shall speak of this later, when we have not an audience." She at once turned to Miss Hawkins, who had closely followed them into the drawing-room. "Do indulge us with some music, Augusta."

"Oh! I shall be glad to do so, dear aunt Lucas. I am not surprised to be asked. At Maple Grove, I was always asked to perform, was I not, Miss Simmons? Such a dear creature, Miss Simmons, you must agree! She does not mind to turn my pages, of course. She always did so at Maple Grove." After making a few remarks upon the quality of the instrument, which naturally could not compare with her own at Maple Grove, she sat down at the pianoforte. Miss Simmons stood beside her to turn the pages of music.

Charlotte sat down with her mother, her sister Maria beside her, and settled herself to listen to her cousin's performance. By the time Miss Hawkins had finished a long concerto, the gentlemen had entered the drawing-room and the opportunity for such explanations as must be made was lost. Charlotte was glad of it, for she had no more wish than her mother to expose her reasoning to her cousin's opinions. Nor did she feel that what she would relate should be aired before her sister Maria and Miss Simmons.

In recalling all that had transpired the day before, Charlotte knew that she would soon be required to give a full account, and have her own actions canvassed. She entered the breakfast parlor, which she saw was occupied only by her parents, and with an apology for her tardiness. "I did not mean to lie abed so late."

"Never mind, my dear, for I told the maid to allow you to sleep."

Charlotte was astonished. She was not often cosseted by her parents. *Allowed to sleep!* She smoothed her expression, covering her astonishment, as she seated herself, across from her mother at the table and to the left of her father.

Lady Lucas addressed her again. "Charlotte, what is this about Mrs. Bennet? Mr. Collins related a most distressing tale. I could scarce credit my ears. Upon your return yesterday you added but little detail. We wish to know what information you can supply."

The inquiry was a natural one; she had been at Longbourn.

"It is all too true, Mama. There was a most horrible accident." Unbidden, her brain formed a kaleidoscope of impressions and images. A strong shudder passed through her.

Sir William placed a hand on her forearm. He glanced at his wife and gave a slight shake of his head. "Allow the girl to have a sip of tea and a bite of toast before you question her further, my dear."

Charlotte was grateful for the few moments granted her. She felt she needed the fortification of the hot tea, liberally sweetened and taken white. It also gave her an opportunity to form her thoughts.

She needed to be as succinct as possible, so that the full gravity of the situation was understood. "Mrs. Bennet caught her heel in a rent in the carpet. She fell and hit her head with great force on the hearthstone. She was all over blood on her head and face." Charlotte shuddered again. "I do not think I shall ever forget it."

"Oh, my poor dear girl! I am very distressed for you!"

Sir William went straight to the point. "Is Mrs. Bennet dead?"

Charlotte shook her head. She wet her lips. "When I left yesterday, she was not. Mr. Bennet had sent for the physician. Before I left Longbourn, Eliza said she had overheard him expressing the gravest misgivings, before he had even quitted her mother's bedchamber. Indeed, I do not believe I misstate when I say Mrs. Bennet is not expected to survive her injuries."

Lady Lucas half-raised her palm, instinctively repudiating what she had heard. "Oh, no, no! Such a terrible tragedy!"

Sir William drew together his bushy brows. "A tragedy, indeed! I rode over to Longbourn at first light, on the basis of Mr. Collins' report, but Bennet would not see me. I did not like to linger. I saw Eliza but she seemed unlike herself, so I came away without putting questions to her. What was going forward, Charlotte? I assume you made yourself useful at Longbourn."

"Indeed, Papa, there was much to see to and no one seemed able to decide what was to be done. Shocked out of their senses, all of them." Charlotte marveled now over her own composure. *My sensibilities must have been wholly suspended. I cannot account for it otherwise.* "Even Eliza seemed too bewildered to form two thoughts together!"

"I can well imagine! Mr. Collins described a household thrown into the greatest confusion and chaos." Sir William's expression was shadowed by unusual gravitas. "How was my old friend? Did he say anything to the purpose?"

"Oh, poor Mr. Bennet! He was not at all like himself. He scarcely uttered a word."

"Lydia in the throes of wildest hysterics! Poor dear Jane, fainted dead away! Mrs. Hill shrieking and wringing her hands!" exclaimed Lady Lucas, distressed. "And worst of all, those militia officers picking up poor Jane and placing her on a settee! I was scandalized on Jane's behalf when Mr. Collins told us of it!"

"Well, Mama, how else was Jane to be gotten up off the bloody rug?"

Lady Lucas gawped at her, seeming unable to muster up a suitable response. Charlotte added, "Jane was in danger of her mother's blood seeping under her."

Lady Lucas made an odd gurgling noise in her throat. She pressed a napkin to her lips. "Really, Charlotte! How repugnant! Must you describe it in such...such a ghoulish manner?"

Charlotte dipped her head, acknowledging the rebuke. "I *am* sorry, Mama! I was the one who directed Mr. Wickham and Mr. Denny to move Jane. I was very glad they were there. As for the rest, everything had to be sorted. Mr. Collins kept petitioning Mr. Bennet about some matter or other, driving the poor gentleman to distraction, which is why I suggested that he come here. Mr. Bennet expressed his gratitude and ordered out the gig for Mr. Collins. Kitty, so fragile and ghastly pale! She appeared to be on the verge of collapse, but I talked gently to her and with such encouragement she did very well. And Mary! If you could have but seen her! She was cool as a cucumber. She threw a pitcher of water over Lydia and slapped her out of her screaming hysterics."

"Rough and ready treatment," observed Sir William.

Charlotte nodded. "And I was so thankful for it! Mary and Kitty between them got Lydia upstairs – she had to be dosed with laudanum. Eliza and Jane needed me, for a time. I even had to direct poor Mrs. Hill to make tea for Mr. Bennet."

Lady Lucas was most taken aback by the last revelation. "Why, Mrs. Hill is such a level-headed woman! Why ever would she not think of her duties first?"

Charlotte did not like to hear censor of the Bennet housekeeper. *Poor Mrs. Hill. The woman had a right to have been as overset as the rest.* However, as a dutiful daughter, it would not do to openly reprimand her mother. "A shock to the nerves often scatters the wits, I believe."

Sir William's eyes gleamed appreciation of her rejoinder; he smiled at her. "Given the extraordinary circumstances and the undoubted shock to your own sensibilities, you performed admirably, Charlotte."

Charlotte inclined her head. "Thank you, Papa."

Lady Lucas raised her brows. "I did wonder, dearest, at your sending Mr. Collins here, when he could easily have gone to the inn in Meryton."

"I am persuaded Charlotte acted for the best, my dear wife. The Bennets are our near neighbors and our close friends," pronounced Sir William. "We are all civility here at Lucas Lodge. I doubt not that Mr. Collins is most gratified by our hospitality; so much better than what he would have found at a public inn."

"Perfectly true, Sir William," nodded Lady Lucas, pursing her lips. "*We* air our sheets. *And* we provide a good, substantial board. Mr. Collins can have no complaints whatsoever."

"Indeed, Mr. Collins has certainly proven he can tuck away his dinner," grumbled Sir William.

Charlotte felt impelled to further justify herself. "The Bennets are in no fit case to entertain a guest, even so near a relation as Mr. Bennet's heir. They had completely forgotten him. He stood like a block, not helping in the least, as you would expect of a churchman. Indeed, he was very much in the way."

"An indictment against the man, to be sure," remarked Lady Lucas.

Charlotte turned out her palms. "I am sorry, Mama. I should have asked permission of you or my father first, but there was such confusion and I *could* not leave, not right away, nor did I feel it my place to instruct one of the Bennet servants to carry a message."

Sir William gave a nod. "You did right, daughter. If we can ease our neighbor's burden in this small way, we will have done our Christian duty. In any event, we shall have the gentleman's company for but a few days. Mr. Collins informed me over the breakfast boards that he stays only until Saturday."

"Oh!" Charlotte was taken aback. "I had expected that Mrs. Bennet's misadventure might shorten his visit in this neighborhood."

"Mr. Collins' plan does not appear in the least affected by it," said Lady Lucas, her mien as calm as her tone. "He was always to have gone on Saturday, and to Saturday he still means to stay."

Sir William frowned and harrumphed. "The man is tedious. Once the details of Mrs. Bennet's accident were exhausted, he could speak of nothing afterwards but of his parsonage and his garden and his patroness, Lady Catherine de Bourgh!"

"I did gather, at the Netherfield ball, that Mr. Collins is a rather garrulous man," murmured Charlotte.

Sir William gave a snorting chuckle. "Yes, even for a clergyman! What a longwinded speech he made that evening!"

Charlotte had been glad to find her parents alone, in order to discuss such sensitive matters, but now she wondered at the coincidence of it. Of course, her brothers' tutor and the governess for her other siblings would have them at their separate lessons, but that still left the unexplained absence of their houseguests. "Bye the bye, where is Mr. Collins, Papa? And my cousin Augusta?"

Lady Lucas supplied the answers. "Augusta is upstairs adding trim to one of her gowns, with Maria to help her. Mr. Collins expressed such a keen interest in gardening, I sent him to seek out our gardener for a tour of the formal gardens."

"But it is nearly December! There is nothing to see!" exclaimed Charlotte, glancing towards the nearest window, which framed the low, leaden sky and the leafless treeline in the middle distance. "Everything will be dead from the hard frosts."

"Quite true, daughter," said Lady Lucas complacently. "However, I informed Mr. Collins that he would find the superior layout of the beds to be of interest, perhaps even rivaling those at Rosings Park, which he decried, and was immediately off to prove me wrong."

Sir William chuckled. "Your mother has great presence of mind."

[14]

The hearth fire had died down to sullen red coals. Flickering tapers had long since guttered, leaving behind the oily odor of burnt wax. The dark of night had given way at last; long, slow shadows had retreated across the graying ceiling as daylight penetrated the chilly bedchamber.

Thomas Bennet shifted. He ached from the cold and the long hours spent sitting in the straight-backed chair. Yet he would not leave his wife's bedchamber. *It is my penance.* He looked down at his wife, lying so still in the bed. She looked small under the bedclothes. Her eyes were closed – *a mercy, that* – her mouth slack. He knew she was dying. *Even if the physician had not said so, I would know it.* He saw it in her paper-white countenance, in her utter immobility. When she breathed, her breast barely stirred the bedcovers that lay folded across her body. She was reduced somehow, as though her soul was already gone.

The door opened, the hinges squeaking, but he did not turn his head. "Father, you must come away. You must rest." It was Mary, pleading in her subdued voice, but he did not answer. After a while his middle daughter left. He was glad. He had his vigil to keep.

The clock struck the quarter hour; his life was marked by quarter hours. He had listened to many through the first nightmarish night, and the day following, and the long night just ended.

The door creaked open again. He knew that light, quick tread on the floor boards, knew it was Elizabeth before she spoke. "Papa, Sir

William has come to call again. Come down, sir." She did not stop speaking but her words made little sense. It was like the annoying buzzing of an insect, yet it was difficult to tune her out.

There is nothing but my guilt to consider.

He wanted her to go away and leave him to it. His head throbbed. His throat was dry. It was with a massive effort he replied. "No, no, I shall not come down. Convey my apologies."

She shook his shoulder. "Papa! Attend to me! You have been here too long. You have had no rest. You have not taken anything to drink or eat. You cannot go on like this!"

He carefully turned his head, pained by the crick in his neck, and beheld her angry face. He said, with detached amazement, "Why, Lizzy, you are crying."

She brushed the tears from her cheeks with jerky fingers. "Am I, indeed! Well, it is your fault, Papa. I fear for your sanity, *and* your life, if you go on in this stupid way. Then we will be without a father as well as a mother! It is selfish of you, sir! And you *smell!*" She whirled around and rushed from the bedchamber, slamming the door behind her.

Bennet sat for several minutes, impassively listening to the *tick-tock* of the clock. He decided that his daughter's complaint bothered him. Though he was by no means a dandy, he had always been fastidious about his linens. He lifted his arm, to give a deep sniff of his days'-old clothing, under his wrinkled frock coat. He dropped his arm and mournfully shook his head. "Lizzy has the right of it. I do smell – nay, I am ripe."

This does no honor to Mrs. Bennet.

He pushed himself up from the chair, an action that his stiffened back and aching hip joints mightily protested. His head swam and he staggered, much like a man the worse for heavy drink. He reached for the bell rope and pulled it to summon a servant.

I shall bathe. I shall eat. Then I shall come back to poor Fanny.

Gossip had come to Lucas Lodge, but after their informant had left, the Lucas ladies chose not to give it full credence, unless and until there was separate and definitive confirmation. "I shall say nothing about it. I think it a very good thing to wait and see," pronounced Lady Lucas. "The Bennets have endured a crushing blow without this added unpleasantness. I do hope they do not hear it! Not just now, at least."

"Agreed, dear Mama."

Miss Hawkins bustled into the parlor, an open sheet held between her fingers. An expensive shawl draped from her elbows, one which at a glance Charlotte knew to have cost more than the whole of her allowance for a year. "Oh! I have such a happy letter from Selina – she is delivered of a son, is that not the happiest of news? Mr. Suckling is beside himself with pride, says Selina, and fairly dotes on the infant. How she does go on, in such glowing terms! She is quite, *quite* turned into the little mother! My brother Mr. Suckling has written a few lines to you also, in a postscript, dear aunt Lucas. But here! – read the whole for yourself!"

Lady Lucas took the letter, and as she read it, a small smile began to grace her face, a smile which vanished when she reached the postscript. She looked up to stare at her niece. "Why, here is a surprise! Mr. Suckling makes request for you to remain with us, possibly as long as to the end of the year!"

Miss Hawkins gave a tinkling laugh. "Yes, yes, poor Selena is feeling low and weak after her ordeal! She will not be able to resume her duties until the physician pronounces her fit again. Such a strange thing to have written, for I am sure – you will agree, Lady Lucas! – I am sure you *must* agree, that I could be of infinite help to my sister when she is in such megrims. However, I suppose I must bow to my brother Mr. Suckling's wishes."

Lady Lucas and Charlotte met one another's eyes in a pregnant look. Lady Lucas replied, though without visible enthusiasm.

"Indeed, I suppose you must. Well, what a surprise! I shall inform Sir William that we shall have the honor of housing you for the foreseeable future."

Charlotte primed her lips to a genteel smile. She had discerned the resignation beneath her mother's civil reply. *Ah yes, our vaunted civility, here at Lucas Lodge!*

Miss Hawkins smiled, seeming oblivious to underlying currents. "I shall go upstairs at once to my desk and pen a reply to my sister. I must be sure to commiserate with Selena, for I know how disappointed she will be not to have me returned quickly to dear Maple Grove. My se-night here at Lucas Lodge was to be ended on Tuesday, just a few days hence! Oh! I *am* disappointed, for I did so long to return to Maple Grove."

"We are disappointed on your behalf, niece."

Charlotte waited a day and a half before she returned to Longbourn. She was well wrapped in her cloak against the cold and was conveyed in her father's carriage. She had not asked anyone to come with her, and, indeed, had rebuffed her cousin's company with a decisive word. "Stay here, Augusta. I am churlish, yes, in my desire to visit my dearest friends without you! They will be freer to confide in me, even shed tears, without being forced to make polite conversation with a mere acquaintance!"

Miss Hawkins had laughed in her light-hearted manner. "I shall not regard your rudeness, cousin; no, I shall not! But I shall give way, on this one occasion, for it is too brutally cold for me. I do implore you to bundle up well, for here is Mr. Collins in residence, and you must not show him a red nose! While you are gone, I shall endeavor to build you up in his estimation. We are agreed, are we not? I fear for you. Your case is desperate and time grows short – you must agree it is so! – for he is to leave on Saturday! Really, I see my duty plain before me, dear cousin!"

Charlotte shook her head over that scene now; it appeared that her civility was to be continually tested well into the holiday season since Augusta Hawkins was to remain at Lucas Lodge. *Goodwill to men, and may the good Lord have mercy upon us all.*

The coachman handed her down to the gravel driveway. She held tight the handle of a large covered basket. When she spoke, puffs of white appeared in the air. "I doubt I shall be long, John Coachman."

"Aye, miss. Oi'll walk the horses for a bit."

Charlotte walked up onto the shallow porch and pulled the bell. The front door was opened not by Hill or a footman but by the housekeeper. Mrs. Hill was red-eyed but she seemed to have regained her steady manner since Charlotte had last seen her. Charlotte stepped into the welcome warmth of the entry hall, the basket hanging heavy from her gloved hands. She turned as the housekeeper shut the door. She set down the basket on the floor in order to remove her outer garments. "I trust you are well, Mrs. Hill?"

"Aye, miss." The housekeeper gestured her toward the front parlor. At her patent hesitation and appalled look, Mrs. Hill managed a wan smile. "Tis all right, Miss Lucas. It has all been scrubbed clean and the rug burnt. I will go upstairs to let Miss Elizabeth know you have called."

Charlotte entered the parlor with reluctance, having been given little choice, and gingerly sat down on the settee. She placed the large basket at her feet. Strong traces of scrubbing ammonia lingered on the air, prickling unpleasantly within her nostrils. She glanced around, seeing that except for the noticeable absence of the rug, neither the fresh-scrubbed hearth and floor, nor anything else, hinted at the terrible drama that had taken place in the room.

I am glad. I do not think I could bear it otherwise.

In a few minutes, approaching from outside the parlor, she heard quick footsteps and Elizabeth came into the room. Her dark curls were pinned in an untidy fashion and she wore an old merino daydress, with a serviceable but nubby shawl wrapped tight round her shoulders. Charlotte was disconcerted. *Eliza, who is always so neat and tidy in her toilette!* Charlotte then saw how drawn her beloved friend appeared, and at once exclaimed in concern. "Why, Eliza, you are so pale." She started up, but she was waved back to her seat.

Elizabeth sat down beside her. She reached out to seize Charlotte's gloved hands in a tight hold. "Dearest Charlotte! I am so glad to see you. What you did for us...I cannot begin to express the gratitude of us all! Indeed, Jane sent her own thanks with me."

Charlotte returned the pressure of the slender clinging fingers. "How is dear Jane? I was so much concerned for her. The shock to her sensibility was extreme."

Elizabeth sighed, shaking her head. "She suffered from more than shock. Jane had a fever. She had told no one that when she arose that morning, her head hurt and body ached. A bout of severe influenza coming on! And she would not confide in any of us. And then after...afterwards, she said her own frailties seemed unimportant. I scolded her but my heart was not it, as you may imagine. Mrs. Hill put her to bed and I sent for the apothecary. She has been vomiting up nearly everything she swallows."

"Poor Jane! Does she go on better?"

"Physically, yes; but otherwise, I have doubts."

Elizabeth let go of Charlotte's hands at last and wound her fingers together in her lap. "Jane would have us all believe she has perfectly recovered her equilibrium, but it is obvious to me that she is still much shaken. But then, so are we all! Lydia is so shattered she will do little else but weep. And Kitty, too!" Elizabeth raised a hand and passed the back of it across her brow. "We were all so stunned. We were none of us in fit state to take charge. All except Mary! She must have ice-water in her veins!"

"Mary dealt with Lydia's hysterics readily enough," said Charlotte with a nod. "I was grateful for it. She kept her head."

"Oh, I will say nothing in disparagement of her! She is so good! Mary's steadiness has become our rock." Elizabeth looked at her, a glistening of tears in her dark eyes. "Charlotte, the physician has been here again. He gives us no hope, none at all. Mama is in coma now and she is dying. It is a matter of days or perhaps even hours."

Charlotte put her arm around her friend's shoulders and she felt the trembling of her body. The weight of Elizabeth's head dropped to rest on her own shoulder. Her heart was wrung. "I am very sorry, Eliza. As you know, my father came to see Mr. Bennet twice, but both times he had to come away before he had speech with him. He asked me to relay his sympathy to all and to charge me with a message to Mr. Bennet that he holds himself ready to perform any service that he might. Is there any reply you wish me to take back to my father?"

Elizabeth straightened away and shook her head. She brushed her fingers under her eyes, wiping the wet away. "At the moment, I can think of nothing." She lowered her hands and Charlotte watched the twisting of her fingers together in her lap. *So unlike Eliza, that nervous habit.*

"My father sits with my mother. He has scarce left her bedside. I have finally persuaded him to lie down for a few hours. Indeed, he is sleeping for the first time now." Elizabeth hesitated, before she burst out, "I think it to be guilt alone which animates him, Charlotte! Nothing more! He has no affection for her!" She gave a shake of her head and compressed her lips, perhaps against saying something even more damning.

Charlotte believed the correctness of Elizabeth's estimation; *she* had never observed a particle of affection between the Bennets. However, Charlotte did know of the real affection existing between Elizabeth and her father, so she was careful in her reply. "Whatever the state of Mr. Bennet's feelings, then or now, surely his present actions are commendable."

Elizabeth's low voice vibrated with feeling. "Thank you, Charlotte, you remind me to be charitable." She appeared to gather herself, tucking away her emotion. "Then there is Lydia, poor unhappy girl that she is! I am glad she has Kitty to cling to, for I have little enough strength left to tend her. She had to be given more than the one dose of laudanum, Charlotte."

Charlotte was astonished. "Lydia? Why, she is such a stout, self-assured girl. Indeed, I was surprised she fell into such strong hysterics. It seemed so unlike her. And she continues in such an agitated state?"

Elizabeth lifted her shoulders in a tired shrug. "She is very like Mama in temperament, excitable and heedless, though she is much sunnier in disposition, and because of their similarities, she was our mother's favorite. Mama's accident has hit her the hardest, I think."

"Then I most sincerely pity her. How do you go on, then? You must be worn to a frazzle, Eliza, when I know you are caring for Jane in the midst of your own grief."

"Oh, I am well enough. But I do fear for Jane. Mr. Bingley was here, you know, to take leave of her, and after she saw him, she had such a shuttered look on her face! She would say nothing to me of what was said. I believe – I suspect – Charlotte, I believe he came to tell her goodbye."

Charlotte's heart sank. She had hoped not to have been the one to convey the latest gossip, which had reached Lucas Lodge via a visit from Mrs. Long. She took Elizabeth's hand and squeezed it. "I fear it to be so, indeed. Mrs. Long has been to call on Mama this very morning and she brought the latest intelligence to be had in Meryton. Mr. Bingley left for London, and so has all of his party. Netherfield is closed up. I am so sorry, Eliza!"

"Yes, yes, all of Jane's hopes are dashed." Elizabeth wiped a tear away and managed a little smile. "I must thank you for sending Mr. Collins to Lucas Lodge! I trust he is not a burden, but truly he would have been very much in the way. He was in the middle of a marriage proposal to me, when Kitty burst into the room and told me of Mama's accident. He is not a sensible man. I very much fear he must have renewed his addresses if he had remained. I *could not* have borne it along with everything else!"

Charlotte tried for a bit of gentle levity. "A proposal, Eliza? Why, the man must have been completely smitten! Mr. Collins has not been here a full two weeks!" At Elizabeth's tiny spurt of laughter, she smiled. She was glad to see the lightening of Elizabeth's tired countenance. "But tell me the truth, Eliza. How do you go on? What can I do to help?"

"It is just like you to offer, Charlotte." Elizabeth smiled warmly at her. "Mary and I spell each other in persuading Papa to rest or to eat, and sitting with our mother. Jane insists she is well enough to sit up or to do small tasks. I cannot allow Jane to overdo, however, not when she is so downcast over Bingley. And such an awful letter was sent by Miss Bingley! Jane seems so – I cannot explain it to you! She goes about with this blind look in her eyes."

"It is sorry of Mr. Bingley to treat her so!"

Elizabeth nodded, a pained expression flickering in her eyes. "She had not slept well. Poor Jane! Some little while ago, she fell asleep over some stitching in the drawing-room and I *could not* bear to waken her!"

Charlotte understood at once why she had been shown into the front parlor, with all its dreadful memories. "How do the others?"

"Kitty does the best she can with Lydia and calls on me when she needs the help. As for the rest, Mary sees to everything. I think she is in the kitchen now, talking to Cook."

Elizabeth rose to her feet and held out her hands. "I cannot stay any longer, Charlotte. Jane will be needing me."

Charlotte stood, reaching for Elizabeth's hands. "I must go as well, for John Coachman is walking the horses." She pressed Elizabeth's fingers in true sympathy, before she let go and bent to take up the covered basket. "I shall take this to the kitchen before I go, so that I might say a word to Mary. My mother sent some comfits and a roast for your dinner. Eliza, you must send to me if there is anything I can do."

"I will. Pray convey my thanks to Sir William and Lady Lucas. I must go."

[15]

At Lucas Lodge, in one of the smaller back parlors, Charlotte was seated close to the cheerful fire. Despite the several tall windows, the wintery afternoon light which slanted into the chamber was inadequate to her task. Several tapers had been lit and the candelabras were set about to disperse the gray gloom. She was engaged in darning sheets, a tedious exercise which none of her sisters would join her in so she was quite alone.

Somewhere in the middle distance, she could hear the tinkling notes of the pianoforte. It was either her sister Maria who played, or her cousin. After listening a few minutes, she rather thought it was Augusta, for the piece seemed too complicated for her sister's level of skill.

Upon hearing a heavy tread on a floorboard, Charlotte looked up, to see the tall, heavy-looking young gentleman who entered the room. She acknowledged him with a brief smile. "Mr. Collins."

The gentleman bowed. "Miss Lucas." When he closed the paneled door behind him, shutting off the strains of the music, she was surprised. An unwed gentleman closeting himself with a young lady unrelated to him, without a chaperone present, was simply not done. *It is quite scandalous! I am astonished at Mr. Collins* .She set her needle and folded up her work on the table, before rising to her feet, ready to make her excuses and leave the room to him.

"Miss Hawkins directed me here, once she learned I wished to speak with you."

Charlotte raised her brows. "Did she, indeed?" *My cousin is a little too busy.* A random supposition occurred to her, astounding her. *Does she set up a compromise? Surely, surely, her insistent desire to aid me does not stretch so far!* Charlotte gestured at the door and took a step toward it. "Is she to join us shortly, Mr. Collins? Perhaps we should seek her out before you unburden yourself. I should feel infinitely more comfortable to have someone else present."

"No, no, Miss Hawkins was very understanding of my desire for privacy." Mr. Collins did not appear to realize he was in serious breach of etiquette. He was possessed of a somber and stately air, and his manners were very formal; though at the moment, he seemed to be caught up in some kind of frowning perturbation.

He made another low bow to her, to which civility she responded with a curtsy, and was further detained when he addressed her. "Miss Lucas, may I be frank with you? My private reflections are such that – it is a grave matter which exercises my mind and I must seek advice. In short, there is no one else that I may speak to, so far removed from my patroness, Lady Catherine de Bourgh, and I must settle it at once!"

Charlotte hesitated, weighing the matter, but then sat down again. "Very well, Mr. Collins." Curiosity had overcome her better judgment. *After all, I am past the age for a private tête-à-tête to damage my reputation.*

Mr. Collins clasped his hands behind his back. He took a nervous turn around the room before speaking. "I came to Longbourn at Lady Catherine de Bourgh's express wish, and for two reasons, one to offer the olive branch to my cousin Bennet and thus end my father's feud with him, and the other to mitigate the effect of the entail, which has made me my cousin's heir. I suppose you are aware of the entail, Miss Lucas?"

"I am, sir. Indeed, I believe all the neighborhood is aware of how things are arranged." Charlotte did not believe it was her place to explain that this knowledge was so widely known due to Mrs. Bennet, who had not been silent on the subject, but for years had dolefully bewailed the gloomy fate of herself and her daughters, whenever Mr. Bennet passed on to reap his heavenly reward; this fate, which would be meted out by the very gentleman who was standing in the room before her. Mr. Collins was the heir presumptive and he could put them out of the house that had been their home, leaving them all homeless and nearly penniless. Mrs. Bennet and her daughters would then be forced to rely on the generosity of her relations and the charity of others.

Mr. Collins inclined his head. "I am not surprised. The fate of an important estate such as Longbourn is of consequence to the whole of the county. But I digress; with the approval of my patroness, Lady Catherine de Bourgh, my second goal in coming to Longbourn was to make what recompense I could to Mr. Bennet's daughters, in the expectation of taking one of my cousins to wife. My object was to secure an amiable companion for myself, with due consideration given to the advantage it would afford all the family Bennet. Indeed, I was speaking to Miss Elizabeth on this very subject, when the unfortunate accident occurred."

Charlotte was astounded. *That he speaks of such a private endeavor!* She hoped she was successful in concealing her feelings. Not for worlds would she reveal that her dear friend had already told her of his offer of marriage. "Forgive me, Mr. Collins, but may I inquire if you were successful in your suit?"

Mr. Collins shook his head. Frustration weighed heavy in his overall demeanor. "The accident was most ill-timed, most ill-timed, indeed! I was interrupted in my proposals before I could ask for Miss Elizabeth's hand. As you may imagine, I had been in hopes, since Mrs. Bennet had assured me that her daughter would be most amenable."

"Oh!" Charlotte was amazed by what he said; in a flash, she knew just how it had all come about. *Mrs. Bennet and her outrageous scheming! Eliza and Mr. Collins! Such a pairing!*

She could not imagine a worse match. Elizabeth's wit and liveliness yoked to such a pontificating dullard! *Eliza would not ever have accepted him.* She well knew what her friend's feelings must have been to have been forced to hear the gentleman out. At the Netherfield ball, Elizabeth had freely expressed her low opinion of Mr. Collins. Of course, she could not blurt out *that* truth, and of a certainty, Mr. Collins had shown himself in the worst possible light – his ineptness on the dance floor, his presumption in addressing Mr. Darcy, his odd speech to the whole company. *Many stared. Some smiled. Mr. Darcy did not.* In any event, Mr. Collins seemed to regard Mrs. Bennet's ghastly fall as a mere nuisance to his own interests, which struck her as callous, and her response was cool. "It was unfortunate, to be sure, Mr. Collins. No one could have foreseen such an awful accident."

"Resignation to inevitable evils is the duty of us all, Miss Lucas. It is the peculiar duty of a young man who has been so fortunate as I have been in early preferment; and I trust I am resigned."

"Oh!" Charlotte was not sure what she was supposed to make of his pious pronouncement.

Mr. Collins paused in his perambulations, his heavy brows drawing down over a deepening frown. "I hope I am not bitter." He shook his head. "No, no, it cannot be from pique or stung pride – these are not worthy emotions; therefore, it is resignation. Perhaps not the less so from feeling a doubt of my positive happiness *had* my fair cousin honored me with her hand." He nodded to himself, satisfied, and turned to his audience. "I have often observed that resignation is never so perfect as when the blessing denied begins to lose somewhat of its value in our estimation."

Charlotte stared at the gentleman, her lips half-parted. *His regard for Eliza is quite imaginary. He would not speak so if it was otherwise.*

"You are all astonishment that I should address you, an unmarried lady, on such matters. Indeed, I surprise myself, Miss Lucas, but you are an intimate of the Bennet family. I beg you will forgive my forwardness, for such is my dilemma that – as I have divulged to you, I was in certain hopes of securing an amiable companion for myself and such remains my object."

Charlotte's amazement segued into embarrassment. Foolish he might be but Mr. Collins was a respectable man and it was not right that he should reveal so much to one who had no familial connection to himself. "Mr. Collins, I must ask you to stop speaking."

Mr. Collins did not heed her; he took another turn round the room. "My situation in life, my connection with the family de Bourgh, and my relation to the Bennets, are circumstances highly in my favor. To fortune I am perfectly indifferent "

Mr. Collins continued to speak, but she did not hear him. *Indifferent to fortune.* Those words acted powerfully upon her. Perhaps even more so after being forced to listen to her cousin's several reiterations of her bleak future. *I am seven-and-twenty. All I ask is a respectable, comfortable home.*

As Charlotte recalled the conversation between herself and Elizabeth at the Netherfield ball, and their differing opinions on marriage, the germ of the idea planted by her cousin formed full in her brain. Her heart beat a little faster. *Dare I cut my dearest friend out of the chance of a respectable marriage?* Surely, it would not be a betrayal. Not when Elizabeth held such an adamant opinion against Mr. Collins. She interrupted the gentleman, her mind set on but one thing, to broach the subject in a roundabout way. Her own daring amazed her. "Mr. Collins, perhaps it is not the best time. That is to say, for you to approach *Eliza.*"

Mr. Collins whirled about, the tails of his dark frockcoat flying. He shot out his forefinger, exclaiming, "Not the best time! That is precisely what Mr. Bennet said to me." His lowered expression was considerably lightened. "I must thank you, Miss Lucas."

She faltered, "I do not understand, sir."

"My dear Miss Lucas, you have but confirmed what must assuredly be my best course! I conjectured that Mr. Bennet's intellect was too shaken by Mrs. Bennet's accident to know what it was he said. But now *you*, Miss Lucas, have said to me those very same words and I know you for a sensible woman. It has become obvious that Mr. Bennet's rationality was *not* impaired. Therefore, I conclude he is but thinking of the conventions at such a terrible time."

"Oh! Yes, yes, he must be," she stammered. She was still in the dark.

Mr. Collins smiled at her. "I am grateful to you, indeed. I had it half in mind to prolong my stay in this neighborhood, the civility shown me by Sir William and Lady Lucas having persuaded me that I might continue to rely on the hospitality of Lucas Lodge."

Charlotte blinked at this assumption.

She was not called upon to either confirm or correct it, for Mr. Collins swept on. "Perhaps Mrs. Bennet's health will quickly improve; at which time, I can again approach Mr. Bennet on this most delicate subject, and with his permission renew my proposals to my cousin, Miss Elizabeth. My uncertainty arose as to how long I should delay my departure before such a happy conclusion could be had, when I had leave but for a sen'night, and especially in light of the duty I owe to my esteemed patroness, Lady Catherine de Bourgh. I shall not delay, however, and I return to my parsonage with good conscience. I shall instead write to my cousin Bennet and fix a future date for another visit, perhaps later in the month, when the business may be addressed in a congenial atmosphere. I have certainly meant well through the whole affair."

Charlotte had not time to reply before Mr. Collins bowed and left the small parlor. She remained seated, stunned by the odd interview. As her stupefaction faded and was replaced by wry amusement, she shook her head, and aired a small, self-deprecating laugh. "Well, it seems there is no chance for me. Mr. Collins is still set on Eliza. My cousin Augusta will be most disappointed!"

She retrieved her work, picked up her darning needle again, and returned to her mundane task. Disappointment and relief competed in her pensive reflections; yet perhaps a mild regret was uppermost. *It would have been pleasant to have a home of my own.*

She did wonder what feelings would have been animated if Mr. Collins had informed Sir William and Lady Lucas that Lucas Lodge was to host him for an indeterminate time. She gave a small spurt of laughter. Charlotte decided not to relate that startling tidbit to her parents, nor indeed, when she thought about it some more, any part of Mr. Collins' astonishing conversation.

On Saturday morning, Mr. Collins took punctilious leave of Sir William and Lady Lucas and their eldest daughter, expressing to the trio who had walked out with him to see him off, his fervent desire to return to his parsonage. "I must convey my humble gratitude for your most welcome hospitality, and certainly would have extended my stay, except I am persuaded that my duties to my esteemed patron, Lady Catherine de Bourgh, cannot be put off any longer. I trust you will forgive my departure at such an unseemly early hour, and it is my expressed hope that I will see you again. You will be flattered, I know, when I tell you that I will speak of your many excellent qualities and civilities to her ladyship."

"No, no, dear fellow," said Sir William soothingly. "I assure you, nothing more need be said. Indeed, must not keep the horse waiting."

Mr. Collins made a low bow. He climbed up into the gig and from his perch on the bench beside the driver, he gave further pledges. "Rest assured that I will not leave the neighborhood without making a dutiful call upon your near neighbor, for I feel a strong regard for all within my sphere of influence. I shall naturally take leave of my relations at Longbourn with much solemnity, and condole with them; and wish my fair cousins health and happiness; and I shall promise to write another letter of thanks to my cousin Bennet. These will be the proper things to do, I believe, as I know Lady Catherine would certainly demand it of me."

By their expressions, Sir William and Lady Lucas appeared to be overpowered by his good intentions. Miss Lucas had lowered her eyes, no doubt in modest admiration of his benevolence. Mr. Collins was satisfied that he had conveyed everything needful and smiled down at them.

Sir William recovered himself, shaking off the effects of such fulsome periods. Uttering all that was polite and wishing Mr. Collins a safe journey, he was glad to watch the back of the rector's hired gig bowling away at last.

Sir William turned to Lady Lucas and his eldest daughter. "Well, my dear ladies, my ears are left ringing. Such a long-winded fellow!"

[16]

Besides her sister, married to Mr. Philips, who had been a clerk to their father, and succeeded him in the business in Meryton, Mrs. Bennet had a younger brother, Mr. Gardiner, who was settled in London in a respectable line of trade. Urgent letters from Mr. Bennet and the Philips were sent by express riders to Gracechurch Street in Cheapside to appraise the Gardiners of Mrs. Bennet's dire condition. The Gardiners set forth posthaste from London, but within hours of their arrival, the sad vigil at Longbourn was at an end.

For near four days, Mrs. Bennet had lingered. Then she breathed her last and her family got on with the business of the living. For Thomas Bennet, much passed in a blur, through the haze of his shocked senses, and yet he made decisions. His breeding as a gentleman rigidly propped him up in his duty, to carry through with it all. Mourning clothes. The funeral. The canceling of engagements. The polite acknowledgement of condolence visits. In short, all of the adjustments into mourning. All for a narrow, petty woman, one who had ruled the household through temper and high melodrama, the insistent orbit around which all else must revolve.

Mr. Collins' promised letter of thanks arrived. Mr. Bennet laid it aside with indifference, but then, with a mechanical punctilio, penned a brief reply informing of Mrs. Bennet's demise.

It was the oddest thing. Thomas Bennet pondered it many times. Without the shrill voice, the intemperate outbursts, the incessant demands – no one quite knew what to do. It was like an anchor had been ripped away and they were all adrift, not knowing how to act or react. All their former ways of dealing with one another had been shaded by Mrs. Bennet. It was *she* who directed conversation, *she* who had to be placated, *she* who had driven their social life.

I am glad my brother and sister Gardiner stayed on after the funeral.

Bennet was grateful for their presence and quiet, steadying influence. Otherwise, he might have sunk back into his ineffective fugue. As for his daughters, he could see the increments of improvement in them under Mrs. Gardiner's gentle influence.

Sir William Lucas was one of the first to come on a condolence call. When he emerged out of his carriage, he was accompanied by his two eldest daughters, Miss Lucas and Miss Maria. The young ladies made their curtsies to Mr. Bennet and at once went upstairs to be with their friends. The two men shook hands, Sir William conveying Lady Lucas' excuses. "Lady Lucas remains at home with a trifling complaint and she begs forgiveness for not coming."

"Not at all! I trust a few days will see her in better health." Bennet was pleased to welcome his closest friend and appreciated the genuine sympathy and concern which had brought Sir William to Longbourn. "You have just missed my brother Gardiner and Mrs. Gardiner. They have gone to Meryton to call on the Philips."

"I would have liked to pay my respects." Sir William was invited into Mr. Bennet's inner sanctum, his beloved library. His host said he was about to take tea and asked if Sir William would care to join him. Sir William assented gratefully. "It is cold even for December. A hot cup will be most appreciated."

"Hill, send for refreshments, if you please."

The butler bowed and pulled shut the door, leaving Bennet with his visitor. He gestured his guest forward. "Pray be seated, Sir William, and welcome."

Before the warm fireplace, Sir William settled into an armchair. He shook his head. "I am sorry for this, my friend. It must be difficult for you. And the girls, of course! What will you do now that Mrs. Bennet is gone?"

Bennet bent to stir the burning logs with a poker. Sparks hissed and whirled up into the chimney. He set aside the iron tool before taking a similar chair. His spaniel laid down near his booted feet. "It is an odd thing to lose a wife, Sir William," he said thoughtfully. "Mrs. Bennet was like an appendage that has been suddenly amputated. I still feel her presence."

"And no wonder! More than twenty years!"

Before more could be said, a knock was heard on the door; Mrs. Hill entered with a tea tray, which she sat on the occasional table between the two armchairs. The housekeeper arranged the tea pot and plate of biscuits to her satisfaction, then folded her hands at her ample waist. "Will there be anything else, sir?"

"Thank you, Mrs. Hill, that will be all." The housekeeper exited, quietly shutting the door behind her. Bennet poured the tea and made certain his guest had everything as he liked it before he addressed what was ever at the forefront of his mind. Perhaps his unease and worry were irrational. "In truth, I am glad to be private with you, Sir William, for I am in need of advice. As one of my oldest friends, I appeal to you. What should I do? I am now a widower, the father of five unwed daughters, some of marriageable age. You are aware of the entail, of course. And you have had the dubious honor of housing my heir for a few days."

Sir William shot him a glance, and Bennet mustered a faint smile."No doubt you formed an opinion, Sir William. I suspect it aligns much with my own. On his progress back to Hunsford, Mr. Collins stopped here to extract what information he could from my daughters and to extol your hospitality, which I am told took the better part of an hour. I was spared his excessive periods as I was laid down on my bed taking some rest. He promised to write me a letter, a civility which I regard with indifference."

Sir William harrumphed. "I am a blunt man, Thomas. It is a pity you have not another to step into your shoes when you are gone. Such a tedious, garrulous fellow! After spending time with Mr. Collins, I must say I am reluctant to see him succeed you. But I have several years on you, so I doubt I will see that sad day."

Thomas Bennet replied with a twist to his lips. "We were to have a son, who was to join in cutting off the entail, as soon as he should be of age. The widow and younger children would by that means be provided for. Five daughters successfully entered the world, but no son."

Sir William made sympathetic noises. The father of several children, among them promising sons, he could sympathize with his friend's regret. "Well, well! It is a pity. Mr. Collins is a foolish man. I do not know that he will improve."

"Longbourn does deserve better. However, for reasons known only to God, it is not to be." Bennet set aside his teacup and returned his gaze to his friend's attentive expression. "Now to the crux. I left the upbringing of my daughters to Mrs. Bennet. Her sole ambition was to get them married off, and she scarce cared what consequences her machinations might have upon our daughters or their reputations. I was complacent." He pressed his lips together, before grimacing. "It was not comfortable to run counter to any of Mrs. Bennet's wishes. As my oldest and most intimate of friends, you and Lady Lucas will best understand."

Sir William slowly nodded, with a degree of embarrassment in his expression. "You need not elaborate, Thomas. Indeed, Lady Lucas and I often spoke about – well, never mind! I do understand your concern. The entail sets Longbourn away from your daughters. It is a pity they have no fortune."

"Felicitate me, Sir William! *That* is one good thing to arise out of the mess. With the death of Mrs. Bennet, her dowry is to be divided equally amongst her five daughters, but only upon the occasion of their marriages. Before, they had each a mere *L*50 for dowry, derived from interest; now, each will have a respectable portion of near *L*1000, so their prospects of marriage have risen exponentially!"

Thomas Bennet abandoned his ill-timed derisiveness; he lifted his shoulders and spread his hands. "If only there were any suitable gentlemen to press their suits! Meryton is barren of such necessary individuals, the Netherfield party having departed, and the arrival of the militia regiment notwithstanding."

"Ah, indeed! Suddenly, the ground is littered with scarlet-coated officers. Many are the impoverished younger sons of respectable landed families," observed Sir William, adding apropos, "My own dear Charlotte is a good, sensible girl. I hope I value her as I should, but she is a spinster and she will be a burden on her brothers."

Bennet nodded, acknowledging it. However, Miss Lucas' plight could not be said to hold his attention. He was all too aware that his two youngest daughters had been thrown into high alt over the military presence. For weeks, their exuberant chattering had been an irritant over the breakfast cups, when he wished for nothing but quiet. Upon their careering entrance into any room, his ears had been freshly assaulted with their giggling inanities; unfortunately, their girlish fancies had been encouraged by Mrs. Bennet, who had said that she had always been fond of a red coat. Though Lydia and Catherine's spirits had been bludgeoned by the tragic loss of their mother, he did not doubt their natural ebullience would reassert itself. *It is not a realization I relish.* He rubbed the back of his neck. *As for the others...Lizzy favored Wickham, Jane has had her heart broken by Bingley, and I know nothing of Mary's thoughts.*

Shaking his head free of his mind's drift, Bennet was blunt in his outline of the discomforting situation. "If my daughters are not settled in their own homes, they will be left in straightened circumstances. I do not expect – nor *should* I expect – that Collins will support them. Do you suggest, then, that I entertain every scarlet coat in the county?"

"Not at all, sir! Not at all! That would be rash, indeed. It would be impossible to distinguish the chaff from the wheat. I doubt there are more than a handful of men of character and means amongst the whole lot." Sir William shrugged. "As for *entertaining!* My dear fellow, it will be impossible for you to entertain, even if you were not in mourning. Yours is now a bachelor household. Our ladies will be unable to attend any parties you might get up because you have no hostess. Ah, I see it has not occurred to you! Have you a female relation, a genteel lady, someone you may ask to come reside at Longbourn?"

Bennet frowned with the fresh problem presented to him. "There is no such person. Perhaps my sister Philips might on occasion – no, no, that will not do!" He rolled his shoulders, feeling the tension. Fastening his gaze on Sir William, he sought reassurance."But surely, as the eldest and being of age, Jane could fill that office. She is such a good girl and she can chaperone for her sisters."

"Oh, yes, if you wished to condemn her to spinsterhood. She will have to set aside all thought of marriage. She will have to sit with the matrons, never to stand up in the dance or accept a gentleman's escort. She will have to sacrifice her youth and her beauty. Surely, you cannot wish this for Miss Bennet."

"No, of course I do not! My poor Jane!" Bennet was appalled. *Why is there no word from Bingley?* He said heavily, "My God, it is worse than I thought. How then will I do right by my unwed daughters? I wish I could have left this all in Mrs. Bennet's hands! It is too much for me!"

Sir William shifted in his chair. "You must remarry."

"Remarry?" Thomas Bennet mouthed the syllables as though they were foreign. He jerked around in his chair to direct a fulminating stare at his friend. "Are you mad? And Mrs. Bennet gone less than a week!"

"My dear Thomas, do not glare! You make too much of it! Why, a man may marry within two weeks of the death of a wife. You know this, as well as I do! It is accepted that a man must attend to his business, and certainly, five unwed daughters is a great business!"

Bennet was shaking his head. He was shocked, yes, but more than that, he found the very notion to be repellent. He had not been interested in the marital bed in years. *I am not a dotard, of course.* However, the swirling image in his mind of his wife's pouting face, the remembrance of her shrill voice, her hysterics – *no, no, I will not subject myself to wedded bliss again.*

Sir William leaned over the tea things on the occasional table to place an urgent and strong hand on his friend's tensed forearm, giving it a shake. "Think, man! I pray you, do not reject the notion out of hand! You need a hostess to entertain. A respectable widow, perhaps. A sensible lady who will know how to run your household, to allow you to attend to your studies, and who will be a firm, guiding hand for your daughters. How will you manage otherwise? You said it yourself – without being wed, they will be destitute. Is that what you want?"

"No, no, of course not." Bennet felt as though he was struggling in a rough northern sea and the cold waters were closing over his head. His chest tightened and his breathing accelerated. "This is what you advise me to do?"

"I do, most sincerely."

Bennet knew Sir William Lucas to be a shrewd, pragmatic man; it was why he had asked for his friend's advice to begin with. However unpalatable it was, he had the honest assessment he had sought. He was seized by a strong desire to retreat and go somewhere, anywhere but where he was. *Perhaps the Antipodes.* He drew in a ragged breath. "Thank you, Sir William."

Sir William's visit ended with mutual utterances of cordiality and Bennet was left to unpalatable reflection. The advice was surprising; its substance was unwelcome. Yet the more he contemplated the advice he had been given, the more sound it became. It seemed to him that his daughters staggered through their days, seeming lost without Mrs. Bennet's querulous direction. *If not for my sister Gardiner's presence, I do not know how we would be managing.* However, the Gardiners would not remain indefinitely; they would return to their lives, to their children. As for his own state, he shuddered at the impossible task of bestowing all of his daughters into advantageous marriages.

The earliest days of December ushered in a frigid cold, the kind that froze a man's breath in his lungs. Though Thomas Bennet took exercise, he was careful to stay out but a short time and to remain close to the manor. His spaniel suffered from the plunging temperatures but she howled if she was left behind, so he allowed her to accompany him, afterwards taking care to gently warm her paws to remove the ice.

Bennet's disquieting cerebrations were consumed by his conversation with his old friend, which was buttressed by a subsequent talk with his brother-in-law, the subject broached by Mr. Gardiner himself. "Thomas, what will you do with your daughters? They need a woman's advice and guiding hand. My sister Fanny was a foolish woman but she *was* dedicated to their interests. Marriage is the proper disposition for gently bred girls like Jane and Lizzy. They are the eldest, and it becomes imperative that the matter be addressed." Mr. Gardiner shook his head. "A half-year mourning for their mother! Their chances diminish with each passing year."

"I do know it. Of late, it is much in my mind." Bennet threw out an open palm, indicative of his helplessness. He wanted to avoid making any decision, but it was not possible. *I wrestle as Jacob did with the angel.* The wretched business was one of gathering urgency, and he gave voice to his internal conflict. "I will be blunt, Edward. I am ill-equipped. Indeed, I am awash with apprehension! Have you a suggestion?"

Mr. Gardiner shook his head. "I fear not, not one which is inclusive of all my nieces. Between us, Madeline and I have discussed the matter, and willingly, we would take Jane or Lizzy, or even Mary, and offer them a home with us. Their chances of meeting decent young men will be greater in London, though likely the candidates will be in trade. We do not have connections in high social circles, as you know. Perhaps a stern governess might be gotten to help you at Longbourn with the younger girls. They are still young to be of an age to marry, so there is time enough to be thinking of them."

Bennet was grateful, but he knew at once that he could not agree. "Your offer is generous, Edward, and though I do appreciate it, I know well the burden it would impose upon you. Yours is a large, hopeful family and you must provide for them. As for a governess, I am persuaded Lydia and Kitty are beyond accepting the discipline of the schoolroom, when they have already been so much out in society."

Mr. Gardiner sighed and shook his head. "A mistake, I fear."

Bennet frowned and fiddled with his watch fob. "Recently, I have had advice from my good friend, Sir William Lucas." He proceeded to disclose his conversation with Sir William and at the last, asked, "What think you, Edward? Should I remarry for the sake of my daughters? And if so, should it be immediately?"

Mr. Gardiner had listened with concentrated attention. His reply held an obvious inflection of relief. "My dear Thomas, I applaud Sir William's suggestion. Indeed, I am surprised I did not think of it myself! As a man of business, I pride myself on my astuteness, but I did not perceive what was before my face."

Bennet gave a long exhale. "Then you agree with Sir William."

"Yes, yes, it is exactly what you must do, Thomas, and rather sooner than later. In the meantime, if it suits you, Madeline and I shall invite Jane to return with us to Gracechurch. We have observed she is not happy, and Madeline has learned, from my sister Philips, of Jane's disappointment with this Mr. Bingley, and also that it is much talked of hereabouts. This gossip must abrade Jane's finer sensibilities. Perhaps the change of location will do her spirits good, especially in light of my sister's tragic passing."

Bennet bowed his head in acquiescence; the suggestion was a most welcome one. "Very good, brother. I agree with you, going away from here must help Jane. It will be a blessing to give my poor unhappy Jane into your sensible care. " She would recover from her disappointment much easier away from the incessant talk of her abandonment by Bingley.

All in consequence of Mrs. Bennet's boastings!

Further, he appreciated his brother-in-law's assessment of his own situation. *The advice is good.* An unexpected release of tension washed over him, easing his whole being. Mr. Gardiner's opinion, aligning exactly with Sir William's advice, seemed to clarify his own reasoning. *My preference is to remain a widower. But I cannot indulge my own wishes. I must see to their future happiness.*

That evening, after all the rest had sought their beds, Bennet sat up late in his library. His torturous internal debate was ended, true, but it had been supplanted by a question of equal urgency. He would remarry, and as swiftly as possible. The only question remaining was to what lady he should make an offer of marriage.

He was well-acquainted in Meryton and the surrounding county. He knew the respectable widows and the other unmarried ladies, if only by reputation. He rejected most out of hand, deeming them to be of the same cut as his late wife, when what he wanted was a lady who could handle the household duties at Longbourn and manage his daughters. Most important to his own comfort, he wanted peace, peace in which to pursue his studies and to dwell in the world created by the books he read. Sir William had urged him to a second marriage for just such reasons as these. However, there was one other consideration which was taking up a bit more of his meditations than it might have been supposed it would.

The spaniel snored at his feet while he stared into the crackling fire.

He had finally met his heir presumptive, his cousin Mr. William Collins, and he did not like him. *Such an obsequious fool. I will deprive him of Longbourn if I can.* Sir William had not brought up the getting of a male heir for Longbourn; nor had Mr. Gardiner. However, the possibility could not be overlooked. He had another chance at it, if he was fortunate in choosing the right bride.

She must be young enough to still be able to bear children, but not so young that she cannot manage a household and my grown daughters.

He fancied that he was not yet in his dotage, being two-and-forty years. He could not completely banish a niggling insecurity, however. He had not felt an iota of physical attraction for Mrs. Bennet for years. Indeed, after Lydia's birth it had been a rare occurrence for him to visit his wife's bed. Five daughters and his wife's inability to quicken again, when added together with an inexorable, profound dislike for her character, had essentially gelded his libido.

He worried that he would not be able to perform.

"I've a lobcock," he murmured. For several minutes, he was sunk in his dour ruminations. Finally, he gave a fatalistic shrug and left that anxiety to the future. "God willing! Even so, I will still attain my other goals. A respectable mistress for Longbourn and a proper chaperone for my daughters. This time round, I must simply be wiser in choosing a wife."

Charlotte Lucas. Her name came to his mind as naturally as a cooling breeze on a hot summer day. Thomas Bennet drew in a long breath, letting it out slowly. He could think of no other lady who so admirably suited his criteria.

[17]

Thomas Bennet chose to ride the short distance to Lucas Lodge, and anxiety rode with him, but he was resolute. He was fortunate enough to find Sir William Lucas at home and was immediately ushered inside the house. His friend waited for him, standing in the open doorway of a ground floor room, while he gave his hat, gloves and riding crop into the butler's care and the footman divested him of his drab wool overcoat. He was assured that his horse would be taken to the stable and he was at last free to turn to his host.

Sir William beamed and clapped him on the shoulder. "Bennet! Come along into my study. I am glad to see you. We had good hunting the last time out, did we not?" He ushered his caller inside the room, made cozy by a crackling fire, and shut the door. "I would take you to make your bow to Lady Lucas, but she is gone to Meryton."

"Pray convey my compliments when she is returned." Bennet cleared an odd throat constriction. "I have come to talk with you, Sir William. Our last conversation has stuck in my mind. I have discussed it with my brother Gardiner. He concurs in your opinion, by the by."

Sir William's bushy brows rose. "Well, then! Let me pour a sherry for each of us and then you may open the budget."

The gentlemen made themselves comfortable, seated in wingbacks facing one another before the fire, and in silence tasted their wine. Bennet shifted in the chair, ill at ease. Erratic thoughts and irrational fears beset him, which infuriated him. *I pride myself on my mental powers!*

Sir William eyed his old friend closely. "It appears you are laboring under some tension, Thomas. You must tell me, what is on your mind? Have you decided upon remarriage?"

"Indeed, I have." Thomas Bennet tightened his jaw. He ignored the hard thump of his heart. "I have given careful thought to all the advantages you pointed out to me and I have concluded you are quite right. With that said, I wished to inform you of my intention to make an offer to your daughter, Miss Charlotte Lucas."

Sir William blinked. "My Charlotte?" A peculiar expression flickered across his face. "You wish to offer for my daughter, Charlotte!"

Bennet was assailed by an awkward discomfort, such as he had not experienced since he was a very young man, where his shoulders bunched, and the whole of his body was on edge. He brought the wineglass to his lips, swallowed sherry without tasting it, and coughed a little. He set aside the glass and looked straight at his friend. "Yes. I hope you do not dislike it. I believe Miss Lucas is the best-suited female of my acquaintance."

Propriety set a barrier against revealing his renewed hopes for a male heir to break the entail. He might have entered upon the subject if speaking in the abstract, but he would not do so to the man's face regarding his own daughter. *My oldest friend's daughter, for the Lord's sake!*

Sir William put an abrupt question. "Have you spoken to Charlotte?"

Bennet shook his head. "I have not. Miss Lucas is naturally of an age to make up her own mind, but I first wished to broach the matter to you." His mind flashed to the worst possible consequence of his declaration. "I trust our friendship will not be affected, whatever the outcome of my suit."

Sir William smiled. He shook his head. "No, our friendship means as much to me as it does to you. As for Charlotte, I will speak plain, Thomas. For all of her good qualities, at seven-and-twenty years, her mother and I had given up hope that Charlotte would ever receive an offer. You are a good man, a gentleman, one whom I am proud to claim as my friend. If this is truly your desire, then I wish you well. It will please me to see Charlotte so well-situated."

"Then you do not think Miss Lucas will look unfavorably upon my suit?" Bennet fiddled with his watch fob. He felt honor-bound to point out the obvious. "I am fifteen years older than she is, after all."

Sir William snorted. "She is not such a noddy! My Charlotte is a sensible girl. She will see the advantages of the match, never fear. And as for the difference in age, bosh! I snap my fingers at it! You are still in your prime, while she is fast approaching her last prayers."

Bennet would not have chosen to phrase it just that way, but he appreciated the sentiment. "When would be a good time to meet with Miss Lucas? I should like to make my offer in proper form, as soon as possible."

Sir William slapped his knees. "Now is as good a time as any! She is upstairs darning sheets or some such thing. I shall send for her now." He got up to tug the bell-pull and when a footman entered, he requested the presence of his eldest daughter.

Upon her entrance, Mr. Bennet rose to make his bow.

Charlotte curtsied, murmuring a greeting. She sent a look of inquiry towards her father. "Did you need something, Papa?"

"No, but here is Mr. Bennet, who has a question for you. Come sit down, daughter." Sir William led her to a comfortable chair and saw her disposed before addressing Mr. Bennet. "I shall leave you to it." He patted his daughter on the shoulder and went out of the room, firmly shutting the door.

Charlotte watched her father's exit and turned her surprised gaze to the gentleman standing before her. Mr. Bennet seemed strangely ill-at-ease. She wondered, with concern, if there was some irregularity at Longbourn. She could not imagine what her father and Mr. Bennet thought she could do unless it was to give advice for a domestic crisis of some sort. *With one of the younger girls?* She wished her mother was available, but perhaps in her absence, that was why the two gentlemen had chosen to consult her.

"Sherry, Miss Lucas?"

"No, I thank you, sir." She folded her hands in her lap.

"You have a restful quality, Miss Lucas." Mr. Bennet cleared his throat. "It is one of the reasons I have asked for this audience with you."

"I see." Charlotte did not see, not at all. She was growing even more concerned and beginning to feel confused. "Mr. Bennet, what is it you wished to ask me?"

"Miss Lucas, I shall be blunt. I am in need of a wife."

She stared at him. She was so staggered, all of her faculties seemed to be suspended. Of all things he could have said, she had never imagined to hear *those* words.

What is he saying? Oh, what is he saying!

His gray-blue eyes seemed to pin her to her seat.

"We spoke not so long ago, and you assured me that you were not of a romantic nature. I am asking you to become my wife."

"What?" Suddenly, her heart gave a bound and began behaving very oddly. Her middle quivered and an inner tremor affected her limbs. She felt a peculiar lightheadedness. "Mr. Bennet." She sounded breathy, quite unlike herself. She cleared her throat and tried again. "Mr. Bennet, I should like that sherry now."

"Certainly." He poured a half-glass for her and brought it to her. She took small sips of the wine, as much to revive herself as to give herself a few precious seconds to bring her disordered brain into some semblance of rationality. She set aside the wineglass and drew a deepened breath. "Mr. Bennet, I am not certain how I should reply. You-you have surprised me."

Mr. Bennet sat down in the wingback chair opposite. He leaned forward with an earnest expression. "Pray let me speak, then. I have come to respect your character and your sensible nature, which figured so well at the time of Mrs. Bennet's accident and during the awful, chaotic days afterwards. In those first hours, I suspect all of us at Longbourn must have collapsed without your support and practical guidance. Miss Lucas, I need someone to sensibly manage Longbourn and to give good advice to my daughters. I believe it to be an advantage you are so well thought of by Lizzy and Jane. They will not need you, but must surely be companionable, and help you with the younger girls."

Charlotte sternly reminded herself that she was *not* a romanticist. It was her first proposal; undoubtedly, the only one she would ever receive. There were no flowery speeches, of course. She did not expect there to be. *Still, should there not be some lip-service to sentimentality?*

She swallowed a sigh.

Mr. Bennet spoke of managing Longbourn, of being of use with his daughters. He had not implied anything more in a union. She thought she knew exactly what the gentleman was proposing, but it was best to have it all out in the open. She was too practical a creature to do anything else. "Then-then you wish for a marriage of convenience?"

Mr. Bennet flushed. "No, Miss Lucas. Not quite that."

She flushed in turn, the heat scorching her cheeks before spreading down her neck. "Oh." She quickly looked down at her folded hands, unable to meet his eyes. It seemed an inadequate reply. She was conscious of it. Tightness burned inside her chest – she dragged in some air. As a maiden, she was not supposed to know what went on between a man and a woman, and though she was somewhat hazy about some of the details, she was familiar with the mating of farm animals. Of a sudden, unbidden, she imagined herself – *with Mr. Bennet!* Her face grew hotter. She felt exposed and on display by her own outrageous thoughts.

Mr. Bennet took her monosyllabic reply to mean further explanation was required. "I-I shall not unduly press my rights, I assure you." At that, her gaze darted back to him. He was looking anxiously at her. "I hope that does not put you off, Miss Lucas?"

Charlotte shook her head. She honestly could not put a name to her feelings. She clasped and unclasped her hands. *I am plain of face and on the shelf.* She knew these things about herself to be true. Mr. Bennet did not approach her as a man in love.

Something inside her wailed. *Oh, how I wish it was different!* Perhaps the silly young girl she had once been still existed, buried somewhere deep inside of her. *Foolish, Charlotte!* She could scarce expect him to admit to passion for her, yet she felt a strange measure of hurt.

She castigated herself for such foolishness. She resolutely set aside the slur against her femininity and began to consider the incredible opportunity which was so unexpectedly being offered to her. She would be mistress of her own home. She would no longer be a burden and a drain upon her family's purse. She would not become an aging spinster, losing year by year her social stature and the dwindling of her small portion, sinking finally into genteel poverty.

Of course, with the way Mr. Bennet's affairs were bound up with the entail, and if he were to die prematurely, she could well end up in equally bad straits – as would his unwed daughters. The Bennet sisters were dependent on their father's benevolence. Charlotte gave a sharp nod. *I would make certain to do all in my power to see that Mr. Bennet lived to be a ripe old age.* And if their union was blessed with a son, then her future and those of his daughters would be assured.

Longbourn and the estate's income would not pass out of the Bennet family. It was at that point in her reflections that she realized she had made a decision. An outward calm belied her swift-shifting thoughts and emotions. "Mr. Bennet, I accept your offer of marriage."

"Then I am a fortunate man." Mr. Bennet rose to his feet. She stood as he came over to her. He lifted her hand to his lips for a brief salute. At the warm contact on her bare fingers, a tingle ran up her arm. He retained her fingers and smiled down at her. "You have gratified me, Miss Lucas. We must now decide when the marriage is to be. I would have it before Christmas."

"Before Christmas?" Charlotte looked up into his face, giving a small, disbelieving headshake. "But sir, there is not time for the banns to be read. And besides, you are in mourning."

"Ah. Perhaps we should sit back down, Miss Lucas."

Mr. Bennet stepped backward and gestured at the wingback she had just vacated. She sank down onto the cushion, wondering at him. Her gaze remained fixed on his impassive face as he sat down across from her. "I do not understand, sir. You will be in mourning for a year. Surely, we must wait to wed."

"I have formed a different intention, Miss Lucas. I propose to wed as soon as may be, by common license. I have five unwed daughters and I am unfit to direct their futures. I cannot wait twelve months. The law allows me to wed two weeks after the passing of Mrs. Bennet. It has not yet been a fortnight, but it will be, by the time I ride to London to procure the license and return. Then we have only to wait seven days."

Charlotte's eyes widened. Her palms crept to her cheeks. "And-and this is what you propose? To wed just three weeks *after Mrs. Bennet's death?*"

"Well, it depends on the date of the license; but yes, this is what I propose."

Charlotte's breathing hitched. She stared at him. The callousness of it stunned her. Indeed, she was repelled. The haste was unseemly – *marry in haste, repent at leisure!* A conflict of emotions churned. *And yet, what am I to say? Do I refuse his offer?*

"Miss Lucas, by your appalled expression, I see this is an unwelcome surprise." Mr. Bennet tightened his lips. "You are horrified, you believe me unfeeling, that what I suggest is improper." He formed a tight fist on one knee. "Pray believe me, I have shared in these same thoughts! My own sensibilities – but I have not made this decision lightly. I first sought the advice of both Sir William and my brother-in-law, Mr. Gardiner."

Charlotte felt another jolt. "My father advised you to such haste?"

"He did, Miss Lucas."

She bowed her head. "Then I must have no objection, sir."

"Then I am satisfied. I will seek your father and give him the good tidings. Sir William will wish to settle everything between us. I will leave you now." Mr. Bennet got up and bowed to her.

Charlotte rose to her feet in turn and curtsied. Her brain was in a whirl but she was still capable of thought. *My betrothal will occasion surprise in so many quarters.* In particular, Elizabeth Bennet would not take kindly to hearing the news from any lips but her own. Coming from her aunt Philips or another such busybody, she would react badly. *The shock of it. I must give Eliza some warning!*

"Wait, sir!"

Mr. Bennet turned towards her, surprise writ on his countenance.

Charlotte stammered a little. "Pray, will you wait upon me again after you have seen my father? I have something of import I wish to say."

Mr. Bennet's dark brows rose, and a wave of anxiety rolled through her. Charlotte wondered if he would deny her request.

However, he was a gentleman born and bred, and he civilly acquiesced. "As you wish, Miss Lucas."

Upon his exit, the door was shut behind him. Then she had nothing to do but wait. She could not compose herself and paced the carpet.

[18]

When Thomas Bennet was ushered upstairs into the private sitting room, he found that the lady of the house had returned from Meryton. Sir William had obviously informed Lady Lucas of the momentous occasion, for as one they turned toward him with hopeful expressions. He was at once hit by the reality that his long-time friends were now to become his in-laws. *What amazement is mine! Never could I have imagined it.* He bowed to Lady Lucas and exchanged civilities before coming to the point. "Miss Lucas has consented to my proposal."

Sir William surged forward to seize him by the hand. "My dear sir! I am pleased, yes, very pleased indeed!" Lady Lucas threw up her hands, exclaiming with delight. Applied to for their blessing of an early marriage by common license, Sir William and Lady Lucas bestowed it with a most joyful alacrity. Mr. Bennet's worldly circumstances made it a most eligible match for their daughter, to whom they could give little fortune, and her prospects were now exceedingly fair.

"I shall have my attorney draw up the settlements, Sir William."

"Of course, Bennet, of course! I shall look forward to receiving the papers," said Sir William in all cordiality. He offered his hand again, Bennet took it, and so their bargain was sealed to their mutual satisfaction.

After Mr. Bennet had taken his leave and bowed himself out, Sir William and Lady Lucas were free to discuss the great news between them.

"Oh, my dear, I never thought to see our eldest do so well for herself! Especially if dearest Charlotte should give Mr. Bennet a son, doing away with the entail," exclaimed Lady Lucas. "Her future would be established!"

"Well, well! That is in the hands of God, madam," said Sir William. "But I shall say this much! Our girl is too sensible not to do her duty, and Thomas Bennet is not yet in his dotage. He will see a boy raised up, never fear, before too many years pass."

Lady Lucas began at once to calculate, with more interest than the matter had ever engendered before, how many years Longbourn's master was likely to live; and Sir William gave it as his decided opinion that it would be highly expedient for Mr. Bennet and his new wife to make their appearance at St. James Court in London.

Unaware of the excitable transports he had left behind, and relieved to have the major portion of the business done with, Thomas Bennet set out downstairs to dispatch the unexpected request from Miss Lucas. As he re-entered the study and closed the door, she whirled to face him. He noted her anxious expression, and he hesitated, before he stepped away from the door. "I trust you have not had second thoughts, Miss Lucas? I have just come from Sir William and Lady Lucas, who have assured me of their delight with our betrothal."

"Oh, no! It is nothing like that!" Miss Lucas clasped her hands before her. She pulled in a breath. "Mr. Bennet, the news of our-our betrothal will be discussed everywhere. It will occasion surprise, not the least to all your daughters, and in particular, to Eliza. It is a difficult time. I fear the news will be a shock, coming so soon after Mrs. Bennet's passing."

Bennet was swift to discern her meaning, and grimaced. "Yes, yes, I perfectly comprehend you." He clasped his hands behind his back, his expression somber. "There is something rather unfeeling on my side, what with the grave scarcely grown cold, is there not? Indeed, *I feel* it to be so. I daresay others will say as much and more. Do you think Lizzy will take the news better from you?"

"I do, sir."

"I suppose you may be right. The three younger girls are silly enough that gossip will not matter. Jane will receive the intelligence with her usual sweet-tempered placidity; it will not occur to her to wonder at anything." He raised a brow as he regarded her. "But Lizzy's temperament is quick, and though she has a rational mind, she will wonder at this hasty betrothal, and freely express her amazement, perhaps with indiscretion. In such a case, it is best to make the announcement in private. Is this what you wish to say to me, Miss Lucas?"

His frank supposition appeared to discomfit her.

Miss Lucas colored. "The bonds of friendship are such...in short, I am resolved to tell her myself."

"It is understandable, I suppose."

He smiled at her, a contemplative gleam in his eyes. "If that is how you wish it, then you must do as you think best."

Charlotte's tension subsided. She said, gratefully, "Thank you, sir. May I charge you, when you return to Longborn to dinner, to drop no hint of what has passed before any of the family?"

Mr. Bennet raised his brows. "I pledge secrecy, Miss Lucas, at least for the remainder of this day and night." He placed a palm over his heart, executing a shallow bow, and continued with a sudden, marked hyperbole. "My promise will not be kept without difficulty, for the curiosity excited by my long absence will burst forth in very direct questions on my return. It will require some ingenuity to evade, and I will at the same time be exercising great self-denial, for I long to publish my prosperous love abroad."

Charlotte's cheeks flamed. She half-turned her head, pressing her lips together against her consternation. She had gained her point. However, Mr. Bennet's sardonic drollery at her expense forcibly brought to mind how he had dealt with Mrs. Bennet. A dreadful sinking in the pit of her stomach – she recalled once thinking she would know how to handle Mr. Bennet's many quick-silver parts better than had his late wife. *Oh, how I am foolish!*

Mr. Bennet's satirical smile faded. "Forgive me, Miss Lucas, for my churlishness. I do not treat your concern as I should. Rest assured, I will endeavor to do my solemn best in your service." He moved forward to take up one of her hands and she looked up, meeting open kindness in his gray-blue eyes. "I shall see you on the morrow, Miss Lucas."

Mr. Bennet bent to brush his lips over her bare knuckles. The warmth of his light salute sent a *frisson* through her skin. Charlotte stood with rushed breathing and a rapid heartbeat. She murmured something, she was unsure what, but it seemed to satisfy the gentleman. Dazed, she watched his tall, retreating back, heard his boot steps as he exited. The door shut behind him with a click. He was gone, and with him went the shaken feeling that she had perhaps erred; but in what way, she did not know.

Of a sudden, her legs failed to support her. She dropped inelegantly into the chair she had been sitting in before and for several moments she remained immobile. Over and over, her mind ran through the interview, marking nuances of Mr. Bennet's expression and bearing, and what had been said between them. Her racing thoughts swept on. Though she still had reservations about the haste of the wedding, she had none about her decision. Mr. Bennet was a kind man and he would make a good husband; of that, she had no doubts.

In a few moments, having reassured herself of the rightness of her decision, she became tolerably composed. Her private reflections were in general satisfactory. At the age of seven-and-twenty, without having ever been handsome, she felt all the good luck of it.

A gathering contentment pervaded her. She smiled to herself as she relaxed her spine against the chair cushion. She was growing accustomed to the idea that she would be wed before she even had an opportunity to order her bridal clothes.

Charlotte got up and walked to one of the tall windows, to watch the occasional flurry of snowflakes swirling over the grounds. *Without thinking highly either of men or of matrimony, marriage has always been my object.* She suddenly discerned a distant, fleeting glimpse of Mr. Bennet on horseback, trotting away in the direction of Longbourn.

My betrothed.

She touched a cold glass pane with her fingertips. In a low murmur, she reiterated the sum of her reflections, "And however uncertain of giving happiness, marriage must be our pleasantest preservative from want. It is the only honorable provision for well-educated young women of small fortune." This provision she had now obtained, and with a more agreeable man than the one whom she *might* have acquired for herself.

The heir presumptive to Longbourn. Mr. Collins was neither sensible nor humble, his society was irksome to many, and his shallow attachment to his cousin, Elizabeth Bennet, was surely engendered by little more than self-importance. *Our conversation did not advance as I had intended.*

"And I am very glad of it!" Indeed, she was fiercely glad. She could not have accepted Mr. Bennet's advantageous proposal otherwise.

The door opened behind her and Charlotte turned, to be informed by the footman that she had been summoned by her parents. She said quietly, "I will come at once."

When she entered the sitting-room, Sir William advanced to take her hands, and bussed her cheek. He guided her to sit down beside her mother, warmly congratulating her. "I am vastly pleased by your surprising good fortune and so is your dear mother."

Lady Lucas corroborated it. She smiled at her eldest in approval. "It is a good match for you, Charlotte. Indeed, I had not expected such luck! It is most, *most* astonishing!"

Charlotte swallowed against the sudden tightness in her throat. *I can well believe Mama's amazement!* She had not forgotten the pain given her at the exchange she had overheard between Mrs. Bennet and her mother: "Charlotte *would* have made some man an excellent wife."

Sir William's bushy brows twitched together while he looked at her. He puffed out his cheeks. "Bennet is not in the flush of first youth, I grant you, but I am persuaded you will not care for that. He is still a fine figure of a man, at two-and-forty! You would not like a callow youth, Charlotte, not at your time in life."

"No, Papa." Charlotte was stung. *At my time of life, indeed!* She added, with a faint brush of acid, "I do not look for romance, Papa, if that is what you wonder."

Sir William snorted. "I should think not! Rubbishing stuff, romance and whatnot. Girlish fancies have no place outside the covers of a novel."

Lady Lucas added her mite. "I do so enjoy a good horrid novel, but your father is quite right, Charlotte. Romantic notions are so very silly. And though Mr. Bennet is reserved and bookish and even *thoughtless* on occasion, it will not matter to you. You will be the mistress of Longbourn and may order everything to your taste. And to think, it is all because Mrs. Bennet hit her head! Well! One never knows when a tragic occurrence turns out to be not as bad as one first thinks!"

[19]

Upon his return to Longbourn, as the footman relieved him of his riding crop and outer garments, Bennet was ill-pleased to be informed by the butler that Mr. Collins had arrived. He spied a traveler's corded trunk. "The devil you say! Plague take the man. What has he come for?"

"I cannot say, sir. Mr. Collins asked many questions. He was insistent to have speech with you before he was announced to anyone in the house."

Bennet grunted. He stripped off his tan riding gloves and gave them inside his hat to the butler. "Where is he? In the front parlor?"

The butler shook his head, his expression pained. "Regrettably, Mr. Collins knew it was where the fatal accident...in short, he refused to go in." Hill delivered what was sure to cause severe disapprobation. "Mr. Collins insisted on awaiting your return in your library, sir."

Bennet felt the planes of his face stiffen. *Encroacher!* Outrageous, that his retreat should be invaded by the man! "Did he, indeed!" His boots rapidly striking the floor, he turned away, striding the short distance to the library. The half-open door swung inward under the hard push of his hand. Bennet stepped across the threshold into his inner sanctum. Without preamble, he said, "My dear Mr. Collins. I am all astonishment. What do you here?"

Mr. Collins, who had been seated, made haste to stand up to make a deferential bow. "I received your letter in which you related the saddest of news. Poor, dear Mrs. Bennet! The news was most shocking! Indeed, I could not believe it upon first reading! I have come to condole with you, cousin."

Bennet shut the door with a sharp click and stalked to the fireplace. He bent to spread chilled hands in the welcome warmth radiating from the fire. Over his shoulder, he said, "I thank you, sir. However, your visit is singularly ill-timed. I would have preferred you had informed me of your intention previous to your coming. Mrs. Bennet's brother and sister-in-law are staying with me, and I think you will agree, their claims to Longborn's hospitality take precedence."

Mr. Collins bowed. "Just so, sir, and it is why I took the liberty of coming into your library to wait for you. A peculiar delicacy is required! Mr. and Mrs. Gardner are quite unknown to me, and being informed by your butler of how seldom the young ladies leave their private chambers, I dared not trespass on my dear cousins in their grief. But how is this? Your surprise at my arrival! Had you not my letter?"

Bennet at once glanced over at his desk, where there were stacked several papers, a ledger, and missives scattered in a haphazard fashion. He was at the best of times a desultory correspondent; it would scarce surprise him if he had tossed aside a letter from Mr. Collins.

The man's unexpected visit is unwelcome and very much a nuisance. And it appears that I have but myself to blame for it.

He sighed and straightened himself, reaching up to rest a hand on the mantel. The fire warmed his side. "Forgive me, Collins. I may well have had your letter but it must still be unopened. There has been much else to occupy me besides a simple correspondence."

Mr. Collins frowned. "It is most understandable, sir. But what is to be done? I feel peculiarly unsettled. I acknowledge it, I am most unsettled, Mr. Bennet! I have already sent away the job horses and carriage."

"I shall arrange all. For how long was your projected visit to be?" Mr. Collins launched into a long-winded speech, much of which in Bennet's opinion could have been left unsaid, since it extolled Mr. Collins' self-sacrifice in coming to Longbourn on what the clergyman viewed as an errand of mercy. Mr. Collins at last came to pertinent point. "...However, her ladyship made plain that she can spare my services for but a week."

During the long-winded speech, Bennet had taken up a tool to poke at the burning logs, crackling sparks rising up the chimney. He abruptly turned, hearing it in disbelief. *An invasion of a week, forsooth!*

Thomas Bennet stared hard at the man, his mouth compressed. *I have just come from speaking to Miss Lucas. I must away to London tomorrow for the marriage license.* He would not put off his business, and confiding in his heir was impossible, for he valued his privacy. He intensely disliked the notion that Mr. Collins would of a certainty report all that came to his attention to his patroness, Lady Catherine de Bourgh.

He replaced the poker on the hearth. He needed to ponder over what was best to be done about Mr. Collins. *I cannot very well throw him out of the house, unfortunately. The indignity would be extreme.* The Gardiners occupied the guest bedchamber; there was another, smaller room into which Mr. Collins could be put, but he rejected that solution. *I cannot have him here at Longbourn. We are too many and we are too sorrowful.* The obvious alternative was to house Mr. Collins for a week at the inn in Meryton, at Longbourn's expense. That possibility also displeased him. The strain placed upon the estate that quarter, what with the expenses necessary to bury Mrs. Bennet and the procurement of mourning clothes for five ladies, was considerable. His own needs had been minor, for his coats were mostly dark, and it had been a simple matter to add black bands to his sleeves and to his hats.

Bennet went back to the door and opened it. "I must change out of my riding clothes, Collins. We shall speak again later. But first, come into the drawing-room. I should like to make you known to my brother and sister Gardiner. Tea will have been served, I daresay."

The clergyman bowed. "I shall wait upon your pleasure, cousin."

Bennet introduced his heir to the Gardiners and after a few moments, during which his subdued daughters in their black attire entered, tea was brought in, and Mr. Collins was happily settled to partake of it and civil conversation. He excused himself to change his attire. A reminiscence by Mr. Collins, that on his first visit to Longbourn, he had become acquainted with the Philips, had given Thomas Bennet a happy thought. He went at once to his library to pen a short note to his brother-in-law Philips, which he sent off post-haste to Meryton by a servant. Then he went upstairs to change out of his riding clothes, in hopes of getting a favorable reply. If the Philips were agreeable, Mr. Collins could be lodged at their townhouse in Meryton, where he could condole with *them*, and *would not* be underfoot at Longbourn.

The Philips sent back an obliging reply, extending an invitation to Mr. Collins to partake of their hospitality, an invitation couched in a way that much pleased him. "How well I recall the great civility of Mr. and Mrs. Philips! But cousin, though I am confident of my comfort in their house, I am reluctant to abandon those residing here at Longbourn, for it was for the purpose of consolation that I came."

"You will be able to do much in that regard, here and at Meryton, for you must remember that as sisters, Mrs. Bennet and Mrs. Philips were very close. While the girls have one another to lean upon in their bereavement, and I have the Gardiners, my poor sister Philips has no one to sustain her, for my brother Philips is often gone to his office."

Mr. Collins appeared struck. "The excellent good sense of what you have said, cousin Bennet! I can better apply my efforts, in this way, by condoling with Mrs. Philips, and with Mr. Philips in the evenings, which would not be possible from Longbourn. Nevertheless, rest assured, dear sir, I will not neglect my duty to all those under *this* roof." Mr. Collins was consequently persuaded to remove himself and his traveler's trunk to Meryton, and with many thanks and promises to call on his dear cousins, he was driven off in Mr. Bennet's gig.

Elizabeth exclaimed, "*Thank you,* Papa, for relieving us of the burden of his company. It is always irksome but at such a time as this it would be insupportable!"

"You are too hard on Mr. Collins, Lizzy," remarked Mary. "He does by his lights only that which is good."

"He will come again," sighed Catherine.

Lydia had her say. "Lord! I hope he does not read to us!"

"We shall bear with Mr. Collins with due patience," murmured Jane.

Bennet was well-pleased by the decampment, which left him able to attend to other, more important, matters, and he beckoned his in-laws to follow him. In the privacy of his library, he informed the Gardiners of his intention to wed Miss Charlotte Lucas by common license. "I waited on the lady to solicit her hand this very day." Mr. and Mrs. Gardiner took the tidings with every appearance of approval.

Mr. Gardner smiled broadly, and offered his hand in congratulation. "This is welcome news! You do well by this, Thomas."

Mrs. Gardner's felicitation was also warm. "Indeed, Miss Lucas is an exemplary young woman. She will make you an admirable helpmate."

"I am glad you think so," said Bennet, bowing to the lady. He was gratified by their instant approbation. "At first light, I shall ride to London to procure the license. I do not wish to make an announcement to the girls until I have it in hand."

A movement caught the corner of his eye. He half-turned his head. A sheet of writing paper slid to the corner edge of his desk and fell from it, kiting slowly side to side. Another sheet of paper followed the first to the carpet. *Odd. There is no draft.* Then a cold eddy brushed against his face. He crossed to the window to lay his hand on the sash, thinking that the latch was not set. He frowned. The casement was well-closed.

"What is it, Thomas?"

"A draft, I thought." He shrugged his shoulders. "I was mistaken."

§

That evening, when all Charlotte's siblings had gathered after dinner in the drawing-room, Sir William announced the betrothal. Charlotte was drowned in the noise of an animated cacophony. The whole of her family was overjoyed. Charlotte cast down her gaze, listening with a pinch of hurt to what was being said around her with such abandon. Her brothers were loud in expressing their relief that Charlotte would not die an old maid, an opinion in which Sir William was in hearty agreement, and her younger sisters expressed their excitement at having new dresses made up for the wedding.

"I have formed hopes of bringing out the younger girls a year or two sooner than they might have otherwise," pronounced Lady Lucas.

It seemed that her marrying would profit everyone even more than herself, and with such conditional felicitations, Charlotte thought it hardly surprising her spirits should be wilted. She was startled when her hand was taken in a warm clasp and squeezed. She slid a sideways glance at her sister, who was sitting beside her on the settee. *Maria guesses something of my feelings.* Separated by eleven years and the birth of brothers, her nearest sister possessed a full measure of empathy for others. She was grateful for Maria's unexpected support, acknowledging it with a small nod.

Miss Simmons proffered quiet congratulations.

Miss Hawkins laughed lightly and shook a finger at her. "Such a sly boots as you are, cousin! Only think! Well, it is infinitely provoking! I never suspected such good fortune for you, I am sure! I have heard only good of Mr. Bennet. And I assure you, I have very little doubt that my opinion will be decidedly in his favor."

Sir William called order. When the excited chatter had abated, he approached his eldest daughter, took her hand and brought her to her feet. "A shout for our dear, dear Charlotte!"

In the resulting huzzahs, Charlotte was at last moved by her family's genuine happiness on her behalf. She blushed and laughed. Upon meeting her mother's gaze, she recognized beaming approbation and pride. *Well, Mama, I shall make a gentleman a good wife after all.*

Charlotte was well aware that her mother looked upon the betrothal as a triumph and it was one which Lady Lucas would not keep to herself. It would not be long before all of their acquaintances were made privy to the extraordinary news. She was not wrong. As the family party broke up to retire for the night, Lady Lucas beckoned Charlotte to accompany her up the stairs. As they ascended, Lady Lucas informed her, "We shall be visiting all of our friends on the morrow to announce your good fortune."

To announce my amazing escape from spinsterhood!

The surprise it must occasion to Elizabeth Bennet! She experienced an odd fluttering in her middle. If she wanted to be the one to tell her dearest friend of her change in fortune, she must do so without delay. *I know her so well.* Elizabeth, whose friendship Charlotte valued beyond that of any other person – Elizabeth would indeed wonder at it. *But Eliza is sensible. She will accept it.*

A restless night brought clarity to her intuition. *I know Eliza's romantic nature. I fear she will not perfectly understand.* The dawn revealed lowering clouds, perfectly mirroring her pensive rumination. At the first opportunity after breakfast, Charlotte set out for Longbourn. Fitful gusts harassed the edges of her cloak, inserting sly chill fingers. More than once, she reassured herself, yet an apprehensive dread oppressed her. It was possible Elizabeth would leap to one of her swift judgments. Charlotte's resolution was not to be shaken, but her feelings must be hurt by any censorious utterance. Her announcement was received as badly as she had feared; indeed, she saw the revelation stunned. "I see what you are feeling. You must be surprised, very much surprised. But when you have had time to think it all over, I hope you will be satisfied with what I have done."

"Betrothed to my father! My dear Charlotte – impossible!" Elizabeth drew back, staring at her, her voice shaking. "I do not believe it! Charlotte, no, no! You cannot be serious!"

The palpable, horrified disbelief etched on Eliza's face!

Charlotte clung to her composure, but her voice wobbled. "I-I believe I shall be tolerably happy in the lot I have chosen."

Elizabeth sprang up from the settee. As she stared, wide-eyed, down at Charlotte, her voice rose. "Marry my father? You cannot do it!"

Charlotte clasped her hands, tightened her fingers. "Why ever not?"

Elizabeth's face reflected a flashing of myriad of emotion. She made a hasty gesture. "It is appalling! Every finer feeling revolts!"

"I am sorry you feel that way, Eliza. Perhaps if you set your mind to it, you might see things from my perspective," said Charlotte tersely; her stomach roiled. "I am not romantic like you. I am seven-and-twenty, and I am plain, and I have no fortune. And I am *afraid*, afraid of what will become of me. Now I am offered a comfortable home of my own."

"But Longbourn is not your home! It will never be your home!" exclaimed Elizabeth passionately. The flush of her face contrasted with her black beaded fichu. "It is ours – it belongs to me and my sisters! *We* are now the mistresses of Longbourn."

"You are cruel, Eliza. And you are mistaken. Longbourn's mistress will be whomever your father sets in place." Still seated and looking up at her, Charlotte challenged her. "Would you say the same if Mr. Bennet had made his choice elsewhere?"

"Of course not! But you - *you* are my friend." Elizabeth violently shook her head, her lips puckering. "Why, he is *old!* He is old enough to be *your* father!"

Charlotte spluttered a laugh. "Old! Pray do not be ridiculous, Eliza. Mr. Bennet is but fifteen years my elder." She was astonished that anyone could look at Mr. Bennet and see a declining, fusty old fellow. *As though he has one foot in the grave!* Even his daughter must surely acknowledge that Mr. Bennet was a man of vigor. "That is absurd."

However, Elizabeth was beyond acknowledging any such thing. Her bosom heaved. "*You!* And my father! It-it is repellant."

Charlotte's smile died. She twisted the strings of her reticule. She was at last angered by Elizabeth's vehemence, but fearful, too. A hollow pit was opening up. She slowly got to her feet. "You become insulting, Eliza! Pray, think carefully of what you are saying."

Elizabeth repudiated her warning with a quick gesture. "It does not bear thinking about! It must destroy our friendship. Oh, Charlotte, can you not see that?"

Charlotte was shaken. The rejection cut deep. "I am sorry for it. A falling out between us will not be at my instigation." Her voice broke. "I had hoped you would be better than this, Eliza."

"But I am not!" Elizabeth gave a little, amazed laugh. "*You* to become my step-mother! I do not know what my father is thinking! He has run a little mad since Mama's accident." She struck her palms together. “Yes, yes, it is the only explanation. What a ridiculous start!”

“It is you who are ridiculous!”

Elizabeth’s dark eyes flashed. She tightened her lips. “I shall talk to him, be assured of that!"

Charlotte’s eyes burned. It was worse than she had imagined; it was a betrayal. Unshed tears thickened her throat. "You must do what you think best." She wanted only to escape. Anguish in her heart, she rushed from the parlor. She ran across the entry hall to the front door, the hasty pace of her half-boots audible in her hurried passage.

Elizabeth did not follow her, nor even call out.

The butler approached. “Miss Lucas? Allow me to open the door for you.” Throwing decorum to the wind, Charlotte yanked wide the door and fled Longbourn.

It did not take long before the cold searing air in her lungs made her slow in her headlong flight and swipe at the cold tears on her cheeks. She was agitated and the scene played out over and over in her afflicted mind. She pressed a closed hand over her lips. “Horrid, so horrid!” Fortunately, by the time she had returned to Lucas Lodge, she was outwardly composed.

“Charlotte! Where have you been? I have had the horses put to these ten minutes past.”

“I was at Longbourn. I wished to tell Eliza of my good fortune.”

“Ah, I see! Well, go up and repair the damage to your hair. You are quite windblown and I would like you to appear at your best when we make our calls.”

“Yes, Mama.”

[20]

Thomas Bennet sat at ease before the crackling fire. He was content with what he had accomplished that morning. The marriage license was in a drawer of the desk. It but remained to hear from Miss Lucas that she had informed Elizabeth of their betrothal before a formal announcement could be made to the rest of his daughters.

An imperative knock sounded on the library door. "Enter."

The door was thrust open. Elizabeth came in, a dark whirlwind. She shut the door behind her. "Papa! I must speak with you!"

"Why, Lizzy! What stir is this?" Bennet marked his place in his book. Regarding her, he smiled. "Your cheeks are very rosy. Have you been out walking?"

"Yes, yes, I have but just returned. Mr. Collins was good enough to give me a lift in his gig from the lane, where he caught up with me."

"Pray do not tell me that he has come for the midday meal." Bennet shook his head and sighed. "It is inevitable; he *will* come to condole with us. So, I must gird up my loins to receive him with civility.""

Elizabet made a hasty motion of her hand. "Mr. Collins did not come in, but has returned to Meryton."

"You surprise me. You must have mistook him, Lizzy.

"Mr. Collins took something I said in bad part. Some-some *gossip* I have heard this morning." The spaniel rose and trotted forward, wagging its tail. But Elizabeth did not stoop to pat the dog as was her usual habit. All of her attention was focused on her father as she crossed the room. "I must speak to you – about Charlotte Lucas.'

Bennet raised a brow. "Indeed?"

Ah, Miss Lucas has been to the house. And Lizzy spoke of this to Mr. Collins! What ailed her to do such an idiotic thing?

Elizabeth reached him then and sank down on her knees beside his chair, her black skirts gracefully settling around her on the rug. She placed an urgent hand on his forearm, where he rested it on the arm of the chair. "Charlotte has said she is to wed you. It cannot be true, Papa! Say it is not!"

As he studied his daughter's upraised, distressed expression, Bennet realized he had been backward in appreciating the concerns of his betrothed. *Miss Lucas was correct. The news appears uncommonly upsetting to Lizzy.* "Miss Lucas speaks the truth. We are to be wed."

Elizabeth uttered an exclamation. She tightened her hold, her fingers digging through the fabric of his sleeve. "No, no, you must not! Papa, pray do not wed Charlotte! Anyone else would be more acceptable to me! Oh, why must you remarry at all? Mama is scarce in her grave! It-it is unseemly! It is a mistake. Surely you must see that."

I cannot endure wild, emotional utterances. Mrs. Bennet – he bit off that thought. Thomas Bennet addressed what he saw as the main point. "Lizzy, even if I wished it, honor will not allow me to draw back." He wondered at his tolerance for her histrionics; but this *was* his dearest daughter and she was not usually given to such foolish demonstrations. At the moment, her irrational intensity reminded him of the theatric outbursts of her younger and sillier sisters. Instead of rebuking her, however, he addressed her in a mild inflection. "I should think you would be pleased. Miss Lucas is your very good friend, after all."

Elizabeth jumped to her feet. Her hands closed into fists at her sides. "Pleased! How could you think so?

That quick wit of hers...it has gone begging.

Troubled by her attitude, Bennet set aside his book. He said gravely, "Why such heat, Lizzy? Surely, you must understand that my marriage to Miss Lucas is to all of our advantages. Every one of us will profit by the addition of Miss Lucas to our family."

"You cannot love her!"

"Love her? Pray, do not be a simpleton, Lizzy." He was impatient with her at last. "Though I regard Miss Lucas with respect, and she must feel something similar for me, there is nothing of the romantic in our agreement. It is a mutually beneficial business transaction, as so many matches are. I will gain a proper mistress for Longbourn. In exchange, Miss Lucas will secure a substantially better position in life. It is of a certainty a much better future than she would have had by remaining the spinster daughter of her parents, and the sister who must subsist on the future benevolence of her brothers."

Elizabeth stared at him, a strangely blank look in her eyes.

She must comprehend me. I am not speaking in tongues.

Bennet sighed. Much as he disliked it, he went further, with brutal bluntness. "I am marrying for *your* sake, Lizzy."

Her face drained. She took a step backwards. "Mine!"

"For you and your sisters," he amended. "The conventions require a proper hostess at Longbourn, if we are to be able to entertain and to accept invitations. For all of her faults, Mrs. Bennet chaperoned and made every effort to put her daughters in the way of making advantageous matches. I hope Miss Lucas may fill this office on behalf of you and your sisters."

Elizabeth clasped her hands together, and in all earnestness, she said, "No, no, you must not make such a sacrifice."

"Sacrifice!" Thomas Bennet shook his head, marveling again at her foolishness. *I hope to sire a son on Charlotte Lucas and break the entail. Yet this I cannot say.* Instead, he offered a smile. "There you are off, Lizzy. I believe Miss Lucas and I shall suit very well. I have been patient with you, Lizzy. Apply to your aunt Gardiner to further your worldly education, for I have done with explanation. Now, I will thank you to have back the use of my library."

Elizabeth left her father's presence as swiftly as she had entered it. She could not yet accept what she had been told. *Such shocking communication!* Charlotte had long held a place in her affections as a friend, and more, very much as a sister. Her disordered thoughts were such that she felt she would burst if she did not express them, and at once she thought of her eldest sister, but just as swiftly rejected confiding in her. Jane was her dearest sister and her closest confidante, but Jane was already struggling with such a strong disappointment that Elizabeth could not bear to further burden her. *My aunt Gardiner.* Her father had suggested talking to her aunt, and indeed, Elizabeth could think of no one better in whom she might take counsel.

Elizabeth immediately sought out her aunt and poured out her feelings over the betrothal that was so unacceptable to her. "From my earliest memories, Charlotte has been as a sister to me! There can be no love in this!"

"What would you have me say, Lizzy?" asked Mrs. Gardiner quietly. "It is a wise and desirable measure for both."

"I could never address her without feeling that all the comfort of intimacy is over."

Mrs. Gardner fastened a grave regard on her. "You are a sensible girl, Lizzy, and, therefore, I am not afraid of speaking openly. Do not involve yourself or endeavor to further inflict your contrary opinions upon your father and Miss Lucas. By speaking to your father in such a manner, you have displayed a sad lack of prudence."

"I have nothing to say against *him.*"

"You must not let your ungoverned feelings run away with you. You have sense and we all expect you to use it. Your father would depend on your resolution and good conduct, I am sure. You *must not* disappoint your father."

Elizabeth managed a constrained smile. "My dear aunt, this is being serious indeed."

"Surely, Lizzy, you must see such a marriage is important to the preservation of Longbourn."

"Importance may sometimes be purchased too dearly!"

"Nothing, on the contrary, could be more natural. Your father hopes to break the entail."

At her aunt's calm assertion, Elizabeth gaped. "The entail? What has it do with..." Suddenly, heat surged into her face. Elizabeth flattened her palms against her hot cheeks.

"You are shocked, Lizzy, but why should you be? Miss Lucas is some years younger than my brother Bennet. She is still of childbearing age. It should have occurred to you."

"Believe me, it did not!"

"Well, give some thought to it now and cease airing your outrage. Believe me, my dear niece, you and your feelings are insignificant beside this hope for the Bennets."

After the surprising, distasteful interview with Elizabeth, Bennet thought it prudent to reveal his successful suit as swiftly as possible. He would have preferred to speak to his immediate family first, but it was not to be. That afternoon, Mr. Collins returned, to beard him in his den, and waxed eloquent upon the ill consequences of the match. The clergyman took out his handkerchief and blotted his brow. "Indeed, sir, I cannot stress it enough. I have written immediately to Lady Catherine de Bourgh, but I believe I know what her ladyship would say. The timing – so soon after Mrs. Bennet's demise – why, it is unconscionable! I shall go so far even to say unchristian! Some few hours, have I wrestled with the morality of this matter and I cannot condone it."

"It is perhaps unconventional; but I believe you will agree, my girls will profit from having a step-mother, one who will see to their future bestowal into marriage." Thomas Bennet allowed himself a sardonic smile. "My daughters will not then become a burden upon your purse."

Mr. Collins opened his mouth, then closed it. He frowned, before giving a slow nod. "It is a point, cousin Bennet. I must say, a very fair point. I flatter myself that I am able to adjust my thinking when it is pointed out to me, by others of such quick intellect, that I have been too rigid in my own perception. As your heir, and in deference to yourself, I must give some weight to this consideration. Indeed, I am left amazed by your benevolent foresight on my behalf. It is good of you, I protest."

"Pray do not give it another thought, dear fellow. I shall not, I assure you." Bennet took him by the elbow and gently ushered him toward the door, exiting with him from the library. "You must have much to think on, Collins. In fact, I should not wonder at it if you wished to write to your esteemed patroness, Lady Catherine de Bourgh, and lay all before her."

Mr. Collins at once expressed his full agreement. He was still talking when he reached the front entry. Accompanying him all of the way, Bennet smiled and nodded. He signaled the butler. "Mr. Collins is taking his leave of us, Hill. Send for his gig to be brought round to the door. Ah, here is your overcoat and hat! We must have you bundle up well, Mr. Collins. We would not wish you to catch your death of a cold!"

Mr. Collins was torn between his desire to get to his correspondence and his duty to those in his sphere of influence. "But I feel I leave you too soon, sir. I have not properly condoled with you."

"Our relationship is such that very few minutes suffice to console me."

After dinner, when all had congregated in the drawing-room for the evening, Thomas Bennet made the announcement of his engagement to all of his daughters. Four pairs of rounded female eyes regarded him with amazed incredulity. Elizabeth bent her head, avoiding his questing gaze.

"Good Lord! Why, it is a joke!" exclaimed Lydia. She brayed a loud laugh. "Papa, how can you tell such a story!"

"You forget yourself, Lydia," said Mrs. Gardiner in quiet reproof.

Lydia went goggle-eyed. "But it cannot be true!"

Catherine uttered not a word but she knit her brows. She darted a glance at her aunt and seemed to weigh the lady's unsurprised calmness at the announcement against Lydia's outburst. For once, she did not parrot Lydia's outspokenness.

"I have had it from Charlotte herself," said Elizabeth in a subdued voice.

Jane's sweet smile spread over her lovely countenance, a genuine pleasure sparking to life in her deep blue eyes. "Congratulations, Papa. I am certain you and Charlotte will deal well together."

"Thank you, dear Jane. I expected your whole-hearted acceptance, for yours is a good and kind heart." Though he addressed his eldest daughter, Bennet gazed straight at Elizabeth, so he saw the red staining her cheeks at his oblique barb. *My subtlety is rewarded. Lizzy is reprimanded.*

"I offer my felicitations, sir," said Mary with a grave air. "Indeed, I am very glad of it. I had wondered how we would go on once my aunt Gardiner had returned to London. We have no one to chaperone us or to receive visitors."

"You are very right, Mary, and you speak with great sense." Bennet smiled at her. He was surprised by her astuteness; but then, Mary had shown a different side of herself since the death of Mrs.

Bennet. She was unexpectedly matured and accepting of responsibility.

Of a sudden, Elizabeth jumped to her feet and left the drawing-room.

Mr. Gardiner was surprised. "Why, what is wrong with Lizzy? It is unlike her to behave in such a precipitate manner. I trust she is not unwell."

Bennet connected with Mrs. Gardiner's gaze. He raised one of his brows in mute question. She frowned and gave a little shake of her head. He believed he knew what she was thinking. *Yes. Give it time. Lizzy will come around.*

[21]

Mr. Bennet's betrothal to Miss Lucas was spread quickly the length and breadth of the countryside, primarily due to Lady Lucas, who was not backward in announcing her spinster daughter's good fortune. Mr. Bennet observed the result with mingled amusement and much annoyance.

The engagement excited enormous interest. When it became known that a date was set for the wedding, before Christmas, it roused to a furor. Little else was talked about in the whole of the county. All four-and-twenty families seemed to have formed an opinion. Of course, Sir William and Lady Lucas expressed their prodigious happiness. Most approved of the match, and were not behind in proffering sincere congratulations to Mr. Bennet and Miss Lucas. Amongst them was Col. Forster, who commanded the militia, billeted for the winter in Meryton, and had recently married. Some others, like Mrs. Philips and her particular cronies, declared it was scandalous for Mr. Bennet to enter again into the wedded state with such indecent haste.

"Folly, and so I told Mr. Philips!" cried Mrs. Philips. "My poor sister! Oh, such pains and spasms she must endure in her heavenly reward! Her nerves were fragile, you know. She had such sensibility! I doubt even the glorious Lord's table can distract poor Fanny from Mr. Bennet's folly!"

It was perhaps unfortunate that Mr. Collins was staying with the Philips, and was the recipient of such exclamations. He could not moderate the good lady's opinion, not when his own was so equivocal; on the one hand, he thoroughly agreed with Mrs. Philips, but on the other, his condemnation had been tempered by Mr. Bennet's pointing out the future advantage to himself. His quibbling therefore served more to prop up the lady's outraged disapproval than to discourage it.

At Longbourn of an evening, Bennet remarked on the swell of gossip to Mr. Gardiner. "I fear our sister Philips is not happy with my taking a wife so soon after Mrs. Bennet's death."

"I shall speak to her again, Thomas, but my sister is such a foolish woman, as you know. She may bewail the marriage now, but I daresay she will quickly become reconciled. She will not wish to create a permanent rift with Longbourn."

"The shortest route to reconciliation with Longbourn is in the value of gossip. My sister Philips will not allow such a small thing as her avowed animadversion get in the way of it." Bennet's sharp response was acid. "She may throw up her hands, declaring herself unable to enter the church for the blessed occasion, but she will welcome the opportunity to witness the scandalous nuptials. All for the coinage of gossip!"

Mr. Gardiner chuckled, but shook his head. "I acknowledge it with a heavy heart, Thomas. I do not take offense at your words because I harbor no illusions about my eldest sister. She is an inveterate gossip. She knows of everything that passes in and through Meryton, and what she does not know for certain she embellishes from her imagination."

Mrs. Philips' disapprobation *was* somewhat blunted by the obvious support of the Gardiners, who presented a calm unity with their brother Bennet. Though Longbourn's inhabitants were cut off from general society by the etiquette of mourning, mercifully saving them from the worst of the rude curiosity, they were in attendance at Sunday services, where craned necks and whispers behind raised hands followed the Bennet family to their pew.

Mr. Bennet adjusted his black neckcloth by hooking a finger under the tight edge and giving it a tug. In an irritated aside to his brother-in-law, who sat beside him on the bench, he muttered, "It is a damned nine-day's wonder. I feel like a two-headed calf at the county fair!"

Mr. Gardiner covered his chuckle with a cough into his fist.

An unwilling Mr. Bennet had been thrust onto a public stage, but he was not the lead actor. Charlotte Lucas was the cynosure of all eyes.

At Lucas Lodge, Miss Hawkins professed herself to be delighted. "Dear cousin! The awed wonder you have excited! So very flattering! Why, it must turn your head, if you were not such a retiring creature – is she not retiring, Miss Simmons? – but, she is *too retiring*, in her manner and her dress, I am sure you must agree! She simply *fades* into the wallpaper!"

Charlotte managed to suppress a sigh. *I should not be astonished any longer at anything she may say.*

"Miss Lucas is a modest young lady."

"Oh, just so! A veritable *card* of dull modesty!" Miss Hawkins gave a silvery trill. "You have adroitly expressed my precise point, Miss Simmons. We must break her of this distressing habit, really we must! It will not do for Mr. Bennet! Perhaps a new modality –" Miss Hawkins exclaimed anew, and removed a brightly-colored Paisley shawl. "Here, Charlotte, you must have my third-best shawl. It is not my favorite, so I have scarcely worn it. No, no, I insist! It will add *just* that touch of elegance your present daygown lacks!"

Charlotte issued a quiet laugh. She was torn, irritated by her cousin's insensibility, and yet overthrown by her generous gift of such a fine article. The expensive woolen weft was supple in her hands. *It is a handsome piece.* "Very well; I thank you, Augusta.'

Charlotte had never experienced so much attention in the whole of her life and it *was* disconcerting. However, she *had* anticipated the intense interest so she went about in much of her usual calm manner – but she was not as sanguine as she appeared.

My heart aches at the loss of such a dear friendship.

The rupture was severe. Since the hour she had fled from Longbourn, behind her placidity, she hid a churning anguish. *Eliza! As dear as a sister!* The former warmth between them was utterly extinguished. Charlotte had no way of knowing if Elizabeth had indeed gone to her father, as she had threatened, and expressed her opposition against the marriage; but she suspected that she had and the conversation had not gone as Elizabeth had hoped. Charlotte had reason to believe that Jane had gently reproached her sister, gathering as much from an oblique, melancholy remark made by Mary; whatever Jane had said, however, had fallen on deaf ears. Whenever Charlotte met her, Elizabeth's dark eyes flashed. Though she was civil, she spoke with an alien coolness. *Her anger is poorly hid. All affection is gone.*

The schism was becoming remarked upon by the gossips, speeded by Mrs. Philips' much-reiterated opinions. Charlotte overheard the woman for herself after Sunday service. "My brother Bennet is shameless, *unnaturally keen* to remarry. Why, see how my dear niece Lizzy looks so disapproving of her friend, Miss Lucas!"

A tide of heat flooded Charlotte's face. She bent her head to hide her flush beneath the brim of her velvet bonnet and she hurried to one of the Lucas carriages. Catching up her skirts in one hand, she clambered into it, glad of the chatter of her siblings and her anonymity amongst them.

Accompanied by her mother, Charlotte paid a few social calls on the Bennet sisters and Mrs. Gardiner. It was very much done so that Charlotte and Mrs. Gardiner could have conversation, to become better acquainted. Elizabeth went about tight-lipped, her vivacity dampened, seeming unable to sit still. Some might have attributed her restless demeanor as being an outward grieving for her mother, but Charlotte was not deceived. Elizabeth avoided her gaze, *avoided her*, murmuring excuses to exit the drawing-room within minutes of Charlotte‘s entrance. Once only, Elizabeth approached her for a private word, leaning down close to look into her face, and her low tone was accusatory. "Papa danced with you at Netherfield."

Charlotte knit her brows. *What is that to the purpose?* "Mr. Bennet was kind to solicit my hand."

"Had you designs on my father even then?"

Charlotte recoiled. "Eliza!" Shocked, horrified, she stared at her.

Elizabeth shook her head, frowning, her fine brows knit. "No, no, it was not possible, Mama was still alive; there could not have been anything between you *then*. But later...when I recall the ways you inserted yourself here at Longbourn! – it *must* have been then! You seized upon the wretched situation and made of yourself the heroine."

Elizabeth's terrible charges were beyond her comprehension.

Charlotte could scarce draw breath past the constriction in her throat. She pressed a hand to the base of it. "You are wrong! You are *wrong*, Eliza!"

Mrs. Gardiner's penetrating gaze was on them. Elizabeth must have seen it; she straightened and moved away. After a glance at her retreating niece, the lady walked over to Charlotte and sat down beside her; in a lowered, concerned voice, she asked, "Are you ill, Miss Lucas?"

Charlotte shook her head. She tried to smile, but it trembled upon her lips. "I mourn our friendship, Mrs. Gardiner."

Mrs. Gardiner reached out to take her hand and give her quivering fingers a reassuring squeeze. "Be patient with our Lizzy, Miss Lucas. She is strong-minded and impulsive and still green in her judgment. But she is a sensible young woman and she will not deceive herself for long."

Charlotte blinked back tears. "I do hope so, ma'am."

The Gardiners expressed their intention of attending the wedding, which would take place in a bare handful of days, and Mr. Bennet invited them to remain to the end of month. "It will be a somber Christmas, what with the black crepe ribbons on the front door, and all of us in mourning color, yet your presence in our household will be most welcome."

Bennet was glad when the Gardiners agreed, for their company was a buffer against the tempest of gossip. *Such ado about nothing!*

As visits were exchanged between the Gardiners and the occupants of Lucas Lodge, Charlotte became comfortable with Mr. Bennet's relations. She had met the Gardiners during their visits in past years on a number of occasions. However, as Mr. Bennet's betrothed, she was accorded a warmer civility by the Gardiners, and in turn, she satisfied her deepened curiosity about the couple from Gracechurch Street, in Cheapside, London. Charlotte discovered Mr. Gardiner to be a sensible man, much superior to either of his sisters by nature and education. He was well-bred and agreeable. Mrs. Gardiner, who was several years younger than either Mrs. Bennet or Mrs. Philips, was an amiable, intelligent, elegant woman. Charlotte already admired and respected her; she hoped to someday count Mrs. Gardiner as one of her dearest friends.

The lady was a great favorite with all her Longbourne nieces. However, there was a particular regard existing between Mrs. Gardiner and the two eldest sisters. Lady Lucas remarked on it. "Mrs. Gardiner is very fond of Jane and Eliza. I recall that they have frequently stayed with their aunt in town."

"Yes, that is so," agreed Charlotte.

"Perhaps that explains their better manners. Mrs. Gardiner is a very good influence. It is a pity the younger girls have not modeled themselves after her, as well."

Charlotte quietly concurred. "Indeed, Mama, Mrs. Gardiner is such a refined lady, and if she so wished, I daresay she could easily move in the highest circles of society."

Charlotte kept to herself her decided opinion that Mrs. Bennet had done a dismal disservice to her untutored, youngest daughters by allowing Catherine and Lydia to enter too soon into society; the two girls comported themselves badly in company. *Careless, unrestrained – especially Lydia. And Kitty follows her lead in all things.* She hoped in her new role as step-mother, she could curb their wildness. As for the middle sister...*Mary is merely pedantic, but oh, how much better she could be!*

Days before the wedding, Sir William and Lady Lucas extended invitations to the Bennets, the Philips, and the Gardiners to a private dinner party. "All of our guests are in mourning, and in regular circumstances, it would not be acceptable. But we are becoming family, so it will not be thought so very odd," pronounced Lady Lucas. "We will consider it a betrothal dinner."

Charlotte did her duty; she smiled and conversed with everyone, but all the while she could not but observe the listless attitude of Jane Bennet. At the earliest opportunity for a private word, Charlotte sat down beside her and asked in a lowered tone, "How do you fare, Jane?"

Jane smiled, but her pleasant expression did not erase the shadows in her eyes. "I am well enough, Charlotte. I do not pretend to misunderstand you. My aunt Gardiner has invited me to stay. I shall be glad to go to town. People do talk so."

Charlotte was not surprised to hear of Jane Bennet's going away. The Gardiners were exceeding fond of Jane, and her unhappiness would be of natural concern to them. Charlotte suspected Jane was suffering from more than heartbreak. *Mrs. Bennet's boastings have held up poor Jane to public humiliation.* Mr. Bingley's defection and abandonment had been the subject of much discussion; not even the astonishment of the betrothal had entirely displaced it.

It was her belief Mr. Bingley's marked attentions had been merely the effect of common and transient liking, which ceased when he saw Jane no more. She did not air her conviction, as it would not bring comfort. *If only she had put herself forward more, she might even now be engaged. How different it might have been!* She did her best to console Jane. "Perhaps Mr. Bingley will come again in the summer."

"It is kind of you to say so, Charlotte, but Miss Bingley has written. They will not return." Her friend's calm face and tone were much as usual, but Charlotte discerned a look of devastation deep within her eyes, and she felt like weeping in pity for Jane.

I am glad, glad, that I have put away all notions of romance!

[22]

Mr. Thomas Bennet, widower, and Miss Charlotte Lucas, spinster, were wedded by common license on Saturday, Dec. 21st., in Longbourn church.

Charlotte wore a new Spanish hat, white velvet with a Corbeau rim, a green so dark it was almost black, adorned with a demi-wreath of white snowdrops. She was gowned in her best morning dress, cut square across her bosom, set with the fashionable, fuller-cased long sleeves. Her sister, Maria, stood beside her. Mr. Bennet was distinguished in a well-cut black frock coat and trousers. A mourning band was stitched on the sleeve of his coat. Mr. Gardiner stood up for the bridegroom.

The nuptials were attended by Mr. Bennet's five daughters, a row of feminine figures dressed in blacks. In the next pew back, the Gardiners and the Philips were seated together. Removed to the far end of the pew was Mr. Collins, with his arms folded across his chest. On the bride's side, the Lucases filled two pews, beaming their universal happy approval. Behind them were Miss Augusta Hawkins and her companion, Miss Simmons.

Mr. Collins left directly after the ceremony and the signing of the parish register. After expressing regrets to everyone to be taking leave so soon, he promised letters of thanks. He had planned journeying into Kent, to arrive at his Hunsford parsonage before dusk.

The church bells were rung for the newly married couple, Mr. Bennet being able to afford the ringers.

At Lucas Lodge, a lavish wedding breakfast was provided. A fine wedding cake had been baked by the cook and was much admired. Music, and games for the younger set, enlivened the atmosphere. Despite the felicitous occasion, an incongruous pall hung over the small gathering. The Bennet sisters were gowned in lusterless black twilled bombazine and their hands were encased in black gloves. Their bonnets were covered in black silk and tied under their chins with black ribbons. Surveying the flock of soberly-clad young ladies, Lady Lucas remarked, "Such a pity the Bennets are in deep mourning."

Charlotte responded quietly. "But if they were not, there would be no wedding."

"Just so. An uncomfortable observation."

Charlotte regarded the meager company, half of whom were dressed in similar funeral garb. The members of *her* family had worn their Sunday best, in hues of biscuit, bottle green, rose, chocolate brown, and jonquil. Her cousin's morning gown was *a la mode* in the new color, Sardinian blue. *My wedding celebration. A collection of dour crows and happy jackdaws.* In any other circumstances, Sir William and Lady Lucas would have spared no expense in sending her off. A large part of her wished she *could* have had the grand wedding – the yards-long white Brussels lace veil; the semi-décolleté glace silk wedding dress to be paired with arm's-length white gloves – how pleasant it would have been to be admired for once in her quiet life! And afterwards, the crowded celebration, with guests from all about the county, the music and dancing, overflowing with good wishes.

A small sigh escaped her. *I am a practical creature. I will not repine.*

Charlotte had begun her new life as a respectable married woman.

The generous flow of wine induced jocularity. A succession of toasts were made, a few ribald in nature, which Mr. Bennet received in good part as Charlotte blushed. *My father! And Mr. Philips! Even John! What does my brother know of such things?* She decided she did not want to know how her eldest brother had come by such knowledge.

The hour was well-advanced before outer garments were put on, and goodbyes were said. Then Mr. Bennet bore his second wife off to Longbourn in his carriage. His daughters and the Gardeners remained at Lucas Lodge, where their trunks had been delivered and unpacked for a visit of several days, it having been decided beforehand, for privacy's sake, to leave Longbourn to the newly-wed couple.

Charlotte's things had been transferred to Longbourn.

Mr. Bennet handed her out of the carriage and extended his arm. She laid her gloved fingertips on his sleeve. His opposite hand came across to cover them in a warm clasp. As he accompanied her inside the manor, he smiled down at her. "Welcome home, Mrs. Bennet."

"Thank you, sir," she murmured. The ribald remarks at the wedding breakfast had set up a circling in her brain. She kept thinking about what Mr. Bennet had said in that extraordinary interview, which had culminated in her acceptance of his proposal of marriage.

A marriage of convenience. But not entirely so.

She went hot, then cold, goose-bumps rising on her flesh.

In the entry hall, the butler and footman were waiting to relieve them of their outer garments. Charlotte surrendered her muff and was helped out of her fur-edged pelisse. She shivered as cool air brushed the exposed skin above her bodice.

Mr. Bennet searched her face. "You are wearied, my dear lady. It has been an eventful day. Might I suggest a warm bath and a rest before we meet again?"

Charlotte gratefully accepted the recommendation. He called for Mrs. Hill to see to her comfort and she followed the housekeeper upstairs to the bedchamber that had become hers. The cans of hot water were brought in and poured into the tub placed close to the cheerful, crackling fire. After bathing, she put on her nightshift. Charlotte curled up in the wide bed, drawing covers to her shoulders, almost at once falling asleep. Hours later, a maid roused her to change into fresh clothing and tidy her coiffure. At five-thirty, Charlotte went downstairs.

A two-course dinner was served. She was seated at the foot of the table, in the place of honor, as was her right as mistress of Longbourn, but she felt terribly awkward and nervous. *It feels so strange! The dining room is familiar but not my place in it.* However, Mr. Bennet took pains to set her at ease and once she lost her reticence, she enjoyed the conversation. Not having partaken of anything since the wedding breakfast, Charlotte *was* hungry, and she did justice to the first dinner she presided over.

Afterwards in the drawing-room, she found that the gentleman was not driven to polite conversation. Mr. Bennet engaged himself with a book. Charlotte quietly embroidered. The spaniel snuffled in sleep, as the ormolu mantel clock ticked. It was peaceful, and she had ample time for reflection. *I am so ignorant. How will it go? I do not know what to expect... Will it bring pain? Will he stay...after?* By degrees, a strange agitation prickled her skin. She shifted from side to side in her chair.

"What is it, my dear?"

Startled, Charlotte lifted her gaze. Mr. Bennet was looking at her with a quizzical expression, his gray-blue eyes fixed on her face. He had lowered the volume in his hands, one finger marking his place on the page. She realized he must have been observing her. *He is not as fully engaged in his book as I believed!*

"Nothing, sir! A wayward thought only," she stammered.

Mr. Bennet smiled, in an enigmatic way that sent blood rushing to her cheeks.

At last, it came time to retire to her bedchamber – the one that had once belonged to her predecessor. The bedclothes had already been turned down. The maid silently helped her to undress and don her nightshift, before exiting and closing the door.

Charlotte sat on the little stool in front of the dressing-table, turning around so that her back was to the mirror. She had finished brushing out and plaiting her hair, tying the braid off with a ribbon.

Charlotte looked slowly around, noting details in her surroundings. Earlier, she had been too tense and tired to do so. *The furnishings are not to my taste.* Mrs. Bennet's preference had been for frills and ruffles and dark-colored wallpaper. She occupied her mind by imagining what she would change, and when she was done, she had nothing else to think about.

Except Mr. Bennet...my husband and master!

She waited, her hands clasped tight in her lap.

A sitting room connected the master and mistress' bedchambers. Mr. Bennet knocked, before opening the door and entering. Charlotte leaped to her feet. She watched as Mr. Bennet walked toward her, before he stopped a few arm-lengths away. In the privacy of the bedchamber, lit only by the ruddy firelight, they somberly regarded each other. Her heart raced and her breath fluttered. He was wearing a loose-sleeved dressing gown over his long nightshirt. She had never seen a man in *dishabille* before.

Thomas Bennet looked her over, and under his thoughtful scrutiny, deep color swept across her cheeks. He uttered measured words that would set the course of their union. "I have reflected much on the matter. I want more from you than what we agreed. I wish to press you often and often until I have gotten you with child."

Her gray eyes widened. She visibly swallowed. "It is your husbandly right, Mr. Bennet."

"Take off your nightshift. I want to see you."

She slowly pulled the neck-to-ankle voluminous gown over her head and stood bare before him. The heat in her cheeks spread down her neck, blooming lower still. She did not seem to know what to do with her hands, first covering herself, then dropping them to her sides. She averted her gaze, unable to meet his eyes.

The firelight limned her naked body.

Bennet's breath stuttered in his chest, then speeded up. He took keen notice of a quickening in his lower trunk, an arousal he had not felt for a long time. His new wife might not be a great beauty in countenance, but her flesh was firm, her breasts were high, and her curves were womanly.

Thomas, you lucky cur.

He led her to the bed and laid her down. Despite his rising erection, he was not altogether sure that he could do justice to her.

Lobcock or no, I must and will explore every curve of her beauteous body!

He did not hurry the business; as a consequence, he gently and thoroughly initiated her into her marital duties. He wrought pleasure on her with lips and hands, more than once, until her body quivered like a taut bowstring, and her pith was wet as rippling water. Finally, his heart pounding and his breathing ragged, he settled into his rightful place. The muscles of his body tightened – no longer a lobcock, he thrust strong into her center. In a hoarsened voice, he exclaimed, "At last, I make you *mine*!"

He greatly surprised her, yet once more. His heated weight on top of her, lying thick between her parted thighs, the powerful, rhythmic friction of his possession, drove her back to the sparkling heights where he had sent her before. She cried out, her spine arching. Shudders stretched and rent her apart as he went rigid and found his own groaning release in her.

Afterwards, he held her in his arms. Her slickened back was settled against his sweating bare chest, her plump buttocks in the cradle of his hips. He rested an arm over her waist, palm upwards, and cupped full her warm, yielding breast. Verses swam into his contented brain; verses he had not recalled for years. *Song of Solomon.* He uttered them into her ear. "*Behold, thou art fair, my love; behold, thou art fair; thou hast doves' eyes. Behold, thou art fair, my beloved, yea, pleasant: also our bed is green.* You are beautiful, my Charlotte. You have pleased me, very much."

Bliss suffused her brain, much as it had coursed, so recently, through her aroused, tight-wound, aching body – a sense of completeness. He must have spoken only out of carnal satiation; yet she treasured up the words. *My cup runneth over.* Contentment filled her. She closed her eyes, a smile resting on her face.

For four days, during which they learned of each other, Mr. and Mrs. Bennet had Longbourn to themselves. The household servants discreetly went about their duties.

On Christmas morning, Bennet ordered out the carriage for the short drive to Lucas Lodge to participate in the holiday festivities there; it was not even to be thought of to hold a lively celebration at Longbourn, where the front door was draped in huge dismal knots of black crape, instead of being decorated with a fragrant wreath of greenery.

"Since all of our relations are already houseguests at Lucas Lodge, it seems only sensible to join them." His wife readily agreed. "Indeed, sir. I will very much like being with my family for Christmas day."

It was a happy reason to return to her former home for a visit.

The couple's arrival was exclaimed over by Lucases, Bennets, and Gardners alike, and they were warmly welcomed.

Sir William heartily shook Bennet's hand. "Well, Thomas! Well!"

Lady Lucas kissed her daughter's cheek. "My dear, *dear* girl! I am happy to see you! You look well, very well indeed."

Charlotte was treated to the commotion and glad cries of her siblings. Besieged by her family, Charlotte laughed and blushed, greeting them all, and especially the younger ones, with whom she was a favorite.

Maria fiercely hugged her. "You have been missed, Charlotte."

She returned her sister's hug with equal fervor. "We will remain close, dearest Maria, always!"

Thomas Bennet was himself surrounded. He kissed the cheeks of his daughters, saying a kind word to each of them, and exchanged friendly greetings with the Gardiners.

Miss Hawkins did her upmost to engage Charlotte in confidences, "I shall one day have my own *caro esposo*. Oh! The pains I shall be at, to dispel gloomy ideas and give him cheerful views, which will be enough for anyone! You must tell me, how goes it with Mr. Bennet?

I see the glint in her eyes. Her nose fairly quivers with inquisitiveness. Charlotte was not of a mind to satisfy her cousin's pushing curiosity. "I am vastly content." *Does she expect me to spill the secrets of my marriage bed?*

"Dear cousin Charlotte! You may speak well or not of him, but speak you must! I am disposed to like Mr. Bennet, I assure you! At the same time it is fair to observe that I am one of those who always judge for themselves, and are by no means implicitly guided by others. I give you notice, that as I find your Mr. Bennet, so I shall judge him – I am no flatterer."

Charlotte smiled. "I know well you are no flatterer!" *Indeed, I know it all too well. She sets her barbs indiscriminately.* "I shall allow you to judge for yourself, Augusta, for I am determined to preserve discretion."

For the most part, Charlotte enjoyed herself; the conviviality was universal, being marred only by her cousin's intrusive questioning and the bare nod given her by Elizabeth. *She has not forgiven me.*

Well into the afternoon, she and Mr. Bennet returned to Longbourn. They would have what remained of ten days, until the end of December, when Mr. Bennet's daughters and the Gardiners would remove from Lucas Lodge and return to Longbourn.

[23]

Upon the printing of the wedding announcement in the newspapers, written felicitations arrived in the post. Col. Forster's note was typical in its form, being sent on behalf of himself, his wife, and the entire regiment. Mr. Collins penned a lengthy contradictory letter, expressing his compliments on securing Miss Lucas' hand, intermingled with reproaches for marrying in such unseemly haste – a letter which Thomas Bennet tossed into the fire. *He blows hot and cold. Pomposity and equivocation! The reek of Lady Catherine de Bourgh's influence is stamped in near every period.*

He was supremely satisfied with the beginnings of his marriage. *Ne plus ultra. That which is peerless.* He decided that he could not have made a better choice of bride. *I enjoy her company. She is a good helpmate.* Inevitably, Bennet's musings led him into familiar territory. He quirked a smile at the flames. *A good bedmate.*

Bennet glanced up at the mantel clock, saw the advanced hour, and turned from the fire, to step over to where sat his wife. As was her custom in the evenings, she was sewing, this time a very delicate piece of lace and net. With her marriage, she had taken to wearing lacy matron caps and had fashioned several for herself. He approved of the results. *She is always neat as a pin.* He held his hand down to her. Matter-of-factly, he said, "Let us go upstairs, Charlotte."

A blush rising in her face, she allowed him to draw her upwards "As you wish, sir." Together, arm in arm, they left the drawing-room to ascend the stairs.

The five Bennet sisters and the Gardiners returned to Longbourn. Bennet was glad of it, yet unsettled. His first wife's vacuous conversation and her temper had grated on his nerves and forced him to flee to his exile, his sanctuary. *Not so with Charlotte.* So, there was the strangeness explained.

The evenings fell into a recognizable pattern. Mr. Bennet picked up a book or perused a new agricultural treatise. The Gardiners sat down together to play backgammon. Charlotte embroidered, as did Elizabeth and Jane, and desultory conversation with the two sisters followed.

Charlotte felt the awkwardness of it as she quietly placed tiny stitches on the piece stretched on her hoop. All of her former ease with the Bennet sisters was vanished. Elizabeth was cool and distant; Jane seemed sunken in painful reflections; and Mary was a cipher, reading *Fordyce's Sermons* in the corner by the fire. The younger girls ignored everyone else to exchange giggling, whispered confidences.

Am I become the hated step-mother of fable?

At the fanciful reflection, her lips twitched.

Bennet spent more time in the drawing-room, in the company of his family, than he had been his wont, and as a consequence, saw more and discerned more than he had previous. It was swiftly born in on him that with the return of his favorite daughter, strife had entered his house. Elizabeth's manner was cold towards his new wife. He was surprised and exceeding puzzled by it. He wondered whether he should exert himself to reprimand Elizabeth or simply allow matters to take their natural course. In the end, he did nothing.

Those residing in the neighborhood were curious about how the second Mrs. Bennet was settling into her new responsibility and place. For a short time, a spate of callers enlivened the dull atmosphere of Longbourn. But it was not only Longbourn's neighbors who paid calls. Some members of the militia traversed the short distance from Meryton. Captain Carter and lieutenants

Denny, Wickham, Pratt and Chamberlayne came to pay their respects to the newly-wed Mr. and Mrs. Bennet and stayed to chat with the daughters of the house.

Mr. Wickham sat down beside Elizabeth and particularly attended to her. She received him with a welcoming smile. The handsome lieutenant's attention was obviously flattering to Elizabeth. The two had leisure for a full discussion, and for all the commendation which they civilly bestowed on each other. It was most acceptable as an occasion of bringing him again to the notice of her father and – yes! – her step-mother.

Thomas Bennet did not think it remarkable his daughter should be forming a regard for the officer. Mr. Wickham's appearance was greatly in his favor. He had all the best part of beauty, a fine countenance, a good figure, and a very pleasing address. He wondered whether it was possible that the lieutenant was destined to become his son-in-law.

I shall not lightly bestow my daughter's hand. No; not until I am certain of her future happiness. Now all that remains is to discover his situation in life!

Charlotte heard from her sister, when Maria came to visit, that Miss Hawkins had departed from Lucas Lodge. "Mr. Suckling wrote to Mama, and a week later he arrived to collect Augusta. He frowned the whole time. I suspect he was not best pleased to have to fetch her at all, but it seems Mrs. Suckling is fond of Augusta." Maria shrugged, with a grin spreading over her comely countenance, inviting her sister to share in the joke. "Augusta was very willing to return to Maple Grove, however."

Charlotte chuckled. "But Lucas Lodge is *so very like* Maple Grove!"

The Gardiners had intended to extend their stay, for a week or more, but Mr. Gardiner received letters which changed their plans. Mr. Gardiner said regretfully, "I am sorry, Thomas. The correspondence I have received has become urgent. I can no longer put off some business matters."

"I will regret your absence, Edward, yours and my sister Gardiner's. Quite beside the pleasure I take in it, your benign influence will be sorely missed. However, it will be the best thing for Jane to be gone from here."

The Gardiners set out to return to their home at Gracechurch Street, accompanied by Jane Bennet. She had not improved in her spirits and she had lost weight. Father and step-mother bid Jane a fond farewell, as did Elizabeth. The two sisters wept at the separation, clinging together until Jane gently disengaged and stepped up into the travel carriage.

Charlotte's own eyes were welling. She *was* glad Jane could leave behind the place of her disappointment; but once Jane's calming influence was taken from Longbourn, she felt her own situation would suffer.

The sprightly clop of hooves and rumbling of the carriage wheels receded. Thomas Bennet addressed his favorite daughter. "So, Lizzy, I find your sister is crossed in love. I congratulate her. Next to being married, a girl likes to be crossed in love a little now and then. It is something to think of and gives her a sort of distinction among her companions. When is your turn to come? You will hardly bear to be long outdone by Jane." He rallied her. "Now is your time. Here are officers enough at Meryton to disappoint all the young ladies in the country. Let Wickham be *your* man. He is a pleasant fellow, and would jilt you credibly."

Elizabeth's dark eyes flashed. "Thank you, sir, but a less agreeable man would satisfy me. We must not all expect Jane's good fortune."

He smiled, pleased by his daughter's quick *riposte*. He mocked her gently. "True, but it is a comfort to think that, whatever of that kind may befall you, you will have an affectionate step-mother who will always be ready to condole with you."

Bennet was rewarded by Elizabeth's darkling look before she hurried back into the manor. He had observed her antagonism toward the young woman he had set up in her mother's place. He was displeased by it, but held patience. He hoped that with time, their former friendship would reassert itself and there would be peace in his house. *Such sublimity in those ten days we were alone.* Jane had been rather indifferent to the situation, rousing herself on rare occasions to offer a soft rebuke either to Elizabeth or her two youngest sisters, half-hearted efforts which had no lasting effect. Lydia and Catherine exhibited their pettishness in such childish ways. *This tedious slamming of doors!*

Mounting the front steps, he offered his arm to his wife and her soft sigh came to his ear as she leaned against him. In a lowered aside, he said, "Never mind, my dearest. It will all come right. Jane will recover and so will we all, here at Longbourn."

"I hope so, dear sir."

[24]

Charlotte settled fully into her duties as mistress of a large house. The servants at Longbourn were in number similar to that of Lucas Lodge, consisting of the Hills, butler and housekeeper, respectively; a footman, two housemaids, the cook and a scullery maid. Others were outside her parvenu; the denizens of the stable and the farmhands at the croft farm. She did not fear problems that might arise with the household staff, in the upkeep of the house, or budgeting for expenses. She was brought up and well-trained for her responsibilities. Refurbishing her bedchamber to reflect her own taste was a happy project, one which she managed with economy, and which garnered Mr. Bennet's approval.

The only fly in the ointment are the Bennet sisters.

Elizabeth's illiberality was marked. Her antagonism was displayed in snubs and crushing remarks that cut Charlotte to the quick. Catherine and Lydia readily followed her example and their incivility was much more intemperate. Mary was the only one who seemed to regard her step-mother with complacency. However, *she* preferred not to take sides, or perhaps it was fairer to say that she had no influence over her sisters to make any difference in the commotion. The tumultuous outpourings, the shrill accents, the slamming doors – all of it made the atmosphere hideous. Charlotte was strongly reminded of how Mrs. Bennet had dominated Longbourn.

Charlotte often and often made overtures of peace, believing that if only Elizabeth could be brought to some accord, then her younger sisters would follow her lead; but her erstwhile friend would have none of it. *If only Jane was come back to Longbourn!* Charlotte thought it more than once. She felt it must have made a difference. Jane's good sense might have prevailed with Elizabeth. However, Jane remained with the Gardiners in London, still suffering her romantic disappointment over Mr. Bingley.

Mr. Bennet had told her to do whatever she wanted to establish her rule over the household and subsequently disappeared, either into his library or out taking exercise. She wished for his support in consolidating her position with his daughters, but he was not present for most of the tension-filled scenes, the raised voices, or slammed doors. Perhaps he was so accustomed to such occurrences that he could ignore them. Perhaps he did not know how she suffered. *Dear Heaven above, I begin to sound like Mrs. Bennet! Full of self-pity!*

Charlotte resigned herself and soldiered on.

However, her plight was not so unnoticed as she supposed.

On a cold, overcast morning, well into January, Thomas Bennet called his wife into the library and addressed her. "My daughters cannot make social calls so soon after their mother's passing. However, I see no reason why *you* should not, Charlotte. Though we have wed, you are not expected to observe mourning for a woman who is of no relation to you."

Charlotte's gray eyes steadily regarded him. "Are you certain, sir? I do not wish to give offense to anyone, especially not your daughters."

Bennet took her hand and held it between both of his own. "I am aware of the animosity they are showing you." At her flush and unhappy look, he smiled and shook his head. "Pray do not take it so much to heart, Charlotte. I assure you, it will not last, once they have all adjusted to our marriage. In the meantime, I believe it will refresh you to leave Longbourn to make visits in the neighborhood. And I wish you to make full use of the carriage. It is too cold to walk."

"You are very good."

"Besides, you will be able to satisfy the gossips," he said lightly.

She laughed, as he had meant her to, and went away obviously cheered. "I shall leave you to your work and your studies, sir."

Even after she exited, his smile lingered. *She is the perfect wife.* She was composed by nature, her low musical voice never grated on his ear, and she was graceful in her form and walk. She never rebuffed him.

Bennet was thoroughly satisfied. He had made a wise and, for him in a very personal sense, an advantageous marriage. She had awakened a hunger he had kept buried for years. He sought to occupy his new wife in a manner that guaranteed the firmness of his cock and spewing of his thick mettle. She was a warm, willing partner. In the dark, when he mounted *his* Charlotte, it was as though he had his youth handed back. *I marvel!* He was reacquainted with manly vigor. *I exult!* There was never a question in his mind now that he would fail in his performance.

He had set to with a will, using every skill at his command. She was incredibly responsive to his advances. He kindled in her a latent passion. In turn, it stimulated him whenever he discovered yet another sensitivity in her sleek body which induced a convulsing culmination. He did not know when, or if, the novelty would ever wear off. A succession of nights, as the sweat dried on their satiated bodies and she fell asleep yet again in his arms, he thanked God for her, as he had many times before.

The getting of an heir. It is a pleasant business.

It was difficult, but Bennet returned his attention to the documents on his desk.

Elizabeth trapped her in the confines of the breakfast room, where Charlotte had gone to retrieve a list. She clasped and unclasped her hands. "If all you wanted was a comfortable home, why did you not set your cap at Mr. Collins! Shown *him* more interest than you felt!"

"Have done!" Charlotte threw up a hand. *I am wearied by her.* "I beg of you, Eliza, let us not feud! Indeed, it is uncomfortable for all."

Elizabeth was deaf to her plea. She regarded her with color mounted high in her face. "I recall very well what you once told me, that a woman must show more affection than she feels to fix a man's interest."

"I spoke of Jane!" Charlotte was provoked out of her tattered calm. *"We spoke of Jane!"*

Elizabeth was unchecked in her hostility. "My poor father! You took advantage of him, Charlotte. His senses had become disordered, as I think you knew. You preyed upon him! I shall never forgive you."

Charlotte stared, her lips half-parted. *Her brain is fevered.* She forced a reply; her voice strangled in her throat. "You cannot believe that, Eliza!"

Elizabeth shot her a contemptuous glance and exited the room.

Charlotte grasped a chair back. She sucked in gasps of air, fighting vomit as her stomach roiled. *Eliza believes me cold, unfeeling, to be a scheming monster!* She had hoped and prayed for their differences to be smoothed away, to reach some détente; but Elizabeth's mind was closed against her. A vast despairing miasma pervaded her. *It is the end. We shall never more be friends.*

Shrill combative inflections caught her ears, coming nearer. Charlotte could not bear facing anyone else. *Especially Kitty and Lydia.* Attempting to put on a face of calm pretense was beyond her powers. Instead, she fetched her velvet bonnet, her gloves, and her woolen cape and fled Longbourn.

The raw blustering cold was bracing and a relief to her heated face.

I have begged. I shall beg no more! Her ragged breath caught in her lungs. Her heart beat rapidly. *I must resign myself. I must let Eliza go.* In her anguish, she paid no heed to where her feet carried her. The short distance to Lucas Lodge, the walk so familiar to her, was accomplished in a trice. She stopped in her tracks, while her gaze swept the familiar exterior. Longing swept through her. *Home! I am home!*

Mindful that she was no longer a daughter of the house, Charlotte inquired whether Lady Lucas was in to callers. The butler bowed, with a benign smile. "Certainly, Mrs. Bennet. At present, Lady Lucas is private in the upper sitting room. Allow me to show you up"

"Thank you, Hobson, but I shall find my own way." She left her outer garments with an attentive footman and went upstairs to find her mother.

Lady Lucas greeted her with warmth. She took her hands and kissed both of her cheeks. "My dearest Charlotte! It seems an age since I saw you last. Why, you are chilled! Sit down before the fire, here on the settee with me, and tell me all your news."

Charlotte obeyed; she prattled on about inconsequential things, about settling in and managing her household, about how pleased she was with the result of making over her bedchamber. Lady Lucas's regard did not waver. Charlotte could scarce meet her mother's unblinking, silent attention, and her own gaze darted here and there around the sitting room.

Of a sudden, she felt stifled, trapped. *I should not have come!*

"Then you have had no difficulties with the servants?"

"Oh, no, Mrs. Hill and the rest of the staff are perfectly amenable to my direction." Charlotte's chest heaved before she cried out, "Oh, Mama! It is hideous. I am so unhappy!" And to her horror, she burst into tears.

"There now, my poor girl! I thought you looked wan." Lady Lucas soothed and petted and brought her daughter to a calmer state. "Here is my handkerchief. Dry your eyes, my dear."

Charlotte wiped her eyes and blew her nose. She felt better but she was mortified. "I am sorry for my excess of emotion, Mama. I do not understand...I do not know what came over me."

"Is it Mr. Bennet? Has he treated you ill?"

Charlotte shook her head. "Oh, no! Mr. Bennet is all that I could have hoped for in a husband, kind and gentle." Honesty compelled her to add, "Though I could wish he did not recluse himself in his library so often."

"Mr. Bennet is reserved and scholarly. You knew this before you wed him, Charlotte. It is not right that you should be disappointed now in his habits."

Charlotte twisted the handkerchief between her fingers. She dipped her chin, and said in a low voice, "I do not resent his studies, Mama. I do not mind his attention to estate business or his taking exercise. He is a gentleman of parts and interests. I should not mind anything in the least, except that he does not bestir himself to speak to his daughters. I can bear anything but that omission."

Lady Lucas pursed her lips. "His daughters! So, *that* is where the trouble lies. Lydia and Kitty resent you taking their mother's place, I'll be bound."

"You are perfectly right, Mama, they do resent me. But as unpleasant as that is, I think I *could* bear it." Charlotte bit her bottom lip at her heart's pain. *It is hard to even speak of it.* "It is Eliza's unkindness which is so cruel. She-she believes that I...that I *entrapped* Mr. Bennet. She quarreled with me again, this very morning. I felt sick, Mama, positively sick!"

Lady Lucas' posture, always erect, further stiffened. After a pause, and with a slow, disbelieving shake of her head, she rendered a judicious observation. "Eliza Bennet is reputed to be clever and in possession of an uncommon degree of wit. I cannot credit it, not when she makes such a foolish accusation. However, let us leave that for the moment. I shall spare you by withholding my decided opinion of Mr. Bennet's carelessness of his household, for it is nothing we have not observed these several years. Indeed, again I say to you, Charlotte, your eyes were wide open before you accepted his suit. Mr. Bennet's neglect of you is merely an extension of his overall negligence."

"Mr. Bennet does not neglect me!"

Lady Lucas was silent for a long moment, during which she stared fixedly at her daughter. "My dear Charlotte, you do surprise me. Kind and gentle, I believe you said, was it not? I suppose he has bedded you often?"

A flush crept across Charlotte's face. She could scarce credit that her mother had broached such a private subject. Apparently, married ladies discussed all sorts of things. She supposed it *should* not surprise her. After all, her mother had sat her down and explained what would happen on her wedding night. *But it was not at all as Mama led me to expect. Not at all!* Charlotte attempted to match the matter-of-factness, but her sensibilities were shocked and her embarrassment bled through. "Yes, very often."

Lady Lucas studied her daughter. "When were your last courses, Charlotte?"

Charlotte was taken aback. "Why, with all that has happened, I do not know exactly." She knit her brows, trying to remember until coming to a startled realization. "Near the end of November, Mama. I cannot recall it more recent. Of a certainty, not since I was wed."

Lady Lucas gave a crisp nod. "I suspected as much. You are pale and you speak of feeling sick. You may be coming, daughter."

Charlotte's heart fluttered in her breast. She did not know whether she was frightened or thrilled. "Truly, Mama? It-it never occurred to me."

"You must have taken almost at once." Lady Lucas suddenly looked arch. "Mr. Bennet must have been uncommonly attentive."

Charlotte lowered her eyes, a scorching heat in her cheeks. "He has come to me every night."

"Every night? Does he *still* do so?"

At her daughter's mute nod, Lady Lucas was amazed. "Well! Such vigor at his time of life! And you are seized so soon! His virility is evident. Such welcome news, Charlotte! Mr. Bennet will be pleased. May I be the first to wish you happy, my dear!"

Charlotte made an inarticulate sound in her throat.

Lady Lucas fixed her eyes on her speechless daughter to address her in a direct manner. "A man's pride is intimately tied to his manhood. Mr. Bennet will desire to prove himself many times. Once you have done with your laying-in, he will be after you without ceasing – your womb will not be left fallow. I hope you do not *dislike* the bed-sport, Charlotte."

Charlotte's face flamed to a degree she would not have believed possible. She pressed her hands to her cheeks. *This is plain speaking, indeed!* In a suffocated voice, she admitted, "No, I do not dislike it, Mama."

Lady Lucas arched her brows, but to her daughter's infinite relief, she did not pursue the topic. "Does Mr. Bennet know you are breeding?"

"How could he, Mama, when I did not know it myself?" Charlotte dropped her hands and clasped her fingers together. "What should I do? Should I inform Mr. Bennet at once?"

Lady Lucas weighed the matter before she offered her opinion. "You have been so occupied, Charlotte, by the changes in your life – the hurried wedding, your new responsibilities and duties, your tribulations with the Bennet girls. Such created an undue stress upon you. My advice is to wait. If you miss your courses again, or if you feel a quickening of the babe, then it will be certain. You would not wish to disappoint Mr. Bennet with a precipitous announcement."

"No, no, I do not wish to do that." Charlotte's heart thudded as a fragile hope unfurled. She splayed a hand against her breast. "Oh, Mama, if I am to bear him a son!"

Lady Lucas nodded. A delighted smile formed on her face. "Yes, my dear, bear an heir and your future will be secure, for the Longbourn estate will remain within the Bennet family. And the Bennet sisters will have a home until they marry or for as long as an affectionate brother will allow." She reached over to give her daughter's hand a fond squeeze. "Perhaps when Eliza is informed you are to be a mother, she will be kinder. We shall hope for it, indeed."

Charlotte fervently returned her mother's comforting clasp. "Oh, I do hope you are right, Mama."

[25]

Charlotte returned to Longborn, her brain still awash with possibility and wonder. She was informed by the butler that Longbourn had a visitor. "Mrs. Philips is sitting with all of the young ladies in the upstairs parlor."

"And Mr. Bennet?"

"The master is out riding, madam."

Charlotte sighed. She wanted to be alone for happy reflection, but civility deemed she should do otherwise. She cast a glance at the casement clock, noting it was all of two in the afternoon. "I will join them when I have put off my things and tidied myself. Pray have the tea tray brought up as soon as possible, Hill, for I do not wish to delay Mrs. Philips from taking her leave. She will wish to make all her rounds this afternoon."

A quiver of suppressed amusement passed over the butler's visage. "Very good, madam."

When Charlotte entered the upstairs parlor, she exchanged curtsies with Mrs. Philips. She apologized for her tardy appearance. "I have just come back from calling at Lucas Lodge."

The lady's eyes glinted. "Oh! I do trust the Lucases are well? Such dear friends, Sir William and Lady Lucas! I quite dote on them."

"Indeed, I found all was well at Lucas Lodge, thank you for asking." Charlotte smiled, gesturing with a graceful hand. "Pray be seated again, Mrs. Philips. What brings you to Longbourn?"

At once, Mrs. Philips launched into a spate of *on-dits*; not even the entrance of Hill with the tea tray caused her to falter. She was in fine form. She had much to say about officers in the regiment and about Colonel Forster's bride. "Oh, such a *delightful* creature! She quite reminded me of you, Lydia, when you were of a more *cheerful* disposition. What a glum face you are wearing!"

"I miss Mama," responded Lydia resentfully, hunching a shoulder.

"Of course, my poor girl, it goes without saying! Kitty, you are too pale and you cough too much. A delicate consumptive habit, I daresay. A few bottles of elixirs will set you up again! Lizzy, you must send for the apothecary for poor Kitty!"

"I am not ill!" Catherine reddened and crossed her arms. "I only took in a bit of smoke from the fire! There! See, aunt, I am not coughing *now*."

Mrs. Philips paid not the least heed. She turned her sights on her hostess and bestowed upon her an insincere smile. "My dear Mrs. Bennet – why, how *strange* that sounds! Miss Lucas, that was!" The lady gave a little titter behind her fingers before she continued. "My dear Mrs. Bennet, you must have Cook give me the recipe for these delicious biscuits. I have not had them before at Longbourn. I cannot understand it, but it is true!"

"The recipe is one which I brought with me," said Charlotte quietly. "These biscuits are frequently served at Lucas Lodge."

"Indeed! You do astonish me." Mrs. Philips sipped tea from her cup before she set a smiling barb. "My sister Fanny was a very good mistress of Longbourn and her dinners were renowned. You shall have much to live up to in following in her footsteps, *dear* Mrs. Bennet."

Charlotte kept her polite expression but behind her small smile, she gritted her teeth. *Insufferable woman!*

For several minutes, Mrs. Philips waxed eloquent, regaling the small party with gossip from Meryton, while she consumed several biscuits and drank two cups of tea. "And Mr. Wickham's apparent partiality for Lizzy has subsided, his attentions are over, he is the admirer of someone else."

Lydia's drooping posture vanished, and she demanded, "Who does Wickham admire?"

"Miss Mary King! Who inherited ten thousand pounds!" Mrs. Philips nodded at the gasps of astonishment. "What think you of *that*, Lizzy?"

"My heart was but slightly touched and my vanity is satisfied with believing that I would have been his only choice, had fortune permitted it."

Mrs. Philips appeared discontented with the calm rejoinder, but she rallied, to divulge all she had heard of Mr. Wickham's claims on Mr. Darcy, and all that he had suffered from him; it was now openly acknowledged and publicly canvassed. Mrs. Philips was at one with the general consensus. "Everybody is pleased to think how much they had always disliked Mr. Darcy before they had known anything of the matter."

The lady's primary object in calling, however, was to find out what she could about her eldest niece. She questioned her sister-in-law and nieces closely and was visibly disappointed when none could tell her anything she did not already know. "How unhappy Jane was when Mr. Bingley went away! Netherfield has been closed up ever since and no one has heard if it will ever be opened again."

Charlotte and Elizabeth exchanged a swift, speaking look. Though they were at outs with one another, they were united in a mutual desire to protect Jane from idle gossip, which Mrs. Philips dealt in with excessive energy.

Mrs. Philips rattled on. "For my part, I am determined never to speak of it again to anybody. I know my sister Fanny would not want me to! I cannot find out that Jane has seen anything of him in London. My brother and sister Gardiner write nothing to the purpose."

"She was unhappy, it is true," said Charlotte in a neutral tone. "But all her good sense and her attention to the feelings of her friends must check the indulgence of those regrets."

"Well, he is a very undeserving young man – and I do not suppose there is the least chance in the world of her ever getting him now."

Mary cast a decided look of distaste at her aunt. "Jane is kind and good and her heart is tender. Everyone of sensibility must respect her privacy."

Mrs. Philips bobbed her head. "Oh, of a certainty! We all of us are agreed on *that*." She turned away from Mary's glowering disapproval to fasten her alert gaze on Elizabeth, and heaved a sigh. "Well, Lizzy, what is *your* opinion now of this sad business of Jane's? There is not talk of his coming to Netherfield again in the summer; and I have enquired of everybody who is likely to know."

Elizabeth thinned her lips, and said quietly, "I do not believe he will ever live at Netherfield."

Charlotte tilted her head, darting a sideways glance. She was attuned to Elizabeth's inflections, and she could hear the note of pessimism. *Eliza's belief in Mr. Bingley is not what it once was.* Before their falling out, Elizabeth had told her the contents of Jane's letter from Miss Bingley and what construction Jane had put upon it. It appeared Elizabeth had since come to share in Jane's gloom. Elizabeth had received letters from Jane, one of her safe arrival in Gracechurch Street, which Elizabeth had shared with the family; but the contents of the other, Elizabeth had not shared. She now wondered if it had been about the Bingleys. Her heartstrings were wrung. *Poor Jane! Mr. Bingley has indeed abandoned her.*

Mrs. Philips made a *tsking* sound. "Oh, well, it is as he chooses. Nobody wants him to come. Though I shall always say that he used my niece extremely ill, and if I was her, I would not have put up with it. Well, my comfort is, I am sure Jane will die of a broken heart, and then he will be sorry for what he has done."

Charlotte again glanced at Elizabeth. She wore a frown, her brows were furrowed, and she did not seem to take comfort from Mrs. Philips' expectation. But Elizabeth made no clever rebuttal to her aunt, as she had expected. Charlotte exerted herself. "Mrs. Philips, let me freshen your tea. Perhaps another biscuit? I *could* send for your carriage. Kitty, do pull the bell to summon a servant. We must not keep you overlong when you must have other visits."

"Oh, it is true! I do wish to make several more calls."

Thomas Bennet returned from exercising his hack. Leaving the stables, he crossed the muddy yard and entered the house from the back door, where his spaniel awaited him; it yelped happily at his entrance. Laughing, Bennet stooped to pet the gamboling dog. "There you are, my girl!" Accompanied by the spaniel, he used the servants' stairs to go up to change out of his dirtied riding clothes. Refreshed and in fresh raiment, he then made his leisurely way down the main staircase. At the bottom, the butler informed him of Mrs. Philips' visit.

"Mrs. Bennet requested tea be served a quarter hour ago, sir."

Bennet nodded his acknowledgement. *My sister Philips! No, I think not.* "A quarter of an hour? Mrs. Philips must be on the point of departure, so I will not disturb the ladies. After such a splendid ride, I will have a sherry in my library."

"Very well, sir."

Bennet walked down the hall, his faithful spaniel trundling along with him. He opened the door. On the threshold of his sanctuary, he stood stock-still. One hand was still rounded on the brass door knob. The hinge of his jaw dropped. He could scarce credit the evidence of his eyes. Several volumes of books, even whole shelves of books, were wantonly strewn over the whole of the rug. Rage ripped through him. He spun on his heels, setting up a bellow. "*Hill!* Send for Mrs. Hill! At once!" He bellowed again. *"Mrs. Hill!"*

The spaniel scurried to hide under the desk.

Moments later, the housekeeper hurried towards him. She wore an anxious face. "What is it, Mr. Bennet?"

He stepped backward to allow her space to enter the room. He flung his arm out in a grandiose gesture. "*This,* Mrs. Hill! Who has done this?"

Mrs. Hill stared around, looking appalled and bewildered. "Why, sir, I do not know." She drew in a sharp breath. "No one under my command, sir!"

"Not one of the housemaids, then?"

"Certainly not, sir."

Thomas Bennet tightened his lips. "What you are saying is that it was the fault of one or more of my daughters! Lydia, in a tantrum, most like!"

Mrs. Hill cast down her gaze. Her plump hands worked in the folds of her white apron. "I never did say that, Mr. Bennet."

"No, you did not. Not in so many words. But nevertheless, Mrs. Hill, I heard you." Bennet sighed, his rage bleeding into sudden weariness. "Go away, Mrs. Hill. I will deal with this, one way or another."

"Aye, sir." The housekeeper retreated. She closed the door behind her.

Bennet put away his precious books. The task took several minutes. As he finished, one of the replaced volumes shifted to the edge of the shelf and tumbled off it to the floor. Bennet stared fixedly at it. Another volume launched itself from the same shelf. His heart suddenly stuttered in his chest. He had the sensation of tiny hairs lifting on his arms and at the nape of his neck.

All of his life, Mr. Bennet had read extensive treatises in philosophy and religion and myth, so perhaps it was that which made his mind more elastic than most. *I cannot believe – and yet, here is the evidence of my own eyes.* "Fanny..."

Three more leather-bound books slammed out of the polished shelves in swift succession. Bennet walked around the corner of his desk and sat down in his chair. "I am most curious, Mrs. Bennet. What is it like, being dead? I suppose, given the physical evidence, you *can* wield a pen?" He offered up a trimmed quill. "I have good ink and paper at the ready if you choose to oblige me."

Of a sudden, the door opened and slammed shut. *Ah! The slamming doors!* He was pleased to discover that his youngest daughters' behavior was not as childish as he had previously assumed. *And so is explained the mishandling of my books.* "Mrs. Hill will look askance if I name the culprit."

Thomas Bennet eased his shoulders to rest back against the chair. He still experienced an increased heart rate. He curled his lips. *Of a certainty, she has engaged my attention!* The driest chuckle escaped him. "Death has not mended Fanny's poor nerves one whit."

[26]

An important event occurred. Behind the closed door of Mr. Bennet's library, Charlotte seated herself and informed her husband, with blushing cheeks, that she was with child. "I hope you are pleased, sir."

Bennet came out from behind his desk. He sat down in the adjoining chair, turning his body to face her, and took her slender hands in his, to kiss one palm and then the other. Her blush deepened at his tender salutes. He smiled at her. "Dearest Charlotte! I am pleased beyond measure."

In that moment, Bennet cared little that he had five daughters who were nearly all of marriageable age or that it could be called folly to begin a new young family. *It is why I chose her, what I hoped for.* This time, with this woman – a woman who was becoming more and more essential to his happiness – he might beget an heir for Longbourn. Of course, the child could well be another girl; but still, it would be a child of his and Charlotte's making.

A bothersome conversation rose to his mind. He felt compelled to air it. "My one regret is what I told you on our wedding night."

"What is that, sir?"

"That I would press you *only* until I got you with child." He looked closely at her face, watching her expression. "I wish I had not, for I do not believe I can give up our carnal concourse."

Her color fluctuated, deliciously so. She laughed low in her throat. "My dear husband, I do not *wish* to be bereft of your attentions."

"Well, then." Thomas Bennet stood and went to the closed door. He turned the ornate brass key and it clicked in the lock. He returned to her and drew her to her feet. Heated blood ran thick in his veins, throbbed in his groin. "Charlotte, my dearest Charlotte."

She had watched him, her face wondering. When he drew her into his arms, her expression changed to astonishment. She held him off with her flattened hands on his chest. "But-but it is middle of the day! We are not in our chambers!"

"Indeed, my lovely wife. I shall enjoy seeing your plump mounds and wondrous curves with the sunbeams dancing over your soft skin."

At his words, she flushed red. He kissed her gently, coaxingly, as his hands roamed over her. "Let down your bodice, my sweet." She undid the ribbons with trembling fingers and drew down the fabric. He palmed her warm, full breasts. "Such lovely bubbies." He sucked on one, then the other, making the dark nipples stand up like hard, round little berries.

Charlotte threw back her head, uttering a soft moan.

He knew her body well and it was not long before he heard the hitch in her breath and felt the trembling in her limbs. He turned her to face his desk. "Grasp the edges, Charlotte." He was breathing heavily. He bunched her skirt and petticoat over her hips, exposing her lovely bare bottom to his avid gaze. His lobcock rose rapidly into a thickened Roger. He undid the front of his breeches. *I am become a satyr, a libidinous fellow.* As he slid his engorged organ into her snug moist heat, she shuddered.

"Oh, *yes,* Thomas!"

It was all the encouragement he required. *I am gone mad.* But if he was, she was equally so, for she fully responded. Pleasure suffused his body as potently as in the fullness of his youth. His spending racked his bollocks. He dismounted, panting, with his heart racing; she was rosy and glistening. He held her in his arms, murmuring his approval in her ear, stroking her until she was calmed enough to go on with her daily activity. "Thus do I express my joy, dearest, sweetest wife!"

Her gray eyes were alight. A small smile curved her lips – reddened lips that were still plumped from his ardent kisses. "Have I permission to inform your daughters and my family?"

"With my very good will! Indeed, you may tell the whole of the county." He felt expansive in his pride and his recent physical satiation.

She laughed, a musical sound which delighted his ears. "I doubt, sir, I shall need to do so, for the news will fly like the wind without any further help from me!"

For several days thereafter, whenever Thomas Bennet entered his library, his glance fell at once on his desk, over which he had so vigorously tupped his wife. *Smug bastard!* The smile tugged anew at his mouth at the *frisson* of remembered pleasure. *A satisfying bout. She shuddered so winsomely as I spewed inside of her.*

The happy news of Charlotte's interesting condition was not long a secret. The Longbourn household knew of it first. Elizabeth appeared taken aback. She uttered a few disjointed words but Mary was warm in her congratulation. Lydia and Catherine were swift to run to Meryton to convey the intelligence to their aunt Philips, who bugled it to all and sundry. It was as well that Charlotte made an announcement to her own family or otherwise Lucas Lodge would have received the news as secondhand gossip.

Lady Lucas kept Charlotte with her for a good hour, making much of her eldest daughter. "I was intending to take your sister shopping. You must come with Maria and me, and we shall look for some cloth suitable for infant gowns."

"I should very much like such an outing, Mama." Charlotte said her goodbye to her father, who had come into the room a few minutes earlier and been told the news, which had engendered his hearty congratulations, before she went off with her mother to collect her sister.

Sir William at once set off on his horse and called at Longbourn. As soon as he was ushered in to his host, he sent a sly look at Mr. Bennet. "So, old friend, you make of me a grandfather.'

Bennet flushed. "Yes, I do."

Sir William seized his hand and shook it. "I am glad for it! I could not be better pleased. Let us all pray for a boy – a son and heir! Ousting Mr. Collins! A very good thing that would be!"

Thomas Bennet laughed. He firmly believed that God, in His infinite wisdom, had blessed him. *Charlotte Lucas was made for me. Sensible, passionate, dear girl that she is.*

§

The shopping expedition was such a success that plans were made to repeat it. Charlotte ordered out the carriage, and taking up Lady Lucas and her sister Maria at Lucas Lodge, she spent a second pleasant afternoon shopping in Meryton. Mrs. Philips waved to them from her window and they stopped the carriage to oblige her with a visit. Mrs. Philips was good enough to offer refreshment and she made many doting comments to the second Mrs. Bennet. Charlotte was amused. *She is all conciliation since hearing of the babe.*

As Charlotte returned to the carriage with her mother and sister, she remarked, "I had a visit from Mrs. Philips only yesterday. She quizzed me, much as she did just now, on whether there is any word of Jane. I could not satisfy her curiosity."

Lady Lucas smiled at her. "And *have* you had any word?"

"Mr. Bennet has heard from Jane and he has had a separate letter from Mr. Gardiner. Jane is still low in spirits."

"Not surprising. Poor girl, one can only feel for her."

Upon her return to Longbourn, she directed the footman to carry her packages up to her private sitting room. She had barely put off her bonnet, gloves, and spencer in her bedchamber before she was summoned to the library. She went downstairs at once. "Sir, you sent for me?"

Mr. Bennet gestured sharply. "Close the door, Charlotte."

Charlotte did so, wondering at his peremptory manner. *It is so unlike Thomas.* She fixed her gaze on him. The intemperance of his expression, the furious air radiating from his being, gave her some cause for alarm. She clasped her hands together at her waist. "Oh, what is it, my dear?"

"An express rider has come." He held crushed in one hand a closely written sheet. "My brother Gardiner has written me. You must read it for yourself!" He thrust it into her hands.

Furrowing her brows, Charlotte sat down in a wingback armchair to make herself mistress of the express. Meanwhile, he paced with his hands clasped behind his back. She knew that he watched her face, watched her features pale as comprehension broke across her expression. She jerked up her head to stare at him with horrified amazement. "Jane! And Mr. Bingley!"

"Yes! I must away to London at once. There are decisions to be made, matters to be discussed." He bit out, dripping with cold sarcasm, "I must speak with this fine, upstanding buck!"

Charlotte exclaimed, "I cannot believe it of Mr. Bingley! He is so amiable and his manners so gentlemanlike. I cannot believe we were all so mistaken in him." She rapidly scanned over the letter again. "There is some mystery here. Jane never saw Mr. Bingley in London. She would have said so in her letters or the Gardiners would themselves have mentioned it."

"Exactly so!" Bennet caught her meaning. He narrowed his eyes, saying slowly, "I am struck by your percipience. What is in your mind, Charlotte?"

"I cannot be certain. The days following the accident were so chaotic! Eliza told me before Mr. Bingley quitted Netherfield that he had come to see Jane. She saw him alone." Charlotte hesitated before adding, "Perhaps it was not the first time they lacked chaperonage."

Bennet's nostrils quivered. He slowly and forcibly expelled his lungs "My eldest daughter – my beautiful, serene, modest Jane! Engaging *in an affair?*"

"It is an outrageous notion, to be sure. Jane is so good." Charlotte anxiously watched her husband's face. Revulsion was in his expression. Yet it took bare seconds before he had adjusted to ideas so wholly foreign to him.

"It never occurred to me." He took another hasty turn, his hands tight-clasped behind him. Anger vibrated in his snapped queries. "Where did they meet? When? Did they meet clandestinely in some glade? At Netherfield when she was ill? *Here – at Longbourn?*"

He stopped in his tracks and cried, "My God! I shut myself away with my books. I left all to Fanny. And the good Lord knows, *she* was not above plotting! She would have been glad to see Jane compromised!"

Charlotte was unsurprised by his furious charge against his dead wife. Indeed, *she* would not have put it past Mrs. Bennet. However, his self-recrimination was astonishing. *He takes responsibility?!*

A vein throbbed in his temple. His voice grated on her ears. "Bingley and Jane! They *must* wed."

Charlotte said pensively, "Yes; but not from Longbourn."

He pinned her with a razor-sharp scowl. He demanded, tight-lipped, "What is this, madam?"

Charlotte steadily met his fierce glare. She had never known him to exhibit such temper. Without volition, her fingers curled in her lap. She took a long breath. "My dear sir, they cannot be wed here, not when everyone knows Mr. Bingley abandoned Jane." She shook her head. "Three Sundays to read the banns. Another month, sir!

A birth so soon after marrying! The scandal and talk will kill Jane." She caught her breath at his altered expression. *It is as though I have struck him between the eyes.*

Of a sudden, grief twisted his features. "Wise Charlotte. You have discerned all in a flash. No, you are quite right! Jane cannot return to Longbourn – ever."

The second month of the year 1812 was marked by an unusual progression of rainstorms. The excessive rain that hampered Thomas Bennet's travels suited the bleakness in his mind. All of his thoughts dwelled on the recent happenings in London; his meetings with Jane and his brother Gardiner; his rather tense interview with Charles Bingley; and finally, the dignified, subdued wedding of his eldest daughter. *Jane should have married in her own church, where she was baptized, with her sisters to attend her.* He believed the regrets and resignation would plague him for a little while yet.

The carriage jolted and jounced over deep ruts. He held tight to the roof strap to keep himself being flung from the seat. The clouds had finally broken and the sun peeped out, but such encouraging signs could do nothing to change the tenor of his reflections. He was returning somber and physically worn.

At sight of Longbourn, however, his depression lifted and he alighted from the carriage with more energy than when he had entered it for the journey home. He pressed a palm to his glad heart as he went into the house. With the footman's help, he divested himself of his drab overcoat and gave his hat and gloves to the butler. He kissed his wife, who had met him in the entry hall, and said, "It is done. They are wed by common license." He tightened his hands on her shoulders, looking down into her heavily-lashed, anxious, gray eyes "I missed you, my Charlotte."

Her beloved face lit up; a smile curled her lips. "I am happy to hear it, dear sir. Now do you go upstairs and refresh yourself. I have already asked for bath water. We shall have hot tea when you come down."

The announcement of Jane's nuptials, which he made in the drawing-room, after imbibing his tea, was startling enough to set off squawking outcries from Lydia and Catherine, and to make Mary stare. Elizabeth exclaimed, "Jane said nothing of Bingley in her letters! Oh dear sir, how could she have wed without her family in attendance?"

Bennet felt tightness in his chest. He said flatly, "I was there, Lizzy, as were her uncle and aunt Gardiner."

Elizabeth's gaze clashed with her father's and whatever was writ in his face caused her to suck in a quick, audible breath. She sprang to her feet. "I must write Jane." She swept out of the drawing-room.

Lydia's china-blue eyes were rounded. "Good Lord! I must away to Meryton. My aunt Philips must know of this! Come, Mary, make haste! We shall all go together to our aunt."

"It is cold and the ground is too wet."

"La! What is a little mud? I have stout boots"

No one tried to keep Lydia back. She rushed off, exclaiming she had to put on her bonnet and pelisse at once and the pace of her passage echoed from the stairwell, followed by that of Catherine. "Wait for me, Lydia!"

Thomas Bennet curled his lips into a grim smile. "We can expect a visit from my sister Philips ere long."

Within a very few minutes, Lydia and Catherine clattered back downstairs and set off for Meryton to relay the incredible news to their aunt Philips. Mary was more of a mind to stay and discover exactly what had precipitated the marriage. "For we *are* still in mourning."

Bennet made a pained, brief explanation. He saw he had profoundly shocked his middle daughter. *Aye, your sister is already with child, and by your lights, a fallen woman.* "Mary, you are a sensible girl, so I do not hide anything from you. Say nothing of the truth. A parent is mourned for six months, as you know. Say, therefore, an engagement already existed and a private ceremony was had as Bingley has business that will keep him gone to the north for an extended period. Our family must endeavor to spare Jane any taint of scandal."

Mary nodded, her expression grave. "I will do as I am bid, sir."

With a deep sigh, Bennet turned to his wife. "I am fatigued from my travels, my dear. I shall rest before dinner." She murmured her understanding. As he ascended the stairs and went along to his bedchamber, he hoped that she did understand; but he need not have doubted her intelligence. From a distance, he heard the beginning notes of a sonata on the pianoforte. His daughter Mary's practice of the long piece was well underway when Charlotte came to him. She welcomed him home in an intimate and most satisfying way. Then he slept the sleep of exhaustion.

Charlotte left her slumbering husband's bedchamber to pass through the sitting room that connected it to her own bedchamber, where she refreshed herself and straightened her clothing. She sat down at the dressing-table to brush out and redress her tousled hair.

Beside her reflection in the mirror, she saw a white, spectral face – black holes where the eyes should be – a black slash of screaming mouth. She clutched at her throat, terror-stricken. Charlotte twisted on the stool. But there was nothing behind her. *I am alone in the room!*

Heartbeat thundering in her ears, she turned back to the dressing-table. She watched in horror as her hairpins began lifting out of the ceramic box. The sharp metal hairpins rose, a whirling, clicking, menacing entity. Charlotte's rapid breathing rasped on the air. She was sickeningly aware, if that deadly cloud came flying at her face, she could be mutilated, even blinded.

An intuitive flare illumed her terror, and she blurted, "You left before you achieved their marriages."

The metal hairpins stalled in midair. The malignant hovering clicking swarm riveted her. *But I cannot think of it!* Her single-minded focus had to be that of saving herself. "The height of your ambition! All of your daughters wed." She flicked a glance into the mirror but could not see the horrible apparition. She felt the frigid cold, though; her clammy skin prickled with chill goose-bumps. Tiny hairs stood up at her nape and on her arms. *The ghost is here, listening.*

"I vow to do my best to see them wed." Charlotte wrapped instinctive, protective hands over her belly. "I am breeding. If I am brought to bed of a son, the entail will be broken."

The hairpins dropped, pitter-pattered pinging, scattered across her dressing-table.

Charlotte's heart raced. *It is indeed her!* She pressed her hands against her stomach. *Mrs. Bennet is appeased, for now.*

She stared at her own whitened reflection. She licked her dry lips. *Dear Lord, am I gone mad?* But she had only to cast down a horrified look at the hairpins scattered willy-nilly over the surface of her dressing-table – to know for a certainty that Longbourn had acquired a ghost.

With no greater events than these in the Longbourn family, and otherwise diversified by little beyond the walks to Meryton, sometimes dirty and sometimes cold, did January and most of February pass away.

[27]

The post had come and Bennet carried it with him into his library. He sat down at his desk and flipped through the several sealed missives. One in particular drew his attention. Bennet raised his eyebrows. He picked up a small knife to slice through the dried red wax wafer and unfolded the letter. As he read the closely written lines, he began to enjoy every period. He snorted. "Mr. Collins, you continue to amaze and amuse." Folding up the letter again, he put it into his frock coat pocket and went in search of his consort. *Charlotte will appreciate the absurdity.*

Instead of his wife, he found Elizabeth in the drawing-room. "Ah, Lizzy! I see you are reading some correspondence of your own. I did not see a letter for you in the post."

Elizabeth looked up. "A letter from Jane, from a few days ago."

Bennet nodded. He now recalled the delivery; the letter was one his daughter had not shared with anyone else. *No doubt it relates something of Jane's private affairs.* "I have received a letter from Mr. Collins, which I shall tell you of later. Have you seen Charlotte?"

"No, Papa, I have not."

"I shall leave you to it, then."

Mr. Bennet found his helpmate upstairs in her private sitting room. The chamber faced east and had good morning light, which she often took advantage of, in her sewing of tiny white garments. Her workbasket was on the table top next to her, but her hands were idle. At his entrance, she looked up. Her expression was anguished.

He was not pleased to discover his sensible wife in tears. "What is it, my dearest one?"

Charlotte hastily brushed her fingers over her eyes, averting her face. The huskiness of her voice betrayed her. "Nothing, nothing."

"I must insist, my love. Is it the babe? No? Then what has overthrown your spirits?" Bennet was alarmed. He could not recall that she had ever wept. It took several minutes, but Charlotte was finally persuaded to confide in him. She confessed how unbearable had become the broken friendship between herself and Elizabeth, and of the continued antagonism shown her by Elizabeth and his two younger daughters. It provoked him so much that he took a quick turn around the room.

His first wife would have been astonished by his agitation. Indeed, he was himself aware of the irony. *This unprecedented interest in petty squabbles!* However, he deemed his young wife's well-being to be of uppermost importance. "I *will not* have you upset. It is not good for you or the child."

"I am being-being oversensitive." Charlotte seized an embroidered handkerchief and dried her face. Straightening her wilted posture, she offered a tremulous smile. "There, now I shall do better."

He contracted his brows; his dear wife was prepared to gently push aside his concern. He pressed his lips together. *And I cannot allow it.*

"No, no, I must take steps." He focused his singular mental acuity on the perplexity, and an epiphany burst in his brain. *A ready solution is at this moment stuffed in my pocket!* "My dear Charlotte, I have hit on a worthy notion."

Bennet told his wife he had that day received correspondence from Mr. Collins. "I had been coming to tell you of it. I found it rather diverting, for he has expressed an interest in renewing his suit with Lizzy. Yes, you may well stare! As I understand it, Mr.

Collins was unable to finish reciting his reasons for marriage before the disruption caused by Mrs. Bennet's accident. He writes he is mindful of his cousin's tepid reception of his attentions during his visit to Longbourn – and here is the point! – he proposes that Lizzy, in the company of one or more of her sisters, come to visit for a few weeks at Hunsford. Then Lizzy may fairly judge for herself the several advantages of wedding him."

Charlotte had forgotten her misery. "But Eliza will never wed Mr. Collins! And you cannot want it!" she exclaimed, staring at him in mingled amazement and consternation. "No, I can see from your telling glance that you *would not* wish it. But besides that, she cannot entertain a suit while the family is still in mourning! What is Mr. Collins thinking?"

He shrugged, his careless manner illustrating what little importance he attached to it. "I hope Lizzy is too intelligent a girl to accept his suit, but maidens can be foolish. We must not jump so far ahead, Charlotte. Mr. Collins is well-aware the family is in mourning, but he hopes a visit to *so near a relation* would be seen as suitable at such a time. My heir presumptive, in fact! He has proposed a tentative date for this sojourn"

"It is an extraordinary idea!"

Bennet patted his coat pockets. "Where is that letter? I thrust it in – ah, here it is! I had thought Mr. Collins' periods might amuse you so I have it with me. Here, I shall read the rest. It is all most persuasive and rational. *The parsonage is a most sober place, I do assure you, Cousin Bennet; and there cannot be a more respectable, nor a more somber, manor than Rosings Park. My illustrious patroness, Lady Catherine de Bourgh, is herself in deep mourning for her beloved daughter and would enter with utmost sympathy into the grief of my cousins at losing their dear mother.*"

He looked up with a triumphant smile. "All unwitting, Mr. Collins provides an answer to this unpleasantness. My dear wife, we shall divide and conquer! Lizzy and Kitty shall go to Kent. Mary does not grieve you and between you and Mary, Lydia must surely become more conformable. I judge this matter to be of some urgency, so I shall write to my cousin Collins at once and accept his invitation on behalf of my daughters."

"You astonish me, dear sir." Charlotte let out a huge pent-up breath. "I fully support your plan, husband. It is *truly* a worthy notion." However, she doubted Elizabeth would readily acquiesce. *Sent away from Longbourn to entertain Mr. Collins' suit!* She believed Elizabeth would oppose it. Perhaps she would cajole her father into changing his mind.

But oh, how wonderful it could be! Eliza's trying conduct set at a distance!

Mr. Bennet crossed the room to close the door and firmly latched it. He turned to smile at her. There was a certain predatory gleam in his gray-blue eyes. "I am pleased you approve, dearest Charlotte. Dare I ask for a kiss in reward from you?"

The first time Mr. Bennet had made overtures outside the conjugal bed, in full light of day, she had been shocked and astonished. Since then, she had discovered she enjoyed these irregular bouts of daytime passion. *Indeed, since I have felt the quickening of our child, I am most enthusiastic.*

Charlotte returned her husband's smile. She undid the laces at her bosom and pulled down her bodice, exposing her plump breasts to his darkening gaze. She was plain but he made her feel beautiful. She did not know when she had become so wanton but it pleased her that she could inflame his ardor. "You may ask for much more than that, sir, if you choose to act the ladies' maid."

Bennet's expression altered, his cheeks flushing. His eyes blazed and his voice deepened. "I have learned to like the role very well."

He came to her swiftly and gathered her into the strength of his arms. Kisses, caresses, the sliding and rustle of fabric – at last, at last, he entered her, and in the fever of their coupling, Charlotte forgot the problems that had beset her.

Afterwards, when they had properly arranged their clothing again, he bent to pick up her lace-and-net cap from the floor, and handed it to her. "A pretty confection, this." He rested his hands on her shoulders, looking down at her, and said wryly, "I have mussed your hair thoroughly, dearest Charlotte."

"Never mind. I shall fix it. There is a mirror over the mantel."

Bennet bussed her soundly and with a roguish smile lingering on his face, he left her.

The reply from Mr. Collins was swift.

Thomas Bennet grimaced down at the letter that had come to his hand. He expected some objection to the scheme. Catherine and Lydia did not run after the militia officers, as they did before their mother's death, since mourning was a blight to social interaction, but there was always *hope* of seeing a redcoat. He addressed his snoozing spaniel. "I must gird up my loins! Kitty will not like leaving the militia officers behind, though we do not see them often at Longbourn. Lizzy will not be best pleased, but she will accept it with her usual cheerfulness." He sighed. "I do dislike having a rumpus kicked up. However, I daresay I will weather it well enough."

Over the game course at dinner, he announced that he was sending Elizabeth and Catherine to Hunsford, and Mr. Collins' explanation for proffering the invitation. "Quite beside that, I believe it is a fair exchange in hospitality for my cousin's visit at Longbourn last autumn. I have no doubt, daughters, that you will enjoy yourselves excessively. Sojourning in a different society and in a different part of the country than you have seen before will broaden your horizons."

Catherine's fawn-brown eyes widened. Her mouth dropped open, before she squeaked, "Oh! But...Hunsford Parsonage? A*nd Mr. Collins!*"

Lydia snickered. "Lord, Mr. Collins! What a joke on *you*, Lizzy!"

Elizabeth's expression was a sketch in horrified disbelief. "Papa, you cannot be serious!"

"On the contrary, Lizzy. Mr. Collins has made a very proper request. I expect you to conform to it, as a young unattached lady should, and give him a fair hearing. If you do accept his proposals, bear in mind that you are still in mourning and insist upon a long engagement."

Bennet's dry recommendation elicited delighted chortling from his youngest daughters. However, Elizabeth did not appear to share in their amusement, which mildly surprised him. *Lizzy is usually quick to take enjoyment in the ridiculous.* When her face remained clouded, he realized that she was seriously discomposed.

He believed he understood her outrage well enough and tendered a smile at his favorite daughter. "Come, come! Spending a few weeks in my cousin's company and experiencing the hospitality of Hunsford Parsonage will do you no harm, Lizzy. And we must not forget, you and Kitty will be presented to Lady Catherine de Bourgh at Rosings Park! A high treat, indeed, and certainly one that must not be missed."

Elizabeth glared, lifting her chin high. "This excursion is absurd, sir! I have not the least inclination to marry Mr. Collins!"

Bennet was taken aback by his daughter's vehemence. He frowned as he studied her obdurate expression. He had anticipated objections from Catherine, but had not expected that Elizabeth would set herself against his will. *I truckled to Mrs. Bennet too often. This is what comes of it! Disrespect for my wishes!* He narrowed his eyes. He had made up his mind and it was not even for *his favorite daughter* to gainsay him. He said sharply, "What you want does not signify! You will do as I bid you. I am displeased by this contrariness, Lizzy. If there was any other argument needed to persuade me that you should go, it is this truculence of yours!"

Elizabeth lowered her gaze, her features flushed. She said nothing more but her mouth was pressed into a thin line. She lifted her wineglass to her lips and took a swallow, her throat working.

Satisfied he had carried his point, Bennet returned his attention to the tender roasted venison on his plate.

The clink of cutlery on china was loud in the heavy silence. Discourse gradually resumed, becoming dominated by Lydia's talk of the red-coated militia officers and lording it over Catherine.

"I shall have them all to myself now!"

Catherine pouted, but after casting a wary glance at her father's unusually stern face, she sheltered her mouth with her hand and issued a fast whisper into her sister's ear, which set Lydia off into a paroxysm of giggles.

Charlotte had observed it all in mingled curiosity and trepidation. She was most interested in the reactions of the two sisters affected. Neither Mary nor Lydia warranted much of a glance from her since the proposed journey had nothing to do with them.

Throughout, Mary had kept silence, but her surprise at her father's dictum was evident. Of a sudden, her eyes narrowed and her gaze flickered between Charlotte and her elder sister. A small smile curled her mouth before she directed a knowing look into Charlotte's eyes.

Charlotte felt the tide of rising heat in her face.

Mary had more wit than anyone supposed, and she had obviously come to a conclusion which amused her. When they had risen from the table and removed to the drawing-room, in a private aside, Mary expressed her sentiments. "I am all admiration, Charlotte. It is masterfully done. We shall all have a measure of peace. Only consider this evening! Lizzy has pleaded a headache and gone upstairs early."

Charlotte did not pretend to misunderstand her. "I have done nothing, I assure you. It was your father's idea, not mine."

"Nevertheless, I am glad for it. Lizzy will not listen to me. She believes she is the superior in understanding." Mary shook her head and sighed. "If only Jane was here, it would be different. She could have talked sense to her." Mary patted her on the arm. Charlotte was astonished, for this sister was the least demonstrative of them all. "I am glad you have come to us, Charlotte. I will try not to distress my father or upset you in any way."

Charlotte had taken for granted Elizabeth's strong opposition to the scheme. However, what she did not expect was that Elizabeth would come to her, on the following morning, and demand that she intercede on her behalf.

"I have spoken to my father, but he is adamant. I have reasoned with him, but no argument of mine can move him!" Elizabeth closed her eyes for an instant; it appeared to gall her that she felt impelled to make an appeal to her step-mother. Achieving an air of calm, she said, "You must talk to him, Charlotte. He might lend an ear to your counsel."

Charlotte shook her head, a little incredulous. After all of the coldness and incivility and barbed remarks, Elizabeth thought to come to her for succor! It said much about Elizabeth's frame of mind that she would appeal on the grounds of their friendship, however damaged it had become. As much as Charlotte longed to rebuild that dear friendship, she would not put their fragmented relationship before the wishes of her husband. "You have always been my friend, Eliza, but now my first loyalty must be to my husband."

"*Who is my father!*" exclaimed Elizabeth. She drew in a long breath and tightened her lips, attempting to maintain her composure. "When the letter from Mr. Collins came, Papa was looking for *you*, Charlotte. So I *know* he discussed this stupid notion with you. Tell me the truth! Did you influence him to accede to Mr. Collins' suggestion?"

"No, I did not."

"I do not believe you!"

"Your resentment clouds your judgment, Eliza."

Twin flags of color mounted into Elizabeth's cheeks. Her anger erupted. "How *could* you wed him, Charlotte? I thought I knew you! You were like a sister to me! Your arts and allurements may, in a moment of infatuation, have drawn him in. Of a certainty, you did not love him! And he does not love you. He told me so!"

"This is no way to recommend yourself to me!" Charlotte realized Elizabeth had never understood her reasons for marrying. Perhaps she *had* understood but had rejected such common sense as unworthy. Her prejudice against the marriage was as strong as ever.

Arts and allurements! Oh, Eliza! How you wrong me!

As for the hurtful words just hurled at her...*I know he does not truly, truly love me. Ours is a marriage of convenience. But oh, how I wish he did.*

Charlotte was struggling to keep her emotions in check, while her stomach churned. She lifted her chin. "Mr. Bennet is well-satisfied in his choice, as I am in mine."

"An heir for Longbourn! Yes, it would be a fine thing!" Elizabeth's dark eyes flashed. "I have found the library door to be locked during the day. I have heard you and my father, through the wall at night. Making-making *rutting* noises like-like farm animals!"

The look of disgust on Elizabeth's face sickened her, shamed her. It also angered her. *I have nothing to be ashamed of.*

Charlotte leaped to her feet. She cried, "I am not used to such language as this!"

Elizabeth backed a step. A somewhat conscious look fleeted across her face. "I should not have..."

Charlotte threw up her hand. Her voice shook, from anger or tears, she did not know. "You can *now* have nothing farther to say. Let me be rightly understood! We shall not speak of this, Eliza –

ever! Nor shall we speak again of your leaving Longbourn. *I am not against it!* Indeed, I count the hours!"

The two women avoided one another, as much as it was possible in a small household. Tension thickened the atmosphere, affecting almost all at Longbourn, and the only relief was when Elizabeth absented herself with frequent and long rambles in the countryside.

After Bennet had written to Mr. Collins, accepting the proposed date for the visit, the journey had been arranged easily enough. Sir William Lucas had business in Kent and he was taking his daughter Maria with him. When he offered a seat in his carriage to the Bennet sisters, Thomas Bennet accepted the kindness. "It could not be better. My mind will be relieved of any anxiety with your protection, Sir William."

On the day of departure, while the Bennet trunks were corded onto the carriage, Sir William and Maria came inside, into the warmth of the front parlor where they were received cordially. Charlotte stretched out her hands in welcome. "Papa!"

Sir William took her hands and bent forward to kiss her cheek. He looked intently into her face. "Well, well, Charlotte. You are looking pale. I trust you are well?"

"I am well enough, Papa." Charlotte smiled and disengaged her hands to turn to her sister. "Maria! Promise you will write to me."

Maria was fairly vibrating in her excitement. Her bright eyes and her wide smile showed her delight. She hugged Charlotte. "Oh! I do promise! Such an adventure! I have never been beyond Meryton in my life!"

Lydia tossed her head in much her old manner. "I am glad *I* am not going to stuffy Hunsford!"

"You are simply envious, Lydia." Mary looked at her sister with a knowing expression. "Kitty is doing something that does not include you."

Lydia tossed her head again, but for once had not a pert word to say. Catherine was teary-eyed, but at Mary's observation she looked surprised and even a little pleased.

After goodbyes were said, Bennet escorted the departing party to the carriage, conversing amiably with Sir William. Charlotte did not go outside to see the party off. She had spoken a few kind words to Catherine, but she and Elizabeth had not exchanged farewells.

"Well! I am glad I am not going." Lydia tossed her head and flounced out of the front parlor.

Despite the fire crackling in the fireplace, an eddy of cold air caused Charlotte to shiver. *Leave me be, Mrs. Bennet!* Pulling her long shawl closer about herself and standing at the front window, with Mary standing beside her, she watched the two sisters stepping up into the Lucas carriage. Sir William followed them in, the carriage swaying as he entered it. Mr. Bennet himself folded the iron step and shut the carriage door. Through the glass panes Charlotte heard the driver's command. "Hie up!" She saw the horses jerk in their traces and then the carriage rolled away. Charlotte's heart ached. She turned from the window. *I do not know if Eliza and I can ever resolve our differences.*

Mary touched her arm. Charlotte turned her head and saw that she wore a sympathetic expression. "I am sorry about Lizzy. Pray excuse me, Charlotte. I have a new pianoforte piece to practice."

Charlotte nodded. "Certainly, Mary."

As Mary exited the parlor, she heard the front door being closed, and a brief exchange between father and daughter. She heard quick, firm boot steps. Bennet appeared in the open doorway and crossed the threshold into the room where she stood. He smiled across at her. "It is done, my dear."

With a great sigh, Charlotte walked into the warmth of his embrace.

In the following days, a welcome tranquility descended upon the house and its remaining inhabitants. Thomas Bennet was conscious of it, and it grieved him that Elizabeth had become such a contentious agent that he welcomed her absence. He had never felt such a way before about her. Elizabeth had always been one with whom he could share his amusement over the ridiculous, and rely on for her cheerfulness. He greatly missed the daughter he remembered. He hoped her former nature would reanimate in her.

He bent to pat his spaniel, confiding into its upraised, uncritical, silky ears. "I love her, but I do not much like the obstinate, unkind female she has become in these past months."

[28]

Charlotte received a thick post from her sister. She took it into her private sitting room and sat down immediately to break the wafer. Since they had left over a week prior, she had not heard from Maria or her father and she was anxious to have news of them. As she read the lively narrative of all that happened since her sister's arrival in Hunsford, her lips curved. "Oh, Maria, you do not disappoint!"

Charlotte chuckled over certain passages, rereading them and marveling again at their content. Despite their painful estrangement, of particular interest to her were her sister's remarks about Elizabeth Bennet.

"Eliza spends much time rambling out of doors, just as she did at home. She speaks with enthusiasm of the delightful walks of Rosings Park...

"Of us all, only Eliza is not betrayed into nervousness in Lady Catherine's presence...

"Eliza's air was so composed! She answered all of Lady Catherine's penetrating questions with such self-possession, until Lady Catherine exclaimed, "Upon my word, you give your opinion very decidedly for so young a person."

Charlotte folded up the sheets into the original square and tucked it into her beaded reticule. She put on her bonnet and fur-edged pelisse, with over it a woolen cape, and collected her gloves and muff. Leaving word with a servant that she was going out, she sallied forth to Lucas Lodge, where she expected to spend a leisurely half-hour or so with her mother.

Lady Lucas was very ready to receive her and kissed her on her cheek. "Charlotte, my dearest! Come, sit down. I shall ring for tea. Then we shall have a long visit, for I wish to hear how you go on."

Charlotte sat down beside her mother, making herself comfortable. She had already given cape and muff to the footman belowstairs and now unbuttoned the top of her pelisse. She pulled off her tan kid gloves, laying them in her lap. "I go on very well, Mama. The conflict that was so upsetting to me is gone. I hope that when Eliza and Kitty return, all will be different after the period apart from us at Longbourn."

"Mrs. Long was here only a day or two ago, wanting to know if I had heard anything from Sir William and Maria. I have heard little enough. Your papa is not one to pen volumes of letters. But Mr. Bennet must have heard from Eliza! Surely *Eliza* is a good correspondent."

Charlotte shook her head, smiling a little. *The hurt is akin to a pricking thorn lodged in my flesh.* "No, Mama, she has not written her father. Nor did I expect Eliza to write to me." Opening the strings of her reticule, she took out her sister's correspondence. "But Maria has written! She sends her love to all and asks that her letter be shown to you."

Lady Lucas leaned over to nip the folded square from her daughter's hand and at once unfolded the creased sheets. "I do thank you, Charlotte!" She made herself mistress of the contents before giving back the letter. "Well! I must say, Lady Catherine de Bourgh sounds to be a formidable lady. She has quite overawed your sister."

"Indeed, Mama! I gathered Papa felt somewhat out of his depth, too."

Lady Lucas nodded her agreement. "Though Sir William has been presented at St. James, he is not accustomed to the nobility. It will be to Maria's advantage to have a glimpse of higher society. She is not yet out much in company, and the experience will show her how best to go on. From Maria's letter, I took particular note that Kitty did not exhibit herself in Lady Catherine's presence."

"Yes, very unlike Kitty to be so subdued!"

"Perhaps this visit will serve to tame her company manners."

"I do hope so, ma'am." Charlotte sighed and raised her shoulders in a small shrug. "My unhappy reflection has been that once Kitty returns to Longbourn, she will be swayed again by Lydia's stronger disposition, and they will go on with as little sense as before. Truly, it is worrisome! They are still in mourning and those conventions *must not* be contravened."

"Those girls are sad romps, it is true. Wanton women are often called gigglers, and by their indulging in such unrestrained merriment, a stranger might mistake them for such. It is fortunate everyone in Meryton knows them and overlooks their behavior."

"Mama!" Charlotte was awash with consternation. *I never knew this was in her mind. She has not divulged such reservations of the Bennets before.* A horrid surmise presented itself to her mind; and she suddenly wondered, with not a little dismay, what some others might believe about Lydia and Catherine.

Careless girls!

"Yes, my dear, I *do* know how shocking it sounds. Mrs. Bennet was foolish and far too indulgent in permitting them to enter society so young. Lydia and Kitty's reputations remain intact solely due to respect for the Bennet name." Lady Lucas snorted. "I shall not air my opinion of Mr. Bennet's abdication from responsibility, for it does no good, and must wound you." Lady Lucas voiced a measure of her displeasure. "Although, his youngest daughters are now become a rather tiresome embarrassment to *our* family, since we are now related to the Bennets."

Charlotte flushed, heat infusing the whole of her face and neck. She was greatly embarrassed that her family was exposed to censure through her marriage. She said earnestly, "Mama, you know I will do all in my power to cure their worst faults. Indeed, Mary and I are in accord to work with Lydia on her deportment as much as we can before Kitty returns."

Lady Lucas laughed. "You may *try*, my dear girl. Lydia and Kitty are set in their ways, so I doubt you will have much success. No, I say expend your energies rather on your household and your child. You will be happier. That is my advice."

A soft-footed servant brought in the laden tea tray, exiting as silent as upon entering. Lady Lucas poured the tea. "I was rather astonished by one of Maria's tidbits...that Eliza was sent to Hunsford to hear Mr. Collins' proposals." She handed a cup and saucer to her daughter. "What is that about, pray?"

Charlotte was glad to turn topic. She was greatly disturbed by her mother's chilling opinion of the younger Bennet girls. *Is it true? Wanton gigglers! The militia officers...* She shook off the unpleasant abstraction. "Well, Mama, it is rather amusing. On the very morning of Mrs. Bennet's fatal accident, Mr. Collins was declaring his intentions to Eliza. But he was quite ignored in all the confusion, and he wishes to renew his addresses. Mr. Bennet has agreed that his cousin should be given the opportunity."

Lady Lucas stared at her, her mouth slightly agape.

Charlotte gurgled laughter. "Oh, Mama, *such* a droll expression!"

Lady Lucas regained her equilibrium. "My dear! Does Mr. Bennet *expect* Eliza to accept Mr. Collins?"

Charlotte shook her head. "Oh no, not at all! However, he decided the invitation was a fortunate one, since it would absent Eliza and Kitty for some weeks." She sipped tea, before adding, "It is much more...tranquil at Longbourn, even though Lydia remains."

"Ah, I comprehend you! And Eliza is such a favored one." Lady Lucas smiled, appearing pleased. "Well! That Mr. Bennet should be moved to such effort at all! It is a compliment to you, Charlotte."

Charlotte agreed with considerable satisfaction. "Yes, Mama, I do believe it is." *He may not love me in a romantic sense, but he does hold me dear.*

"I have some news also. Your cousin Augusta will be returning to us. Mrs. Suckling has suffered a constitutional crises and Mr. Suckling begged me in his letter to offer the shelter of my roof to his sister-in-law. The gentleman sounded quite desperate, poor man."

For a moment, Charlotte could only stare. "You astonish me."

Lady Lucas gave a rueful chuckle. "I astonish myself. But I feel for the Sucklings, Charlotte. It cannot be easy to deal with Augusta's excessive personality when they are just become parents."

Charlotte's emotion got the better of her. She declared her opinion. "The best thing for everyone would be for Augusta to be brought out and married off to some unsuspecting gentleman!" She gave it a second's more consideration. "And preferably one who rules the roost with a rod of iron!"

Lady Lucas laughed and agreed to it.

The conversation devolved into more general subjects that were of interest to each of them. Lady Lucas gave her some good advice on caring for herself as her belly ripened and what she could expect with the laying-in. Since her marriage, Charlotte felt her relationship with her mother had deepened and grown easier. Certainly, she left considerably cheered by the hour she spent in Lady Lucas' company.

The confidences exchanged with her mother had made her burdens seem lighter than she had thought possible, as though all of her worries and concerns had evaporated.

Except for my fear of Mrs. Bennet's ghost.

But that was one thing that she would not confide in anyone.

§

Elizabeth had already been at Hunsford for above two weeks when a letter, addressed to Mr. Bennet, came in the post. He was glad to receive it; he had been troubled that they had parted with discord, and he hoped his favorite daughter had gotten over her anger with him. *Perhaps her correspondence will be illuminating.* Regardless, it was the first letter he had received from her, so it was of utmost interest, and he broke the red wafer without delay. As he read the single sheet, a wide grin split his face; there were no reproaches to be found here, only amusement.

Friday, 20 March
Hunsford, Kent

"Dear, dear sir,

As you bid me, and though most reluctant to do so, I have allowed Mr. Collins to address me. I have rejected his several proposals. But the gentleman has shown a marked disinclination to accept my repeated refusals. He believes me to be merely modest, and must soon succumb to the inducements of the fine aspect of Hunsford Parsonage and making up a fourth at Lady de Bourgh's quadrille table.

I beg of you to disabuse his mind of its present self-deception.

Your obedient, loving daughter,

E. Bennet"

"Such excellent inducements, indeed! An intelligent young lady could not bear to refuse them!" Bennet chuckled, relishing the satirical tone of Elizabeth's letter. He had missed her wit, which aligned so closely to his own. Though he was often a negligent correspondent, he was entertained enough to do as his daughter bid him, and as he also wished to spare her further importuning from her foolish suitor, with remarkable alacrity, he penned a letter to his cousin, Mr. Collins.

Thursday, 26 March
Longbourn, Hertfordshire

"Mr. Collins,

I am in receipt of a letter from my daughter Elizabeth. Her report of the flattering proposals which you have made to her is of natural interest to me. I must, however, withhold my consent for my daughter to accept such honor as you would bestow upon her. Chalk it up to the caprice of a father not willing to part from a beloved daughter.

Yours, etc., etc.

Thomas Bennet

[29]

Sir William Lucas, having concluded all his business in Kent, had returned to the bosom of his family, to a delighted and joyous reunion with his wife and several children. He assured Lady Lucas of their daughter Maria's well-being and comfort when he had left Hunsford in mid-March. He accepted the advent of Lady Lucas' niece, Miss Augusta Hawkins, back into his household and greeted the officious young lady with determined civility. He asked whether the new governess, Miss Simmons, was going on well with her charges and was pleased to hear his lady's good report. Then he turned his attention to matters beyond Lucas Lodge. Sir William called at Longbourn, where he received a glad and affectionate welcome from his eldest daughter, and from his son-in-law, warm affability.

The gentlemen shook hands, exchanging the easy banter developed between friends. "Ah, Charlotte!" Sir William bussed his daughter soundly on the cheek. She laughed and drew him over to a chair beside hers.

For a half-hour, Sir William played his part in a cordial conversation, sitting with Charlotte and the other two ladies of the household. At length, Thomas Bennet invited him into his library with the offer of a good brandy and Sir William was amenable. After the gentlemen had seated themselves, with wineglasses in hand, Sir William remarked, "Charlotte looks well. I was a little concerned for her at the time I went away, near a month ago. She was wan and cast down in her demeanor." He cleared his throat. "She was feeling the effects of her condition, I expect."

Bennet inclined his head in agreement. He believed he was astute enough, however, to recognize that Sir William was fishing and that more should be said. "I conjecture you heard something of the many incivilities inflicted by her step-daughters. Not by Jane or Mary, but the others."

Sir William shifted in his chair. "It is solely my concern for Charlotte which motivates me to inquire. I shall not level censure at any member of your household. I hope you understand that, Thomas."

"You do not trespass, Sir William. An explanation is owed to ease your concern." Bennet sighed, shaking his head. "I fear this all took its toll on Charlotte's spirits. In particular, Lizzy's unkindness was hard for her to bear; the rejection was so very grievous to her. My concern for Charlotte's welfare was such that I divided my household." He slowly swirled the dark amber brandy in his glass. "It did not occur to me that my daughters would feel resentful of any lady whom I thought to wed."

Sir William made a commiserating sound deep in his throat before offering an apologetic explanation. "Charlotte is not one to complain. Lady Lucas pried it out of her."

"I believe it will all come right, in time." Bennet, raising a faint smile, deliberately closed the subject. "But tell me of your visit to Kent! What were your impressions of Hunsford Parsonage and Rosings Park and my cousin's grand patroness, Lady Catherine de Bourgh?"

"I confess, Lady Catherine is a very impressive lady! My first sighting of her was in a crested brougham stopped at the garden gate. Mr. Collins stood at the gate in conversation with the great lady, and I was stationed in the parsonage doorway." Sir William mournfully shook his head. "I felt compelled to bow whenever Lady Catherine looked my way!"

Bennet cracked a genuine smile. "I can imagine the scene!"

Sir William chuckled and lifted his hand in a staying gesture. "But *that* was as nothing to our first visit to Rosings Park! Mr. Collins was careful to instruct us in what we were to expect, that the sight of such grand rooms, so many servants, and so splendid a dinner might not wholly overpower us. We followed the liveried servants through an antechamber, to the room where Lady Catherine was seated, and a gentleman stood beside her ladyship's chair, as though he was a courtier attending a queen. A faded creature in genteel clothing was also present, serving as lady-in-waiting. Her ladyship, with great condescension, arose to receive us, as though we were ambassadors from foreign parts. Mr. Collins performed the office of introduction. I made a very low bow and took my seat *without saying a word.*"

Bennet laughed heartily, highly entertained by Sir William's self-deprecating account. "And yet *you* have been presented at St. James!"

"I was in a veritable quake then, too, I assure you!"

"But who were the gentleman and the lady?"

Sir William waved his hand in dismissal. "A widowed son-in-law; he was an affable fellow. The lady was some sort of companion." He set aside the wine glass, a residue of brandy in the bottom. All joviality faded from his expression. "Now, Thomas, I must tell you that when I returned, Lady Lucas handed me a London newspaper, folded open to a certain wedding announcement. I must say, it surprised me very much to read it. She told me there was not a peep of gossip preceding the event. Indeed, not even Mrs. Philips hinted at a thing! It is rather remarkable, when I think on it."

Bennet gave a snort. He was neither surprised, nor offended, by Sir William's query; his concerns were inextricably linked with

Lucas Lodge now through marriage. However, he *was* offended by the flapping loose lips of such ilk as his sister-in-law Philips, inflicting untold misery. *Poor Jane! Subjected still to vulgar wagging tongues! It is very well she is not here.*

The cold curl of his lips conveyed his contempt for gossipmongers. "The gossips are putting in all their oars now, are they? After all the talk of Jane's abandonment, I do not doubt that Charles Bingley marrying her *was* a wonderment to everyone in the county!"

"But how did it all come about, sir?"

I do not wish to lie to my old friend.

"Ah, the nuptials." Bennet's mind raced, weighing the information he would share and what he chose to hold back. *He will confide in his good wife. She will gossip to others.* He rubbed his thumb over the rim of the wineglass, weighing how the words sounded before he uttered them. "They met again in London and their affections were reanimated; but theirs was a private betrothal, in deference to our family's mourning."

I will see her no more at Longbourn, at least until the child is of good size

He looked up again and shrugged. "Despite the conventions, I was persuaded to give my blessing for marriage, as pressing business will remove Bingley from our sphere for some time. They were wed from my brother Gardiner's house."

"Jane is of age, of course."

"Yes; Jane is of age and may do as she likes."

Sir William's shrewd blue eyes surveyed his friend and son-in-law. "Come, Bennet! I perceive something hidden beneath your explanation."

Bennet felt his body stiffen, yet he controlled his face, preserving his bland expression. *Blast Sir William's percipience!* He cocked a brow. "I do not know what you mean." He sipped slowly of his brandy, thus rendering himself silent, and waited for Sir William to continue, which he knew that voluble gentleman would.

Sir William lowered his bushy brows. Without roundabout, he said, "I suspect you are not best pleased by this match, Bennet. Why, you have just stopped short of admitting as much! *Jane may do as she likes!* Indeed! Has your good opinion of Bingley changed? My good fellow, you may tell me with the utmost confidence, you know."

Bennet hesitated, being acutely aware of Sir William's steady regard, knowing that he must make some reply. *The lie encapsulated in the truth.* Setting down his wineglass, a simple action to give himself another second to organize careful words, he shrugged and settled back in the chair. He fiddled with his gold watch fob. "My Jane was taken from me too soon. She was to return home, but now I do not know when I shall see her again, and I am resentful. Jane and Bingley will not be settling at Netherfield. Indeed, I do not think it is decided yet where they will set up household."

"Ah! I see it clear. Indeed, indeed! In these several months, what sea changes have occurred for Longbourn. And more yet to come, I doubt not." Sir William shook his head, heaving a gusty sigh. "Jane will naturally be missed. She is such a dear, kind girl. I am glad her happiness is assured."

Bennet lifted his shoulders in another studied shrug. He dropped his watch fob. "I trust it is so, indeed. More brandy, Sir William? I must tell you of a recent letter, received from an old friend in Edinburgh. Snow a foot deep fell, followed by drifting in a northeast gale the 21st to the 23rd."

A few days later, Charlotte received another lengthy letter from her sister, the contents of which she summarized for Mr. Bennet while sitting in his library. She doubted Maria's flowing pen would regale him as much as it had her. However, this letter did contain some observations she believed were of particular interest, and which she would come to before ere long.

"The entertainment of dining at Rosings is repeated about twice a week, and there being only one card table in the evening, every such entertainment is the counterpart of the first. Now and then, they are honored with a call from her ladyship. Maria says their other engagements are few, as the style of living of the neighborhood in general is beyond Mr. Collins' reach."

Bennet shook his head. "Lizzy would not have been happy in such a limited sphere. Surely, even one as foolish as Mr. Collins must discern that! I do not know what the man was about, to set his sights on Lizzy!"

"Indeed, sir, but listen to this. Maria reports that Mr. Darcy did come to Rosings Park to visit his aunt, Lady Catherine de Bourgh. He was seen at church; and on Easter Sunday, and those at Hunsford spent the evening at Rosings. The next day, Mr. Darcy called at the parsonage."

"A simple courtesy, surely." Bennet looked pensive, before saying with a wry twist of his lips, "I trust Lizzy received Mr. Darcy's civilities in a proper spirit. He did insult Lizzy at the Meryton assembly. Though she joked about it often and often, I suspect that she was made resentful.'

"I believe her sensibilities were wounded, and to such a degree that she would not wish anyone to guess." Charlotte shook her head. "Indeed, at the Netherfield ball, I found it puzzling that she placed such emphasis on having his good opinion. She dreaded his censure and that of Mr. Bingley's sisters."

"Perhaps she believed that it might influence Bingley's regard for her own sister. As perhaps it did, since the whole party left Netherfield the next morning."

She regarded him in astonishment. "Do you believe it to be so?"

As he looked at her, his eyes crinkled at the corners with his sudden smile. "I must say, I do approve of your toilette this morning. That is a very fetching cap."

Charlotte was wearing a new French foundling cap of alternate stripes of lace and white satin, ornamented with ribbons and flowers, with her morning dress. She put up her fingers to touch the confection, very pleased by his notice. A glow warmed her. "I am glad you like it."

Some volumes flew off of the bookshelf, clapping hard on the carpet. Charlotte jumped in her seat and pressed a hand to her breast.

Bennet gave a dismissive wave. "Do not heed it, Charlotte. It is only Fanny's way of making her presence known."

"Mrs. Bennet?" Charlotte stared at him. "Oh, have *you* seen her, sir?"

His gaze arrested, Bennet returned her stare. He raised his brows. "I have not seen her, no, but you must tell me of your experience. She appeared to you?"

Charlotte eloquently shuddered. "As an apparition in my mirror! And she lifted my hairpins out of the box. She-she has unfinished business, Thomas, the marriages of her daughters."

Bennet showed his teeth in a malicious grin. "Mrs. Bennet's boastings of catching Bingley for Jane was certainly abhorrent to Mr. Darcy and Bingley's sisters. No doubt they kept him from returning to Netherfield." The library door abruptly opened, and slammed shut. Bennet chuckled. "We are alone, my dear."

Charlotte regarded him in some consternation. "You do not seem particularly exercised by the fact that your dead wife haunts us!"

"I am exercised by the metaphysical. I have been trying to persuade her to write of her experiences on the other plane of existence."

Charlotte spluttered a laugh. "Sir! You are joking me!"

"She can throw a book and slam a door. Surely she can lift a pen! Her temper is the same. She was certainly upset when I mentioned how her bad behavior harmed Jane's chances with Bingley." Bennet smiled again, a twist to his lips. "Bingley's sisters were such peacocks. I wonder, how have those prideful ladies dealt with Jane and Bingley's marriage?"

Charlotte quite forgot about the ghost in her concern for the living. "Jane does not write as she should. I suppose it is too much to expect of her, or for her to reveal anything to the point. I should like to hear how the Bingleys are getting on." *It was a blessing that Mr. Darcy offered his hospitality.*

Bennet replied sharply, "Jane pens her milky sentiments. Depend upon it, she is placid enough in her dealings with her new sisters."

Charlotte was surprised by his acerbity. "My goodness, sir! Your sentiment is alarmingly choleric. I am persuaded you cannot be angered at Jane so much as your tone implies."

He shrugged away his pique, fleeting as it was. "I am sorrowed for Jane – it is Bingley who has incurred my bitter temper. As for Mr. Darcy, I did not take him in dislike as did most of our neighbors. He is reserved and proud, but I observed that his manners were in general good. Certainly, he has acted the gentleman in throwing open the doors of Pemberley to the Bingleys!"

Charlotte was reminded of the point she wished to make. "About Mr. Darcy...Maria writes that Mr. Darcy and his cousin, Colonel Fitzwilliam, have visited the parsonage several times." She tapped a forefinger against the pertinent line on the closely-written sheet. "And Eliza has said to my sister that she *often chances to meet Mr. Darcy* on her walks."

Charlotte examined her husband's handsome face. She found little in his aquiline features to hint at his thoughts. She pressed him. "I find this last to be most remarkable, do you not? Maria would not have written about these encounters unless they were taking place often enough to be remarked upon by others."

Bennet quirked a brow in a sardonic expression. "They chance to meet often? Lizzy and Mr. Darcy? Without anyone else about or a chaperone accompanying them – scandalous! Enough to start tongues wagging."

Charlotte nodded, satisfied that he had at last grasped what she wanted to convey. "Just so, sir."

Bennet closely regarded his wife. A quizzical gleam was in his eyes. "Are you concerned for Lizzy's virtue?"

"No! Of course not," exclaimed Charlotte, taken aback. "Such a thing never entered my mind." As she stared at him, absorbing his meditative expression, her amazement grew. "Surely, *you* do not believe it possible?"

Bennet grimaced. "I own, after Jane's discomposing lapse, I regard these things with a more jaundiced eye." He shook his head. "However, I trust both Lizzy and Mr. Darcy enough to believe that there is nothing of impropriety between them. But you are right, it is curious, indeed."

"Yes, so I thought." Charlotte had sometimes toyed with the notion Elizabeth was not so set against Mr. Darcy as she had claimed. *Eliza had a peculiar dread of his bad opinion of her family at the Netherfield ball. Though she was vehement in spurning my teasing, I still wonder.*

She chose to reveal something of her private speculations to her husband's examination. She had a high regard for his penetrative understanding. "Perhaps it is not Mr. Collins, but rather, Mr. Darcy who will win Eliza's regard."

"Oh, I should not think so. Has not Lizzy always hated the man?"

[30]

At Longbourn, Catherine's absence was not keenly felt in the family circle. Indeed, she was scarcely missed. She had been little more than Lydia's shadow, a parrot of her younger sister. She was not a prolific correspondent, and on the whole, confined her few letters to her sisters. Mary was faithful to relate anything of note to everyone else.

"Kitty writes that Lizzy is in a strange mood, very unlike herself, and suffers from some affliction of the spirit. Mr. Darcy is going away from Rosings Park."

But Lydia was not much interested in Catherine's news and tossed aside her own letters after reading them. "Hunsford Parsonage! Rosings Park! So boring and stuffy! I do feel for Kitty, stuck in Kent, away from all the officers!"

Such hasty remarks delivered by Lydia indicated she was fast regaining her spirits. Despite being in mourning, and for the most part retired from society, Lydia had formed a friendship with Colonel Forster's young wife, who was seventeen years old and possessed a similar ebullience in personality. They had met at Sunday services, and passed swiftly from being mere acquaintances to fast friends.

In private, Mary pointed out the obvious. "Mrs. Forster has replaced Kitty in Lydia's affections."

"Yes, and it concerns me." Charlotte furrowed her brows over her uneasy reflections. She let her hands, and the tiny garment she was embroidering, fall to her lap. "Lydia is not likely to lend an ear to *us* when there is much more entertaining conversation to be had with a high-spirited girl, no matter that she is married!"

"In a bare month, my sisters and I shall come out of mourning. Lydia and I will be able to make calls and attend entertainments. We will naturally see more of the officers then." Mary made a face. "Lydia is already wild to get back into society. She will be traipsing off to Meryton as many times as she is able, to visit my aunt Philips, to hear all the gossip, and run after the officers."

"Thank you, Mary. You have quite put me to the shudder!" Charlotte jerked the hand hidden under her handiwork. "Ouch – now look at what you have made me do! I have stuck my finger with the needle!"

Mary laughed, her face lighting up. "Oh, my dearest Charlotte! How did I not guess before that we would become such good friends?"

Charlotte regarded her with genuine affection. "We have become friends *and sisters*. I feel the richer for it."

Mary flushed red to the roots of her hair. She murmured inaudibly and hurried away, her ankle-length black bombazine skirts rustling. Charlotte smiled after her, feeling the balm to her spirit that only a close friendship could apply. *I have lost Eliza but I have gained Mary.*

Thomas Bennet received a most astonishing letter and told of it over the midday meal. "The author is one whom I have never heard from before in my life. Mr. Collins' great patronage, Lady Catherine de Bourgh!"

At the amazed exclamations of his wife and two daughters, he gave assurances that it was true. "Her ladyship writes that with the going away of her nephew, Mr. Fitzwilliam Darcy, and the approaching leave-taking of the Hunsford party, she feels a young companion to be indispensable. Lady Catherine requests permission for Kitty to remain for a few more months – indeed, through the whole of the summer – at Rosings Park! My word, our Kitty must have been uncommonly pretty in her manners to have earned such a grand lady's approval."

The original plan had been for Elizabeth, Catherine, and Maria Lucas to leave Hunsford Parsonage, after a visit of six weeks, and journey to Mr. Gardiner's house in London, where they were to remain a few days. Jane was to have been there. Then the young ladies would set out together from Gracechurch Street and be met by Mr. Bennet's carriage at an appointed inn. Of course, now that Jane was married, she would not make one of the party.

At the news conveyed by Mr. Bennet, Charlotte and Mary exchanged a startled glance, but Lydia merely shrugged. "Lord! What a joke on Kitty! I would not be in her shoes for all the world."

She flounced out of the breakfast parlor with a want of courtesy that caused her father to tighten his lips. *Lydia displays a lack of breeding in her manners!* Since he had begun spending a larger amount of time in company with his new wife and his daughters, such observations had become more common to him. His irritation with his youngest daughter smoldered. *If I knew of a place to send Lydia...a convent, perhaps!*

A soft-voiced query cut short his irritable reflections.

"Will you give your permission, sir?"

Thomas Bennet angled his head toward his sweet lady wife. "Of a certainty! I shall send a swift reply to her ladyship. Our Kitty will come to no harm in such a great house. Indeed, I have every expectation that she will return to us greatly improved."

"I hope it will be just as you say, sir." Charlotte glanced toward the doorway through which Lydia had disappeared. She gave an audible sigh.

He smiled at his wife. "In any event, it will spare *you*, my dear, her crochets and the shrill, incessant squabbles between her and Lydia. I am of the same mind as ever. I shall have peace in Longbourn."

He made his way to his library, his faithful spaniel trundling at his boot heels. It was an unusually cold April, and he was glad of the roaring fire in the fireplace that warmed the room. *The cold ground will have a severe effect on the germination of the spring crops. I pray the warmth of the sun returns.*

Sitting down at his desk, he penned a short note.

"Monday, 13 April
Longbourn, Hertfordshire

Lady Catherine de Bourgh,

"I am much obliged to your ladyship for your kind invitation. When one has five daughters, they are never of so much consequence to a father. My daughter Catherine was to be in Kent only six weeks; however, there can be no occasion for her going home so soon when she is the object of such an honor. Mrs. Bennet can certainly spare her.

Yours in cordiality,
Mr. Thomas Bennet"

Sanding the page, he folded the sheet into a square and sealed it with a wax wafer. He lent back in his chair and stared through the tall windows, not seeing; rather, he reflected on the changes that had come to Longbourn. *Such upheavals after the Netherfield ball.* He touched the black satin mourning band stitched on his coat sleeve.

"Fanny has not been gone a year yet," he murmured, marveling at it.

The noise of a book hitting the floor behind him did not make him turn in the chair. He ignored it, as he had learned to do.

With the death of the first Mrs. Bennet, there had been floundering and adjustments, as none of them quite knew how to deal with each other. Jane had always played the serene peacemaker. Elizabeth had been his foil, and her wit, his delight. Mary had buried herself in the pursuit of imperfect accomplishments and readings of *Fordyce's Sermons*. Catherine and Lydia had run free without restraint.

It was strange how a sudden death affected those left behind; their roles shifted, either subtly or with the force of a blunt instrument.

Bennet pondered the mutations. Jane had remained the same gentle creature, but she had been desperately unhappy. *She is wed, at least. I hope she will be contented with Bingley. Damn the man.* Elizabeth had set herself against Charlotte, and so against him. Catherine's letters home reflected a more serious turn of mind. Lydia, once she began to throw off her grief, was become the same silly girl she had always been. She alone remained true to her former self. *I have become aware of all the improprieties of Lydia's general behavior.* Perhaps Mary showed the greatest change. She had turned useful. She lent her support to her step-mother and filled in some of the role that Jane and Elizabeth had abandoned. His middle daughter, once much ignored, had become a steadying influence.

And Charlotte, dear Charlotte, had only been Lizzy's friend.

He had himself changed to a startling degree. He had been a man who hid himself away from his family, preferring isolation to the company of a shrewish wife, whose violent scolding and nagging temperament had unbearably chafed his finer sensibility. These days, he chose to take an interest in the direction of his daughters; more even than he had intended, for reason had forced him into another, greater role. His affection for his second wife was entirely responsible for his evolution. She had wrought peace and a sacred passion.

Charlotte is everything to me. She is my happiness.

[31]

On a wet day in the middle of May, Elizabeth returned to Longbourn. Charlotte was torn by mixed emotions – stabbed with longing for her old friendship yet fearing the renewal of hostilities. She drew the warm folds of her Paisley shawl closer about her shoulders.

Mr. Bennet seemed not to share in her anxiety. He welcomed home his daughter with a considerable show of feeling. He held her hand and kissed her on the cheek. "I am glad to see you, my dear girl. After you have refreshed yourself, you must come back down to tell us all of your news." Elizabeth looked astonished by her father's kind greeting.

I am not alone in my apprehension, I see.

Charlotte drew in a deep breath. "Welcome back, Eliza."

For Mr. Bennet's sake, she was happy Elizabeth had come home. She wished she could receive her with similar felicity, but their greetings to one another were constrained. Elizabeth barely met her eyes and her face did not relax into her easy smile.

I share in the fault. I am reserved, stilted in my greeting.

In the bustle of welcome, the footman carrying in the trunks, and the lively talk among the sisters, as the two accompanied their elder sister upstairs to put off her traveling garments, she was glad to be forgotten. The housekeeper hovered nearby, and with an outward calm she was far from feeling, Charlotte addressed the woman. "Mrs. Hill, bring tea and cakes to the drawing-room."

Mary and Lydia soon came down, to join her and their father in the drawing-room. When Elizabeth returned downstairs, and she quietly asked her for a private word, her heart jumped. Apprehension chilled her. Before Elizabeth's going away, she had endured too much hurt at her hands. *But I shall not cower.* Charlotte steeled her spine. "Certainly, Eliza."

Charlotte led Elizabeth into the front parlor and closed the door. She did not go to sit on the settee, however, but remained standing. She clasped her hands together, aware of her own defensiveness. Elizabeth had walked past her when entering the room. She swept round with a swish of her skirts. And so, across the expanse of the new rug, they faced one another. Charlotte's state of mind was turbulent. The grief was fresh again. *Oh! How wrong this wall between us!*

Elizabeth drew in a deep, audible breath. "Charlotte, since I have been away, I have given much time to reflection. I shall not hide it from you. It was long before I became at all reconciled to the idea of what I considered so unsuitable a match. The strangeness of it!" She hesitated, before continuing. "I knew your character, Charlotte, but still I judged wrongly. I have now recollected myself, and I am able to assure you, with tolerable certainty, that the relationship now existent between us is highly gratifying to me, and that I wish you and my father every happiness."

For the interview, Charlotte had commanded a steady control over herself. It cracked in her confusion at Elizabeth's concession. She soon regained her composure. "I am all astonishment. What has brought about this turnabout?"

Elizabeth's eyelids flickered, her straight gaze faltering. "While I was at Hunsford, there were...certain things brought to my attention. My-my perceptions were faulty. I found myself questioning everything of which I had ever been sure." She lifted her gaze and her inflection firmed. "I knew not myself before. Now I know myself to be guilty of prejudice."

Charlotte stared at her; her brain was awhirl, unable to find adequate words in reply to such an extraordinary statement. *I am stood on my head by her utterance!*

Elizabeth pivoted, restlessness in her graceful figure, and moved to the window. She spoke over her shoulder. "It was in my mind...you see, I had always felt your opinion of matrimony was not exactly like my own, but I could not have supposed it possible that when called into action, you would have sacrificed every better feeling to worldly advantage."

Charlotte tightened her lips. She said icily, "I never declared myself in love with Mr. Bennet." *My feelings are not what they were then. But I will not – cannot! – confide in her.*

"No, you were honest in that." Elizabeth turned around. Her fine brown eyes were somber. "The thing of it is, Charlotte, you were not the only one who entered into this marriage from a worldly standpoint. My father explained it to me – that you had both entered into a business transaction of sorts, and that this was the nature of most marriages. I cast you in the roll of villain and I should not have. I am sorry. I accused you of taking advantage of my father while his mind was disordered. It was not his wits which were disordered, but my own."

A fraught silence fell, while Charlotte digested what had been said and what had not. Apart from the astonishing olive branch offered her, she felt herself fairly bursting from curiosity. *Why is Eliza so changed?* She was persuaded in her heart whatever had happened, it had been tremendously unsettling, for she could discern shadows in Elizabeth's dark eyes.

I must speak to Maria, and read her letters again, for I do not dare ask for Eliza's confidences.

Charlotte offered a small, tentative smile, and extended her own olive branch. "You were still romantic, then."

Elizabeth quietly replied. "An insensible romantic" Raising a smile, almost in her old manner, she said, "I present again, and with greater warmth than before, my good wishes. You are to be a mother. My father must be pleased."

Charlotte laid her splayed palm over the small swell of her stomach. The change in her figure had lately become more apparent. She raised her chin, mindful of the shaming, hurtful utterances Elizabeth had once hurled at her. "We hope for a son."

Elizabeth nodded. "Yes; to break the entail."

There was an awkward pause.

"Shall we return to take tea with the family?" Elizabeth agreed and Charlotte led the way back to the drawing-room. In former times, they would have entered the room together, arm in arm, confident in their mutual affection; but not on this day. She and Elizabeth moved away from one another, an instinctive distancing that was by mutual desire. Charlotte knew the reason. Their discourse had been so short, yet of some import. *Our raw emotions are too strong for us. But the festering wound has been lanced.*

Bennet touched her shoulder; in a lowered voice, he asked, "Are you all right, my dear? I saw you and Lizzy withdraw to be private."

Charlotte slowly nodded. She was still digesting the extraordinary thing that had happened. "Eliza proffered an apology, of sorts."

Her husband's relieved sigh was audible in her ears. "I am glad to hear it, Charlotte, very glad, indeed. We will speak more of this later. I wish to hear every word that was said."

During the ladies' absence, visitors had arrived and had already been ushered in by the butler. Lady Lucas had come with her daughter Maria and her niece, Miss Hawkins. Charlotte welcomed her guests and recalled Elizabeth to her cousin's attention.

"Oh, yes! I have heard your elder sister is wed and *you* are become Miss Bennet! So very pleased to see you again. We are both returned to Meryton, are we not? Such a sweet little market town! I am quite fond of it. We must go shopping together one day, I positively insist we must!"

Elizabeth complimented Miss Hawkins on her stylish bonnet, which had long and broad strings crossed under the lady's chin and tied across the crown. Miss Hawkins smiled with delight. "Is it not the dearest thing? My sister Selena sent it to me. The crown is much higher than formerly, as you see. I do not know if Meryton has such fashionable headgear yet."

Mrs. Hill rolled in the tea cart. Charlotte said a gracious word and stepped away to take her seat and pour for the company. Mary positioned herself beside her and distributed biscuits, tiny sandwiches with the crusts cut away, and slices of a heavy plum cake.

As the eldest daughter at home, Elizabeth was duty-bound to help with dispensing the tea. She had started to move forward, but she stopped short, her astonished expression quite clear at having been usurped by her sister. Thomas Bennet observed how she rearranged her features. Elizabeth said not a word, however. Instead, she sank down on a settee and watched the smiles, conversation, and ease between Charlotte and Mary. Once, she shook her head.

Yes, my Lizzy. Things have changed at Longbourn.

Bennet watched his newly returned daughter, looking for and hoping to find visible signs of change in her. *Is my kind, cheerful Lizzy restored to me?* However, as much as he studied her, he could not tell what she was thinking. Any regrets she might harbor she kept to herself. Nothing of her feelings could be discerned behind the small smile that played over her lips. *She has become enigmatic.*

Lydia showed off her newest purchase. "Look here, I have bought this bonnet. I do not think it is very pretty; but I thought I might as well buy it as not. I shall pull it to pieces and see if I can make it up any better."

When Mary teased her and abused it as ugly, she added, with perfect unconcern, "Oh! But there were two or three much uglier in the shop; and when I have bought some prettier colored satin to trim it with fresh, I think it will be very tolerable."

Bennet looked with disfavor at the bonnet. A sprightly confection of knotted ribbons and ruched satin, quite unsuitable for a young girl wearing blacks. *As silly as ever. She has not the grace to respect convention.* He delivered a temperate rebuke. "Pray recall, Lydia, you are still in mourning."

Lydia shot a sideways glance at him before she scowled down at her new bonnet. Her chin wobbled. "Such stuff! Mourning! I hate it! Dull, dull, dull, we are all so dull. Oh, how I *long* for it to be over."

Lady Lucas folded her lips. Behind her hand, Miss Hawkins hid a lilt of laughter. Maria cast down her gaze, color coming up in her cheeks.

"Oh, Lydia," murmured Elizabeth.

Lydia had exposed herself before their neighbors; it was not entirely without precedent, and Bennet could overlook it. But her lamentation set ill with him. *Her mother's favorite. Does she grieve so little?*

For a suspended beat, he met Charlotte's beautiful gray eyes, and she gave a low chuckle. An involuntarily curve came to his lips.

My dear wife discerns my exasperation.

She did not address him, however. "Do not despair, Lydia! If you must have new satin, a muted hue will be perfectly acceptable. Then you may trim it again in a fortnight when you come out of mourning."

Lydia's face brightened. "That is so!"

Hill ushered in Mrs. Philips. The lady at once divulged that she had seen the Bennet carriage pass through the village, so she knew her niece had returned. "I hurried to welcome you home, my dear Lizzy!"

After a round of hugs and affectionate words with all of her nieces, making curtsies to the Lucas party, and exchanging a cordial greeting with Charlotte and Mr. Bennet, she sat herself down on the settee beside Elizabeth. She removed her gloves, signaling that hers was to be a lengthy visit.

The lady chattered away to her niece in her inconsequential manner, finally ending, "It is odd not to find Jane here, is it not? So extraordinary! The surprise of hearing from Lydia about Jane's marriage! I was that astonished to learn she had met Mr. Bingley again in London, for I could not discover anything about it previous. It was quite thought by everyone that he had abandoned her, you know. Poor dear Jane! But now she is wed!"

"Yes, my sister is married," said Elizabeth quietly.

Bennet exchanged a quick glance with Charlotte. He knew she shared in satisfaction that Jane's reputation did not suffer from the hasty marriage. *My sister Philips would of a certainty report if it was otherwise.*

He delivered a repressive remonstrance. "Gossip is sickly food for the empty, idle mind."

Charlotte swiftly interjected. "It is a happiness, indeed. Will you take tea, Mrs. Philips?"

Lydia aired her sentiment. "I wanted to wed before all my sisters, but Jane is first." With a little pout, she bit into a lemon biscuit.

Mary's response was mild. "You must not begrudge Jane, for she is the eldest."

"My dear Miss Lydia, you must not repine! Really, you must not!" exclaimed Miss Hawkins. "You must and shall be delightfully, honorably and comfortably settled before the Bennets or I have any rest."

In an undervoice, Lady Lucas reproved her niece. "Really, Augusta, you insert yourself too readily into our neighbors' affairs."

Mrs. Philips accepted tea but she had taken only a few sips before she was off and running again. "Oh, my dear Lizzy, I wish to know all about your visit to Hunsford Parsonage. I met Mr. Collins previously at my own dinner party, as you must recall. I was quite impressed with him and what he had to say of his situation. Such very good manners! He likened my drawing-room to a small summer breakfast parlor at Rosings. You see, I have not forgotten! Now, are we to hear of a betrothal between you and dear Mr. Collins?"

Elizabeth rolled her eyes. "No, you will not, Aunt Philips."

"Why, how is this?" cried Mrs. Philips, her amazement writ large on her face. "Mr. Collins danced with you at Netherfield. I took particular note of his gallantry. He scarcely left your side all that evening. I was sure there was something in the wind."

"What a dear creature he is – I assure you, I liked him excessively, Miss Elizabeth. I admire all that quaint, old-fashioned politeness; it is much more to my taste than modern ease; modern ease often disgusts me," said Miss Hawkins with an arch smile.

Elizabeth did not appear at all gratified by her endorsement.

Bennet struck in. "Mr. Collins is not able to aspire to better society, with the exception of the occasional afternoon tea or making one of a table for quadrille at Rosings Park. Lizzy is not suited to such a restricted life."

"I am fond of my friends and good society, it is true," said Elizabeth.

Her aunt gave a regretful shake of her head. "It is a pity, Lizzy, for you would have been well-settled. But there! My sister Bennet always said you were an unaccountable girl. And what news of Kitty?"

Mrs. Philips was astonished but pleased to learn that her young niece was to remain at Rosings Park. "*The entire summer!* Why, such excellent tidings! I know all about Lady Catherine de Bourgh, from

Mr. Collins, and he told me at the Netherfield ball that she is the aunt of Mr. Darcy. Well! You could have knocked me down with a feather. Lizzy, did you see anything of Mr. Darcy in Kent?"

Elizabeth said calmly, "I did, aunt. But he went away before I did."

Mrs. Philips sighed, satisfied at last that she had squeezed out every drop of information. "Oh, I had quite forgotten in all the excitement!" She sat her cup aside in haste, slopping tea over the rim into the saucer. The plume on her bonnet swayed and her eyes gleamed as she leaned forward in a bid for everyone's combined attention. "I am fair to bursting with news! The militia are leaving Meryton. They are to be encamped near Brighton, and they will be gone in a fortnight."

"Are they indeed!" exclaimed Elizabeth with what appeared to be the greatest satisfaction.

Charlotte looked at her, struck by her response. *Why is she not cast down? She had such a partiality for Wickham.*

At her aunt's news, Mary made no comment but she looked pensive.

As for Lydia, she uttered a loud cry of dismay. She tossed aside the new bonnet. "It will not much signify what one wears this summer, then!"

§

It was a fine May morning, and Miss Hawkins had come in the Lucas carriage to carry Mary and Lydia off to Meryton. The Bennet sisters were shortly to put off their mourning and had expressed a desire to purchase some lengths of muslin to make up some new morning dresses. It was just such a project to appeal to Miss Hawkins and she insisted upon making a party of it. "I have very good taste, I assure you! My sister Selena says I have an *expert eye* for color. I shall be quite an asset to you!"

Elizabeth had been expected to go along but she begged off, saying that she had letters to write, albeit promising to accompany Miss Hawkins on another occasion.

Charlotte intended to take advantage of her cousin's excursion to call on her mother and sister Maria. *The opportunity for privacy is priceless.* She found her short walk to be enjoyable. She lifted her face and breathed deep of the fresh, clean air.

At Lucas Lodge, Charlotte was received by Lady Lucas with a fond kiss of her cheek, and with genuine affection and pleasure by her sister.

Maria expressed her delight at her eldest sister's rounding figure. "I am so pleased for you, dear Charlotte. When I went away in March, one could not tell it at all!"

After a few minutes of sharing what she was doing to welcome the birth of her child, describing the details of her sewing of several tiny embroidered garments, and of a laced cap and christening gown, Charlotte turned the conversation to her sister's recent visit to Kent. Responding to Charlotte's curious inquiries, Maria chattered away about her experiences, her impressions, and in particular, what she had observed of Elizabeth Bennet and Mr. Darcy. "The morning we set out for London, Eliza seemed peculiarly quiet." Maria tilted her head, in contemplation. "I wondered if it had to do with Mr. Darcy."

Charlotte was taken aback. "Why, whatever can you mean, Maria?"

"We went to Rosings of an evening, except Eliza, who said she had the headache. When we returned to the parsonage, it was to see Mr. Darcy rushing from the parlor, with *such* a black look on his face! Eliza was vastly upset – so white I feared she might faint! – and she at once went upstairs though it was still early in the evening."

Charlotte listened with the greatest astonishment. *"A quarrel?"*

Maria looked from her mother to her sister. "I did not see her again until sometime in the morning after. She had already returned from her usual walk and she appeared agitated."

Lady Lucas raised her brows and pursed her lips. "This is a strange sequence you are relating, Maria."

Maria nodded, acknowledging it. "In her discomposure, Eliza had dropped a crumpled letter. I picked it up from the floor to hand back to her, and in glancing at it, I recognized Mr. Darcy's signature! Eliza *snatched* the letter out of my hand and would not say anything about it."

Charlotte furrowed her brows. *A puzzling sequence of events, indeed!*

"I am thunderstruck at what you have told us, Mara. It is shocking that a single young woman is receiving correspondence from a gentleman who is not related to her," pronounced Lady Lucas. She cleared her throat in a delicate fashion and looked at her eldest daughter. "But perhaps, there is an attachment between Eliza and Mr. Darcy?"

Charlotte shook her head. "Not to my knowledge, Mama. Mr. Bennet has not hinted of any such attachment. And if it was so, I believe he would relate it to me."

She quite clearly recalled what he had said.

Has not Lizzy always hated the man?

Charlotte had not been many minutes returned to Longbourn, before the front door opened and a chattering was heard. Shortly, Mary and Lydia came into the drawing-room, accompanied by Miss Hawkins. The footman followed after them, carrying several packages wrapped up in brown paper and string. Mary quietly directed that the parcels be put down on the card table.

Lydia, rather louder in voice than any other person, was enumerating the various pleasures of the morning. "Oh! Charlotte, I wish you had gone with us, for we had such fun! I have spent all my allowance! We visited all the shops and when we got to the George, we three had the nicest cold luncheon in the world, and if you would have gone, we would have treated you too. I thought we never should have got into the coach for all the parcels. And then we were so merry all the way home!"

Miss Hawkins placed one bulky package on the occasional table standing beside Charlotte's chair. "Pray open this one, cousin, for I am eager for your opinion."

Charlotte obeyed, snipping the string with her embroidery scissors, and unfolded the paper. Inside were a few ells of dress material. "Why, how lovely! A most attractive shade of blue.

"It is Clarence blue! Really, I was most astonished to find such a new color stocked in Meryton. *We* go to the emporium Harding and Howell in town; Maple Grove is 165 miles from London, so you may judge what an expedition! My sister Selena says it is positively one's *duty* always to look a fine lady. She had a number of gowns made up as she increased, so I made up my mind, dear cousin, that you must do the same. The fabric is for *you*, to sew up a new daygown.

Charlotte was astonished and taken aback. "Oh! I never expected – but, indeed, Augusta, I could not possibly accept. Such an extravagant gesture! The challis is too dear."

"No, no! Not another word, for we agreed – did we not, Miss Lydia, Miss Mary! – that you are so very deserving. You must let me gift you. I had no bride-gift for you before I went away, so you must, *must* allow me to give you this!"

"This is truly kind of you, Augusta," said Charlotte, stroking the fine texture of the twilled silk and wool. Already, her mind was busy making plans for the new garment to be formed out of the beautiful fabric. *A walking dress embroidered up the front, a French gray cottage mantle to be worn with it.*

"You must put on a few ornaments now, because it is expected of you. A bride, you know, must appear like a bride." Miss Hawkins held up a hand. "I know what you would say, cousin! Your natural taste is all for simplicity; a simple style of dress is so infinitely preferable to finery. But you are quite in the minority, I believe; few people seem to value simplicity of dress, show and finery are everything."

After a few gracious words of thanks to Miss Hawkins for the outing, Mary, with the suggestion of carrying their separate purchases upstairs, took Lydia off, leaving Charlotte to further entertain her cousin.

Miss Hawkins watched their exit and sat down opposite her. "I am glad to have this opportunity to talk with you, dear cousin. I would not for worlds push in where I am not wanted, you know I would *never* do that! But I do feel I must drop a word in your ear. I was very much surprised at the way Miss Lydia positively *ogled* the officers whom we met. So familiar in her manners, too! I was positively put to the blush, I assure you! And so mortifying for Miss Mary!"

Charlotte was bereft of speech. She disliked very much that her cousin should have occasion to say anything at all. She was aggravated with Lydia for making such a show of herself, and especially, placing *her* in a position to bring on her own mortification. *Augusta, one who is so likely to put her relations to the blush, is the critic!* All she could think of to say was, "In a fortnight they shall be gone."

Miss Hawkins blinked at her, and then gave her usual trill of laughter. "Such sangfroid does you credit, cousin, - oh yes, it does!"

[32]

The last days of the militia's stay in Meryton marched forward. All the young ladies of the neighborhood bemoaned the loss. "Drooping spirits abound, my dear. The assemblies will seem sadly flat without partners in red coats. Augusta has quite changed her good opinion of our Meryton society and compares it unfavorably with Bath."

"A higher society, to be sure! Augusta talks often of her come-out in Bath. When does she return home?"

"Mr. Suckling's last letter hinted that his wife's constitution is not yet strong enough for such exertions."

"If Mr. Suckling has his way, my cousin will be left on your hands for good! Dear Mama, *you* will be forced to bring Augusta out!"

Lady Lucas' pensive demeanor lightened with a smile. "You joke, but it is something to ponder, indeed! How does it go here at Longbourn?"

Charlotte's response was dry. "*Elizabeth and Mary* are still able to eat, drink, and sleep, and pursue the usual course of their employments."

Lady Lucas chuckled. "I am glad to hear it!."

Charlotte laughed also, a bit ruefully, shaking her head. "They are frequently reproached for their insensibility by Lydia, whose own misery is extreme, and who cannot comprehend such hard-heartedness."

Lady Lucas's pleasant expression altered. "It does not surprise me. A wild, sad romp of a girl – just coming out of mourning, and already she has been sighted flirting with the officers! Mrs. Long observed Lydia's forward behavior for herself, and called her a bird-witted baggage."

"My goodness! I do hope Mrs. Long was jesting."

Lady Lucas aimed a straight, serious look at her daughter. "Well, you know how people are, Charlotte. There have been other things said. Lydia is well-known in the county and allowances are made, especially in light of her mother's death. Otherwise, the talk of her would be less tolerant."

Charlotte made a *moue* of distaste. "My cousin has spoken to me of Lydia's behavior."

"Has she, indeed? Augusta is too forthcoming with her opinions! She writes often to her sister, so tales of Lydia's lack of decorum must already be known at Maple Grove. This displeases me very much!"

Charlotte felt the weight of guilt. She lifted her hands, palms open. "Mary and I have done our best to correct her, but our efforts have been met with indifference." Neither she nor her mother alluded to Mr. Bennet and his authority. His record for checking his daughters was negligible. Recalling the gentleman's proposal to her, Charlotte was fairly certain that, if she appealed to him to correct Lydia, he would point out that he had made her responsible for his daughters and their futures.

"It is unfortunate Lydia is related to Lucas Lodge."

Charlotte was shaken by the blunt sentiment. But she said nothing.

Lady Lucas kissed her on the cheek, remarked how well she looked, and took her leave. Long afterwards, Charlotte was disturbed. She did not doubt her mother's concern over Lydia's reputation and fully entered into her sentiments. *I wish Lydia was not so enamored of the militia!*

"Good heavens! What is to become of us! What are we to do!"

Charlotte tried to ignore Lydia's tedious harping on the removal of the militia from the neighborhood. Her patience was stretched near to its limit, so she was thankful when Elizabeth took her youngest sister to task.

Elizabeth addressed her tartly. "Lydia, your agitations are useless. Pray cease these silly exclamations! I tell you to your head that you make yourself irksome."

"If Kitty was here, she would enter fully into my feelings!"

Mary looked up from her book and rolled her eyes. "And no doubt would treat us to the same loud, useless histrionics."

Lydia gave a gusty sigh before pouting "I am sure I shall break my heart." She fidgeted around the drawing-room, picking up a ribbon, letting it drop from her fingers. "If one could but go to Brighton! A little sea-bathing would set me up forever. My aunt Philips is sure it would do me a great deal of good."

"Papa will not go to Brighton," said Mary with a small, audible sigh.

"No, indeed." Elizabeth shook her head, without looking up from drawing her needle and thread through the piece on her embroidery hoops "The expense of such a diversion is most prohibitive. You must cease teasing Papa about it, Lydia! He has already said we will not go."

"Papa is so disagreeable!" exclaimed Lydia.

Charlotte glanced at Mary in private speculation. Mary must have felt it almost as keenly as her younger sister, not because she was mad over all of the militia, but because she had formed a partiality for one officer. It had not escaped Charlotte's notice that Captain Denny, whose promotion was recent, had been to call several times. *And it is not Lydia's liveliness that draws him.*

Lydia's gloom was shortly cleared away, for she received an invitation from Mrs. Forster, the wife of the colonel of the regiment, to accompany her to Brighton. An invaluable friend, Mrs. Forster was a very young woman, and very lately married. A resemblance of good humor and good spirits had drawn her and Lydia to each other, and out of their three months' acquaintance they had been best of friends for two months.

Lydia immediately sought her father's permission to accept the invitation, and it was given. "I declare Papa is not so disagreeable as I had thought!" The rapture of Lydia and her adoration of Mrs. Forster served to send her flying about the house in restless ecstasy, calling for everyone's congratulations, and laughing and talking with more violence than ever.

Upon learning of Lydia's good fortune, Elizabeth sought an interview with her father. When she emerged from the library, Charlotte saw at once that she was distressed. Charlotte followed her into the drawing-room, but she hesitated to address her, for there yet remained enough coolness between them that she feared rebuff. Despite her trepidation, she went over and said in a lowered voice, "Are you all right, Eliza?"

Elizabeth shook her head. She spoke impetuously, with a degree of the warmth and openness of former times. "Oh, Charlotte! I am much in fear of what might happen. My father does not see the evils attached to this trip of Lydia's to Brighton."

Charlotte was sharply reminded of things her mother had said and of her own uneasy concern. *Wanton gigglers. Bird-witted baggage.* She sat down beside her. "I own, I am not comfortable. Lydia is so feverish in her speech and actions. Mary and I have spoken of this friendship of Lydia's before. Mrs. Forster is too young to be a chaperone. She will not be a hindrance to Lydia's embarrassing herself. Lydia is too headstrong."

"No, indeed! Vain, ignorant, idle, and absolutely uncontrolled!" She struck her palms together. "Oh, Mr. Darcy was right! The members of my family have exposed themselves by their bad behavior to be vulgar and underbred!"

"Mr. Darcy!" Charlotte gazed at her in amazement. "He never said such things when he was in Hertfordshire or you would have told me! Whenever did you speak with Mr. Darcy again? Oh, of course, it was while you were in Kent! Maria wrote to me from Hunsford and she mentioned Mr. Darcy's visit to his aunt. How long was he at Rosings Park?"

"Nearly three weeks."

Elizabeth's reluctance in her reply was obvious, but it had nothing to do with the awkwardness still existing between them. Otherwise, Elizabeth would simply have cut short their exchange. *She is strangely wrought-up.* Charlotte wondered at it. *There is some mystery of feeling here.* "And you saw him frequently?"

Elizabeth lowered her eyes. "Yes, almost every day."

"His manners are obviously just as disagreeable as ever."

Elizabeth's color rose. She looked up, saying steadily, "I think Mr. Darcy improves upon acquaintance."

"Indeed!" Charlotte stared. This was a far different tune than the one Elizabeth had played when Mr. Darcy had been in Hertfordshire. Then, she had disliked the gentleman and taken a delight in poking fun at his great pride and at his arrogance in holding himself so far above his company. It was as much for paying off some old hurts as for curiosity that she chafed at her. "And pray, is it in address that he improves? Has he deigned to add civility to his ordinary style? I dare not hope that he is improved in essentials."

"Oh, no!" Elizabeth shook her head. She spoke in a low, serious tone. "In essentials, I believe, he is very much what he ever was."

Charlotte's amazement increased. "But he laid such unhappy charges against your family! Eliza, *what exactly* passed between you? Maria spoke of a quarrel between you and Mr. Darcy."

Elizabeth flushed scarlet. She pressed her palms against her blazing cheeks. "Oh, do not ask me! It is not a conversation I wish to ever recall." She twisted her body to face her. "But do you *remember*, Charlotte, at the Netherfield ball? Lydia and Kitty, giggling and romping without restraint. My mother's vulgar boastings of Bingley for Jane! My cousin, Mr. Collins, importuning Mr. Darcy in such an impertinent way. I even blushed for my father! Interrupting Mary in the middle of a piece and stopping her from performing anymore!"

Elizabeth's agonized reminiscence explained the grounds for Mr. Darcy's opinion. It had indeed been disgraceful behavior by most of the Bennet family. *But it is not so iniquitous as Eliza makes it out to be.* Besides, nothing was to be gained by dwelling on it and she said so. "You must not refine on it, Eliza. Little good will come of such melancholy reflections, I assure you."

However, she did denounce Mr. Darcy's cruel censure. "As for Mr. Darcy's conduct! What impertinence! Indeed, I am surprised by it. I would have expected the proud Mr. Darcy to behave in a more gentlemanly way." Elizabeth winced and she looked guilt-ridden, to Charlotte's considerable surprise.

Then she made an impatient, dismissive gesture. "Never mind Mr. Darcy! My present concern is with Lydia! I cannot agree with Papa's decision. I do not disguise my melancholy conviction that it is a mistake."

Charlotte believed the same. She reached out and pressed Elizabeth's hand. "I share your concern, Eliza. I shall speak to your father."

"Thank you, Charlotte. You are very good."

A light knock and Charlotte entered the library. Thomas Bennet was made pleased by his wife's presence. However, his pleasure was tempered by the solemn look on her face. He thought he knew why she had come. Nevertheless, he welcomed her with a smile and set aside his pen and the accounts ledger. "Ah, Charlotte! Have you come to reproach me as well?"

"Eliza was very downcast when she left you."

Charlotte lowered herself down into the same chair his daughter had vacated. The rounding of her lithesome body gratified his manly pride. *Near to seven months in the basket.* He watched her, feeling a tenderness for her which had but grown in the brief months of their marriage. *She is the wife of my bosom.*

"In truth, I gave but little consideration to my assent. The prospect of having reprieve for several weeks from Lydia's moping and loud whining is impossible to resist. Let Colonel Forster exercise responsibility for her. "

I had been wishing for a place to send Lydia. Now it has presented itself.

Charlotte's low, musical inflections were as ever pleasant on his ear. "Excuse me, for I must speak plainly. If you, her dear father, will not take the trouble of checking Lydia's exuberant spirits, and of teaching her that her present pursuits are not to be the business of her life, she will soon be beyond the reach of amendment."

Bennet vented a sigh. "In Lydia's imagination, a visit to Brighton comprises every possibility of earthly happiness. She fancies the streets of that bathing place covered with officers. She sees herself the object of attention, to tens and scores of them at present unknown."

He swept his hand through the air, as though he gestured at the wondrous sight. "Imagine it, Charlotte! All the glories of the camp, its tents stretched forth in beauteous uniformity of lines, crowded with the young and merry, and dazzling with scarlet, and to complete the view, herself seated beneath a tent, tenderly flirting with at least six officers at once."

Charlotte listened, her gaze fixed on him, her face overshadowed by a frown. "If that is what you believe is in her brain, then I do wonder at your agreement to this precious scheme."

He chuckled. "We shall have no peace at Longbourn if Lydia does not go to Brighton. Let her go then! Colonel Forster is a sensible man and will keep her out of any real mischief. She is luckily too poor to be an object of prey to anybody."

In the face of his decided opinion, Charlotte would not persist. She contented herself with only a dry observation. "I am glad Kitty is not here. Though two years older, she *will* follow wherever Lydia leads, and she was as mad after a military coat as her sister! She would have been in the sulks not to have been included in Mrs. Forster's invitation."

"Yes, we are spared that at least."

Charlotte hesitated. Her mind was teased by what she'd heard from Elizabeth, and because she wanted to know her husband's opinion, she spoke of it. "I have come from a most astonishing conversation with Eliza. She met Mr. Darcy several times at Rosings Park, as we know from Maria's letters, and now she speaks of him with extraordinary forbearance. Indeed, I would almost say with respect."

Mr. Bennet put up his brows. "I am surprised. She disliked him immensely when he was at Netherfield. I cannot conceive of such a change of heart! Are you saying Lizzy has formed an attachment? Surely not! Not with Mr. Darcy!"

"I do not say she has *lost* her heart. But I think...perhaps it is a little bruised."

"Oh, well then! That is just as it should be, for every young girl must break her heart at least once. She is all the more interesting for having suffered a romantic disappointment."

Charlotte left the library, disappointed and sorry over her husband's decision. It was not in her nature, however, to increase her vexations by dwelling on it. She was confident of having performed her duty, and to fret over unavoidable evils, or augment them by anxiety, was no part of her disposition.

She recommended to Elizabeth that she accept that there was nothing more to be done or said concerning the matter. "Lydia is going to Brighton. You know, Eliza, if Lydia knew of our conferences with your father, her indignation would find loud expression in a ready flow of wrath. I urge you to say nothing to her! I stand in some way as her mother and have a little authority; but if she knew that *you* sought to tear her from such prospects, what would be her sensations?"

"Oh, what do I care for Lydia's temper? It is of no consequence!"

"I cannot agree. Lydia is very like her mother in temperament."

Elizabeth huffed a soft chuckle. "I take your point. Lydia is selfish, thinks only of her own pleasures, and insists upon having her own way. The household will be subjected to just such an emotional storm as Mama used to unleash."

Charlotte's cheeks heated. "I am embarrassed to own, that is exactly my apprehension. Tell me that I am wrong!"

Elizabeth's laugh was throaty. "I shall keep my own counsel, never fear."

Her look is friendly.

Charlotte went away, marveling that a shared concern for Lydia had served to mend a little of the breach between her and Elizabeth.

Lydia remained ignorant of what had passed between her father and her sister, so Charlotte's peace was not cut up. Lydia's raptures continued with little intermission until the very day of her leaving home.

On the last day of the regiment's remaining in Meryton, Colonel Forster, Mrs. Forster, and some of the officers dined at Longbourne. Among the latter was Captain Denny, and Charlotte observed how often his gaze strayed to Mary, and that he managed to seize some conversation with her. Mary was looking particularly well in a new gown made up in a soft moss green, vandyked at the neck and trimmed with black ribbon at cuffs and hem.

When the party broke up, Lydia returned with Mrs. Forster to Meryton, from whence they were to set out early the next morning. The separation between her and her family was noisy instead of saddened. In the clamoring happiness of Lydia herself in bidding farewell, the more moderate adieus of her father, stepmother, and her sisters were uttered without being heard.

The month of June brought a flurry of correspondence. Lydia sent the longest composition of her life, all about celebrating her sixteenth birthday with Colonel and Mrs. Forster, surrounded by *scores* of red-coated soldiers; Kitty wrote from Rosings Park of her humble gratitude to Lady Catherine de Bourgh for her ladyship's care and instruction; and Elizabeth received a communiqué from her most beloved sister.

"Oh! A letter from Jane!" Elizabeth sat down, delight lighting up her face. Scarce minutes passed before Elizabeth looked up from her letter, uttering with shock, "Jane is at Pemberley!"

"Yes, of course, the Bingleys traveled there shortly after the wedding. I thought you knew, Eliza." Charlotte was surprised by Elizabeth's paling face and obvious distress.

Elizabeth shook her head. "No! No, I did not know! But how did this come about? Jane shared so little with me; indeed, I knew nothing of her troubles until I received a letter, written from Gracechurch Street. My aunt and uncle Gardiner said nothing of this when I was in London."

"The Bingleys accepted an invitation from Mr. Darcy." Mary looked equally surprised by her sister's perturbation. "Jane's situation is such that – well, it is good she is away from Meryton."

Charlotte nodded, sighing. "The gossip would have destroyed Jane's reputation, and it would have affected all of us at Longbourn."

Elizabeth leaped to her feet, taking an agitated circuit of the drawing-room, the letter clenched in her hand. "But to involve Mr. Darcy! Whatever were they thinking, to expose their shameful circumstances to Mr. Darcy, of all people!"

Mary frowned, and at once remonstrated with her sister. "Mr. Darcy has proven to be a staunch friend, and a very Christian gentleman."

Charlotte studied her unhappy expression. "Eliza, are you thinking *still* of your humiliation, when Mr. Darcy spoke of the ill-breeding he observed in your family at the Netherfield ball? Months ago, now! What of your visit in Kent, where you saw him and came to know him better?"

At Elizabeth's altered and conscious expression, Charlotte shook her head. She said gravely, "I am disappointed in you, Eliza."

"I am disappointed in myself," said Elizabeth in a low voice. "You are each right to rebuke me. Last autumn, I wrongly sketched Mr. Darcy's character, and though my opinion is changed from what it was, it seems my understanding of him is still faulty."

§

An express letter came for Mr. Bennet. He read it in complete silence, without change of expression, in shock and horror. When he was done, he slowly lifted his head and gave brief summary of the content for his wife and daughters. *I will shield them from the wretched, graphic details.* "Bingley's scrawl is barely legible, but he informs that Jane suffered injuries in a carriage accident and was gravely afflicted. She recovers slowly but she recovers. They will remain at Pemberly for an indeterminate time."

"Oh, poor Jane, to have been hurt," mourned Elizabeth. "I wish I had been with her."

His face quivered. *Poor, dear Jane!*

He would not tell of how near death had come; perhaps later, when he was better master of himself, he would confide all to his dear helpmate.

"She is in her husband's care." Bennet mechanically refolded the letter and slid the square into his coat pocket. *I must write Bingley. But I cannot yet face it. My tears would blotch the ink.* "It is a fine afternoon. I believe I shall go shooting."

[33]

At midsummer, the Gardiners returned to Longbourn, for the express purpose of taking up Elizabeth and setting out on a tour to the north. The Gardiners brought news of their eldest niece. "Jane has written. She reports that she goes on well, and she is recovering from her ordeal."

Thomas Bennet spoke for them all. "We are very glad to hear it. Good news, indeed."

Elizabeth's trunks were packed with new gowns, sewn by herself and Mary. The sisters had put off their blacks and were wearing colors again. The Gardiners also were no longer in mourning and appeared elegant and refined in their usual garb. Mr. Bennet alone still wore mourning bands, and would do so until November, when he could remove them.

Longbourn was diminished, without Lydia and Elizabeth to enliven the atmosphere. The days passed in peaceful pursuits. Mary practiced the pianoforte and could often be found out in the garden, the magnificently covered rose arbor arching overhead, sitting on a bench with a book in her hands; Charlotte finished up her handiwork with the infant's christening cap and gown, covering it in delicate lace and satin knots; and Mr. Bennet was busy with the estate demesne, orchards, and croft farm.

Charlotte's one regret was that Elizabeth was not present. She felt there had been progress in repairing the rift between them, and she very much wished to continue in that direction.

The travelers were gone a little over a fortnight, when disaster struck the Bennets and cut up all their peace. On Sunday, 2nd August, just after they had all gone to bed, at midnight, an express was brought by rider to Longbourn.

At the beating on the door, Bennet leaped out of bed. The whole of the house was alarmed. He ran downstairs, wife and daughter following in his wake, each holding aloft bed candles for illumination. All had tossed on shawls and dressing gowns over their nightwear and shoved their feet into slippers. The butler and footman were in the front hall, relighting candles. The express rider stood upon the threshold of the opened door. In short order, Bennet's purse was fetched, he paid the rider, the express changed hands, and the front door was shut.

Bennet glanced at the penned direction. "It is from Colonel Forster."

Charlotte gasped. "Oh, no! Lydia!"

Bennet cupped her elbow and gently guided her into the front parlor. "Hill! Light the candles in here and have the fire built up. Come, dear lady, sit down. The news will wait a few minutes longer. Mary, I know you will wish to remain."

The two women sank down on the settee, murmuring to one another, retying their dressing gowns tight and pulling their long shawls closer about themselves.

Two candelabras were lit and strategically placed, a fire was coached from the banked coals by the footman, and the butler offered to bring a pot of tea for the ladies. Bennet tethered his impatience. He fairly itched to get to the contents of the letter, yet he waited for privacy. *I wish the servants to the devil.* But at the suggestion, he nodded. "A very good idea."

"No, no! I could not possibly swallow it," exclaimed Charlotte. She touched her throat. "Dear sir, only tell us the news! Oh, I dread some terrible accident!

Bennet bowed acquiescence to her wishes. "That will be all, Hill."

He broke the wax seal and unfolded the express letter.

In the flickering candlelight, he read the brief, terse lines – Bennet looked up, shocked. He felt as if struck by lightening. "Dear Lord! Lydia has eloped! She has gone off with Mr. Wickham!"

"What!" Mary stared up at him, aghast. "Oh, foolish girl!"

"My dear sir! When did this take place?" demanded Charlotte. Her hands were clutched together.

"Yesterday! Mrs. Forster discovered Lydia's note. Colonel Forster has enclosed it." He cast a swift glance over the note. He at once recognized Lydia's careless penmanship. "Here, read it for yourself." He gave Lydia's loopy, schoolgirl scribble into his wife's outstretched hand.

Mary leaned close to Charlotte's shoulder, craning her head. She gave an exclamation. "How could she write such gleeful, stupid stuff?"

Bennet paid no heed, rapidly scanning the lines. "Colonel Forster has set out in pursuit. He will try to trace them." Striking the sheet with the back of his hand, he exclaimed, "I am to wait for word from him!"

Charlotte looked up from Lydia's note, her gaze coming up to meet his, her gray eyes reflecting apprehension in their expressive depths.

"I hope he may come up with them!"

"So do I," he responded grimly.

"Lydia writes they are to be wed! At Gretna Greene!" Mary's face held equal measures of doubt and hope. "Perhaps it will not be so bad."

Bennet shook his head. "Such optimism does your heart credit, Mary, but not your intellect. Gretna Greene is their declared destination, but that is nearly three hundred miles away. I cannot imagine either of them has much money to pay for a chaise, and the turnpikes, and lodgings. They will founder well before they can get to the border. Lydia's ruin is nearly set."

"Rash Lydia! My letter to Elizabeth! I must add this alarming news!" Mary hurried away, her candle flame fluttering.

Then there was only himself and his wife. She held out her hand to him. Bennet dropped down beside her and he clasped her hand tightly, accepting the comfort she offered. In the subdued candlelight, Charlotte's face was a pale oval. "What shall you do, Thomas?"

"I can do nothing until I hear from Colonel Forster," he said heavily. "I must rely upon him, for I do not know where to go or where to look." There was no condemnation in her expression, but nevertheless, he felt it for himself.

No curse for Wickham has passed my lips. I cannot fathom it. But he knew it for a lie. With a twist of his lips, he said, "I should have listened to you and Lizzy. My negligence is to blame. I sent Lydia into harm's way."

"Hush, my love. No one could have foreseen such a thing. We must hope for the best."

Bennet lifted her hand to his lips and pressed a kiss to her soft skin. *I am infinitely grateful for her support.* "Yes, yes, Colonel Forster is a good man. We must hope for the best, but prepare ourselves for the worst."

In what was left of the night, little rest was found. Mr. Bennet insisted that Charlotte go back to bed and escorted her to her bedchamber; but even though she was much fatigued, an awful foreboding kept her turning on her pillows. It did not aid her repose when cold fingers touched her face, her hair. She batted at the dark, empty air. "Go away, go away, *go away!*"

In daylight, an air of exhausted melancholy hung over all Longbourn. Among the Bennets, there was not a thought, nor a conversation, that did not relate to Lydia. The talk and speculations were rife over the breakfast cups, but everything just went round in circles, for there was nothing new that was known. Mary put her letter to Elizabeth in the morning post.

The passing hours were oppressive. Bennet produced conclusions out of his brown study. "Upon serious consideration, Charlotte, it appears to me so very unlikely, that any young man should form such a design against a girl who is by no means unprotected or friendless, and who was actually staying in his colonel's family, that I am strongly inclined to hope the best."

He frowned as he fiddled with his watch fob. "Could he expect that her friends would not step forward? Could he expect to be noticed again by the regiment, after such an affront to Colonel Forster? His temptation is not adequate to the risk."

"My dear sir, it *does* occur to me." Charlotte tentatively voiced what she was thinking, even as it seemed so disloyal that she would do better to remain silent; but she took her courage in her hands, trusting that the mutual bonds between herself and her husband were strong enough. "Lydia has no brothers to step forward, and he might imagine, from-from her father's behavior – from his indolence and the little attention he seemed to give to what was going forward in his family – that *he* would do as little, and think as little about it, as any father could do, in such a matter."

There were several moments of silence, while he appraised her with a cold look in his gray-blue eyes. Under his narrowed, unblinking stare, the scorch rose high in her cheeks. At last, he spoke. "Your rebuke of me is harsh. Yet it is warranted. Indeed, I cannot escape the justice of it."

"I have offended you," said Charlotte in a low voice.

"Yes, you have. But I must forgive you, for you have made me face a brutal truth. It does a man good to have his conscience lashed, now and again." He came to her and lifted one of her hands to his lips. "My dearest one, I chose very well when I wed you."

Tears came to her eyes. She cried easily these days, the latter days before her laying-in. At least that was the excuse she gave herself. It had *nothing at all* to do with the warmth of heart that his words gave to her.

At last, late in the day, Col. Forster came to Longbourn, accompanied by one of his officers. Bennet acknowledged Denny with a civil nod, but he had sparse interest in the captain's presence. The communication brought by Colonel Forster drove everything else out of his mind.

The colonel was received with anxious questions. With the kindest concern, Col. Forster broke his apprehensions to the Bennets in a manner most creditable to his heart. He explained all he had done in attempting to locate the runaway couple. "We left Brighton not many hours after the express. I intended to trace their route. I did trace them easily to Clapham, but no further, for on entering that place, they removed into a hackney-coach and dismissed the chaise that brought them to Epsom. All that is known after this is that they were seen to continue the London road."

Bennet masked his emotions; he could not bear scrutiny at the best of times. He clasped his hands tight behind his back. Charlotte and Mary were white-faced. It was Charlotte who spoke first. "There is no absolute proof that they *are not* gone to Scotland." Bennet feared his wife raised a vain hope, but he understood that she felt obliged to do it, for all their sakes.

"Their removing from the chaise into a hackney-coach goes against such presumption. And besides, no traces of them were to be found on the Barnet road. We went on into Hertfordshire, making enquiries at all the turnpikes, and at the inns in Barnet and Hatfield, but without success."

Bennet's shoulders sagged. "Not making for Scotland, then."

Colonel Forster shook his head. "I regret to say, no, Mr. Bennet. I hold myself entirely to blame, sir. Miss Lydia was entrusted to my care. Mrs. Forster is also much affected by what has happened. She feels very much at fault. Indeed, I left her prostrated upon her couch."

"I am sincerely grieved for you and Mrs. Forster, but no one can throw any blame on you," said Charlotte quietly.

"No, indeed." Bennet was scourged in his soul. He knew well where the fault was to be laid. *Mea culpa, mea culpa.*

Charlotte played devil's advocate. "Well, then, *supposing* them to be in London. They may be there, though for the purpose of concealment...for no *exceptional* purpose. It is not likely that money should be very abundant on either side, and it might strike them that they could more economically, though less easily, be married in London, than in Scotland."

She looked at him, appeal in her glance, but he had no reassurance to give. Bennet shook his head "I cannot retain any vestige of hope." He read her true mind in her welling eyes. *Lydia is underage, as Charlotte knows.* "Wickham seduced my silly Lydia away with false promises."

Charlotte covered a sob with her hand. Mary leaned into her side.

He exploded in wrath. "What claims has Lydia, what attractions has she beyond youth, health, and good humor, *that could make him for her sake,* forego every chance of benefiting himself by marrying well!"

Scandal is likely to engulf us all!

He wrenched back his surging emotions, shamed by his outburst. He altered his tone to one of icy control "As to what restraint the apprehension of disgrace in the corps might throw on a dishonorable elopement with her, I am not able to judge, for I know nothing of the effects that such a step might produce."

Colonel Forster did not hesitate. He replied at once. "Sir, they are grave. Wickham's commission will be rescinded. His livelihood will be stripped away. He will be reduced to penury."

Bennet stiffened his lips; he gave a shortened nod. *It is understood. Wickham cannot support a wife.* He gestured at his wife and his daughter, who wore identical expressions of hopelessness and grief. "Our distress is very great, sir. Can you offer any solace to us?"

The colonel shook his head. "I am not disposed to depend upon their marriage. I fear Wickham is not a man to be trusted."

If only I had not sent Lydia away to Brighton.

Charlotte's admonishment had cut deep. He had acted the weak man with his family, resigning himself to live under the thumb of a harridan. Now see what had come of it! He had become indolent, imperceptive, and altogether reprehensible in his own hindsight. Lydia's unhappy fate was to be laid at *his* door. It was horrifying to realize that her sad fall was not the end. He could see the repercussions – they followed as night followed day.

Inwardly, he shuddered. The consequences of Lydia's transgression were too grave to contemplate. The family would be plunged into scandal. An indelible stain would besmirch the reputations of her sisters, whom no decent gentleman would thereafter ally himself.

Thomas Bennet could not stand to be idle any longer. *Every hour that passes makes her ruin more certain. And that of her sisters.* A grieved conscience flicked its whip. "I shall go at once to London, to try to discover her."

"But what do you mean to do?" asked Charlotte. Heightened anxiety etched her features and colored her low voice. She laid a hand on her full, rounded belly, a gesture as unconscious as it was protective.

Perhaps he was still a weak man, but he would do all in his power to avert the terrible trouble, a tremendous swell of tidewaters, rushing toward them. *My poor girls! Lydia brings us all low.* More than all the rest, however, he would set himself to reverse his young wife's damaged perception of him and become a better man.

He shook his head. "I am sure I know not, but nevertheless I must go! Lydia must be retrieved! Perhaps then scandal will be averted."

"I shall go with you, and gladly, Mr. Bennet," said Colonel Forster. "I am obliged to be at Brighton again tomorrow evening, but until then I shall count myself at your service."

Bennet seized the man's hand and wrung it. "Thank you, sir."

[34]

The gloom at separation was sunk in preparations for departure. Colonel Forster had come too late in the day for travelling to London, so the gentlemen agreed to set off early in the morning. Mr. Bennet offered hospitality for the night and it was accepted. On Tuesday, 4th August, he took solemn leave of his wife and daughter. He expressed the hope that he would shortly return to Longbourn. "Pray, dear ones, that I shall have my wayward daughter with me." He promised a letter upon his arrival in London. The three men climbed into the carriage and it rolled away.

The anticipated letter came. Charlotte eagerly opened it; at once, she was let down. In a disappointed voice, she said, "He writes so little."

"*Any* word must alleviate some part of our suspense."

She stifled her acid rejoinder. *You would think so, indeed!* "I shall read it to you, Mary."

Wednesday, 5th August
London

"My dearest Charlotte,

"I have been to Epsom, the place where they last changed horses, to see the postilions, and try if anything could be made out from them. My principal object was to discover the number of the hackney coach which took them from Clapham. I hoped to discover at what house the coachman had set down his fare. But it has come to nothing. I therefore

cannot give you, nor my poor Mary, any consolation. Colonel Forster is returned to Brighton. I have not slept.

"God bless you.

"I remain yours, &c."

"Is that all?" cried Mary, her expression disbelieving. "Surely Papa could tell us more! What are his plans? Where is he now? *At the very least* he could relate the weather!"

"I feel just as you do, Mary, and more besides! *He has not slept!* Did he roam the streets all night? The dangers he might encounter! But he *must* write again and be more forthcoming."

Mary muttered something astringent.

Charlotte released a sigh. *I cannot blame her. Such an inadequate letter!* "At least we know he is arrived safe in London."

Sir William and Lady Lucas were set down from their carriage. The butler showed them into the drawing-room, where Charlotte was sitting. She was warm in her greeting. "I am glad you have come!" She offered her hands to her father and kissed her mother's cheek. She had seen her parents at church for Sunday services, only four days prior. But so much had happened, so much that distressed, it seemed to her far longer.

"Are not Maria and Augusta with you?"

"I would not bring them," responded Sir William.

Charlotte wondered at her father's short, odd reply. *What is going forward at Lucas Lodge? Has Augusta created some contretemps? And pulled Maria into her disgrace?*

Mary was playing the pianoforte in an upper room. Charlotte wished she had chosen a more cheerful piece. *This dirge gives a very odd notion of the atmosphere at Longbourn.* She made as if to pull the bell the bell. "Mary..."

"Pray do not disturb Mary's pianoforte practice. We wished to speak privately with you," said Lady Lucas.

Odder and odder. Charlotte began to feel uneasy. "Come! Sit with me." She seated herself on the settee, to be joined by her mother. She looked an inquiry at her father. "Sir, will you not take your ease?"

Sir William did not avail himself of her invitation. He stood with his hands clasped behind his back. "I shall not conceal it from you, daughter. All of Meryton is talking of this sorry pass with Lydia Bennet."

"Indeed, my dear, Lydia's elopement with Wickham is everywhere spoken of," said Lady Lucas gloomily.

Charlotte regarded her parents with astonishment. "Why, we had the express only Sunday night! How is it that it is already known?"

"Mrs. Philips heard the express rider in Meryton. Mr. Philips still conducts business with some of the militia officers. A solicitor's work is not over simply because his clients are gone to Brighton! The bad tidings were relayed to Mr. Philips by more than one source in the militia, and he erred in judgment by confiding in his wife." Sir William added, in heavy accents, "Now all Meryton knows every ignominious detail."

"An elopement to Gretna Greene!" exclaimed Lady Lucas.

Charlotte lifted her shoulders. She felt utterly wearied by everything. "I knew it could not for long be concealed, but I *had* hoped that we might have some word of Lydia beforehand. The lady's penchant for gossip could not come at a worse time."

So! Our discussion is not thought fit for the ears of my sister and Augusta. But surely, if all Meryton knows, so must they! I am glad to be spared Augusta's opinion, for her observations set ill with me before.

"Mrs. Philips does her best to make her niece's name a byword," said Sir William grimly. "A harebrained, gossiping, vulgar woman, whose mere speculations become as facts by the time they reach her tongue. Her sister Bennet was just such a one. It is a pretty scandal,

Charlotte, and it must be contained. Yet you say that you have no word of Lydia?"

She shook her head. "We know very little, except it now appears that they have concealed themselves in London. Mr. Bennet is there now, doing what he can to discover her."

Lady Lucas was exceedingly shocked. "But can you think that Lydia is so lost to everything but love of him, as to consent to live with him on any other terms than marriage?"

"It does seem so, and it is most shocking indeed." It was the greatest imaginable evil. Charlotte knew that for truth – she had only to look at her mother's frozen expression.

Sir William growled, "Lydia imperils her place in society by this!"

Charlotte bowed her head in shame and sorrowed reflection. She said in a low voice, "Indeed, I fear it! I have confided this to no one else, believe me! But now her elopement is known here in Meryton – is it so impossible to assume that the worst will not also become known? I am not sure what will save her."

Lady Lucas visibly shook herself free. "I am sending Augusta home to Maple Grove! I do not care if it is *inconvenient* for Mr. Suckling! She must not hear of *this* wickedness! I will not have *every sordid detail* reported to the Sucklings and all their neighbors!" Lady Lucas nodded to herself. "We will send her in a hired post-chaise, accompanied by one of the maids, who can then travel back on the mail coach."

Sir William took a hasty turn around the parlor, his perturbation so overpowering that he could not be still. "All Meryton seems to be striving to blacken the man. He is declared to be in debt to every tradesman in the place, and his intrigues – all honored with the title of seduction, mind you! – has been extended into every tradesman's family."

Charlotte was rocked by the stunning revelation. "But this is worse and worse! I cannot credit above half of it, but I believe enough to make my apprehension of Lydia's ruin still more certain."

She could not think what was best to be done. Even if Lydia wedded Wickham, such a sordid reputation must follow them, and besmirch all of their connections. She had thought she would be glad, if only she heard that Lydia was safely married, but this intelligence raised new and horrible specters.

Oh, my dear Thomas! What other sorrows are in store!

"It is quite true, Charlotte." Lady Lucas snorted, her derision and disgust plain. "Everybody declares he is the wickedest young man in the world, and *everybody* begins to find out that they had *always* distrusted the appearance of his goodness."

Charlotte pressed her hands to cold cheeks. "Oh! Everything you say burdens my heart!"

Sir William smote the stone fireplace mantel; in fierce frustration, he exclaimed, "I wish I could help Bennet recover his daughter, but I have no connections worthy of the word in town. Lydia! *All of sixteen!* But a year younger than Maria!"

Lady Lucas shuddered. "It does not bear thinking of, my dear sir."

"Thomas Bennet is my friend – more, he is my son-in-law! Whatever affects him or his family must also affect me." Sir William worked his jaw as he stared into the middle distance. He turned his head to his daughter. The angry glint in his blue eyes startled her. "Charlotte, I shall do whatever I can to protect you and the Bennets from worse gossip. I think I shall pay a visit to Mr. Philips, for a start, and recommend to him that it will not do to have his wife running abroad, gossiping about a family connected to a man who was received at St. James!"

Charlotte was torn between tears and laughter. Her jovial, portly sire did not possess a single threatening quality, either in his genial aspect or his nature. Surely, there was no one alive who would take him in a serious vein. "Will it serve, sir?"

Sir William exhaled forcibly. "I put a lot of work in Mr. Philips' way. If he knows what is good for his pocketbook, he shall see the sense in putting a bridle on his wife!"

At an uncommonly early hour the next morning, Sir William and Lady Lucas brought Miss Hawkins to Longbourn to make her goodbyes. "*Dear* cousin Charlotte! *Dear* Miss Mary! *Adieu, adieu!* I am to be *snatched* from your affectionate company, in this same hour! I know well it has to do with Miss Lydia's shocking conduct – *such* a scandal! I do not know what my sister Selena will make of it. Our hopes of an honorable and comfortable marriage for Miss Lydia are undoubtedly all at an end, are they not, Charlotte, Miss Mary? I am sure you must agree! Lady Lucas sends a letter by me to my brother Suckling – she was good enough to let me read it, you know! – and recommended that my Bath come-out not be delayed, a most agreeable sentiment! But *how* I shall miss everyone in quaint little Meryton!"

Charlotte expressed nothing of her real sentiments. *I must keep at the forefront of my recall that she has a generous heart.* She was wearing, after all, the gown she had fashioned from the expensive, beautiful challis given to her by her cousin, and she was grateful for the inanimate reminder. An unseasonably chilly wind was gusting. Wrapping a large fringed square shawl securely around herself, she walked with her cousin outdoors to the waiting post-chaise, and saw Miss Hawkins off with a cheerful wave. She did not wait to watch the vehicle out of sight but hastily retreated back into the shelter of the house. She called for the Bennet carriage to be brought around to carry her somber parents back to Lucas Lodge, and in a very short time, she and Mary were alone again at Longbourn.

"Such splendid good wishes, such harmonious accords, such effusive adieus, Charlotte! Never was Miss Hawkins so overwhelmed by civility!"

Charlotte looked at her sister-in-law. She allowed her lips to curve in a small smile. "Yes, I did rather take the wind out of her sails. I am a Lucas, after all. My family is *famed* for civility!"

Mary gurgled laughter.

Two days later, on Saturday, 8th August, a dusty carriage, splattered up to the wheel shafts in heavy dirt, pulled up to the doors of Longbourn, and the Gardiners and Elizabeth descended. The travelers were the worse for wear and gratefully accepted the suggestion of refreshment, while their luggage was carried upstairs, and water for baths was heated. Swiftly putting off her wraps, Elizabeth said in a rush, "I had your letters, Mary. We were all profoundly shocked. We left Pemberley at once." She held out her hands. "Charlotte!"

Charlotte was quick to meet her – their fingers clung together.

"Oh, Charlotte! What news have you from my father?"

Charlotte shook her head. "Nothing, nothing! He has written only that so far his search has been unsuccessful." She urged them all into the drawing-room, where they could sit down. "Mrs. Hill will bring in a tray directly. So, your tour went so far north as Pemberley! How is dear Jane?"

Mrs. Gardiner answered. "When we arrived she was low in spirits, which is only natural, but she was beginning to recover her equilibrium. Bingley is most attentive and I dare hope that their strong mutual affection will help them through this sadness."

"The terrible news about Lydia was a severe blow to us all," said Mr. Gardiner, shaking his head. "Mr. Darcy was present when Lizzy had her letters; she was unable to quell her tears and he persuaded her to tell him the cause of her distress. He begged her to take his own handkerchief. He left abruptly for London, though not before insisting the Bingleys continue in his hospitality during his absence. Of course, *we* would not remain when such trouble was before us."

Charlotte's arrested gaze traveled at once to Elizabeth. "Mr. Darcy sounds all solicitude. It is a compliment to yourself, Eliza!"

Her cheeks bloomed with color, and she said in a suffocated voice, "Mr. Darcy was exceedingly kind, but the particulars of our family's disgrace must have disgusted him. I do not expect to ever see him again."

The whole party was in hopes of a letter from Mr. Bennet the next morning, but the post came in without bringing a single line from him. Charlotte was left prey to her anxiety. "I cannot understand it! Surely he can spare time for another letter." She flattened her palm against her side. *The babe kicks hard.*

Mrs. Gardiner noticed, and in a quiet aside, she said, "I ask you not to unnecessarily distress yourself, Charlotte. Such turmoil is not healthful for you or the babe. Mary, pour another cup of chamomile tea for Charlotte. It will help to calm your nerves, dear girl."

With a sigh, Mr. Gardiner said, "His family knows him to be on all common occasions, a most negligent and dilatory correspondent."

"But at such a time, I had hoped for exertion," exclaimed Charlotte.

Mr. Gardiner lifted his hands. "I am forced to conclude that he had no pleasing intelligence to send."

"But even of *that* I would have been glad to be certain."

"I will return to town and find my brother. I promise I shall send word as soon as I can."

Mr. Gardiner waited only for the morning post, to be certain there was still nothing from Mr. Bennet, before he set off for London.

"Come to Gracechurch Street, brother. You must rest."

Bennet shook his head. "I cannot, Gardiner. I must find her."

"Man, you are exhausted! You will do her little good if you fall down in the gutter filth. Come to Gracechurch Street, take your ease, tell me all you have done, and we will confer on what to do next."

Bennet was not proof against his brother-in-law's persuasions and he gave way. Sometime later, he was ensconced in a comfortable armchair in his brother-in-law's parlor, with a half-emptied glass of port in his hand and his belly full of a hot dinner. At Mr. Gardiner's urgings, he described the futility of his search. "I have been to Epsom and Clapham, but without gaining any satisfactory information. I thought the circumstance of a gentleman and a lady's removing from one carriage into another might be remarked. I am now determined to enquire at all the principal hotels in town. I think it possible that they might have gone to one of them, on their first coming to London, before they procured lodgings."

Mr. Gardiner leaned forward, the port decanter in hand, and poured another generous measure into his brother-in-law's wineglass. Bennet lifted the glass in a salute before setting it to his lips and taking a swallow of the heavy, dark wine. An anguished rut had been worn into his tired mind. *What a bad father I have been, shirking my sacred responsibilities.*

As he set aside the decanter, Mr. Gardiner's expression had turned dubious. "I shall be plain, Thomas. I myself do not expect any success from this measure; but as you are eager in it, I mean to assist you in pursuing it."

"Thank you, Edward. She is my daughter. I must try."

Mr. Gardiner leaned back in his own armchair. "My dear wife asked me to relay this message – Charlotte is exceeding anxious, and made more so as she is very near her confinement. Elizabeth and Mary are also fraught with worry. Brother, you *must* take into account how much you are needed at Longbourn."

"I am not wishful to leave town." Yet Bennet was torn. *I must do all in my power – but Charlotte, and my poor girls!*

Mr. Gardiner dipped his head, acknowledging his understanding. "Might I make a suggestion? Let me write to Colonel Forster to desire him to find out, if possible, from some of the young man's intimates in the militia, whether Wickham has any relations or connections, who would be likely to know in what part of the town he has now concealed himself. If there was anyone, that one could apply to – with a probability of gaining such a clue as that, it might be of essential consequence."

Sighing, Bennet passed a hand down his face. "I should have thought of it myself."

"At present, we have nothing to guide us. The colonel will, I daresay, do everything he can to satisfy us on this head."

A low tide of enormous relief rose inside him. *I am not alone. Three of us, working to find them out.* Bennet gave a long sigh. "Edward, I am in your debt for your help and good counsel. Between us and Colonel Forster, we will surely discover them."

"I hope you realize, you *must* return to Longbourn."

Bennet reluctantly nodded. "You are right. I know it. I must go, for Charlotte's sake and mine; but allow me to the end of the week, for I am determined to visit every hotel and inn. Edward, my heart misgives me! Lydia left with that seducer on Saturday. A full week ago!"

Mr. Gardiner's compassion expressed itself prosaically. "My carriage is at your disposal. I shall write my dear wife that I have found you and joined in your endeavor."

Bennet covered a sudden yawn, and he apologized for his lapse in manners. "I must rest for an hour or two before I take to the streets again."

"And I must be diligent to get off my letters."

The gentlemen got to their feet to quit the parlor. Mr. Gardiner delayed his brother-in-law, by way of a hand on his arm. Solemnly, he said, "I assure you, Thomas, you may entrust the search to me. I shall not rest in this matter."

"Yes, I know, and I am grateful to you."

[35]

Mr. Gardiner had left Longbourn on Sunday morning; on Tuesday, his wife received a letter from him. He penned that on his arrival he had immediately searched for and found Mr. Bennet, and persuaded him to come to Gracechurch Street; and he had also written to Colonel Forster.

"...Colonel Forster will discover anything he can in the regiment about Wickham. But, on second thoughts, perhaps Lizzy could tell us, what relations he has now living, better than any other person..."

Mrs. Gardiner looked up from her letter. "Well, Lizzy?"

Charlotte also looked over at her. "You always had a partiality for Wickham. Yes; I recall the expression of your sentiments, most particularly at the Netherfield ball. You preferred him to Mr. Darcy, did you not?"

Elizabeth's cheeks reddened. She appeared mortified. "I am at no loss to understand from whence this deference for my authority proceeds, for indeed, it is true. I once held an ill-conceived preference for Mr. Wickham's company." She spread her hands. "But it is not in my power to give any information of a satisfactory nature, as my uncle's compliment deserves. I never heard of his having had any relations, except a father and mother, both of whom had been dead for many years."

"Surely, it is possible that some of his acquaintances in the militia might be able to give more information." Mary's somberness was lightened by hope. "The application to Colonel Forster is something to look forward to, at the least."

Charlotte agreed, her spirits lifting. "Captain Carter, Captain Denny, Mr. Pratt, and Mr. Chamberlayne were in the same company. One of them *must* know something!"

Elizabeth shook her head. "I am not very sanguine in expecting it."

Mrs. Gardiner resumed reading aloud her letter.

Charlotte listened, wholly focused on it with painful intensity, and her heart squeezed with its ending. *"...I add only that my brother Bennet seems wholly disinclined to leave London, for some few days yet. I promise to write again very soon..."*

She covered her quivering lips with the press of her fingers.

All of the ladies sitting with her regarded her with sympathy. Mary slipped her hand into Charlotte's and linked their fingers. "Never mind, Charlotte. We are all here to comfort and uphold one another."

Mrs. Gardiner folded the letter. "I am certain better news will come."

It was Elizabeth who put it most succinctly. "Lydia has succeeded in disrupting all of our lives. I should like to box her ears!"

Charlotte remained in suspense every day, but the most anxious part of each was when the post was expected. The arrival of letters was the first grand object of every morning's impatience. Through letters, whatever good or bad was to be told would be communicated, and every succeeding day was expected to bring some news of importance.

She received a short communication from Lucas Lodge. *"Daughter, I am in receipt of a letter from Mrs. Suckling. My niece has the temerity to scold me for misrepresenting the pristine respectability of our house, and regrets sending Miss Simmons to us! I shall never forgive Lydia, never! Such a female, lost to all decency, to be related to us!"* Charlotte did not feel herself equal to respond. Nor did she think there was anything she could have penned that would have propitiated her parent.

Mr. Gardiner did not write again, till he had received an answer from Colonel Forster, and then he had nothing of a pleasant nature to send. "*...His former acquaintances had been numerous; but since he had been in the militia, it did not appear that he was on terms of particular friendship with any of them. There was no one therefore who could be pointed out, as likely to give any news of him...Colonel Forster believed that more than a thousand pounds would be necessary to clear his expenses at Brighton. He owed a good deal in the town, but his debts of honor were still more formidable."*

"A gamester!" exclaimed Mary in horror.

Elizabeth was equally taken aback. "This is wholly unexpected. I had not an idea of it."

Mrs. Gardiner at once made known her disapproval. "A young man without character. Tradesmen's debts and gambling!"

"And yet, for Lydia's sake, we must hope that he weds her."

At Charlotte's somber observation, all of her companions had visible expressions of distress. In any other circumstances, a match with such an unworthy man, and moreover, one who had no employment with which to support a wife, would never have been sanctioned; however, the scandal had changed everything. *I share in their unhappiness. Poor foolish Lydia!*

The end of the week brought Thomas Bennet himself, Mr. Gardiner's persuasions having at last been successful. Exhausted and spiritless, Bennet returned to Longbourn in the Gardiner's carriage and Mrs. Gardiner, who was pining to see her children, was carried back in it to Gracechurch Street. Late that afternoon, interrupting tea-time, an express rider arrived with another letter. Mr. Gardiner's pen imparted the unwelcome news that his daughter and Wickham had both been seen by his brother-in-law, that they were not married, nor was there any intention of being so. Mr. Gardiner had entered into engagements on Mr. Bennet's behalf, that if he was willing to perform them, then Mr. Gardiner hoped it would not be long before they were married.

On the same evening, Charlotte's travails came upon her. She labored through the night, with her mother, Lady Lucas, and the midwife in close attendance. Shortly after dawn, on Sunday, 16th August, Charlotte Bennet was delivered of a red-faced, bawling, healthy son.

Thomas Bennet was overjoyed. He wept, brokenly.

Mr. Bennet entered his wife's bedchamber, where she rested on her bed against plumped pillows, her light brown hair dressed in a loose braid, and a shawl tucked around her shoulders. She was reading, but at sight of him, and his frowning expression, she sat aside the volume. *He is displeased.*

He said curtly, "A letter has come from Mr. Collins, dated Thursday, 12th August. He feels called upon to condole with us on our grievous affliction *of which they were yesterday informed by a letter from Hertfordshire!*"

"Oh, no! That the sordid story has become known to Mr. Collins!"

"Just so!" Bennet said, with marked sarcasm, "One's neighbors are so eager to gossip. I wonder which of them had the temerity!"

"I understand your displeasure, Thomas." She considered the matter. "A few innocent lines in one of Maria's letters to Kitty? Lydia's elopement with Wickham was a great piece of news, as you must admit. Mary *has* written to Kitty. As Lydia's nearest sister, Kitty had a right to know, and of our shared affliction and distress. It was probably a cry from Kitty's lips, an expression of her own pain and horror, which informed Mr. Collins."

She saw that his smoldering anger had been checked. He offered an apologetic bow to her. "I believed I was a rational man, but your excellent logic puts me to shame. As usual, my love, your good sense triumphs." She inclined her head, a small smile touching her lips at his endearment.

"I ask you to read out the remainder of Collins' letter, so I may decide if its tone is as offensive as when I first read it."

"Very well." Charlotte, with a curious glance at him, took the creased letter from his outstretched hand. She bent her gaze, passing swiftly down the close-written lines. "Mr. Collins is verbose. But here we are!"

"Be assured, dear sir, that Lady Catherine and myself sincerely sympathize with you, and all your respectable family, in your present distress, which must be of the bitterest kind, because proceeding from a cause which no time can remove. No arguments shall be wanting on my part-"

"Remarkable! A windbag who acknowledges it," interjected Bennet.

Charlotte huffed, half-laughing at him, and dropped the missive to her lap. "Sir, do you wish me to continue?"

Bennet responded with a rueful grimace, and he waved his hand at the letter. "Say on, say on."

It took a moment, but Charlotte found her place. *"-that can alleviate so severe a misfortune, or that may comfort you, under a circumstance that must be of all others most afflicting to a parent's mind. The death of your daughter would have been a blessing in comparison of this."*

Charlotte looked up. "Mr. Collins is harsh."

"Read on. You will be all the more edified."

She obeyed, but her pleasing voice could not ameliorate the lengthy obnoxious paragraphs. Bennet broke in and repeated, with acute distaste, "*This licentiousness of behavior in your daughter!* The worst of it, Charlotte, is that I cannot refute his charges."

He dropped onto a convenient chair, placed beside the bed. "Lydia was always her mother's favorite, so cosseted and indulged! A bad result, as we see! But I am to blame, as well."

Charlotte was caught up in Mr. Collins' communication.

"I am inclined to think that her own disposition must be naturally bad, or she could not be guilty of such an enormity, at so early an age. However that may be, you are grievously to be pitied, in which opinion I am joined by Lady Catherine, to whom I have related the affair."

Bennet straightened in the chair. He spiked a forefinger in the air. "Ah! Now we invoke our social betters!"

Charlotte cast a sideways glance at him, with a minatory frown.

Bennet subsided but listened with a gathering, wrathful expression.

"She agrees with me in apprehending that this false step in one daughter will be injurious to the fortunes of all the others, for who, as Lady Catherine herself condescendingly says, will connect themselves with such a family."

Bennet had obviously heard enough. "Yes, yes, and so on, and so on, *ad nauseum.* I was not mistaken in my understanding. It sounds just the same to the ear. It is a masterpiece of insult." With arms crossed over his chest, he demanded, "Well, my dear? What conclusions do you draw from this illuminating correspondence?"

She folded the letter with deliberate care. "Mr. Collins expresses himself extremely ill. Perhaps he writes from a state of agitation. After all, Kitty is situated with Lady Catherine, which makes it more awkward." She lifted her gaze. "Perhaps we should bring Kitty home?

Bennet considered it with a frown, then gave a decisive shake of his head. "She is better off where she is for now. She is at a distance, where she will not be humiliated by Meryton gossip."

Charlotte said honestly, "I cannot disregard all of the points he has made, Thomas. Gossip is harsh and unforgiving."

"I believe I know your mind well enough." He leaned forward, his elbows coming to rest on his knees, his hands clasped between them, and addressed her earnestly. "I do understand you, dear wife. Our son should not be made to suffer the slings and arrows of gossip through the folly of his foolish half-sister."

She shook her head, feeling full of regret for the necessity of her next observation. *But it has been so much in my mind.* "Even if they were married, which I do not at all believe to be certain, Wickham's character and Lydia's nature are established. Together, the duo will always bring trouble in their wake. Married or not, no good could come from receiving Lydia back into the fold at Longbourn. The gossip would come to a white-heat, here, where we live, surrounded by our friends and family. If Lydia is set at a distance, the gossip will eventually die a natural death."

"Your comments are wise, but nonetheless painful."

"Pray do not misunderstand me!" Charlotte reached over to touch one of his hands. "It is not that I wish her ill, sir. Never believe that of me."

"I know it, my dear. She brought it all upon herself." Thomas Bennet exhaled, before he straightened his spine. She offered him the letter back. He did not let go of her fingers until he had kissed the back of her hand. Over their joined hands, he smiled at her. "Dearest Charlotte! I am bereft of your consolation during the long nights. When may I return to your bed?"

She caught her breath. Coloring, she said softly, "The midwife said that I must allow six weeks before resuming my wifely duties."

"I shall endure each week with impatience, my darling wife." Her blush deepened, to his delight. He turned over her hand and kissed her palm; her fingers curled and he laughed, letting go her hand.

However, the main preoccupation exercising his intellect forced his mind back to the unpalatable communiqué from his cousin. He tapped the letter's folded edge into his opposing palm. "Mr. Collins is not altogether wrong – that Lydia expired would be better, for she must be dead to her sisters and to me."

She said, in compassion, "I am sorrier than I can say, Thomas."

He showed his teeth in a sudden, wolfish lift of the lips. "It occurs to me, dearest Charlotte, that I have been remiss. I have not yet informed my cousin of the birth of my heir. I shall take pleasure in penning that correspondence."

He heard Charlotte's low laughter rippling behind him as he exited the bedchamber. Shortly, he entered his library and sat down at his desk. He trimmed his pen, drew paper toward him, and dipped his pen into the inkwell.

Monday, 17th August
Longbourn, Hertforshire

Dear Sir,

I must trouble you for congratulations. On Sunday, 16th August, a healthy son was born to Mrs. Bennet, a son and my heir. So, I am also writing to inform you of the breaking of the entail. As a clergyman, I am confident you must rejoice, as much as any of us at Longbourn, at such glad tidings.

Yours sincerely, etc.
Thomas Bennet

[36]

Bennet frowned at the entries in the ledger, in which he had notated the dates of crops planted; some resowing had been necessary, due to the capricious weather. Heavy, wet skies had marked June and July, and all of summer had been unusually chilly. "The crops did not come up as they should," he muttered to himself. "The yield will be less than last year, and the harvest will be delayed, as well." He scowled, as worry tugged at him. *My income will be reduced. I will have little in reserve for sowing next season.*

A discreet knock on the library door pulled him from his unhappy ruminations. He called enter and the footman quietly came in.

"An express came from Mr. Gardiner, sir."

Bennet thanked the manservant for bringing it, and at once broke open the seal. On reading the lengthy communiqué, Bennet refolded the sheets and pushed the thick square into his frock coat pocket. He called for his overcoat, hat and gloves, and then walked slowly to the copse of woods to one side of the paddock. His spaniel frisked alongside him and was swift to race past him under the trees.

Bennet pondered what his brother Gardiner had outlined, but even more, the significance of what had not been revealed. *Fiend seize it! It was an ill-omened day when Lydia made off with Wickham!* Marriage articles had settled five thousand pounds on Mrs. Bennet and their children; but in what proportions it should be divided amongst the latter depended on the will of the parents. He had already given over Jane's portion, and Lydia's allotment was one point that was now to be settled.

As for the rest, I fear to learn of it. And Gardiner keeps his own counsel.

He addressed the empty wood. "I must answer the letter. It must be done soon." He turned to make his way back to the house, deep in thought. The spaniel returned at a rush to trot at his heels.

Bennet returned to the library, his canine companion preceding him. With a lolling tongue, the spaniel dropped onto a well-pummeled cushion.

He sat down at his desk and began to compose his reply.

"I have no hesitation in acceding to the proposal before me."

In terms of grateful acknowledgement for the kindness of his brother Gardiner, though expressed most concisely, he then delivered on paper his perfect approbation of all that was done, and his willingness to fulfill the engagements that had been made for him.

"I beg not to know further particulars of what actions I am indebted to you, brother."

He ended with the usual salutations, including an affectionate word for Mrs. Gardiner; but he was too angry with Lydia to send any message to her. *I have borne guilt, yes! As for what she has cost us all, in distress and fear, and obligation, I have yet to sort it out. My resentment is strong.*

As he sanded the ink, he said aloud, "Lydia is to be married." A book slid from a shelf and fell to the carpet. The snoring spaniel flicked an ear. Such things had become commonplace and the dog no longer took notice. He heaved a sigh. *No doubt Mrs. Bennet rejoices at the glad tidings.*

He dispatched his letter to Gracechurch Street, in Cheapside, London, by the next post, for though dilatory in undertaking business, he was quick in its execution.

Mrs. Philips had come to admire the sleeping baby. She and Mary were still sitting with Charlotte, when Elizabeth hurried into the room, her face flushed with excitement. "Prepare yourselves for good news. I came in from my walk and my father called me into the library. Papa gave into my hand an express from my uncle Gardiner."

Charlotte signaled the nursery maid to take her baby back upstairs. She smiled at her friend's scarce concealed impatience. "Now you may edify us, Eliza."

Elizabeth read the letter aloud, and there were amazed exclamations all around. When she finished, she cried, "Is it possible? Can it be possible that he will marry her?"

Mrs. Philips could not contain herself; her joy burst forth. "Oh, happy day! My dear, dear Lydia! This is delightful, indeed! She will be married! She will be wed at sixteen!"

"So, they are to be wed." Charlotte marveled at the news, but the rest seemed to her just as marvelous. Mr. Bennet had only to send full powers for Mr. Gardiner to act in his name. Mr. Bennet could stay quietly at Longbourn, and depend on Mr. Gardiner's diligence and care. *Surely there is more for a father to negotiate.*

"Wickham is not so undeserving, then, as we have believed." Mary shook her head. "I must say, I am all incredulity. I had given up all hope of a happy conclusion."

"Indeed, if it had not been for Mr. Gardiner's exertions, we must still be suspended by sorrow and hopelessness." Charlotte's brain seethed with questions and conjectures. *Mr. Gardiner's most welcome letter is glaringly spare of explanation.*

"My good, kind brother! I knew how it would be. I knew he would manage everything!" Mrs. Philips expressed her desire to leave Charlotte and her nieces at once, with the announced intention of spreading the glad tidings throughout the neighborhood.

"I shall see you out, aunt." Elizabeth rose to accompany Mrs. Philips downstairs.

Charlotte was anxious to discover more, especially what her husband thought about it all. At her request, Mary tugged the bell-pull for the maid before she also left the bedchamber, saying, "I have started a litter to Kitty. I think she will want to hear this latest news."

Charlotte dressed with the help of the maid, and went downstairs to the library. She knocked and entered. Her husband's gray-blue eyes lit up when he saw her. "My dear! You should not be downstairs so soon."

"The maid gave me the support of her arm." It struck her that even though he smiled, underneath it, his expression was melancholic. "I have heard the glad tidings, Thomas. Mr. Gardiner has fixed all. In short, you will have another daughter married."

Bennet got up and ushered her to a comfortable chair, then sat down again behind his desk. "I have answered his letter. I lost no time, you see, considering how important every moment is, in such a case."

"You disliked the trouble."

"I disliked it very much, but it had to be done." Bennet's smile turned lopsided. "Lydia's wedding! That *it* will be done with such trifling exertion on my side, too! It is a very welcome surprise, for my chief wish at present is to have as little trouble in the business as possible. When the first transports of rage which produced my activity in seeking her were over, I naturally returned to all my former indolence."

Charlotte heard the pained self-derision in his voice. "Dear sir, you must not punish yourself with guilt. You must not be too severe on yourself."

"Who should suffer but myself? It has been my own doing, and I ought to feel it. I perceive concern in your beautiful eyes! Dear Charlotte, I assure you, it is misplaced. Let me once in my life feel how much I have been to blame. I am not afraid of being overpowered by the impression. It will pass away soon enough."

Charlotte abandoned her efforts at comfort, for it was obvious he would have none of it. "I had never before supposed that, could Wickham be prevailed upon to marry Lydia, it would be done with so little inconvenience to yourself as by the present arrangement."

"Yes, indeed! She is to be wed from my brother Gardiner's house, as was dear Jane." Bennet's mouth tightened to a thin line. "So, that is two daughters married with scarce an expense to my purse."

"Never mind, Thomas. Events conspired to rob you of a father's dear privileges." Charlotte knew his pride had taken a substantial blow in that he had not had the care and expense for his daughters' weddings, but to her mind it was useless to dwell on what could not be. "And may I ask? But the terms, I suppose, must be complied with?"

"Complied with! I am only ashamed of his asking so little."

"And they *must* marry! Yet he is *such* a man!

"Yes, yes, they must marry. There is nothing else to be done."

"What are the marriage settlements?"

"All that is required of me is an assurance to Lydia, by settlement, her equal share of the five thousand pounds secured with the decease of her mother; and moreover, one hundred per annum during my life and fifty after I am gone." His smile turned self-mocking. "I will scarcely be ten pounds a year the loser, by the hundred that is to be paid them – what with her board and pocket allowance, and the continual presents in money which passed to her through her mother's hands. Lydia's expenses have been very little within that sum."

"Yes, that much was in Mr. Gardiner's letter." Charlotte leveled a straight look at her husband. "We have had such bad reports of Wickham's circumstances. Yet Mr. Gardiner writes there will be a little money, even when all his debts are discharged, to settle on

Lydia, in addition to her own fortune. Wickham's debts to be discharged and something still to remain!" She shook her head. "I cannot credit it."

Bennet regarded her with warm affection. "You have been quick to discern the crux, Charlotte. No man in his senses would marry Lydia on so slight a temptation. Wickham's a fool, if he takes her with a farthing less than ten thousand pounds."

"Ten thousand pounds!"

Thomas Bennet's face became etched in grim lines. "So, there are two things that I want very much to know. One, is how much money my brother Gardiner has laid down, to bring it about. And the other, how I am ever to pay him?"

Charlotte gasped. She felt the blood draining from her face. *Ten thousand pounds!* "Heaven forbid! How is half such a sum to be repaid?"

He made no direct reply, only shook his head, and said meditatively, "I have very often wished, before this period in my life, that, instead of spending my whole income, I had laid by an annual sum, for the better provision of my children, and of my wife, if she survived me."

He fisted his hands on his desktop. "I now wish it more than ever! Had I done my duty in that respect, Lydia need not have been indebted to her uncle, for whatever of honor or credit can now be purchased for her. The satisfaction of prevailing on one of the most worthless young men in Great Britain to be her husband might then have rested in its proper place." He tapped his chest with a hard forefinger. "With me!"

"I per-perfectly understand your-your sentiments." Charlotte's lips were stiff. *The shock of what he has conjectured!* She was shaking inside. The tremor of her hands betrayed her. She folded her arms, holding her elbows. "What is it you intend?"

Bennet spoke in a hard voice. "I am seriously concerned, that a cause of so little advantage to anyone should be forwarded at the sole expense of my brother Gardiner. I am determined, if possible, to find out the extent of his assistance, and to discharge the obligation as soon as I can."

Charlotte bowed her head to the inevitable; he was her lord and master and it was not her place to decry his judgment; but a dreadful fear wormed its way into her heart. She stared down at her tense hands, which she had now clenched together in her lap. "Is it even possible?"

Repaying such a vast sum would surely take decades, perhaps even generations; she envisioned her precious infant son asleep upstairs, and she was afflicted by helpless anger, for the debt would be inherited by him.

That Lydia – feckless, wayward Lydia! – should impoverish her family!

"I do not know. I hope I will find it so. Economy must be my watchword." A twist to his lips, he said, "When I first married, economy was held to be perfectly useless, for of course, we were to have a son. Mrs. Bennet, for many years, had been certain he would come. This event had at last been despaired of, but it was then too late to be saving. Mrs. Bennet had no turn of economy and my love of independence alone prevented us from exceeding our income." Bennet fell silent, before saying in a low voice. "Debt is the harshest of masters; it enslaves and swallows economy. We are forced into servitude."

"Oh, dear sir!" Overcome, Charlotte began to weep. She heard the scrape of chair legs. A moment later, her husband's strong hands lifted her out of her seat, bringing her to her feet, and his arms wrapped around her. She turned her face into the shoulder of his coat and clutched his lapel. His tightened embrace was false comfort, she knew, for nothing could dispel the wretched hopelessness.

"My poor dear Charlotte! You made a bad bargain with me!"

[37]

Thomas Bennet was incensed by the missive he had received.

"The Wickhams travel to Mr. Wickham's new regiment in Newcastle. They have written to say they will break journey at Longbourn!" He strode to and fro in the bedchamber, his hands clenched behind his back; his wife was propped on pillows in her bed, nursing their newborn son.

"I shall not let them set foot inside Longbourn," he exclaimed. "I bear spleen against this licentious pair. The infamy must have besmirched all of us, if not for fortunate intervention. Yet nothing is penned of remorse. Indeed, they mention nothing of elopement! All is forgotten by them."

"You *must* receive them this once, dear sir. Otherwise, it will cause unwelcome speculation about the marriage. And Lydia's inheritance was turned over to her husband, in the settlements, but her first annum was not. Since that is true, would it not be prudent to get a receipt from Mr. Wickham upon giving him the money?"

There was silence, for a long moment. Bennet regarded his wife as his choler cooled under the sway of her thoughtful reason. "As always, my dear Charlotte, your good sense proves its worth. Indeed, I must hand over Lydia's money to Mr. Wickham, and it is *a good idea* to have a signed receipt of the necessary transaction. He did not leave a good reputation behind him when he left Meryton. All the tradesmen were left holding his debts! If not for the good graces of my brother Gardener, and particularly those of Mr. Darcy, nothing would have been paid them to this day."

Charlotte was recalling the afflictions caused by the unrepentant pair. *The anxieties. The horrors of revelation.* "The Wickhams do not remain long in Hertfordshire; their shamelessness will be forgot and later offenses will be far removed from us. Such is our consolation."

The acidity of her observation made her husband laugh.

The Wickhams came to visit; they were received graciously enough, but with reserve. Mr. Bennet and Wickham were in the library for several minutes behind closed doors. When they emerged, both appeared satisfied that their business had been conducted in a gentlemanly fashion.

Charlotte had begun coming downstairs again; she was able to take up her usual duties and act as hostess. After showing off her wedding ring, Lydia flitted about, remarking on everything, and that nothing very much had changed. She cried, "Only think of its being three months, since I went away. It seems but a fortnight, I declare." She spied the housekeeper. "Mrs. Hill! What think you of my ring? I am come back married!"

Charlotte marveled. *They seem each of them to have the happiest memories in the world. Nothing of the past is recollected with pain.* Elizabeth and Mary shared in her bewildered despisal.

Elizabeth curled her lip. "I had not before believed Wickham quite equal to such assurance."

Mary made a choking sound in her throat, as though she felt ill, and concurred. "I blush for Lydia, but the cheeks of the two who cause such confusion suffer no variation in color."

It was inevitable that callers came to Longbourn, Mrs. Philips being the first. There was no lack of discourse. The bride and her aunt could not talk fast enough. Lady Lucas entered the drawing-room, bringing along her daughter Maria, ostensibly to see Charlotte's baby; but also, to observe the newly minted Mrs. Wickham.

When Charlotte took her mother and sister upstairs to make over the baby, it did not take many minutes before an opinion was rendered. Lady Lucas looked pained. "It is not to be supposed that time will give Lydia that embarrassment, from which she had been so wholly free at first."

Charlotte grimaced. "No, Mama, I fear not. Her ease and good spirits have but increased. She wishes nothing more than tour the neighborhood and show off her ring and hear herself addressed as Mrs. Wickham!"

"I do not understand it! I would be ducking my head in shame," exclaimed Maria.

"My dear sister, you have been better taught than Lydia."

Ten days of September passed in Longbourn hospitality. Mr. Bennet and his new son-in-law went shooting for birds, and Lydia declared, "I am sure Wickham will kill more birds than anybody else in the country!" Then the Wickhams took leave of Longbourn for the regiment in the north. Mr. Wickham's adieus were much more affectionate than his wife's. He smiled, looked handsome, and said many pretty things.

As soon as they were out of the house, Bennet said sardonically, "He is as fine a fellow as ever I saw. He simpers, and smirks, and makes love to us all. I am prodigiously proud of him." He rolled his eyes, a teasing gleam in their depths, toward his young wife. "I defy even Sir William Lucas himself, to produce a more valuable son-in-law."

Charlotte chuckled. "You are nonsensical, sir."

No one regretted that the Wickhams had left, particularly Charlotte. She was wearied by their stay. *I am glad to have the house quiet.* She parted from her husband and went upstairs. *Lydia never showed an interest in her half-brother.* After nursing her son and laying down the sleeping infant in the spare crib in her bedchamber, rather than calling for the nursery maid, Charlotte fell asleep on her bed. She had not yet recovered her full strength and little daily naps refreshed her. She dragged her eyes open. What had wakened her, she did not know. Then she heard it – the weak mewling cry. Alarmed, she sat up. *Something is very wrong!*

She at once left the bed. On seeing her child, horror sliced through her. *He is blue-faced!* She lunged, shuddering through the unearthly cold. She snatched up her baby into protective arms and backed up.

Charlotte's heart thundered. She snarled, "Stupid! Your icy touch is deadly! Are you mad? *Is it your intent to kill Mr. Bennet's heir?* Do you want Mr. Collins to inherit Longbourn?"

The apparition was reflected in her dressing-table mirror. It covered its frightening, chalk-white visage with long skeletal fingers. The ruffles of the window curtains whipped in agitated fashion. Charlotte could have sworn she heard a long, low moaning.

She spoke more gently. "You may watch over him from a distance."

§

Mrs. Philips came in a hurry to Longbourn. She was big with news. "The housekeeper at Netherfield has received orders to prepare the house, and she expects an arrival in a day or two! No doubt her master is coming to shoot there for several weeks. Mr. Bingley and dear Jane! Oh, how I shall rejoice to see dear, dear Jane!"

Elizabeth pointed out, "But aunt, do you not recall? Jane is recovering from a carriage accident. I saw her for myself little more than a month ago. I doubt she will be traveling again so soon."

The lady's effusions were dampened. "Oh! Well, I am sure she would come if she wanted. But if it is only Mr. Bingley, I shall be just as pleased to see him as not!"

Bennet replied with a marked reserve. "It is not even a twelvemonth since I first waited upon him."

No one said anything in front of Mrs. Philips, but at Mr. Bennet's repressive tone, glances were exchanged between Charlotte, Elizabeth and Mary. They knew very well that Mr. Bennet was less fond of Mr. Bingley than he had been in the past.

However, to everyone's surprise it was not Mr. Bingley, but Mr. Darcy, who had come to stay at Netherfield. He came to call at Longbourn, riding over from Netherfield. As the butler announced him, Elizabeth gave a small, strangled gasp. Charlotte shot her a glance as she rose to greet the visitor. The handsome gentleman bowed to each of the curtsying ladies, congratulated Charlotte upon her marriage, asked after everyone's health, and was invited to sit down. Mr. Darcy took a seat near Elizabeth. When he first came in, he had spoken to her but little; but every five minutes he seemed to be giving her more attention, bending an intense gaze upon her.

Charlotte found it of profound interest. She exchanged a glance with Mary, who raised a brow. Charlotte noted that Elizabeth's color fluctuated. However, it seemed that she dared not lift up her eyes. *So unlike Eliza, to be so quiet and retiring.*

Bennet entered into the drawing-room. Mr. Darcy rose at once, and Bennet greeted him with a friendly handshake. "Mr. Darcy! I am glad to see you." He gestured down at his riding clothes. "You discover me in all my dirt. I have been at the farm. The harvest has begun. The summer was so unseasonably cold; it has thrown the harvest this late into September."

Mr. Darcy responded in his grave manner. "I am not familiar with the crops in this part of the country. When do you expect to have all of the harvest in?"

"I do not expect it until the first week or two in November."

"It goes much the same in Derbyshire. The growing season has been unusual." They spoke several minutes more about agricultural matters, each seeming to derive enjoyment from the conversation. The gentlemen agreed to ride out later in the week to see the crops being brought in; as a landowner himself, Mr. Darcy expressed himself to be keenly interested.

Elizabeth looked on in wonderment.

Bennet excused himself to change his clothing. “Pray do not go away too soon, Mr. Darcy. I have an agricultural treatise I should like to show you.”

So it was that Mr. Darcy’s visit to Longbourn stretched past the usual quarter hour. The ormolu clock struck the hour; more time had elapsed, during which the agricultural treatise was thoroughly canvassed and Mr. Darcy recommended another one that might not yet have come in Mr. Bennet’s way. At hearing the chimes, Bennet looked over in surprise at the clock. He then turned his head to his wife. "My dear, if Darcy has no other engagements, he must stay to dinner.”

Charlotte knew where her duty laid. Besides, she was very curious at Elizabeth’s reaction to Mr. Darcy’s presence and that gentleman’s presence at all. *It is not for talk of agriculture he has come!* “Indeed, Mr. Darcy, you are most welcome.”

Mr. Darcy acquiesced, an expression of gratification on his face, and stood to make a bow. “A pleasure, Mrs. Bennet.”

The seating at the dining table was informal. Bennet was at the head and Charlotte at the foot. Mr. Darcy calmly took a seat next to Elizabeth, leaving Mary to sit opposite.

Elizabeth turned to Mr. Darcy. “Do you mean to make any stay in the country at present?”

“A few weeks,” he replied.

It was discovered that Mr. Darcy had requested of his friend Mr. Bingley, who had not given up the lease on Netherfield Park, the use of the manor. At a question put by Mr. Bennet, he said that the Bingleys were still at Pemberley.

“A rather strange circumstance, surely? Bingley at your home and you here, residing in his house.”

"Indeed, sir."

Nothing more in the way of explanation was forthcoming from the gentleman, but Charlotte was not behind in observing the intense glance that Mr. Darcy sent toward Elizabeth. The hour over dinner was spent in amiable conversation and afterwards resumed in the drawing-room. Before he went away, an engagement was formed, for his coming next morning to shoot. When he had left the drawing-room, Charlotte said to her husband, "He was much more agreeable than I had expected."

Elizabeth darted a glance at her father. She smiled a little at his reply. "There is nothing of presumption or folly in Darcy, that could provoke my ridicule, or disgust me into silence."

Mr. Darcy was punctual to his appointment; and he and Mr. Bennet spent the morning together, as had been agreed on. Darcy returned with him to dinner, and once again he seated himself beside Elizabeth.

Afterwards, for an hour or more, on horseback, Bennet took Mr. Darcy to look over the harvesting at Longbourn farm and the orchards, and at the cuttings in the woods, where timber had been felled, which would be seasoned for a year or two before being utilized for building materials or the making of furniture.

Elizabeth said, with a wry laugh, "Mr. Darcy is courting my father!"

"My nose is put out of joint," responded Mary, with rare humor.

Elizabeth looked astonished, but Charlotte only laughed. She had become used to Mary's unexpected flares of wit.

The gentlemen came back in, mainly so that Mr. Darcy could take proper leave of the ladies. Before he left, Charlotte invited him to dine on Tuesday evening. "It will be a large party, but our guests will already be known to you from your last visit to Hertfordshire."

At once, he said, "I have no engagements at all. I accept your invitation, Mrs. Bennet." The hunt had been successful and Darcy had a brace or two of birds attached to his saddle as he rode back to Netherfield.

Bennet retired to the library, as was his custom, and Mary went upstairs to her instrument, leaving Charlotte and Elizabeth alone together. Since Mr. Darcy had taken up residence, Charlotte had been fairly bursting to be told something of Elizabeth's feelings at being in Darcy's company again. Much of the rift between them had been bridged, through the traumatic events having to do with Lydia, so she felt more confident in her query. "Well, Eliza, what think you of Mr. Darcy's visits?"

Elizabeth's color rose high. "On both sides, we meet only as common and indifferent acquaintances."

"Oh, very indifferent, indeed!" Charlotte gave a soft chuckle. "Come, Eliza! Again today, Mr. Darcy could scarce take his eyes from you."

"Mr. Darcy's behavior astonished and vexed me."

"I am truly puzzled by what you say, for I am finding him to be perfectly amiable and pleasing."

Elizabeth shook her head, and burst out, "But it was just as you said! He *stares* at me! Why, if he came only to be silent, grave, and indifferent, did he come at all?"

"You seem inordinately fixated by what you call his *indifference*."

Elizabeth bit her lip; her cheeks bloomed pink. "Pray excuse me, Charlotte. I am going for a walk."

Before she could quit the drawing-room, Charlotte called after her. "Think no more about the teasing man, at least until he dines here on Tuesday!" Elizabeth did not reply, nor look around, but hurried out of the room.

Charlotte laughed with delight. *Teasing Eliza again! How refreshing!*

Bennet entered the drawing-room. He smiled at her. "It is pleasant to hear you in such buoyant spirits, dear wife. I hope what

I relate to you will only add to your merriment. This very day, I have received an astonishing communiqué from Captain Denny, in which he presents himself as a possible suitor for Mary's hand! He has set down his future prospects in fine form, and has even enclosed the name of a character reference. What think you of that?"

Charlotte chortled. "Why, I am hardly surprised! He had shown a preference for her company before he went away with the rest of the militia to Brighton. Oh, how happy I am to hear of this! Does he ask permission to court her?"

"He does, indeed! And pending my approval, he requests the honor of writing to her. Do you have any insight into Mary's mind?"

"Dear Mary! I believe she will be well-pleased by such a courtship."

"Then I will leave you and make my way upstairs to speak to her."

A few days after this visit, Mr. Darcy called again. He sat with them above an hour, and was in remarkably good spirits. He turned to Elizabeth. "Do you walk out most mornings, as was your habit at Hunsford, Miss Bennet?"

Elizabeth turned red. She looked at him, lifting her chin. "Why, yes, Mr. Darcy. I know all the walks hereabouts."

He smiled. "I am learning my way about the countryside, too."

Charlotte looked from one to the other. *Oh, so that is why Eliza's color is so high when she returns from her ramblings.* She addressed Mr. Darcy. "Have you yet been to Oakham Mount, Mr. Darcy? There is a lovely view to be had of the entire countryside. It is quite one of Eliza's favorite spots."

Mr. Darcy smiled, a rare lightening of his dignified features. "Indeed? The walk has not yet come in my way. I shall look forward to it. Thank you for the suggestion, Mrs. Bennet."

Beside Charlotte, Mary smothered a quiet laugh.

[38]

On the afternoon of Wednesday, 7th October, three weeks after Mr. Darcy had come to Netherfield Park, Elizabeth and Mr. Darcy walked to Oakham Mount. Upon their return, Thomas Bennet narrowed his eyes, observing the couple. He did not know what had passed between them, but their demeanor was very different than when they had set out. *Her* face had looked pensive, and *he* showed a serious expression; upon returning, each wore a smile and an air of contented satisfaction.

In the evening, as had become something of a given, Mr. Darcy dined at Longbourn. Afterwards, an impromptu card party was proposed, but Mr. Bennet excused himself. The week's post had brought letters of a business nature that he had put off answering. He felt comfortable enough to leave Darcy to be entertained by the ladies of the house. *He has formed a friendship with us all at Longbourn.*

However, not long after Bennet had withdrawn to the library, Mr. Darcy knocked on the oaken door. Setting aside a letter, Bennet invited him in to take a chair. *His mien is uncommon grave, even for Darcy.*

His purpose was swiftly revealed. "Sir, I wish to apprise you of my devotion to Miss Elizabeth Bennet. I ask your consent to wed her."

The devil you say! After the first astonished second, Bennet concealed his surprise. "You have spoken to Elizabeth? And she has accepted you?"

"I have, and she has."

Bennet did not oppose Mr. Darcy's suit, but he was unhappy with it. His favorite child distressed him with her choice, and his fears and regrets on her behalf made for wretched reflection. *I know her disposition. Her lively talents will place her in the greatest danger in an unequal marriage.* The calm of his voice belied his misgivings. "Please send in my daughter, Mr. Darcy."

Mr. Darcy bowed and left him. Not a minute or two later, Elizabeth entered. Grave and anxious, Bennet had been pacing. Upon espying her, he said at once, "Lizzy, what are you doing? Are you out of your senses, to be accepting this man? Have you not always hated him?"

Charlotte had watched Mr. Darcy rise and follow her husband, and then return to quietly tell Elizabeth that her father wished to speak with her. Darcy took leave of herself and Mary, in perfect cordiality, remarking that he would return on the morrow.

"Mr. Darcy is all amiability," observed Mary, laying out cards in a game of solitaire.

"He is, indeed." Charlotte's curiosity was entirely piqued; but several minutes later, when she heard Elizabeth's footsteps going up the stairs, she did not follow her. Instead, Charlotte went to the library to discover what had taken place. "My dear sir, you have had a parade this evening! Pray tell me, what has occurred?"

"Why, Darcy and Lizzy are engaged to be married."

Staring at him, Charlotte dropped into a chair. "I had half-suspected, but I had quite thought – you surprise me very much. I had thought they were indifferent, no, *adamantly* set against one another!"

"Lizzy assures me, most earnestly and solemnly, that she has had a gradual change in her estimation of him, and related her absolute certainty that his affection was not the work of a day, but had stood the test of many months suspense."

"It is an evening of wonder, indeed!"

Mr. Bennet laughed. "More even than you know, my dear, for Darcy performed the role of *deus ex machine* for Lydia. Darcy did everything – made up the match, gave the money, paid the fellow's debts, and got him his commission!"

She saw the care-worn appearance, which had dragged down his features for so many weeks, was erased. "Oh, Thomas! Is it better, then?"

"So much the better! It will save me a world of trouble and economy. Had it been my brother-in-law's doing, I must and *would* have paid him. But these violent young lovers carry everything their own way. I shall offer to pay him tomorrow; he will rant and storm about his love for Lizzy, and there will be an end of the matter."

Charlotte also laughed, but with tears in her eyes. Her mind was now relieved from a very heavy weight, for there was no longer anything material to be dreaded, and the comfort of ease and familiarity of life's events was established. "So, Jane and Elizabeth are in a fair way to being settled." Two books slid off of a bookshelf, and Charlotte acknowledged the phenomenon with a small dip of her head and a smile. *Mrs. Bennet is here and understands.* She addressed her husband. "And Captain Denny still seems to be quite taken with Mary. Since you gave permission for him to court her, he has been in regular correspondence."

"Well, well! Of all her sisters, *Mary* is the one who will have an officer!" Bennet was in an expansive mood, and waved his hand in the air. "If any young man comes for Kitty, send him in, for I am quite at leisure."

Charlotte went back to the drawing-room and calmly took up her embroidery hoop. She smiled to herself. *My vow to Mrs. Bennet is coming to fruition with very little effort on my part.*

Mary looked over at her. "There is some secret, I gather. What has happened between Papa and Lizzy?"

"I doubt you will be long left in suspense, Mary."

Mary quietly chuckled. "Oh, I believe I may well guess."

Elizabeth returned downstairs in half an hour's time. She appeared perfectly composed, but there was a happy air about her that had not been there before. Charlotte and Mary shared a significant glance, but neither said a word.

Charlotte wished to hear all about the engagement, but Elizabeth said nothing. She cast her several glances, marveling at her small, private smile. *There is such an expression on her face!* She held her peace.

The evening passed tranquilly. Goodnights were exchanged and all separated to seek their beds. Elizabeth went inside her bedchamber and Charlotte followed. She knocked on the door before entering. "Eliza, I observed you were flustered when you came out of the library. Have you anything to tell me?"

Elizabeth's countenance glowed. "Oh, Charlotte, you may wish me happy! I am betrothed to Mr. Darcy! We are to be wed by special license."

"My dear Eliza! I do congratulate you! But are you certain? Forgive the question – are you quite certain that you can be happy with him?"

"There can be no doubt. It is settled between us already, that we are to be the happiest couple in the world."

"I am glad for you, then."

Elizabeth surprised her with a swift hug. "I am glad for you also. Dear Charlotte, will you ever, ever forgive me? I have been so horrible to you. I believed my father's marriage to you a great piece of folly, but it was the best thing to have happened. You have made him contented and you have given him an heir, besides."

"Of course, I forgive you! I have always been your friend, Eliza. I hope you believe that."

"Yes, I realize it now. Thank you, Charlotte."

The remainder of the conversation went as might be expected, exclamations of happiness on both sides, and a perfect understanding of one another's heart was reached.

Charlotte was satisfied. She went away to her own bedchamber, where she found her husband waiting for her. He sat in an armchair, holding their infant son cradled in his arms. He was cooing foolish words at the baby, but he stopped at her entrance and smiled across at her. "Dear Charlotte, there you are! Our son will soon be demanding his dinner. Another minute and no doubt he will be bawling for his mother."

"I was just congratulating Eliza on her engagement to Mr. Darcy. She is exceedingly happy." Charlotte's own joy could not be contained. "Oh, Thomas! She has accepted me at last! All is forgiven between us. We are to be friends again."

Bennet kissed his son's forehead and carefully laid him down in his crib. Then he arose from the chair and came toward her. She had not noticed it before; he had divested himself of his upper garments, so that he was bare from the waist up, and he wore only his breeches. His boots and stockings were also gone.

She shook her head, putting up her hand. "It is but three weeks, sir."

Bennet sighed. "Well I know it, dear lady. Pray do not mistake me, I am not pressing my rights. However, I do wish to hold you. I thought to sit behind you, on the bed, while you nurse our child."

She considered the suggestion. "Well, I do not see what possible objection I should mount against it."

A wicked glint in his eyes, Bennet smiled at her, and murmured, "Oh, how much I wish *to mount*!"

Charlotte blushed. "Thomas! *That* is not what I meant, as you well know!" He laughed at her, which only made her blush hotter.

He had obviously sent away the maid, so she turned her back to him. He began to undo the tapes of her dress. She spoke over her shoulder. "What goings-on, Thomas! Here is Elizabeth, set to marry Mr. Darcy and by special license! We must take pains to get better acquainted with him."

"He is already rising every hour in my esteem." Bennet drew the long sleeves of her dress down her arms. "It is a pretty blue thing, this new gown you have made."

'"My cousin Augusta gave me the fabric."

"Did she?" Bennet's voice reflected supreme indifference.

The garment fell past her hips to the floor. He undid the light stays, discarding it, and lifted her short chemise over her head. Charlotte caught her breath as his hands slid round her bare ribcage to cup her rounded breasts and plump them. He spoke low and thick in her ear. "I enjoy watching our son nursing at your bosoms. I have cause to know for myself what sweet bubbies you possess."

He pressed a kiss to the nape of her neck, making her shiver.

In quite another voice, he said lightly, "I admire both my sons-in-law highly. Wickham, perhaps, is my favorite."

Charlotte laughed. Her husband was in an odd humor. Indeed, she was sure of it when he backed her to the bed and tumbled her onto the counterpane. He followed her down. "Thomas! What are you about?"

"But I think I shall like Elizabeth's husband best of all." Bennet kissed her with passion. When he lifted his head, he said, "The midwife said nothing against bussing one's wife; nor of playing in her intimate curls with my fingers."

At his expert touch, Charlotte caught her breath. "No, you are right, she did not." For several minutes, there was no more nonsensical talk, but quite a bit of sighing and stifled moans.

Bennet said, with his mouth very near hers, "My Charlotte! How I love to see and feel your tremors."

There came a vociferous cry, emanating from a surprisingly strong set of tiny lungs. Thomas Bennet reluctantly sat up "You see how right I was. He is fair gut-foundered."

Charlotte breathlessly laughed at his vulgarity. "Do you sit against the pillows, Thomas, and I shall retrieve our son."

"Yes, wife of my heart."

Charlotte returned to the bed, and all was satisfactorily arranged. She rested against his bare chest, her rump tucked between his parted thighs, with her infant son suckling at her breast. She cradled her baby and her husband's arms held them both in a strong comfortable embrace.

"Thomas, my love, I am blessed beyond my imaginings."

She felt his deep sigh against her back.

"No more than I am, dearest, beloved Charlotte."

As she looked down at her son and felt the protective warmth of her husband's loving embrace, she marveled at how it had all began – what had come about when she had accepted Mr. Bennet's unexpected and businesslike proposal.

Most of all, she marveled at herself. *A comfortable home was all I ever wanted.* When she cast back her mind's eye, she saw how small had been her ambition. *No, I was not romantic.* Yet she had entered into the very fabric of that nonsensical sentiment, the warp and weft of it, and very dear it had become in the weavings of her life. She was far more than merely content.

I am happy.

Epilogue

Early in November, Miss Elizabeth Bennet and Mr. Fitzwilliam Darcy were married. The Longbourn church was filled with family and friends, many from Meryton or thereabouts. The Lucases sat on the bride's side. Catherine Bennet came home for the wedding. Miss Darcy and three of Mr. Darcy's cousins, all of whom were sons of the Earl of Matlock, were in attendance. Mr. Collins was also there, bearing Lady Catherine de Bourgh's regrets. The Gardiners and their children came from Gracechurch Street in London. The Wickhams wrote that *his duties* were keeping them away but promised a long visit to Longbourn in the spring.

Mr. and Mrs. Bingley also came for the wedding. Even though they remained for more than a month at Netherfield Park and there was talk of their making Netherfield their permanent home, it did not come about. Mr. Bennet and Mr. Bingley met with all civility, and though Mr. Bingley was as amiable as ever, there remained some small breach between them. Mr. Bennet's feelings were still somewhat hardened against this son-in-law, for the sake of his daughter Jane, and Bingley felt all the awkwardness of it. So, the Bingleys left for Pemberley, with the professed intention to pursue the plan of finding an estate closer to the Darcys. Elizabeth and Jane were the closest of sisters, and it seemed a reasonable ambition, that they should live near one another.

Charlotte resumed her wifely duties, to her own and her husband's mutual and deep satisfaction. The Longbourn harvest was finally finished in the second week of November, as Bennet had estimated. Mr. Bennet was diligent in composing a letter to the Wickhams that made it clear that Longbourn was *not ever* to be considered a boarding house by them.

The Gardiners went to Pemberley for Christmas, being interested in spending time with their favorite nieces and furthering acquaintance with their new husbands. At Longbourn, their absence was felt but nevertheless, between the numerous Lucases and those residing at Longbourn, a merry Christmas season was had by all.

Also by Gayle Buck

Pride & Prejudice Chronicles
The Second Mrs. Bennet

Standalone
Tempting Sarah
The Waltzing Widow
The Holybrooke Curse
Season of Joy
Hearts Betrayed
Chistmas Cheer
Old Acquaintances
Mutual Consent
The Chester Charade
The Desperate Viscount
Lady Althea's Bargain
Fredericka's Folly
Love for Lucinda
Lord Darlington's Darling
The Demon Rake
Lord Rathbone's Flirt
Miss Dower's Paragon
Belle's Beau

Cassandra's Deception
Love's Masquerade
The Righteous Rakehell
A Magnificent Match
The Hidden Heart
Willowswood Match
A Chance Encounter
The Fleeing Heiress
Lady Cecily's Scheme
Cupid's Choice
Lord John's Lady
Honor Besieged

www.ingramcontent.com/pod-product-compliance
Lightning Source LLC
Chambersburg PA
CBHW060411030726
47495CB00003B/525

9781952091230